ITCH

SIMON MAYO

CORGI BOOKS

ITCH
A CORGI BOOK 978 0552 56550 9

First published in Great Britain by Doubleday
an imprint of Random House Children's Publishers UK
A Random House Group Company

Doubleday edition published 2012
Corgi edition published 2012

4

The Random House Group Limited supports the Forest Stewardship Council®
(FSC®), the leading international forest-certification organisation. Our books
carrying the FSC label are printed on FSC®-certified paper. FSC is the only
forest-certification scheme supported by the leading environmental
organisations, including Greenpeace. Our paper procurement policy can be
found at www.randomhouse.co.uk/environment

MIX
Paper from
responsible sources
FSC® C016897

Set in Bembo MT 13/15.5
Corgi Books are published by Random House Children's Publishers UK,
61–63 Uxbridge Road, London W5 5SA

www.**randomhousechildrens**.co.uk
www.**totallyrandombooks**.co.uk
www.**randomhouse**.co.uk

Addresses for companies within The Random House Group Limited
can be found at: www.randomhouse.co.uk/offices.htm

THE RANDOM HOUSE GROUP Limited Reg. No. 954009

A CIP catalogue record for this book is available from the British Library.

Printed and bound by CPI Group (UK) Ltd, Croydon, CR0 4YY

To my son Joe,
where it all
started.

Cornwall, England
December

The earthquake was a small one. The post office shook only slightly, the window rattling in its frame and dislodging an Advent calendar. The van outside vibrated just enough to set off its alarm, and if you were watching closely you might have seen the traffic lights shudder in their concrete base.

A local nurse out walking her dog felt a vibration through the pavement and stopped. She would have thought nothing of it but for her Labrador's sudden bark and raised hackles. She could hear at least two other dogs reacting with a torrent of howls and yelps in houses nearby. The nurse looked around, then shrugged and resumed her walk. Her dog followed, tail between his legs.

A man reading his paper in the bath felt a rumbling and, glancing down, noticed a tiny series of waves running from the edge of the bath to his knees. There were three sets of waves in all, each one a centimetre behind the other. He got out of the bath, telling himself it was because the water had gone cool.

Beneath the man's house, the foundations absorbed most of the tremor. One metre below his basement, the peat that lay beneath moved and folded, and the silt that was ten metres deeper still cracked and heaved for the first time in decades.

Under this was ten metres of sand and all sorts of crushed shells laid down over millions of years – all moving, creasing and pushing into new shapes and layers. Below that lay twenty metres of slate and tin which had shaped so much of the county's history. Then came the granite; under pressure from the magma – the liquid rock heated by the Earth's core – its veins and cracks opened and closed.

And from deeper still came a small dark cluster, pushed up higher and higher, forced through the fissures, stopping only when it met the cooler, solidified mass of granite that ran for miles like a ceiling, north, south, east and west.

It stopped there.

One thousand metres beneath the man and his bath.

Waiting.

1

Itchingham Lofte had caused explosions before. There had, in truth, been many bangs, flashes and smells coming from his bedroom in the past. His multi-stained carpet and pockmarked walls bore testament to that. But there had been nothing like this one. It wasn't just the bedroom walls that shook; it was the whole house. Windows and doors rattled, the pots and pans in the kitchen jumped, and two drawers in the dresser opened.

Not that Itchingham was aware of any of that, as he was unconscious. He would have stayed that way too if it hadn't been for the fact that his eyebrows were on fire — and the astute decision of his eleven-year-old sister Chloe to throw a mug of water over his face.

Itch (everyone called him Itch, apart from his mother, whose idea it had been to christen him Itchingham in the first place) sat up sharply,

3

shaking the water out of his eyes. 'What did you do that for, Chloe?' he said. 'I did have it under control, you know.'

Chloe shrugged. 'Yeah, right. Your eyebrows were burning,' and she turned and went back to her bedroom, which was across the landing.

Itch felt for the prickly remains of what used to be his eyebrows – what was left crumbled in his fingers. Then the unmistakable smell of burned hair filled his nostrils and he realized Chloe had been right. He stood up a little gingerly and thought he'd better go after her and admit it, but when he poked his head into her room he found she was already asleep. Itch marvelled at her ability to get back to sleep in seconds – something he had never been able to do. The truth is, if you sleep in the room next to a fourteen-year-old science-mad boy who likes to blow things up, you learn very quickly only to take any notice of the very *big* bangs.

Itch went into the bathroom to dry and inspect his face. Both eyebrows had indeed gone, and about an inch of his fringe too. His wavy blond hair tended to be straggly anyway, but this explosion had forced it into a shape that Itch couldn't remember seeing before. Most of the sooty black smudge on the left side of his face came away with a vigorous rub.

Itch went back to his room and surveyed the mess. A really bad one this time. White smoke hung in the air and clung to the walls. Where the contents of his beaker had splashed, the carpet had turned black; Itch thought it had originally been green, but that was a long time ago. The beaker itself had shattered into a number of pieces, three of which had embedded themselves in the curtains, where they continued to smoulder. Burn marks surrounded each of the fragments. He climbed onto his bed to retrieve them and stood on a fourth piece, which crunched and then poked its way through his sock. Itch winced and pulled it free. Blood began to ooze through the cotton.

There had been a few posters on the walls, all bearing the scars of previous mishaps. All had now been blasted to pieces. He put their remains under his bed, together with the fragments of beaker. He scraped the chemical remains of the explosion off the carpet and wrapped them in his wet towel. These too were shoved under the bed.

Itch changed into his pyjamas and took his clothes, along with his bloodied sock, downstairs to wash. This, he had learned, was the only way to get rid of the smell of smoke. His foot still hurt from the shard of exploded plastic and he hobbled along to get the detergent. He put the washing machine on its quickest cycle and hoped it would all be done before his mother got back. Thirty-one minutes later the machine beeped at him and he hung his clothes up to dry.

With any luck, thought Itch, *Mum won't notice and I'll just about get away with it.* He had got away with so much over the years that this wasn't necessarily wishful thinking.

But Itchingham Lofte had forgotten about his missing eyebrows.

Jude Lofte arrived home just after eleven-thirty. Though she often had to work weekends, this was late, even for her. Itch had been in bed for twenty minutes but was nowhere near sleep. It always took his brain a couple of hours to shut down anyway, but tonight he was lying in his dark room, increasingly aware of how much it stank. Even with the window open, as it had been for the two hours since the explosion, there really was no escaping the smell of burning phosphorus. He was annoyed with himself for many reasons; mostly because he'd used too much of the phosphorus he'd collected from a couple of old ship's flares. Too many match heads as well. And maybe, on balance, mixing them up with a screwdriver had been one of his more stupid ideas. He was also irritated that he had woken Chloe and she had seen the post-explosion chaos in his room.

Itch had a pretty good relationship with his sister, even though she was only eleven and – clearly – a girl. He knew that most fourteen-year-old boys ignored their younger sisters at best and dismissed them as deeply stupid at worst. But Itch and Chloe Lofte tended to stick together. They got called Itchy and Scratchy after *The Simpsons*, of course, but as Itch had explained to her on one of their walks back from school, there are plenty of worse things to get called. Chloe had pointed out that it was OK for him as he had such a ridiculous name anyway.

Itch heard his mother shut and bolt the door and go into the kitchen. She wouldn't inspect anything too closely. Normally she made herself a tea and then worked downstairs in her study until very late. Sometimes so late that even Itch was asleep . . .

He heard the kettle being filled and the clatter of the tea tin being opened. Then a silence, followed by his mother's footsteps in the hall, where she stopped.

Itch tensed. He could hear sniffing. His mother was now coming up the stairs, still sniffing. The smell of the burning phosphorus in his room had been so strong he hadn't noticed that the whole house was filled with the stench.

Jude Lofte paused outside Itch's room. She waited all of two seconds before opening his door. Slowly at first; then, as the still-powerful smell hit her nostrils, she opened it fully. The landing light shone into the darkness of the bedroom. Itch was lying on his side with his back to his mother, curled up in the classic foetal position. Quite why he was bothering to go through this pretence he wasn't sure. He knew exactly what was going to happen next. He knew *exactly* what his mother was going to say.

'Hello, Itchingham. Been busy?' She sat down on the side of his bed. This was, he knew, the calm before the storm. She always started gently but it usually didn't last long.

'Oh, hello, Mum. Er, yes, I've done my French homework – though I did get—'

'I wasn't thinking of your homework. I was thinking of the smell of bonfires, which as we're nowhere near the fifth of November almost certainly means you've had another accident.'

His mother got up and turned on the light. Itch had made a reasonable job of clearing up, but he hadn't calculated on a late-night maternal visit. Fixing Itch with a stare, Jude crouched down beside his bed and peered underneath.

I really need to think of somewhere else to hide stuff, thought Itch as she pulled out the damp remains of the evening's experiment-gone-wrong.

'You really do need to think of somewhere else to hide stuff, Itchingham,' his mum said, as though reading his mind. 'Did you honestly think I wouldn't look here? Did you think I wouldn't know where to find the source of the stench – the latest you have blessed us with?'

The sarcasm was the final stage before eruption. In geography Itch had just learned about volcanoes and the Volcanic Explosivity Index, which was used to measure the power of eruptions. Mr Watkins had said that it went from 'gentle' to 'severe' to 'colossal' and finally 'mega-colossal'. From his mother he could expect 'colossal' – though he wouldn't rule out a full-blown 'mega-colossal'.

Jude Lofte's top lip quivered; Itch's stomach tightened.

'How many times, Itchingham? HOW MANY TIMES? I told you the last time when you set fire to your bed that any more – ANY MORE – accidents, and that was it. We only escaped then because Chloe had started keeping a fire bucket in her room.'

'That was the classic volcano experiment!' said Itch. 'I just hadn't realized how close the duvet was to the flames—'

'Enough! Stop! No more experiments. At all. NONE.'

Itch said nothing, and now his mother slowed down. 'Have I made myself clear? I want all your kit – chemicals, powders, potions, flasks, and whatever else you have hidden away in your wardrobe – outside in the garden after school tomorrow. No explosions, no "volcanoes", no burning hydrogen bubbles. *Nothing.*'

Itch's jaw dropped. 'But I can't just leave everything in the garden. It isn't safe!' He felt a bit panicky now. His 'kit', as his mother called it, had taken a long time to assemble and was his pride and joy. His friends at school talked mainly of football and surfing; he had no interest in the first and only a passing one in the second. *His* passion – his 'really lame hobby', as Chloe called it – was about to be cleared out of his room for ever.

'Well, you should have thought of that before you tried to blow up the house. And what *have* you done to your face?!' Jude had stopped looking around her son's bedroom and had just noticed his eyebrows. Or lack of them.

'Oh, they burned off. Sorry.'

'*SORRY?*' shouted Jude. '*Sorry?* You could have been blinded! Really, Itchingham, you are an idiot sometimes.' She put her hand under his chin and tilted his head up to the light. 'Well, they're gone.'

'How long till they grow back?'

'Depends what you torched them with.'

'It was phosphorus.'

Itch's mother put her head in her hands. 'Good grief,' she said. She sat silently for a few moments. Itch thought he should stay silent too. Then she stood up and turned for the door. 'All of it – in the garden. Tomorrow.' She walked out of the bedroom, switching off the light as she went.

Itchingham Lofte's obsession was a strange one. It thrilled him to his core, but he was coming to the conclusion that he might be on his own. He couldn't understand why no one else got it. As soon as he tried to explain, everyone yawned and changed the subject.

Some people could name every single computer game released in the last year; others could describe every goal scored by Manchester United in the current season. Itch could name, explain and was collecting *the elements*. The Table of Elements. The Periodic Table. Whoever came up with those titles, Itch thought, had done a spectacularly bad job. It was as if they were trying to put people off by disguising a great subject with the world's dullest name. If it had been called 'The Rocks Factor', more people would get it. If his hobby was marketed in newsagents with: 118 TO COLLECT! WHO WANTS GOLD AND SILVER? GET YOUR PLUTONIUM HERE! maybe things would be different.

There was, he thought, no point in collecting anything else; this *was* everything else. It was the catalogue of everything that existed in the universe, stripped down to its 118 basic ingredients. If Itch was honest, part of him was relieved that most people just left him to get on with it. How boring to be the same as everyone else. Did the world need another football fan? He didn't think so.

He had tried to keep up when he started at the local secondary school – the Cornwall Academy – just so that he could take part in the conversation. He had read the sports pages of his mum's paper, talked to his older brother, Gabriel, about what happens in *Call of Duty* and watched the odd match on TV, but his heart just hadn't been in it and his classmates soon realized he was a phoney. He didn't get their passions, they certainly didn't get his, and Itch had slowly realized he'd just have to accept it.

He had always enjoyed collecting things. Tucked away in a drawer somewhere, he still had folders and albums stuffed with Pokémon cards, coins, maps, marbles and frogs (that one didn't last long). They all seemed a very long time ago. For two years now, Itch had considered himself an element hunter and it had slowly taken over his life.

It had taken over from friends too. He had never found it easy to make friends, particularly since his family had moved to Cornwall from London when he was eleven. He had felt an outsider from day one. All his new classmates were a good three inches shorter than him, spoke differently and, to Itch's bafflement, many said they weren't English but Cornish. He had learned not to argue and had given up trying. They all got on fine without him and he could get by without them.

Itch woke up as his sister banged on his door. They had a well-established routine. Chloe always woke first, and after she had dressed for school she would knock loudly as she passed his door. She would go downstairs and, if their mum hadn't appeared, would start breakfast. Itch normally came down ten minutes later, but this morning it took him longer to get dressed and find his school things. The twin explosions – of the phosphorus and his mother – weighed heavily on his mind. He hoped his mum had worked late and slept in.

He was to be disappointed. He hadn't been in so much trouble since the stench-bomb moment six months ago. He had got hold of some American army spray that had made the whole house smell like a toilet. It had taken a professional cleaning company three days to get rid of it.

'Hello, Itchingham,' said his mother. 'Still no eyebrows, then.'

There should be a law against parents using sarcasm, thought Itch as he poured his cereal. He looked up at his sister. Her expression suggested that it was best to stay as quiet as possible over the next few minutes. He felt sure Chloe wouldn't have said any more than she had to, though she did mouth '*Boom!*' at him whenever she was sure their mother wasn't looking.

Jude Lofte stood at the stove in what Itch was sure were the same clothes she had been wearing yesterday – her usual dark grey skirt and white shirt. They looked a bit rumpled, as did she. She was tall and broad-shouldered, with the same mousy-blond, wavy hair as Itch.

'From now on,' she said, 'no experiments in the house. Ever. At all. Is that clear?' Before Itch could reply she carried on, 'And I will be inspecting your room. Any bits of equipment or' – she paused – 'strange rocks will be taken to the tip. I can't have you endangering your sister or the house again. From now on, if you have anything to mix, anything to smash, anything to play with that's more dangerous than, say' – she looked around – 'a bowl of Cheerios, then you do it in the shed.' She went over to the kettle.

Itch's mouth fell open. 'What?' he said. Hardly believing what he had heard, he pressed for some clarification. 'You mean I can carry on as long as I only experiment in the shed? Really?' He was trying to keep the relief out of his voice for fear that his mother would realize she had been surprisingly lenient. Working in the shed had the huge advantage of being at the end of a twenty-metre garden. Itch would have suggested it himself but had assumed there was no room and the answer would be no.

'It seems last night's bang has affected your ears as well as your eyebrows,' Jude said.

Chloe sniggered. Itch shot her a 'thanks for nothing' glance.

'OK, fair enough. I agree,' he said, slightly too quickly. Such was his relief that he then gave the game away completely by trying to give his mother a kiss on the cheek. She was unprepared for this and moved her head away so that Itch ended up half kissing the air where his mother had been. Displays of affection when their father wasn't there were rare in the Lofte house, and this attempt at one left both mother and son slightly embarrassed and feeling awkward.

Jude covered the difficult silence by putting on the radio. The kettle boiled and she made another mug of tea. She sat down at the table and blew on it. Itch was about to explain how pointless that was and how it would never lower the temperature of the tea unless she blew continuously for twenty minutes, when again he checked himself and said nothing. Chloe continued to eat her breakfast. Jude sipped her still very hot tea and looked up at her son.

'Please, Itch – nothing dangerous. You got away with it this time. Just stick to rocks that don't blow up, OK?' She sounded genuinely concerned.

Itch, taken aback, agreed. 'OK, just the safe stuff, Mum – promise.'

She managed a half-smile and started to clear the dishes.

It was then that Itch remembered the arsenic.

2

This wasn't a good start for the new 'nothing dangerous' regime. Itch's arsenic was contained in a recently acquired piece of green leaf-patterned wallpaper. The guy who sold it to him had explained that in the nineteenth century arsenic had been used as a dye; it had been called 'Paris Green' and was considered the best green pigment it was possible to buy.

After breakfast Itch went back to his room to get his school rucksack — somehow it had survived the explosion of the night before. He blew some ash from the strap and dusted off the rest. When he returned from school he would begin the transfer of his collection, his 'kit' and his books to the shed, but in the meantime he had to decide what to do with his more dangerous items. Personally Itch didn't think they were dangerous at all, as long as you didn't try to eat them or set fire to them, but he knew his mum would not agree.

Under the new closer-inspection regime, these items might not survive. He had always kept the riskiest elements of his collection out of sight. In his bedroom ceiling was a small recessed square of wood which, when pushed up, gave access to the loft and the water tanks. One of the first things he had done after they moved into this house was to write ITCH'S LOFT! in biro on its white paint. It had made his father laugh, and he was still proud of the joke. Standing on a chair, he eased the plywood cover back into the darkness. His hands quickly found the packages he was looking for and he eased them out. They were dusty, damp and, Itch thought, smelled of garlic. One was a large A3 envelope, which he folded in half; one was a jiffy bag and the other was a small, tightly wound plastic bag with a rubber band round it. He placed them all at the bottom of his rucksack, his school books going on top. For the moment they'd be safer with him.

Itch was now walking the mile to school with Chloe, an envelope stuffed with the arsenic wallpaper, a matchbox with a teaspoon of gunpowder in it, and two radioactive clock hands in a jiffy bag. These hands had apparently been painted with radium in order to make them luminous. Itch had bought them from a mineral seller he had first met at a Surfers Against Sewage fair in St Austell that Jack had taken him to.

The mineral seller had said his name was Cake. Just Cake – no first name. Or was that his first name? Itch wasn't sure. He had wanted the gunpowder because it had sulphur in it and he hadn't collected any of that yet. And gunpowder sounded cool. The clock hands looked dull, but the fact that they were painted with radium made them his first radioactive acquisition. The arsenic wallpaper was, apparently, rare, and Itch had been told that he should buy some while he could. The whole lot had cost him sixty pounds in total, which was all his savings.

As they walked down the hill towards the golf course and the sea, Chloe said, 'You know that people will notice your face.'

'Your friends might, but the kids in my class won't,' said Itch. 'Boys don't look at eyebrows very much.'

'But your face looks all weird now; of course they'll notice,' Chloe replied. 'Any fool would notice.'

'Not the fools in my class, Chloe, trust me. Unless Potts, Paul and Campbell spot it, of course – in which case I won't hear the end of it.'

James Potts, Bruno Paul and Darcy Campbell were the main Itch-baiters in the school. They thought that Itch's dislike of sport was proof of his weirdness. Of course, they were the sportiest pupils in the school and liked everyone to know it. It seemed to infuriate them that Itch had no desire to be like them, and for that reason alone they had decided to make his life difficult. Chloe was included in this just for being his sister, and even their cousin Jack, who was in Itch's class, got some stick. It had been Darcy who had first used the 'Itchy and Scratchy' line that was now in common usage across the school. Even Mrs Tooley in Year Seven English had been heard to use it. Other nicknames had come and gone; 'Snitch' and 'Lofty' had lasted longest. Eventually they petered out; most of the pupils just ignored Itch, so they had no reason to call him anything at all.

The golf course sat in the middle of the town, with most of the houses further up the hill to the north. If they were early enough, Itch and Chloe could get across the course without being shouted at. Walking around it added another fifteen minutes, and they were cutting it fine as it was. The almost new Cornwall Academy lay at the southern end of the town, beyond the shops.

It had previously been called Pitcowenn Secondary – which was generally declared to be rubbish – and had now been turned into a swanky academy. Clearly a lot of money had been spent: all the buildings were new and full of top-of-the-range equipment. Only the main hall of the old school had been deemed good enough to survive the upgrade. The school had been designated a 'Science Academy' and attracted many sponsors:

charities, eminent scientists and a global oil company. The academy logo proclaimed: *Together. Inspired.* No one seemed quite sure what it meant.

Chloe and Itch turned off the golf course and headed down the high street. Most of the shops were still shut, with only the newsagent's and two cafés open. Many of the tourist shops hadn't bothered opening since last October, but with summer only a few weeks away they were showing signs of life, with coats of paint and new surfing-gear displays.

'What was that bang last night anyway?' asked Chloe. 'I thought you'd blown yourself up.'

'Only a little phosphorus. Well, a little too much phosphorus actually,' said Itch, rubbing the place where his eyebrows had been.

Chloe looked up at her brother. Like all Loftes, she was tall for her age, but she was still nine inches shorter than Itch. She had short pixie-like brown hair but the same blue-green eyes as him.

'You could borrow some mascara.' She started rummaging in her bag, but Itch stopped her.

'That's the most stupid thing you've ever said. I might get away with *no* eyebrows – but painted ones? Are you mad? And since when did you wear mascara?'

Chloe shrugged and stopped looking. 'You're going to have to stop drawing attention to yourself at home, you know,' she said.

Itch sighed. 'I know, I know. I need to only do the

quiet stuff for a while. At least I'm in the shed now. Mum will forget I even exist.'

Chloe laughed. He had a point. Their mum's work as a solicitor kept her out of the house till late most nights, and if Itch spent the weekend in the shed, he would, to all intents and purposes, disappear completely from her life.

Chloe ran off as they entered the school reception area, and Itch made his way down the corridor. It was the week before the May half term and much of the academy seemed to be in a frenzy of exam preparation. There were timetables everywhere, with last-minute revision sessions advertised on every notice board. None of this affected Itch yet, of course – he was a year away from his first GCSEs – but he sensed the tension that kicks in with the dreaded exam season. He peered into Chloe's classroom as he went past and saw that she was chatting happily to a group of friends. Chloe found the friends thing a whole lot easier than Itch did, but he was pleased she had settled in at the academy in her first year. He walked on past the other form rooms, turned the corner by the science block, with its familiar aromas of gas, floor cleaner and the unquantifiable smell of a thousand different experiments. He turned left again and came to his form room. He paused, closed his eyes and took a deep breath. He always had a shot of nerves before he walked into the classroom, but today was worse. He opened his eyes, pulled some hair forward to where his eyebrows had been and went in.

'Hey, Itch, come and have a look at this.'

He relaxed. It was his cousin Jack, the best thing that had happened to him in all his time at the academy. Jack was short for Jacqueline, and she was tall, like all the Loftes, with short, straight jet-black hair cut with a fringe. She had lived in Cornwall all her life as her parents ran a couple of guest houses. She sat with Itch when classes allowed. They had barely known each other till Itch's family had moved down from London, but now she was his constant companion.

Itch had loved the fact that Jack seemed to accept him as he was and didn't expect or want him to change. For her part, Jack had always wanted a brother or sister and couldn't believe her luck when the 'slightly odd cousin' she had heard about but barely met, turned out to be a whole lot more interesting than most of her school friends. She was happy to have an almost-brother round the corner. Her father, Jon, and mother, Zoe, had helped them all move into their new house and then shown Itch, Chloe and their elder brother, Gabriel, around the town.

With Jack in the same class, Itch could stop trying to make friends. In his first weeks at the academy he had really made an effort. He'd laughed at everyone's jokes, joined the science club and hung around after school. But the only person who was ever pleased to see him was Jack. She realized that Itch was a little different, but she was happy to tolerate that. When Itch started to tell her about the chemical composition of her Twix or why her apple was turning brown, she would just flick his ear or poke him with a pencil.

'Don't be boring, Itch, or I'll tell you more about *Hollyoaks*.' This mention of Jack's favourite TV show was usually enough to stop him in his tracks.

Itch went over to Jack's desk, and was about to throw his bag down when he remembered what was in it and placed it rather more carefully on a chair.

Jack waved a magazine at him; it was a surfing publication called *UP*. 'Latest one,' she told him. 'It's got the new suits in. Check out the O'Neill Psychofreak. It says it's their warmest and most flexible wetsuit ever.'

Itch looked at the windswept and tanned male model who was showing off the Psychofreak. 'Looks great, but the price doesn't.' At £290 it was so out of his price range Itch didn't really want to read about how brilliant it was. Surfing was more Jack and Chloe's thing anyway. 'I'll make do with Gabriel's old one for another year, I suppose. No one's expecting me to be the best-dressed guy on the beach, are they?' His brother's wetsuit had been his for two years now; it had once been ridiculously big, but was now eye-wateringly tight. He'd like a new one, of course, but all his money was going on element hunting. There was also the small matter of not being very good at surfing. Try as he might – and Jack was always attempting to give him lessons – when a wave came, he could be relied upon to miss it.

'Time for a surf after school?' asked Jack. 'Surf's about right at four.'

'Thanks, Jack, but Mum's told me I've got to move all my rocks and stuff out of my room. Had – erm . . . a little accident last night.'

'Did it by any chance involve a flash big enough for you to lose your eyebrows?' She smiled and turned away to speak to some other classmates.

So Chloe was right, Itch thought – it *was* notice-able, but he still reckoned the boys would have no idea.

By now most of the class were in, the last two arrivals being Tom Westgate and James Potts. Tom tolerated Itch, but James Potts most definitely did not. Shorter than most of the class, he was never-theless faster and stronger. He wore trainers with everything and boasted that he had an illegal tattoo 'somewhere really exotic', though no one had ever seen it and many doubted it existed at all. His fellow sports geeks and Lofte-baiters, Darcy Campbell and Bruno Paul, were in the other Year Nine class. Two or three times a day they were in the same classroom with Itch, and unless there was some big sports event to discuss, their attention would normally turn to making Itch's life as difficult as possible.

Their form teacher, John Watkins, hurried in, bags, books and files piled precariously in front of him and a briefcase somehow hooked around his fingers. As usual, he looked as though he had dressed in the dark – orange trousers and a green shirt with permanent sweat stains under the arms. The smell of tobacco suggested that he had enjoyed one last hasty fag before entering the fray of another day as form teacher of 9W at the Cornwall Academy.

He let everything topple out of his arms and onto his desk, where the bags, books and files formed an unsteady pile. Mr Watkins glanced at it long enough to make sure it wasn't about to slide off onto the floor, then turned and smiled at his class. 'Morning, boys – let's begin.'

Form 9W had given up pointing out that the class was more than fifty per cent girls and just accepted that by 'boys' he meant everyone. Mr Watkins had come from an all-boys school in Edinburgh five years ago, and he was clearly not about to change the way he spoke to a class. He was overweight, permanently sweating and always bustling everywhere at full speed. He was head of geography and geology at the academy and one of the most popular teachers they had. His stories were legendary, and many a class would begin or end with a thrilling tale of flooding, earthquakes or riots.

'All present? Excellent! A good weekend, I trust? Splendid! Who wants to get me a tea? Sam, be a love – one sugar, thanks.'

Sam Jennings, who usually sat near the front of every class, rose wearily from her seat to perform the ritual that was a normal part of every morning with Mr Watkins. He always had his own kettle and weird tea bags at the front of the class.

'A reminder from our new friend, Dr Flowerdew, and our colleagues in the science department that biology today is in the greenhouse – you may take bottles of water with you. Some clowns last year thought they wouldn't need any and fainted on a cactus or something unpleasant. It's hot and steamy in there – you can get some water at lunch. Ah, Sam! A lovely brew, thank you.'

Sam Jennings shrugged and sat down again while Mr Watkins took registration with his usual speed.

The first two periods for Itch were history and English, which he drifted through without having to concentrate much. More Tudors, more *Animal Farm*.

Itch struggled in most subjects and only really engaged with any lessons when it came to science. The biology session in the greenhouse was intriguing; they hadn't had any lessons there before.

But first he had double maths and lunch to endure. Lunch would be tough today because Jack was busy with friends and Chloe had a choir rehearsal. Whenever this happened, he ate on his own and then went somewhere the Itch-baiters wouldn't find him – usually the library.

He met Jack just before biology. His cousin already had two bottles of water with her; she handed him one.

'Thought you might forget,' she said as they started to walk round the outside of the school, between the playing fields and the language labs and then past the old school hall. The greenhouse had been part of the rebuilding when the school became an academy, and it featured prominently on the website. The school was very proud of their greenhouse. 'Didn't see you at lunch,' Jack continued. 'My mates had to go early – roped into sorting out tickets for some school-band concert after half term – so I looked for you.'

'Reading,' said Itch.

'With anyone?'

'Well, there were other people there but I wasn't *with* them, no.'

Itch and Jack had got as far as the old hall when they heard the familiar cry of: '*Weirdo cousins.*' It came from a trio of voices – Potts, Paul and Campbell. They had set the words to an R&B song that was all over the radio and TV, but singing

27

wasn't their strong point and it ended up sounding like a rowdy football chant. However, they were clearly enjoying themselves and continued the refrain all the way to the greenhouse. Itch and Jack walked on in silence, Itch with his head bowed and Jack looking away.

During his first months at the CA, Itch had answered back, shouted back and rude-gestured back, but when he hooked up with Jack, she suggested ignoring them in the hope that they would get bored and pick on someone else. But it had just seemed to irritate them all the more. However, until a new strategy could be dreamed up, the 'take no notice' policy remained in place.

As it turned out, Itch and Jack, Potts, Paul and Campbell and most of the rest of the Year Nine biology class all arrived at the greenhouse at the same time. It was an impressive structure, fully thirty metres long, ten metres wide and ten metres tall. The wood was painted white, and from a distance you could see assorted plants filling the interior, though up close the condensation made inspection difficult. A few cracked panes of glass remained from last year's earthquake; the broken ones had been replaced. Small earthquakes were not uncommon in Cornwall, but Mr Watkins had told them that at 3.8 on the Richter Scale, it had been bigger than most.

They all milled around for a while waiting for

Miss Glenacre, the biology teacher, to emerge. Many of the class pressed their faces against the glass to get a glimpse of what was in store for them, but the steamed-up panes frustrated all but the most keen-eyed students.

After a few minutes the door opened and Miss Glenacre appeared, with Dr Nathaniel Flowerdew, the head of science, at her shoulder. The sight of the two of them was enough to trigger a few groans around the edges of the student gathering. Miss Glenacre was, by common consent, approaching her one hundredth birthday and had never had a charitable thought about anyone in her life. The truth was, she was indeed waiting for retirement, but only from the vantage point of sixty-four years, and had actually enjoyed teaching 'until the paperwork and government took over'.

By contrast, Flowerdew was an impressive figure. In his late forties, he was rakishly good-looking with a head full of well-cut, tight curls that had turned completely white. He had deep blue eyes, broad shoulders and the figure of a man who had gym membership. As there wasn't a gym in the local area, everyone had concluded that he had the relevant equipment at home. He was wearing a dark blue suit, brilliant white cotton shirt and electric-blue silk tie. The jacket was undone and a brushed chrome watch showed from beneath his left cuff. His shoes were black loafers. Everything was expensive and somehow out of place in a school field outside a greenhouse.

As a teacher, however, Flowerdew had proved instantly unpopular. Always seemingly in a sour mood, he gave everyone the impression that the academy was somehow beneath him. It was also clear that the rest of the staff didn't rate him. His reputation, so everyone said, was as a brilliant chemist. The staff and pupils of the CA were waiting for the evidence.

He addressed the students, his voice crisp and educated.

'Shut up, Nine W, and listen. You will have one period with Miss Glenacre here, and when you come out you will not have fainted, you will have listened, and you will know what a *Neomarica caerulea* is. Don't touch anything you are not asked to touch, don't put anything in your mouth, Burnham, and for heaven's sake drink water when you need it – you don't need to ask permission. Miss Glenacre is pleased to be your guide; listen well.' And with that he strode back round the old hall in the direction of his labs.

Johnny Burnham, who had once put some magnesium ribbon in his mouth 'to see what it tasted like', flushed scarlet and shrank a little.

They all trooped into the steamy confines of the greenhouse. Miss Glenacre marched to the far end and waited, hands on hips, for everyone to catch her up. She called out, 'All bags to be left at the door. There isn't room for swinging rucksacks in here.'

Itch, Jack and half the class turned round and put their bags in a heap by the entrance. Itch wondered whether it was wise to leave his rucksack unattended, but he didn't have a choice. He left it on top of the pile where he could see it.

They trooped back past the bananas, tomatoes, cacti and other unrecognizable plants to where the glowing Miss Glenacre waited to start the lesson.

'Why are we here?' she said. Silence. 'Anyone. Why are we here?'

'An accident of evolution?' chanced a very brave Ian Steele, standing near some peculiar dangly pink plants. Itch and a few others smiled; Miss Glenacre scowled.

'Idiot boy, Steele. Not why are we on *Earth*, as you well know, but why are we in the greenhouse?'

'Because it cost a fortune?' tried Bruno Paul, smiling and nudging James Potts next to him.

'If the point you are making is that we are very lucky to have such a splendid resource, you are quite correct. But that is not the answer. Anyone?'

Itch knew the answer but kept his head down.

'No one at all?' sighed Miss Glenacre. 'We are studying' — and she said the next word very slowly, as if to five-year-olds — 'pho-to-syn-the-sis. Turning carbon dioxide into sugar and oxygen using light.' She tutted and, motioning for the group to follow her, turned and started her tour of the plants.

They had only been in the greenhouse for fifteen minutes, but the temperature was 35°C. Glenacre's words were punctuated by the sound of water bottles being squished and emptied by the students of Year Nine.

It was after about thirty minutes, just as Miss Glenacre was trying to pull down the top of a giant spiky green and yellow plant, that the first student vomited. It was Johnny Burnham – and it was *spectacular*. He had been swaying and staggering for a few moments. Then, with one hand over his mouth and the other pushing his classmates out of the way, he brought up his breakfast all over a plant labelled *Eucomis pole-evansii*. He knelt down on the floor, his hands gripping the sides of a large pot, his head deep in the foliage. It was clear he hadn't finished.

Then two girls fainted. Natalie Hussain and Debbie Price had turned horribly pale and collapsed on top of each other. There were screams from some of the other girls, and before Miss Glenacre had reached the door to allow some fresh air in, four more students had been sick. The stink of vomit filled the greenhouse within seconds.

'Everyone out!' yelled their teacher. 'Tom, go and get Dr Flowerdew.'

Tom Westgate ran out of the door. The class stumbled outside as quickly as they could, hands or tissues over their mouths and noses. Glenacre propped up Johnny Burnham and called for Itch and Jack to help Natalie and Debbie. Itch picked up Natalie by the shoulders and got her into a sitting position. She groaned, opened her eyes – and was sick over Itch's trousers.

'Nice shot, Nats!' called a fleeing Darcy Campbell.

'Feeling a bit bad myself, miss,' said Itch, looking down at the dampness on his legs.

'Same,' said Jack, who had been struggling to help Debbie Price to her feet.

Itch swiftly lowered Natalie back down and ran for the door. He almost made it too; he got as far as the pile of bags and was sick there instead. He stumbled outside and slumped down on the grass. He closed his eyes; everything was spinning. He could tell without looking that a good proportion of Miss Glenacre's biology class were now in the process of being violently ill.

When he opened his eyes again he saw Jack and Miss Glenacre helping a very wobbly Natalie, Debbie and Johnny out of the greenhouse. Itch tried to stand up, but felt so giddy he sat right back down again. It looked as though his teacher had been sick too.

By the time Dr Flowerdew came running round the old hall, closely followed by Tom Westgate and a short, wiry girl from Year Ten, the entire class – and their teacher – were lying sprawled across the grass. Some were still throwing up, many were groaning with hands clasped around their stomachs, and at least half a dozen were crying quietly.

Flowerdew pulled up sharply, unable to comprehend what he was seeing. It was like a scene from a disaster movie. 'What the . . . ? What on earth . . . ? What has . . . ?' He looked around, trying to find Miss Glenacre. 'Grace? Where are you? Grace?'

She raised her hand. She clearly didn't want to open her mouth just yet.

Dr Flowerdew ran across to her, stepping over students and shouting at Tom to go and get the head. Tom Westgate turned and ran off again.

'What the hell has happened? Grace! Talk to me! I only left you half an hour ago.' Flowerdew managed to sound concerned and furious at the same time.

Grace Glenacre's long grey hair, which had been tied back, was now loose. A few strands were plastered to the side of her face. She put a hand in front of her mouth and tried to speak.

'I don't know . . .' She sounded hoarse. She coughed and spat. Flowerdew looked away and she apologized, then tried again; her voice was stronger this time. 'I don't know – everything was fine. It was hot, of course, but everyone had their water. I think I had got as far as the *Passiflora* when Burnham started being sick.'

'Burnham!' said Flowerdew. 'I might have known. Was he eating the plants as well as studying them?

The boy's a fool. And then hysteria took over, I suppose, and everyone joined in. What a mess this is.'

Miss Glenacre looked incredulous. 'Are you including me in the "hysteria"? Are you suggesting I just "joined in"?' She sat up a little.

'Well, it's possible, isn't it?' said Flowerdew. 'It's very hot in there, you have twenty-seven students in an enclosed space, one of them gets ill and it's easy for others to follow suit. Classic copycat stuff.'

Grace Glenacre had forgotten that she had just been ill. Now she was furious. 'How dare you? How *dare* you!' she shouted. 'I don't think I have ever sworn at a member of staff before but I'm going to now.' She swore at him. 'I have no idea what just happened in there, but twenty-seven sick kids and one sick teacher is *not* hysteria.' Her voice was rising now. '*It's not hysteria*, do you hear me!'

Flowerdew stood up. 'You're hysterical,' he said. 'We'll talk later.'

He went into the greenhouse, but the heat and the acrid stench that hit him forced him back. In front of him was an extraordinary scene. The plants were arranged in long, evenly spaced rows with a wide aisle down the middle. There were fifty different varieties of flora, some huge, green and nearly hitting the roof, others wide and spectacularly colourful. It seemed to Flowerdew that they were all somewhat more colourful than an hour ago. Everywhere he looked there were regurgitated lunches. He'd just realized he was standing in a small pool of gastric juices and sausage when he heard the unmistakable sound of the head arriving.

Dr Felicity Dart was running fast. She was in her early fifties but she kept herself fit and trim, cycling to school and often jogging around the playing fields at lunch time. In general, staff and pupils liked and respected her but knew that she had a fierce temper and a voice like a foghorn. If she started a shouting session, everyone knew about it. Just as Dr Flowerdew had done, she pulled up short as she surveyed her pupils. A couple of them were still retching, and many were still flat out, but a few were now sitting up, texting. She looked beyond the Year Nines to where Miss Glenacre sat, visibly shaking. Then she turned to the head of science, who was still standing in the doorway of the greenhouse.

'DR FLOWERDEW!' she hollered. 'IF YOU WOULDN'T MIND.'

She ran over to Grace Glenacre, who said, 'I'll be OK. Check on the children – some have been very ill.'

Felicity Dart turned to the still puffing Tom Westgate. 'Tom, go and get Mr Littlewood and tell him to call for ambulances, please.'

Tom glanced at his classmates, then headed off for the third time. Jim Littlewood was the new history teacher and a qualified first aider.

Flowerdew came over, closely followed by a staggering, unrecognizable boy, his head down, his mouth covered by his hands. He gave a muffled groan, and Flowerdew turned. The head of science had just enough time to identify Craig Murray before the boy projectile-vomited over Flowerdew's immaculately pressed trousers.

Everyone froze for a moment as the contents of Craig's stomach spread slowly towards the teacher's polished shoes. Everyone, that is, except Sam Jennings, who was recording the moment on her phone.

'If I see that on YouTube, Sam,' called Dr Dart, 'I'll know exactly who to see in my office, won't I?'

'Yes, miss,' said a grinning Sam. (When it did indeed appear on YouTube, she claimed her brothers had taken her phone and uploaded the clip against her wishes. No one believed her.)

Flowerdew wiped himself down with his handkerchief and some tissues which Dr Dart had passed over. He was red-cheeked and obviously uncomfortable as the dampness seeped into his trousers, but he spoke calmly.

'Right, well, it's a real mess in there, Felicity – vomit everywhere. Burnham ate a plant, I think, was sick, and then they all started. Everyone is OK now, though—'

'Really? Are you seriously suggesting, with a whole class ill and prostrate after a lesson, that "everyone is OK"? Now, while we wait for the ambulances, we will need some water. Get as much as you can from the kitchen, please.'

For the briefest of moments Dr Dart thought she detected an 'isn't there someone more junior than me?' look, but then Flowerdew said, 'Of course,' and pulling the clinging fabric of his damp trousers away from his legs, he jogged away.

Itch and Jack were sitting together; both had stopped being ill. The Year Ten girl who had arrived with Flowerdew and Tom Westgate introduced herself as Lucy Cavendish; she gave them both cups of water. Finishing his, Itch got up slowly and offered a hand to Jack, who shook her head and closed her eyes again. He went over to where the head was talking to some of the students.

'Don't know what happened, miss. I just started to feel giddy and I threw up on Matt's head.' This was Timothy Abbott, a rotund, normally cheerful boy. He sounded almost proud of his aim.

'Johnny was sick first, miss, then we all got it,' said Ian Steele.

'I was starting to feel bad before Johnny was sick, miss.'

Dr Dart turned round at that. It was Natalie Hussain. '*Before* Johnny? You felt ill *before*? How long before?'

'About five minutes, miss. Debbie was looking awful, so we leaned on each other for a bit. And that's all I remember. Next thing I was out here.'

Felicity Dart found Debbie Price, who was now

propping herself up on her elbows. Jim Littlewood, Dr Flowerdew and some of the catering staff bearing jugs of water were arriving now, along with assorted sixth formers who had been roped in to help.

'Debbie, this is very important,' said Dr Dart. 'Natalie says you both felt ill *before* Johnny Burnham was sick. Is that right?'

'Yes, miss. Well, to be honest, I don't know. I can't remember him being ill – just Natalie told me she felt rubbish too and then we must have passed out.' Debbie took a glass of water and sipped carefully.

Itch was about to add to the story when Dr Dart looked at him and exclaimed, 'Good heavens, Itchingham, you've lost your eyebrows!' She glanced over at the greenhouse. 'What happened in there?' She put one hand under his chin and lifted his head, exactly as his mother had done last night. Maybe all women did it. 'My goodness, they've gone completely! HAS ANYONE ELSE LOST THEIR EYEBROWS?'

'Er, miss, no – it happened last night. I had, er, an accident at home and they, well . . . they'll grow back, Mum says.' Under other circumstances Itch felt sure he would have been questioned further, but it looked as though Dr Dart had made her mind up about something. She walked over to Miss Glenacre.

'Grace, come and see me when you can face it. Do you have the keys for the greenhouse?' The biology teacher reached into her pocket, produced a fob with two keys on it and handed them to the head. Dr Dart walked over to the greenhouse and looked inside without entering. She called Jim Littlewood and two other members of staff, and between them, with handkerchiefs over their mouths, they reached in and pulled out the bags. They were piled up in a sorry – and in a few instances soggy – heap. She then shut the door and locked it with both keys.

Nathaniel Flowerdew came bustling over, about to question the locking of the greenhouse, but Dart cut him off.

'It's locked and out of bounds to everyone, staff included, until we know what's happened. The ambulances will be here shortly. Come and see me when all the students have been attended to.'

With that she returned to the pupils and escorted two of them back towards the main school.

That afternoon, ambulances ferried the worst – affected pupils to the local hospital. About half of Miss Glenacre's greenhouse class ended up filling the rows of the small outpatients reception. Itch was sitting with Jack and Johnny Burnham, who was still looking the greenest of them all. No one had actually been sick since arriving, but there were a few groaning noises coming from the direction of Bruno Paul on the other side of the room. He was sitting with Matt Colston and next to Miss Glenacre, who was still supposedly in charge but had had her eyes shut for ten minutes now.

'I feel OK,' said Jack. 'I'm not sure why I'm here.'

'Well, they did seem keen to bring us in,' said Itch. 'They've seen Johnny, Natalie and Debbie for tests; they'll get to us by midnight, I suppose.'

Jack leaned in close. 'Any theories?'

'I should have, but no, not really. Some gas given off by one of the plants maybe? There are some pretty weird ones in there.' He paused. 'But they've been in the greenhouse for ages – that doesn't make sense.' He was annoyed with himself.

'A dodgy batch of water, perhaps?' said Jack. 'Everyone was drinking the same stuff.'

Itch shrugged.

They looked up at the sound of running foot-steps: parents were hurrying along the corridor towards the outpatients. The swing doors burst open as Craig Murray's mother and Natalie Hussain's parents burst in. As they looked around the room, Bruno Paul stood up, turned round to face the wall and vomited over the DON'T SWEAR AT THE STAFF poster. This was followed in quick succession by Ian Steele being sick into his cupped hands and Matt Colston being sick on Miss Glenacre, who then woke up. Six pupils dashed towards the toilets and three made for the car park.

'Here we go again,' said Jack, and she got up.

'Are you . . . ?'

'No, I'm just going to help.' She jogged off in the direction of the toilets, and Itch looked at Johnny Burnham who, remarkably, was eating a packet of prawn cocktail crisps. Nurses and doctors arrived from everywhere, and two porters appeared with mops and buckets.

The flustered receptionist emerged from behind her desk and tried to raise her voice above the moaning, swilling and slopping. No one could hear what she said, so she gave up and sat down again.

It was after five o'clock when Dr Dart emerged from one of the corridors, walking briskly with a senior-looking doctor at her side. She was pale but her face was set and she looked determined. She stood at the front of the outpatients area as though it was one of her classrooms.

'I am being advised to close the school.' There were gasps and an outburst of chatter, but she put up her hand for silence. 'Early toxicology tests from the staff here suggest' – she paused – 'that the illness was, in some cases, caused by . . . incredible as this seems . . . a poison gas of some kind. Until they know where it came from, the school is closed for the rest of this week.'

Itch felt his mouth go dry, his stomach tighten and his bowels lurch. He had completely forgotten the packages at the bottom of his bag.

Oh help, he thought. *This is all my fault.*

3

Alone in the house, Itch, shaking, peered again at the computer screen and clicked on DELETE HISTORY. It hadn't taken long to find the information he was looking for. A search for 'arsenic gas' had delivered the information he had dreaded.

What Cake hadn't told him about the arsenic in the wallpaper is that on exposure to damp conditions it gave off arsine, a gas which had, over the years, caused many deaths. When he read that, Itch thought again of his teacher and three classmates still in hospital. From what the head had said, it didn't sound too serious, but could anyone be sure? When was the last time the hospital had dealt with arsenic poisoning? Had they even identified the arsenic yet? The only thing that was certain was that he was responsible. If he hadn't taken his three packages to school – and one of them in particular – none of this would have happened.

After Dr Dart had announced the closing of the school, talking about some kind of 'poison gas', Itch had sat staring straight ahead, not hearing or seeing anything else. Jack had asked him if he was OK, fearing that he too was about to be ill again. But Itch didn't reply. His rucksack was just behind him. He had grabbed it and, excusing himself to Dr Dart, run for the toilets. He had sat down in one of the cubicles with the rucksack on the floor in front of him. He *had* to get rid of the wallpaper. He had considered his options, but flushing it away there and then had seemed to make the most sense. Opening his rucksack, he piled his school books on the floor and fished out the brown A3 envelope.

The roll of wallpaper inside was damp, mouldy and smelled strongly like garlic. *So that's where the smell in the loft came from*, thought Itch, and held his breath. He pulled out the green roll and started to unwind it. He had only looked at it once before, just after he had bought it – a rather boring length of wallpaper with a green floral pattern. Now it was heavier, darker, and thick with mould. He started to tear off strips and flush them down the toilet. Hoping he would remain undisturbed, he ran from cubicle to cubicle, tearing and flushing, until the entire roll had disappeared into the hospital's drainage system.

Itch had started to feel nauseous again, so he sat down on the final toilet and put his head in his hands. He heard the main door open, and Jack's voice asked if he was OK. Itch had reassured her and said he would be back out in a minute. With the danger removed and his stomach settling down, he had washed his hands and walked slowly back to the reception area, his rucksack on his back.

Three pupils – Johnny Burnham, Natalie Hussain and Debbie Price – along with Miss Glenacre had been kept in overnight; the rest were allowed to leave. The school and hospital arranged transport home for those whose parents couldn't pick them up. Jack's father had driven out; he suggested that Itch should stay with them, but Itch wanted to go home – though he promised to call immediately if he felt ill again. He needed to be on his own to work out what to do next.

He had been aware of little on his journey back to the house save for one question: *should he own up?* He hated the thought of three classmates and a teacher being in hospital, but at the same time he wondered about the implications of admitting to taking the arsenic wallpaper to school. Not good, he imagined, and certainly the end of his element hunting. Following on so soon after last night's big bang, his mother would certainly throw the whole collection out. If he didn't own up to the school, should he own up to Chloe or Jack? He was sure they wouldn't tell on him, but the risks were high if they let something slip. He needed more information – which was why the first thing he did when he got home was to do an internet search.

With the science clearer in his head, Itch made himself some toast, then went on to some local-news sites. They had only a sketchy outline of what had happened. He scrolled down to a quote from a hospital spokesman, who had said that all four patients were being kept in overnight for observation, that their condition was stable; there would be more information in the morning. Could he wait till tomorrow? Itch wondered. Should he leave an anonymous message at the hospital?

He called Jack, who filled him in on some messages she'd had from friends. All the Year Nines seemed to be OK now, and Debbie, Natalie and Johnny in hospital weren't any worse. There was no news of Miss Glenacre.

Itch heard his mother's car turn into the drive – he had to decide now! Hearing her key in the door, he opted for silence . . . for now. If in the morning his classmates' condition was no better, he would own up; if they were OK, he would keep quiet. This seemed a logical position, and he started to calm down a bit.

His mother had picked up Chloe from a friend's, and Itch was heading for the sofa with his toast when she hurried in, dropping her bag on an armchair.

'Let's have a look at you.' His mum sat down,

tucking some of her shoulder-length hair behind her ear, and studied him closely. 'How many times were you sick? You still look pale – although the lack of eyebrows doesn't help.' Itch wasn't sure what that had to do with it, apart from letting him know she hadn't forgotten.

'Just the once in the greenhouse, but this is the first time I've felt like eating anything.' He waved his buttered toast at her.

'Thanks for the longer holidays, Itch,' said Chloe as she appeared in the doorway. 'With half term next week, we've now got nearly two weeks off!'

'It's a pleasure – we did it just for you.'

'What do you think happened?' she asked. 'Someone told me that Johnny Burnham ate a poisonous flower and that was the start of it. Everyone else just joined in.'

'And how likely does that sound to you? Johnny might be a fool, but he's not going to start eating flowers in a greenhouse. There might have been some "joining in", I suppose . . . it's difficult to say.' Itch paused for a moment. There wasn't a lot he could say now with his mother still hovering, and he hadn't decided what, if anything, to tell Chloe.

Jude turned on the local TV news. She caught the end of a report showing parents waiting outside the school and the reporter saying that it would remain closed until they found what the gas was and where it had come from. She switched it off again.

'Well, Itch, you're the scientist here. What could cause that? If it wasn't Johnny's flower, what was it?'

This was not something Itch could cope with just now. He was a hopeless actor, and he didn't want to start making up theories. He looked down. 'I dunno, Mum.'

He got up and cleared his plate away. 'I think I'll go and lie down for a bit.' Both Chloe and Jude looked surprised: they had been expecting him to come up with a range of hypotheses about what could have caused the mass sickness. But he didn't offer any and they didn't force him.

As he reached the sitting-room door, Jude said, 'Oh, your dad rang to say he's coming down tomorrow.'

Itch stopped and turned round. 'But he's not due till next weekend – he always says he can't change his shift patterns.'

'I know. He does always say that. But he heard about what happened today and has taken compassionate leave. He's flying down tomorrow and should be here after lunch.'

As Itch climbed the stairs, instead of being excited as he normally was when his father came home, he felt only dread. More explanations, more lying. For some reason, lying to his dad had always been more difficult than lying to his mum.

His bedroom still had that burned smell, even though the window had been open all day. He sat down heavily on the bed, swung his legs up and put both hands behind his head. He was not at all sure that his decision to wait and see was the right one. *Who knows?* he thought. *By the time Dad arrives I might have been arrested and thrown in jail.* He was thinking of Googling 'Youth prison sentences for poisoning' when Chloe knocked and came in.

'You all right, Itch? You didn't look that thrilled to hear that Dad's coming back.'

'Go away, I'm sick.' Itch turned and faced the wall.

'Yes, but you're getting better. What's going on, Itch? Is there—?'

'I've been sick, Chloe, and I'll chuck up on you if you don't leave me alone.'

'Whatever,' said Chloe, and she turned and left.

The next morning was distinctly cool for May, and a strong onshore wind was making it feel cooler still. Itch had been awake for a while, thinking about his dad's imminent return. The whole science thing had really started with him. When Itch was ten, his dad had given him an old book he'd found while clearing out Grandpa Joe's things.

Itch's grandpa had been ill for a while, and when he died Itch went to help his dad sort out the flat. He'd had hundreds of books, most of which went straight into cardboard boxes and then to the charity shop. But there was one his dad had dusted off and started to flick through. He had handed the book to Itch, smiling.

'I remember this from when I was young, Itch – you might like it. Grandpa lent it to me to get me interested in chemistry. It worked! It was probably the start of everything for me. I think it's banned now, though. Too dangerous or something, according to the Americans. Never did me any harm. Though Grandpa might disagree if he was here . . .' Itch remembered his dad trailing off, looking sad again. 'But if you don't want it,' he said, 'just chuck it out with all the others.'

It was a battered, yellowing tome called *The Golden Book of Chemistry Experiments* by Robert Brent. The fact that it was a banned book had, of course, immediately aroused Itch's interest. He had never seen anything that was banned before!

It explained how to turn your house into a chemistry lab – where you could get all the ingredients and equipment you needed to perform the experiments. The first page proudly declared that almost every child alive was *fascinated* by finding out about things.

Well, that's it, thought Itch. *That's all I want to do – find out about things.* However, he had since found out that the book was wrong in one respect at least. Most kids at his school were *not* interested in finding out about things. Not unless it involved a football or a shoot-'em-up game.

The book concluded with a list of all the 102 elements that had been discovered when the book was published in 1960. When Itch put away his Pokémon cards for what turned out to be the last time, it had seemed totally natural to start collecting everything on that list. He wondered why he hadn't thought of it before.

The first ones were easy to find. He'd gone for chlorine, calcium and titanium. They were easy because they were there in the room with him. Chlorine was in the bleach from under the sink, calcium in a seashell Chloe had brought home years ago, and titanium in his brother Gabriel's tongue stud – which he had left in the fruit bowl at Christmas. Gabriel was twenty and in his second year at Warwick University. He came home occasionally, but always seemed keen to leave again at the first opportunity – all the more so when a girlfriend appeared on the scene.

Then came fluorine from the Teflon on an old frying pan, copper from some cable his dad kept in the shed, and nickel in the form of some old coins. Lead had been easy. So was silver – Itch's mum was always losing earrings. He had found three before breakfast one morning and just decided not to tell her. Chromium was next: he had discovered that it covered most cutlery.

And so it went on. Once he had found an element he stored it in a shoe box in his cupboard, and put a tick by it on the TABLE OF ELEMENTS IN FULL COLOUR poster that had come with a science magazine, noting where he had got it from. Very soon, however, he needed more room: stuff like the old piece of lead piping took up half a box on its own. More shoe boxes had followed, and within three months of becoming an element hunter, Itch had thirty-two of the 118 elements residing in his wardrobe alongside his shoes and underwear. According to Chloe, it was a close call as to which smelled the most threatening.

Itch's mum had tried very hard to understand his new hobby. The first time he had put up the poster of the elements in his room she had stood and gazed at it, dirty washing in one hand, a mug of tea for Itch in the other. He followed her eyes as they skipped along the rows and down the columns.

'It's like a crossword,' he said, to break the silence. 'You can read it horizontally as the atomic numbers get higher, or vertically. The columns of elements are all a bit like each other. Cool, isn't it?'

'Er, yes, I suppose so. I don't think I've seen one since I was at school . . .'

'Oh, there's been lots more discovered since then,' said Itch, and he pointed at the bottom right-hand corner of one section. 'Copernicum was only discovered in 1996 – that wouldn't have been there in your day.'

Jude threw her son's pants and socks at him. 'You

make me sound ancient! For that, I'm keeping the tea.' And she sipped it slowly, taking in the blocks of letters and numbers. 'It looks like the plans for a rather odd, unfinished castle. These are like turrets, don't you think?' She pointed to the two ends of the table where the columns of blocks were highest.

'I hadn't seen it as a castle – no,' said Itch. 'More like a map really. Those "turrets" are hydrogen at one end and helium at the other. You see—'

'And this could be a moat at the bottom,' interrupted Jude, pointing her mug to two lines of blocks that underlined the 'castle'.

'No, it really couldn't be a moat. Didn't they teach you anything, Mum?'

She had shrugged and turned to leave. 'What's it going to be, this collection of yours, when it's finished?'

'It's not going to "be" anything. It's just a collection, Mum. You must have collected something when you were young. Dolls, or something?' They both smiled. 'Dad has this book which says the table of elements is a collection of everything you can drop on your foot. Does that help?'

His mother smiled a little. 'In which case I'll take it up with him. Whenever he gets round to seeing us again. Till then, it's a castle.'

Itch heard his sister, and a few minutes later his mother, go downstairs. It was only just gone seven, but although school was closed, they were all early risers. Itch was just thinking he might stay in bed till his mother went to work when his door opened and she put her head round.

'I'm off, Itch – need to be in Exeter by eleven. There's stuff for sandwiches in the fridge, and some bananas. And' – she pointed at the cupboard where the boxes of elements were – 'get that lot in the shed. Maybe Chloe can help you. Call me if you feel ill again, OK? See you tonight.'

'And good morning to you too,' said Itch as his mother went back downstairs. He clicked his computer to life and went to the local-news sites he had been checking yesterday. There was no update on the conditions of Johnny, Debbie, Natalie and Miss Glenacre; in fact, no change to the story at all.

He got dressed and went downstairs. Chloe had been watching TV in the lounge, but she came to join him at the kitchen table.

'I'm feeling fine – before you ask,' said Itch.

'If grumpy,' she muttered. 'Mum says you have to move your stuff out to the shed today. Any news from the hospital?'

Itch made a grunting noise which sounded negative, so Chloe returned to the television.

Back in his room, Itch took his element collection out of the cupboard and arranged it on the floor. To the casual observer it was a rather unimpressive assortment of rocks, corked bottles, bits of metal and everyday household objects.

Counting across the row nearest his bed, he had:

two clear test tubes;
a battery;
the head of a golf club;
some children's play putty;
a pencil;
a sandwich bag with some dark soil-like substance in it;
another clear test tube with a cork in.

However, on his poster Itch had written:

1. Hydrogen (my own!)
2. Helium (balloon gas – Chloe's tenth birthday)
3. Lithium (AA batteries – W H Smith)
4. Beryllium (found on golf course, hole twelve)
5. Boron (birthday present)
6. Carbon (2B pencil – school)
7. Nitrogen (fertilizer – shed!)
8. Oxygen (my own! Electrolysis is amazing!)

They were the first eight elements, and they were stored in the first shoe box. Itch was particularly proud of the hydrogen and oxygen, which he had produced himself (his dad's book had shown how to do it with a few batteries, some copper wire and a flask of water). Into the next shoe box went:

an old frying pan;
a long thin light bulb;
a strip of silvery metallic ribbon;
a brass capsule with a pointy tip;
a small tub of powder;
a computer chip.

As Itch put each one into the box, he said quietly, 'Fluorine, neon, magnesium, xenon, aluminium, silicon.'

He was irritated by this box's contents as there was something missing. Ever since he'd started his collection he had been looking for sodium (which should come after neon), but he had struggled. This was because the sodium he wanted was highly reactive and dangerous. You usually only got to see it at school, when his science teacher would remove a small amount from an oily solution in a jar; he would then drop a tiny amount into water, where it would pop and burst into flames. Itch's birthday was still a month away, but he knew what he wanted, even if he knew he wouldn't get it. He wanted some sodium. Proper sodium.

He finished packing up his elements and put his stink bombs in the front pocket of his rucksack. His collection all fitted into four boxes and a carrier bag, and he was just about to start moving it to the shed when Chloe called out from downstairs:

'They're all being let out, Itch! They're going to

be fine! I just got a text from Arabella and Saz.'

Itch rushed over to his laptop and refreshed the news site he had been on earlier. Sure enough, the headline now read: HOSPITAL RELEASES ACADEMY 'GAS VICTIMS'. There was an image of the CA buildings and an extraordinary photo of Miss Glenacre from at least thirty years ago. He scrolled down. It was a repetition of the whole story from yesterday but it started with a new paragraph:

Cornwall Academy victims of yesterday's mystery gas leak were released from hospital this morning. A spokesman said that they had been monitored overnight and there had been no further symptoms or recurrence of the vomiting. All four have been advised to return immediately if they are feeling unwell. The academy will remain closed until the source of the gas has been identified.

Itch realized he had been holding his breath, and now let out a huge sigh of relief. His classmates and teacher were OK; he wouldn't be going to prison. As he gathered the boxes together he wondered quite how long the academy would be shut. *Until the source of the gas has been identified*, it said.

Well, good luck with that, he thought.

Opening the shed door had taken Itch five minutes. It had warped and twisted so that the bolt was stuck in the locked position. It had finally given way with an almighty creak. Now, he looked at the shed's contents, which were jammed into every corner and onto every shelf, and wondered where his 'kit' was supposed to go.

He started to pull at assorted garden implements tangled up with lawnmower cable. Chloe appeared and helped to move pots of paint and soggy bags of barbecue coal. They worked without speaking for ten minutes, laying the shed's contents out on the grass.

Then Itch said, 'It was arsenic, Chloe. It was in my rucksack.' He hadn't planned to tell her – it just came out. He didn't look at her; he carried on tugging at a rake that was caught up in guy ropes.

Chloe stopped trying to unstick a tin of emulsion and looked up at him. 'OK . . . that sounds bad.'

'Well, yes. It can even *kill*, apparently. But I had no idea, Chloe – honest . . .' He paused. 'I just had some wallpaper in an envelope, that's all, and then it must have reacted with the steam in the greenhouse. I was going to tell someone if they went on being really ill, but I don't have to now.' He glanced over at her. 'You don't seem surprised.'

'Well, everyone chucking up . . . some kind of weird poison or whatever – it sounded to me like another of those stink-bomb things you let off before but without the stink. Your kind of trouble, anyway. And then you were acting weird last night.'

'Do you think Mum noticed?'

Chloe gave Itch a 'what do you think?' look. 'Unlikely, I reckon, don't you?'

'I hope so, especially with Dad about to arrive. Please don't tell, Chloe. Even Jack. It's all too scary otherwise.'

Chloe was quiet for a moment. 'You should have owned up, Itch. Really you should. But as they're all OK this morning, I won't say anything now. Of course I won't.'

They were halfway through some rather raggedy cheese and ham sandwiches that Itch had made when they heard a key in the front door. Chloe flew out of the kitchen, and flung herself at her father. Nicholas Lofte was a good six foot four and Chloe managed to jump half of it.

He dropped his bag and caught her in one easy movement. 'Hi, Chloe!' She had buried her face in his neck but Mr Lofte's eyes found his son. 'Hi, Itch – it's good to see you!' He put Chloe down slowly and walked over to Itch, who met him halfway. They embraced in the way a fourteen-year-old allows, awkwardly but still with meaning.

Once again Itch's head was held in both hands and his face inspected closely.

'Well, I've seen worse, that's for sure. You still look pale, son, but your mother says you're on the mend. I think I've got most of the story, but tell me what happened.'

Itch smiled — it was good to hear his father's rich Cornish voice fill the room. Nicholas Lofte was a rig superintendent on an oil rig in the North Sea, where he had worked for as long as Itch could remember. He was clearly good at his job, respected and in demand, but both Chloe and Itch hated the amount of time it took him away from them. They had felt this all the more keenly since their elder brother had disappeared to university. It had only been three weeks since their dad was last home, but the gaps between visits seemed to have got longer since they'd moved to Cornwall.

Once again Itch told his story about what had happened in the greenhouse, not trusting himself to look at Chloe.

'So we are still none the wiser as to where this gas came from? Any analysis done? No?' Nicholas asked, mouth full of sandwich. 'In a twenty-first-century school, that seems ridiculous. Well, it'll be the end of the greenhouse; I can't imagine any other classes going in there.'

This was all getting uncomfortable for Itch, and Chloe changed the subject.

'How long are you off for, Dad? It's strange to have you here during the week.'

'Just till Monday, Chloe; I managed to rearrange some shifts and took some leave — they all under-stood.'

'How's the rig?' asked Itch. 'Don't hear much about it these days.'

'Oh, you know. Same old, same old. You've heard it all before. I get bored with it myself. What I really need is a surf. Who's up for it?'

Itch had been about to suggest a tour of the rearranged shed but now thought better of it — he wanted to spend some time with his dad. In the past Nicholas had always been full of details of the latest drill, but recently he'd been reluctant to talk about work. Itch had grown up assuming his dad enjoyed his job; now he wasn't so sure.

Then, remembering why he had returned home, Nicholas added, 'As long as you're OK, Itch — don't want to get you out too soon.'

But Itch was already heading to get his wetsuit from the garage.

'I'll come down to the beach but I might sit this one out, Dad,' Chloe said.

Nicholas was about to remonstrate with his daughter but thought better of it. 'How's your mum?'

'She's fine, I think. Busy, you know. A bit stressed.'

Her father nodded but didn't say any more.

Itch appeared in his tight wetsuit. Nicholas disguised his laugh as a cough.

'Heavens, Itch, you can't go out like that! You'll do yourself a mischief. You need a new one. Fancy an early birthday present? Come on, let's go via town.'

Itch changed back, and the three of them walked down to the main parade of shops via the golf course. On the way Itch told his dad about the explosion, his eyebrows and the removal of all his equipment to the shed.

'No wonder your mother is stressed. Easier on the rig than here! We'll have a look at the shed when we get back, but it sounds a reasonable plan to me.'

They had turned onto the high street and had reached the first of the surf shops. It didn't take long to fix Itch up with what he needed, and fifteen minutes later they were beach-bound with his new O'Neill Psychofreak wetsuit in an overly elaborate carrier bag.

'That's a birthday present, right?' said Chloe.

'An early one, yes,' replied her dad.

'Just checking.'

They picked up the boards at their beach hut on the sea front. This wasn't one of those elaborate painted huts you see on postcards and tourist posters but an all-year working hut, its cream paint blistered and peeling. The Lofte children left their surf boards here and considered it their property. Their mother certainly didn't come down and their father only on occasions like this. It smelled permanently damp and musty.

Chloe found an old magazine and followed her brother and father down to some rocks, where they left their towels. Itch and his dad ran out into the surf, boards under their arms. They charged in without stopping, reached thigh-deep water and threw themselves onto their boards. That was the easy bit. Itch could get onto his board as well as anyone; it was what happened next that was a puzzle.

He was desperate to be good at surfing. His sister and cousin loved it, but for Itch it was like living next to Wembley and being hopeless at football. The Cornish waves were some of the best in the world: you were expected to master the basics. But aside from the usual tourist-style belly-board surfing, Itch couldn't do it. He loved the look of his new wetsuit but he felt a fraud. Instead of being the worst-dressed, worst surfer on the beach, he was now the best-dressed, worst surfer on the beach. Big deal.

Itch and his father paddled their way out to where the Atlantic swell began the mysterious process of sorting which would be a breaking wave and which would merely fall back again. They waited for several minutes before a decent one rolled in. Nicholas sensed it first, feeling the undertow and the swelling of the ocean behind him. He used his arms to position the board, making slight adjustments in front of the incoming wave. Itch reacted a few seconds later, and was paddling furiously to catch up when he saw the back of his father's board rise with the wave; Nicholas, crouching now, was accelerating towards the beach. Within seconds he was on his feet and, arms outstretched, waving to Chloe. She waved her magazine back at him.

Itch, of course, had missed the wave and was annoyed with himself; he really should have caught that one. It had taken his father all the way in, and he was even now charging back through the surf, with the wild smile of a surfer who has judged it just right.

'Come on, let's get one together!' Nicholas called as he paddled his board out to where Itch was circling. They lined up and waited there, heads craned round to watch the approaching swell. As the wave piled higher, they both pushed down into the water with their arms to propel themselves forward. Both boards rose together as the wave arced above them. It shot Nicholas all the way in to the beach again. It crashed over Itch.

Although his father was encouraging, Itch had lost heart and just wanted to go home. The top-of-the-range wetsuit made him feel even worse – he had no right to wear it. He had come to spend some time with his dad, but now he wished he'd stayed and sorted out the shed. He knew what he was good at, knew where he was at home. And it wasn't the sea.

They had only been in the water for fifteen minutes when Nicholas suggested they call it a day.

Itch agreed, and they waded out of the water, pulling their boards behind them.

'You've got strong arms, Itch; paddling the board well is a useful skill to have. You'll get the hang of it in time. You forget – I was born here!'

Itch knew his father meant well, but his words were painful. *I'm a good paddler. Wow. You must be so proud*, he thought.

Chloe threw them the towels, and they returned the boards to the hut, where Itch and his father changed out of their wetsuits.

On the way back to the house Nicholas raised the subject of the shed again, and Itch told him what he and Chloe had done that morning. He admitted that quite a few gardening implements still needed a home as a result of his takeover, but at least he wasn't going to be experimenting in the house again.

Once in the shed, Itch showed his father the boxes, while carefully detouring around the surviving 'dangerous items'. The gunpowder and the radioactive clock hands were still in his rucksack, and that hung on a peg where some shears had been.

'Robert Brent would approve,' said Nicholas.

Itch looked up. 'The guy who wrote Grandpa's chemistry book?'

'His father nodded. 'That's him.'

'Well, I could do with him around here: *he* might

approve, but Mum most certainly doesn't. She'd be happy if I chucked it all away today. Chloe wouldn't be that bothered and Gabriel's not here.'

'I'm interested . . .'

'Yes, but you're not here either, Dad, are you? Basically it's me, Mum and Chloe these days . . .' Itch trailed off; he hadn't meant to sound so angry. There was an awkward silence.

'You're right, son, you're right.' Nicholas's shoulders had slumped a little. 'It's not easy sometimes, Itch. I get here when work allows – it's important work we're doing, you know – but your mother . . . well, it's just difficult to . . .' He was struggling to find the words and Itch wasn't sure he wanted him to find them.

Itch changed the subject. Finding a pinkish slice of rock, he held it up so the light caught it. 'Know what that is?' he said.

'Er. Oh. A small piece of feldspar, maybe? So – potassium. Am I right?'

'Yup.' Itch tossed it to his father, who caught it.

'Nice piece.' Nicholas covered the silence with an unnecessarily close inspection of the feldspar. 'Look, Itch, I'll make an effort to get down more often, OK? I'll ask, anyway.'

'Any chance of you hanging round for half term?'

'Oh. When's that?'

'Sort of now really. And next week.'

Nicholas sighed. 'Sorry, son, no; this is just compassionate leave.' He looked sad but then brightened. 'I had a thought on the way down, though. Fancy some work experience?'

'Er, not especially, no. What do you mean?'

'Well, look at all this, Itch! You love this stuff, don't you? It's been your passion for ages now – and there's this guy at chapel, Bob Evert, who runs the mine at Provincetown. He might take you on for a week. Do you have anything planned?'

'Well, no, but what would I do? I'm not old enough to go mining, am I?'

'Of course not, and there isn't much mining going on anyway. They just keep it going for tourists really. But you might be able to help in the shop; I'm sure Bob would love to have someone keen around the place. And you'd have someone to talk to about potassium! Come to chapel and I'll introduce you.'

Chapel was something else they didn't do when their dad was away. Itch didn't mind either way, but remembered that, early on, it had been the first time he realized that his parents didn't agree on everything. Jude Lofte had come once and never returned.

The rest of the week passed like a mini holiday, and Sunday morning found all the Loftes at breakfast. Nicholas explained his work-experience plan to Jude, who seemed quite taken with it.

'I think it's a terrific idea, Itch – and not just because it'll stop you blowing up the house for a few days. I don't think anyone else is thinking of work experience yet but it would look great on your CV.'

This was precisely the sort of thing that parents say all the time, but Itch was warming to the idea. His dad would be back on the rig tomorrow, so why not? He might even get some new bits of tin for his collection.

So Nicholas, Itch and Chloe set off for chapel, and Jude stayed behind to 'work on emails'. Itch didn't mind going to chapel. There was no one his age there – indeed no one within twenty years – but that was the point. He was free of the need to try to make friends, then fail. Everyone always seemed pleased to see him.

Chapel was a small granite building with BUILT 1787 carved in stone above the door. Inside, it had whitewashed walls, dark brown pews and musty old hymn books. There were no candles, no statues and no stained-glass windows. 'That's not our style,' was what his father said. The service didn't require much of the congregation; the minister seemed to do all the work. When he spoke, Itch always counted the hymn books or panes of glass in the main window. Today he reached 95 and 120.

After the service his dad introduced him to Bob Evert, an overweight balding man with a ready smile and firm handshake. He was in his early sixties, Itch thought, and quite the cheeriest old person he'd met.

'So this is Itchingham Lofte! I must have seen you a couple of years back but I barely recognize you!' Bob Evert was one of those men who always spoke so loudly that everyone within a range of twenty metres could hear everything. 'Funny business at the academy this week! Your dad says you were sick but you're OK now – is that right?' Itch nodded. 'And he says you're interested in work experience next week. Well, we could always do with some extra help around the place, and as it's half term we might be quite busy. Better not call it work experience since you're really too young for that – let's try "voluntary work". How does that sound? What do you say, Itch?'

Before Itch could reply Evert jumped in again. 'Actually, you could bring a friend if you like. Know anyone who would fancy it?'

4

Bob Evert had made Itch feel he would be quite the most useful member of his team at South-West Mines. Itch assumed he spoke to everyone like that. As for inviting anyone, well, he didn't exactly have a long list of friends to draw on. The only person he could suggest was Jack, so he had called her after lunch on Sunday. She was unsure to start with, but had agreed as she had nothing planned for the half term.

Work experience – or 'voluntary work', as they were going to have to call it – wasn't something Itch had been planning on. Getting hold of some replacement phosphorus, some mercury and maybe some cobalt would be more fun, but the Province-town mine did sound intriguing. They had had lessons on mining in Cornwall, of course, but Itch had never seen a mine for real. He found he was looking forward to it. They would be picked up on Monday morning by the chief engineer, Jolyon Barth, who lived not far from the Loftes.

The doorbell rang at 7.30 and Itch was dressed and ready. Jack stood at the door wearing jeans and a large I ♥ CA sweatshirt.

'I could never quite bring myself to wear one of those,' said Itch, and invited her in. She had just shut the door when the bell rang again. It was an unsmiling red-haired man.

'You must be Itchingham Lofte. I'm Jolyon Barth, the engineer at Provincetown. How do you do.' They shook hands rather formally, and Itch introduced Jack. Barth was about forty, strongly built, with freckles on his face and forearms. He opened the rear door of his Mercedes and both cousins got in. This felt a bit weird – as though Barth was a minicab driver taking them to the station. They sat in embarrassed silence. It was a relief when Barth put the radio on.

'Your dad get off this morning?' Jack asked.

'Yes,' said Itch gloomily. 'Off at six. He was getting the first flight from Newquay. Not sure when he'll be back – he took some leave after hearing about our fun in the greenhouse.'

'Did you see the video of Flowerdew with sick over him?' laughed Jack. 'It is so cool!'

'Yeah, Dart's going to go crazy when she sees it.' Itch was smiling now. 'She'll probably get it taken down, but it's on twenty thousand hits or something.

My favourite bit is where you can see her trying not to smile when Craig's apologizing to Flowerdew and wiping down his suit with his hand!'

They were laughing so much Barth had started watching them in his mirror. They lowered their voices.

'Apparently,' whispered Jack, 'Ian Steele now has Craig's puking as his ring tone!' That set them off again, and Barth turned up the radio.

They were heading south, but had to travel east and inland to pick up the road to Provincetown. It had once been a busy tin-mining community right on the coast, high above the cliffs, but now almost everything and everybody had left.

The old, unused winding tower came into view first, still an impressive thirty metres high, an iconic image of mining the world over. Not much else of the past had survived. A few houses were lived in and loved; most were dilapidated or derelict. Two of the miners' cottages had been turned into an art and craft exhibition, and a third told the story of mining in the area. New buildings had been built around the edges of the site, with all the accommodation set back from the cliffs. In contrast, the old mine works stretched to the very edge.

Barth drove the cousins straight to the office, which was another converted miner's house, the one nearest the works. It was slate grey like all the others, but had been given a new roof and an extension at the side. A small brass plaque on the door said: SOUTH-WEST MINES. Barth parked his car next to six others, a new 5-Series BMW standing out from the pack.

'Presumably Evert's,' said Jack as they got out and Barth took them into the house/office.

They were shown where to sit and wait for Evert. It had once been the hallway and kitchen area but now housed two sofas, a long, low table, a coffee machine and a series of framed photos on the wall. Most were old black and whites, with miners posing without smiling – as everyone seemed to do back then. *Maybe they didn't have much to smile about,* thought Itch. The last three photos, by contrast, were in colour and featured a beaming Bob Evert in every one: Bob Evert shaking hands with the mayor; Bob Evert underground with a large, bright yellow digger; and Bob Evert looking thoughtful while studying maps.

'Don't tell me,' said Jack. 'My guess is that's Bob Evert.'

'Yup, that's him,' said Itch, and they sat and waited for his arrival.

'Do we come in with Barth every day?' said Jack. 'Couldn't we get the bus?'

'I was thinking that too. But wouldn't it take for ever?'

'About that, yes,' said Jack.

Somewhere in the house a door opened, and the

booming tones of Bob Evert filtered through.

'Here he comes,' said Itch. 'And I think he always talks that loudly.' They listened as the voice got closer and louder.

Evert strode in, finishing a call and putting his BlackBerry away. 'Itch! Hello! Welcome to South-West Mines! And who is your friend?'

'This is Jack Lofte, my cousin.'

'Another Lofte! Very good news! You are both welcome, of course. Let me quickly show you round before it gets busy.'

He led them out towards the mine works. There was a stiff breeze blowing off the Atlantic and it lifted Bob Evert's carefully positioned flap of hair away from his head so that it was at right angles to his scalp. He took a SW MINES baseball cap out of his pocket and put it on, pushing his hair underneath.

'The last tin mine in Provincetown closed in 1950 – it was the end of an industry that stretched back hundreds of years. But in 1981 the council asked me to look into opening it up again as a tourist attraction. I took it on and realized I could go one better than that. I could open it to the public *and* keep it ticking over as a going concern, so that if the price of tin rose enough, we could resume mining in Provincetown.' He beamed.

He took them through some of the old mine works. Crumbling, fenced-off chimneys stood alongside rusting shaft-drilling equipment. They came to the entrance to the new workings – smaller modern buildings of blue corrugated metal housing the lift to take tourists and, if needed, miners down into the ground.

'We don't produce a lot of tin, but enough to be able to say that South-West Mines have brought mining back to Cornwall!' Evert got a small lump of rock out of his pocket and handed it to Itch. 'One of the first bits of ore that we mined here. Dug it myself too!'

Itch held it up to catch the light. It was a piece of shiny dark granite, with a few lines of a lighter substance flecked down one side.

'Cornish tin, that is! Doesn't it make you proud?' Evert took the ore back and pocketed it. 'We produce just enough for tourists to buy in our shop, but if we needed to we could increase production within a month. We need to keep everything ready to go so you'll see a lot of maintenance folk around this week: they're making sure everything is safe.'

'Do you get any help from the students at West Ridge School of Mining?' said Itch. The nearby college had an international reputation in mining, geology and environmental science; it seemed obvious for their students to work with South-West Mines. Mr Watkins was always enthusing about the college, and Itch thought there was going to be a school trip there.

'Ah, yes . . .' said Evert, pausing only slightly. 'Not really. We haven't seen any of them for a while now.' He turned to look at the cousins. 'And you know what? That's fine with me! Don't need them! We are fine on our own, thank you very much!' He smiled at them. 'Now, let's introduce you to Mrs Lee and she can sort you out.'

Mrs Lee, it turned out, was in charge of the shop and exhibition. She was a large lady with greying hair tied back with a black ribbon. She was wearing a green SW MINES sweatshirt which, Itch and Jack agreed, was a cruel punishment to inflict on her. It really didn't fit any part of her upper body, which seemed to be fighting to escape. As Evert came in, she stood up.

'Don't get up, Enid! Good morning to you! This is Itchingham and Jack Lofte – they are doing a bit of work experience with us this week. I think some uniform might be in order . . .' He made a show of winking at Mrs Lee and left.

She called the cousins over to a drawer behind her desk and offered them a cap and a sweatshirt each. 'You'll like these, I think.' She spoke with a strong Cornish accent. 'Just the one colour and just the one size. See what you think.' Itch and Jack exchanged glances and removed their sweatshirts. They pulled on their new ones and Mrs Lee put baseball hats on their heads. 'Lovely. Quite lovely,' she declared.

'You never told me we were going to end up looking like we work in Burger King,' whispered Jack. 'I hope no one we know comes here this week!'

They spent the morning taking money at the till or welcoming visitors at the museum. A slow but steady stream of interested grown-ups and bored children wandered through. If anyone had questions, they were to be referred to the guide, who was called Alice and turned out to be Bob Evert's daughter. Years ago, according to Mrs Lee, they had employed former miners to do the tour.

'They were lovely men,' she said. 'They'd worked here for years. But they were let go; none of them have been near the place for years. Shame, really. I imagine—' Mrs Lee broke off and looked around in case she was being overheard. 'I imagine Alice is cheaper. Nice girl, though,' she added in case she sounded too disloyal.

Alice turned out to be in her early twenties and made the South-West Mines uniform about as glamorous as it could get by customizing it with bangles, designer jeans and UGG boots. 'Traditional mining gear!' said Itch.

Tours left whenever there were a dozen visitors ready to go, and that happened three times that morning. Itch and Jack were offered a twenty-minute break at midday and took their sandwiches outside. They walked to the edge of the mining works, just a few metres from the cliff face, and sat on some loose rocks.

'Odd place,' said Jack.

'Odd people,' said Itch.

'Mainly, I sold postcards,' said Jack. 'And the Americans bought all the toffee.'

'The Japanese seemed most interested in the Cornish tin pixies,' said Itch.

'Classy,' said Jack. 'I saw those. Looked like trolls. But at least they're made from tin. So it's slightly Cornish.'

'Except they turned out to be made out of recycled aluminium from Indonesia. I checked.'

They both laughed at that.

As they ate their lunch, they watched the Atlantic rolling in to smash itself against the foot of the rocks far below. This was one of the stretches of coastline with no beach, the high and low tides marked by a rising and falling sea level. They fed the remaining bread, cheese-and-onion crisps and Twix crumbs to the seagulls and walked back in the direction of the shop. Jack pointed at another series of buildings beyond the mining works, which they hadn't noticed before. Surrounded by equipment and out-houses, it had its own road and car park, and they wandered over to take a closer look. It was similar to the new mineshaft building they had seen earlier – a grey cabin twenty metres above the ground, surrounded by steel frames, with a conveyer angling down into a corrugated iron shed. The car park was empty apart from the Mercedes they had arrived in – Jolyon Barth's. As they approached, the driver's door opened and Barth got out. They hadn't noticed he was inside.

'Can I help you guys?' he said, walking over.

'We were just looking around. We hadn't noticed this bit before,' said Itch.

'Well, it's kind of out of bounds really. It's just for maintenance.' Barth sounded tetchy. 'We need to keep the mine at operational levels of performance at all times, and this is where the teams go in. That's all you need to know. Now I expect Mrs Lee needs you – off you go.'

Itch and Jack turned round and headed back. Itch looked over his shoulder and saw Barth standing and watching them leave.

'Think we were being warned off there, Jack. He didn't sound quite so friendly as this morning.'

'And he wasn't exactly fun to be with then, either. We should definitely explore the option of getting here by bus.'

'Agreed,' said Itch as they re-entered the world of Mrs Lee and mining toffee.

The highlight of their week came after a conversation with UGG-booted Alice, the tour guide. Itch and Jack both wanted to go down the mine and asked her how that could be arranged. It turned out that only Mr Evert or Mr Barth could arrange it, and she would see what she could do. Then, late on the Thursday, just as they were preparing to pack up for the day, Evert put his head round the door.

'Shaft entrance lift in ten minutes – leave your phones.'

Jolyon Barth was standing at the entrance to the lift shaft when the cousins arrived with Evert. Barth handed them jackets and scratched white helmets. Next came heavy battery packs which strapped around their waists, each with a cable that looped over the shoulder to a powerful electric lamp. Barth pulled open the grille for them to enter the lift and they stooped as Evert, behind them, bellowed, 'Welcome to my world!'

They shuffled forward into the 'cage', as everyone called it. There was room for six, according to the sign, but four was quite a squeeze. Barth closed the outer and inner grille doors and pressed one of the many buttons on a brass-coloured panel. With a lurch, the lift shuddered and then suddenly dropped as the cousins gasped and reached for the sides. The men laughed as the lift slowed to a more leisurely rate of descent.

'It's tradition!' yelled Evert. 'All first-timers get that! You won't forget your first trip in a hurry!' He and Barth looked thoroughly pleased with themselves; both Loftes looked distinctly green.

'Right. On with the tour. It's forty metres down and it'll take about a minute to get there,' said Evert. 'We'll need to fix the lighting, but you should get a pretty good idea of life underground.'

Unlike an ordinary lift, you could see through the grille door and watch the different levels of rock they were descending through. This was Barth's cue to speak.

'Once we are through the layers of topsoil and building foundations, it's pretty much granite all the way. It's straight granite at first with nothing else to see, but now' – he pointed to some vertical brown stripes appearing in the black stone – 'you can see the tin veins or lodes appearing.' They trundled their way down further, watching the changing colours and hues in the rock face. Over the din they heard running water, and then saw gleaming wet rock shining back at them.

'What happened here during the earthquake in December?' asked Itch. 'Presumably no one was down here at the time? That would have been scary.'

'We had to shut for forty-eight hours to check that everything was safe, of course,' said Evert, 'but no, there was no one down here at four a.m. The safety and maintenance teams spent a long time studying all the cracks and fissures but they gave us the OK eventually.' He had started to frown now, and fell silent till the lift stopped with a clatter. His face brightened. 'Right, here we are! Not exactly a journey to the centre of the Earth, but as close as you're getting!'

Jolyon Barth pulled open the lift doors. Itch and Jack were pleased that they had jackets on as the temperature had dropped noticeably. Their four lamps bobbed and shook as they ducked out of the lift, sending wild, dancing spotlights into the dark. Barth walked into the gloom and turned on some strip lighting. It revealed entrances to two large tunnels with metal tracks on the ground and a tangle of wires running the length of the low ceiling. Barth, stooping slightly, led the way down the left-hand tunnel, passing a series of alcoves and dark side passages.

'Nearly there!' shouted Evert, his voice louder than ever in the enclosed shaft. They came to an opening with a high ceiling, where an imposing yellow digger was parked. Behind it loomed a black wall with great grooves cut out of it; piles of rock lay on the ground. They recognized the digger from the photographs outside the office. It was surprisingly long and flat, with huge tractor-sized tyres and a large rock bucket pointing up at the front.

'These are the exposed lodes that we are working on — they're the ones that will be mined when the price of tin rises,' said Evert. 'Climb aboard — see what it feels like!'

Itch and Jack took it in turns to sit in the digger like kids on a pier ride. They looked at the control panel. It had two joysticks set in a keyboard, and a computer screen with digital clocks and symbols. Neither of the cousins touched a thing; both felt a bit stupid.

Evert didn't notice. He crouched down, picking up the loose rocks, sifting them through his fingers and letting them fall. 'This is what it's all about.' It was the quietest he had spoken all week. 'This could change us all, you know. There's power in these rocks. Don't you feel it?'

He wasn't expecting an answer, but Itch said, 'I do, yes. They're beautiful.'

Jack looked at him in puzzlement. 'Really? Are we looking at the same thing?'

'Yup,' said Itch. 'Cassiterite. SnO_2. Tin ore.'

Evert and Barth exchanged a look. 'Dead right,' said Barth, 'and if we had more of it we'd be in business again.'

They spent a few more minutes looking around, but Evert was now standing by the lift, clearly anxious to get back to the surface. He opened the doors and the cousins joined him. Jack wondered why Barth wasn't coming back up with them.

'Things to check, Jack – many things to check,' was the reply.

As they waited for their bus home, Jack put her hand in her pocket. 'Got something for you, Itch. Here.' Her fingers were clasped around something and Itch held out his hand. Jack dropped a lump of tin ore in it. He gasped. 'What the . . .? How did you . . .? It's beautiful.'

'If you say so, Itch. I was annoyed they didn't chuck you one down there – times can't be that hard. Evert has a Beemer and Barth has a Merc, after all. So I just, well, helped myself when they weren't looking. Do you have tin in your collection?'

'I do, yes, but nothing like this.' He angled it to catch the light. It was heavy in his hand – about the size and weight of a snooker ball, but square, with jagged edges that had crystallized points. At first it had looked completely black, but brown showed clearly in the sunlight. Itch examined it minutely.

'You like it, then?'

Itch didn't reply; he hadn't heard.

'Should have kept it for your birthday,' Jack added.

'But it's stolen,' said Itch, coming out of his tin-induced trance. 'I should give it back.'

'You should,' agreed Jack, 'but my guess is you won't. You're in love. With a rock.' Again, Itch didn't reply. She continued, 'Anyway, it's pretty common, isn't it? Especially in Cornwall.'

'Tin foil isn't tin,' said Itch. 'Tin cans aren't tin. A lot of things called tin aren't. But this most certainly is.' He was speaking quietly, as if in church. 'Wow. Element number fifty.'

'Have you got fifty now?' asked Jack.

'No, pea-brain, it's *number* fifty on the Table of Elements, in the same column as silicon, carbon and lead.'

'Would now be a good time to remind you that I don't really know what an element is?'

Itch gave a little sigh. 'I can't believe you keep saying that! It's pure *stuff*, OK? It's the most basic stuff you can get. It's stuff that can't be broken down, can't be made any simpler.'

'Like Darcy Campbell?' said Jack.

Itch laughed. 'Yeah, OK, exactly like Darcy Campbell!'

They sat for another thirty minutes, with Itch talking tin and Jack wondering where their bus was. They were normally on their way back by now, but the trip underground had delayed their departure by long enough to miss the 32, which took them most of the way home. The car park was almost empty now. It looked as though only Evert, Barth and a couple of others were still there.

'We could always go back with Barth if we're stuck,' said Jack.

'Let's hang on a bit longer,' said Itch. 'I'm sure there's a later bus. I'd rather that than another trip with Mr Happy.' They sat on the bus-stop bench, watching the road for a sign of the next bus.

'I was on Facebook Chat with Debbie last night,'

said Jack. 'She seems fine now and says that the others are doing OK too. Miss Glenacre had it worst, apparently, but maybe that's an age thing.'

Itch felt himself flush and looked intently at the tin ore in his hand again. The subject of the greenhouse hadn't come up for a couple of days and he was feeling increasingly uncomfortable about not telling Jack what had happened.

'Anyway, the greenhouse is being taken apart. Apparently they are going through all the plants one by one to see what happened, but so far they haven't found anything. They'll all be gone by the time we go back on Monday.'

Itch was just about to explain about the arsenic when four large unmarked white trucks came past in close convoy and turned into the mine works. They didn't go to the main car park but carried on round to the other car park at the back, out of sight of the road.

'Maintenance?' said Itch. 'They've all gone round to the area at the back that Barth turned us off. Seems a bit late to be starting work.'

'Must be shift work or something,' said Jack. 'Easier to do when there's no one around.'

Suddenly Itch spotted a bus coming down the hill. 'Looks like we don't need to ask Barth for a lift after all. Hooray for the thirty-two! Come on, Jack – I've got something to tell you.'

5

Jack listened to Itch's confession open-mouthed. The bus journey took around forty minutes, and their hushed conversation had lasted every second of it. When they got off, they stood at the bus stop as Jack went over it all again. In contrast to Chloe, who had guessed some of the story, Jack was totally flabbergasted.

'But that's so wrong, Itch! You should have told someone! What if the sickness had got worse?'

'Well, I . . .' started Itch, taken aback. 'I wasn't sure what to do. It was only a small piece of wallpaper, so I thought it would only be a small amount of gas—'

'Oh, come on, Itch – you just didn't want to be found out. Which is fair enough, but couldn't you have left an anonymous message at the hospital or something?'

Itch frowned. He knew he could have left a

message, but he had been too scared of being found out. Following on from Chloe's comments, he was irritated by the criticism. 'Well, you've just stolen a rock from the mines,' he said, hating himself even as he was saying it.

'What!' exclaimed Jack. 'I did that for you! And helping myself to a loose piece of tin is hardly the same as poisoning a class with arsenic.'

'Arsine gas,' corrected Itch.

Jack's mouth was open wide, but nothing came out. Eventually she turned and walked off, calling, 'Goodbye, Itch,' angrily over her shoulder. Itch trudged home, his left hand in his pocket, wrapped around the tin.

Both cousins missed their last day at the mine. Jack texted Itch to say she was too tired, and he rang South-West Mines, leaving a message for Mr Evert. He moped around all morning. He was still mad at Jack for criticizing him, but mainly he was angry with himself. He knew she was right. He sent a text:

Sorry, Jack. Messed that one up.

The reply came within ten minutes: OK.

Saturday morning found Jude Lofte making tea, Chloe at the computer, and Itch at the kitchen table with his toast and his lump of tin ore in front of him.

'A new pet?' asked Jude.

'Got it at the mine,' said Itch. He couldn't think of the circumstances under which his mother might meet Bob Evert, so there seemed no risk in saying how he had come by it. 'It's tin. Want to see?'

His mother wandered over and gave it a cursory glance. 'Looks harmless enough. But it still stays in the shed, OK? Any homework to do before school on Monday?' She sat down at the table with her mug, and Chloe joined them with a bowl of cereal.

Itch had, of course, forgotten that he had history and English homework, and these were two subjects he always struggled with. Writing essays took for ever and he found he could only get them done if a crisis was looming – that crisis usually being 'needs to be in tomorrow'. By Sunday afternoon it normally felt too scary to leave it any longer and he would get down to it.

'I'm doing it tomorrow, Mum,' he said. 'It'll be fine. Don't worry. Fancy a surf, Chloe? Swell looked pretty good yesterday.'

'I think that's the wrong way round,' said Jude. 'Homework, then surf. Your priorities are all wrong, Itch.'

Chloe looked at her brother, then at her mother. 'What if we make it quick, Mum? The tide's just right now – it'll have gone flabby by this afternoon.'

'Really?' said Jude. She sipped more coffee and looked between the two of them. 'OK, but some homework before lunch, please.'

'Thanks, Mum,' said Itch, and they cleared away their breakfast.

The wind and cloud had given way to some warm sunshine and a slight breeze, but the Atlantic rollers were still swollen. As they walked down towards the beach they could see nine or ten surfers out already.

'Flabby?' said Itch. 'Do waves go flabby?'

'No idea,' said Chloe. 'It was all I could think of at the time. Worked, though.'

'Yeah, thanks.'

'Why are we doing this?' asked Chloe. 'You don't normally suggest a surf.'

'Mum was building up to a big homework lecture. I wanted to get out and it's all I could think of. I'll just paddle about – I'm good at that.'

They opened the hut and got changed. Itch, still feeling uncomfortable in his brash new wetsuit, let Chloe run ahead of him. The sea was indeed perfect for surfing, with big Atlantic waves lined up and rolling in. New surfers were arriving all the time, and Chloe joined those running into the safe, patrolled area between the red and yellow flags. Itch sat glumly on the rocks, watching his sister catching the waves, and only joined her after fifteen minutes, but by then Chloe was shivering.

'I've had enough!' she called over the roar. 'I thought you were never coming in! What were you waiting for? Go on – give it a go!' And she was gone, wading through the water, heading for the beach hut.

Itch tried a couple of waves, but his timing hadn't improved and, disappointed with himself as usual, he paddled his way back again.

As he ambled up the beach, grateful that their dad hadn't been there, he noticed someone hunched in a deckchair on the paved walkway between the huts and the steps that led down to the beach. The man was staring out to sea, a surfboard doubling as a foot rest. He looked familiar, and as he got closer, Itch realized it was Cake, the mineral seller he had met in St Austell.

There had been quite a few stalls on the fringes of the fair he and Jack had gone to, but Cake had had the most interesting collection, and Itch had spent hours browsing through his rocks and powders. Cake had told him that he had dropped out of college, where he was studying English, and just 'drifted, surfed and sold stuff'. He had an occasionally updated Facebook page which told his customers where to find him next, and turned up at fairs and festivals all over the south-west, setting up a small stall with his latest acquisitions. And that had included, of course, the arsenic-infused wallpaper.

With his board still dripping under his arm, Itch ran over. 'Hello, Cake. You all right?'

Cake looked up, beads around his neck and

wrists rattling as he shifted in the deckchair. Itch reckoned he was about thirty. He had dark, weathered skin and was wearing grubby knee-length surf shorts, a faded red T-shirt that said MAVERICK'S SURF SHOP, and sandals. He swept his long matted hair away from his squinting eyes.

'All right, Itchingham Lofte! The tall kid with the long name! So this is your patch, is it?' He coughed and cleared his throat. He had the coarse, gravelly voice of a heavy smoker, and a London accent straight out of *EastEnders*. There were three satchels tucked under his chair, along with some chip wrappers and a carton of fruit juice. It occurred to Itch that Cake had probably spent the night on the beach.

'Haven't seen you for ages,' said Itch. 'I need to talk to you. Don't go anywhere – I'll just get out of this wetsuit.' And he ran back to the hut, where Chloe was waiting for him, already changed. 'Hey, Chloe, hang on a second, I want you to meet this guy.' Itch darted into the hut and got dressed as quickly as you can when you're in a wetsuit and a hurry. He grabbed a towel and his rucksack and was rubbing his hair dry as he led his sister over to Cake's deckchair. 'Chloe, this is Cake. Cake, Chloe.'

'All right, Chloe? Spit of your brother. Nice to meet you.'

'Nice to meet you too.' Chloe gave her brother a

look which he took to mean, *Your weird friend, not mine.* 'You the guy who sold Itch the wallpaper?' she said.

'Well now, pull up a chair,' said Cake, pointing to a pile of deckchairs against the wall of the last beach hut. Itch dragged a couple over, set them up and settled himself in one. Chloe stood, leaning on hers.

'Well?' she said.

Cake, eyes closed, said, 'Very rare, that – should have charged your brother more.'

'Are you kidding me?' said Itch. 'That wallpaper could have put me in jail! As it is, it put four people in hospital and made all my class sick! You never told me how dangerous it was.'

'And our school got closed,' said Chloe.

Cake opened his eyes and closed them again. 'I heard about that. I did wonder . . .' He paused and looked at Itch. 'The clue, my Lord Itchingham, was in the word "arsenic". One of the world's most famous poisons, favoured toxin of numerous Victorian murderers. How come it ended up in school?'

Itch explained how he had taken it into the greenhouse; how it had caused the vomiting; and how he had flushed it down the toilet.

'Down the bog? What an ignoble end. I shall have to think more carefully before doing business with you in future.'

Itch was exasperated. 'Well, what should I have done, then? Dried it out on a radiator and handed it to my art teacher saying, *Here, miss, you'll like this, it's a piece of famous wallpaper. See those stains? That's where the arsenic seeped out and poisoned everyone in Miss Glenacre's class*?'

'Whoa, whoa, slow down now, Master Itch,' said Cake, looking at him now. 'I'm sorry if I got you into a pickle. But I wasn't to know you'd be taking it into a steam room, now, was I? There wouldn't have been enough gas to poison all of you.' He rubbed his stubbly chin. 'A few of you, maybe.'

Itch was flabbergasted. 'What! I'm telling you, we were all puking everywhere! You should have seen it!'

Cake sat back and closed his eyes again. 'I'm trying to think what else I got you. Oh yeah, you wanted that gunpowder I had – that was you, wasn't it? Please tell me you didn't take *that* into the kitchens and set fire to it.'

Itch smiled at that. 'All right, fair point,' he said.

'Have you got a licence for selling this stuff?' said Chloe, still standing. 'There must be an exam or test you have to pass. Or can anyone sell explosives and poison?'

'Chloe! I'll sort this – really,' said Itch. He wasn't surprised she was being tetchy with Cake – she always took his side, in public anyway – but he didn't want to upset Cake. He not only sold Itch the elements he wanted; he understood why he wanted them in the first place. They had talked at length about other collectors, obscure elements and how to find them.

Itch had never come across anyone like Cake before. He appeared to have no cares or commitments at all. He laughed his way through most conversations, even when he was being serious, and was always interested in Itch's stories and opinions. He regularly asked about Itch's family, though always stayed vague when asked about his own.

Chloe made a harrumphing noise and looked cross like their mother did, but kept quiet.

Itch continued. 'I've had to move all my collection into the shed, but I'm down to thirty now that I lost the wallpaper and phosphorus.' Seeing Cake's puzzled expression, he explained what had happened in his bedroom.

'I can replace that for you. And I've got some other new stuff you might be interested in.' He indicated the satchels under the chair. 'What are you going for next?'

'I was thinking of sodium. Or mercury,' said Itch. 'But I haven't got much cash left. I was going to wait for my birthday next month and see what I could afford.'

Cake leaned forward and reached under his chair for the largest of the three satchels. He undid the two buckles, lifted the leather flap and rummaged around inside. 'Tell you what, why don't I give you this as a gesture of good faith and a symbol of our ongoing retail relationship? To help you get over your . . . wallpaper moment.' He handed Itch a battered round tin sealed with black masking tape. 'Just a small amount of phosphorus. Early birthday present. Don't blow this lot up.'

'Wow, thanks, Cake, that's fantastic! Can I look?' Itch was very pleased at this unexpected turn of events and had started to unpeel the tape.

Cake put his hand on the tin. 'Open it on your birthday, young man, and if I were you . . .' He nodded at the increasing number of people walking past them onto the beach and opening up their beach huts.

'I think what he's saying, Itch,' said Chloe, 'is don't draw attention to yourself. If you see what I mean.'

Itch put the still-sealed tin in his rucksack. 'OK, yeah, you're right, sorry. Thanks again.'

'No worries. Now, mercury might take some time – I'm sure an old thermometer won't cut it – but it shouldn't be a problem. Sodium is easy – usual warnings and precautions required, of course. You could combine both if you wanted – sodium amalgam has mercury in it and is a bit less explosive.'

Itch laughed. 'No thanks. I think they are more interesting apart, really.'

'Of course, of course, but more care needed too. Now, let's see . . .' Cake looked in his second satchel.

'You got uranium ore? I think that's what this is . . .' He took out a rough pebble-sized rock, light brown, almost honeycomb in colour, with patches of darker brown and silver lines through it. 'There's a lot of uranium knocking about under Cornwall; they dug it up here for centuries. Any decent element hunter should definitely have some. Take it – it's quite safe. This stuff is only mildly radioactive.' He handed it to Itch.

'What does that mean?' asked Chloe.

'Radioactivity is everywhere,' said Cake. 'Usually from potassium. A tiny fraction of it is radioactive, which is why bananas are too.'

'Excuse me?' said Chloe. 'Bananas are radio-active?'

Cake smiled, his face creasing. 'Good, huh!'

'So uranium is like a bunch of bananas?' said Chloe, clearly not believing a word.

'Well, no, not exactly, but just as safe. Well, almost, anyway.' He pointed at the rock. 'Ten pounds, if you want it – knockdown price for my favourite customer.'

'Is it always this warm?' asked Itch.

'Just been in the sun, I think.'

'You said you *thought* it was uranium. It looks darker, more like iron, to me,' queried Itch.

'Well, I got it from a dealer in Dorset who said he got it from a gob heap there. So I'm surprised because there's no history of uranium over there, and those lines of silver are different. So maybe it's something else; maybe it *is* iron. That's why it's cheap, mate – I can't be sure what it is.'

'What's a gob heap?'

'Ah. A gob heap. A bony heap. A spoil heap. Stuff that's chucked out of mines, young Itchingham. It's not wanted. So me and my mates have a look around and see if we can find anything of interest. And that's where this came from.'

'OK, deal,' said Itch, but then realized he had no cash on him. 'I could run home and get it,' he offered.

Cake shook his head. 'I'll get you the mercury and you can pay for both next time.'

'How will this fit in with Mum's new safety regime?' asked Chloe.

'Well, it'll be in the shed,' said Itch. 'She won't have a clue it's there.' He was about to leave when he remembered the new piece of tin ore in his rucksack. 'Have a look at this, Cake – got it this week. Cool, isn't it?' He sounded prouder than he had intended but Cake smiled as he turned the tin in his hand.

'Nice piece, nice piece. The tables are turned, my son. *You're* showing *me* stuff. Where'd this come from?'

'From the mine at Provincetown. I've been working there this week.'

Cake held it up to the light. 'And they just gave it to you? Must be more decent people there than I thought. The guys at the mining school haven't got a good word to say about them. I'm impressed.'

Itch was starting to feel uncomfortable again. 'Yes, they took us on a tour of the mine and it was like a souvenir, I suppose.' He stood up and put his deckchair back in the pile. 'We should probably be getting home, Cake. When can I get you the money for the uranium?'

'Well, I'll be back here on Wednesday – probably right here – that'll be fine.'

'And maybe with some mercury?'

'And maybe with some mercury, yes. Fine,' said Cake, and he closed his eyes. That appeared to be that, and Itch picked up his rucksack and he and Chloe jogged home.

'He's freaky,' said Chloe.

'He is a bit,' said Itch, 'but I like him.'

'I could see you doing that in a few years,' said Chloe. 'Giving up a top science job to sell rocks and poisons.' Itch laughed at that. 'Does he have family?' she wondered.

'I ask him, but he never says,' said Itch.

'Like I said,' said Chloe. 'Freak.'

Having attempted to do his homework on Sunday afternoon, Itch put away his books and went down to the shed. He and Chloe had got it into reasonable shape, and his father had found alternative homes for the larger gardening items. This meant that his boxed collection could sit on the workbench, and he removed his new lump of rock from his rucksack.

He found his magnifying glass and examined the rock properly for the first time. It wasn't particularly beautiful but was certainly intriguing. It was darker than he remembered, with both the light and darker browns closer to tan and black. The silvery lines that ran through it looked duller too. It seemed to have retained the heat that Cake had suggested had come from the sun. Itch was puzzled by it, but concluded it was not much of a looker compared with his tin ore. However, if it was uranium, it was 92 on the table, and he needed to start a new box. In time he would group it with the radium clock hands, as they were 88, but all he could find for now was an old cardboard *Call of Duty* case, and he slid it in, closing the flaps. He placed the box next to the others.

The following morning, just as he and Chloe were about to set off for school, he decided on a whim to check his new stone again. While his sister complained that they would be late, he went out to the shed and opened the cardboard case again.

For a moment he wondered if he had the right rock. It appeared to have darkened further overnight. The lighter shades of brown were catching up with the darker shades, so although the silvery veins were less shiny, the contrast with them was more stark. He had never seen a stone change colour before – he was sure Mr Watkins had always said that rocks *never* changed colour. Maybe it was the gloom of the shed, he thought, and took it outside. But the sunlight just confirmed the colour change, and Itch stood there in the garden, staring at his puzzle. This was certainly one peculiar piece of rock. Was there a chemical change taking place? Was it reacting to variations in temperature? Maybe it wasn't a rock at all but something man-made?

He only had questions, but thinking that Mr Watkins might have some answers as he taught geology at A level as well as geography, he put the stone in his rucksack and ran to find Chloe.

6

It was another warm day, more summer than spring, and Itch and Chloe Lofte took their usual route to school across the golf course. Itch would have been nervous anyway the first day back after half term, but following the longer, arsenic-enforced break he was quite on edge. Chloe was as reassuring as a younger sister can be.

'If anything, it'll give you street cred. Make you more cool. They'll be like, *Oh, he's one of the sick boys, he was in the greenhouse, he saw Glenacre with puke in her hair.* You'll be fine.'

'You think so? I get to be cool because we were all sick on each other? Is that how it works?' Itch was sceptical but still glad he had told Chloe his secret and that she was on his side. He hoped the same could be said for Jack.

★ ★ ★

Mr Watkins reversed into his classroom, protecting a mug of tea on his usual pile of books.

'Hello again, boys! A good break, I trust. Longer than expected, obviously, so our thanks are due to Johnny, Natalie and Debbie for their noble sacrifice in getting us a longer holiday.'

Everyone laughed, and Jack, sitting next to her cousin, nudged Itch and smiled at him. Itch, relieved, smiled back.

Watkins continued, 'Everyone is now OK, thankfully, but as you'll have heard, the greenhouse is a goner and the enquiries are continuing. Dr Dart wishes it to be known that if any more posters of Dr Flowerdew's unfortunate encounter with Craig's regurgitated lunch appear on notice boards, she will take swift action.'

All the class laughed again. Stills from Sam Jennings's now-famous video had appeared all over the school – including, so it was rumoured, in the staff room.

Mr Watkins smiled briefly, allowing the class their amusement. 'Apart from that, we have a clear run through to the summer, with the ever so small hurdle of exams to navigate in four weeks' time. If, indeed, one navigates hurdles . . .' He took the register. 'And just before everyone disappears, my geography students need to have read up on their deep mine shafts and those lovely wells for our next meeting together. You may go.'

Itch told Jack that he'd see her later and went over to his form teacher. Mr Watkins looked up from his illustrations of well diggers and mine workers.

'The pump shaft at the Fowey Consuls mine was three thousand feet deep – that's almost one thousand metres, Itch. Imagine that! Driven through granite too! An engineering marvel.'

'Yes, sir.'

'Have I told you the story about the seventeen water wheels . . . ?'

'Yes, sir, you have.'

'And the deepest hand-dug—'

'Yes, sir, that too. A few times.'

'Ah. Are you all right, Itchingham?'

'Yes, sir. Fine, thank you – but I have something I'd like to show you when you have a moment.'

'What sort of a "thing"?'

'Well, it's a rock, actually, sir, but I can't work out what it is.'

'Then I'm your man, Itch, as you know. Lunch time is OK – come and find me in the staff room.' Watkins propped his arms on the table, folded his fingers together and rested his chin on them. 'I am intrigued. See you then.'

'OK, thanks, sir.' Itch hoisted his rucksack over his shoulder and headed off to the dreaded worlds of English and RE, then double cricket with Mr Corrin.

★　★　★

104

Just after one o'clock, Itch knocked on the staff-room door and asked for Mr Watkins. In what must have been the time it took to finish his tea, the teacher emerged.

'Ah, Itch and his mystery rock – let's go somewhere quiet.' His teacher set off in the direction of one of the science labs. They were usually empty at lunch time, but the physics and biology labs were busy with revision classes. That left Dr Flowerdew's chemistry lab: it was deserted. Mr Watkins eased himself onto one of the stools and motioned for Itch to join him. 'So what do you have for me, Mr Lofte? I can't remember being brought a rock before.'

Itch, suddenly nervous for reasons he could not work out, removed the stone from his bag and placed it on the table in front of them. There was no doubt in Itch's mind that it was now considerably darker than when he had bought it on Saturday.

Mr Watkins picked it up and peered at it. 'What's the story here, Itch?'

'Well, it might be uranium, sir – that's what I was told. But I've looked online and I can't see any with those silvery threads in it. It looks too dark, closer to iron. Also, it's changing colour.'

'It's doing *what*?'

'It's getting darker. I got it on Saturday, and the browns were lighter and the silver more shiny. That's why I brought it to you.'

Watkins put the rock down on the table and

rubbed his hands together. Then he cracked his knuckles, something he usually only did when he was coming to his favourite bit of a lesson or about to tell a story. 'Well, well, that's certainly intriguing. It looks a little like uranium ore, as you say. Cornwall is full of it, of course. But those silvery veins suggest something else. Sometimes the veins are quartz or tin. But not here, I think. As I often say in class, there is a lot under the ground here that we don't know about. It is still a mystery. Well, here's another one! Has it been warm like this since you got it? Because that would suggest—'

The door to the lab opened and Dr Nathaniel Flowerdew came in. He stopped when he saw Mr Watkins and Itch at the table.

'Ah, Dr Flowerdew, hello. We were looking for somewhere quiet to look at Master Lofte's intriguing rock. You arrived just in time – come and see.'

Flowerdew, who had looked irritated to find his territory invaded, now came over to where they were sitting. 'What exactly are we looking at?' The sneer in his voice was unmistakable.

'Well you might ask,' said Watkins, handing him the rock. 'Well you might ask.'

Flowerdew examined it while Itch repeated what he had told Mr Watkins. Then he walked across to the window and turned it over and over in his hand. He switched hands and repeated the process. Watkins and Itch watched and waited for him to say something. He turned and came back to the table, replacing the stone. 'Back in a minute. Don't go anywhere.'

For a moment Itch and his geography teacher just looked at each other. Then Watkins stood up and started pacing. 'I think I know what he's doing. Mr Hopkins's physics revision session is about to be interrupted somewhat. Third cupboard, middle drawer, I think. Let's see.' He started pacing, occasionally glancing at the rock on the table next to Itch. Within a minute the door was flung open again and a slightly breathless Flowerdew returned, carrying an oblong box. It had a handle and a tube that looked like a microphone attached by a coiled cable. He waved it around as he approached the table.

Mr Watkins smiled. 'Ah, the trusty Geiger counter,' he said. Itch looked astonished as he continued, 'Uranium ore is mildly radioactive, of course, but the changing colour and heat suggests this is worth looking at more closely. Is it working, Nathaniel?'

Flowerdew was pressing the Geiger counter's 'on' button and shaking it. 'Dead as a dodo. Blast.' He removed the non-functioning batteries, threw them in the bin by the door and left again.

'What kind of reading would be normal, sir, if this is uranium?'

'It'll click every time it detects a radioactive

particle. I'm a geographer, not a scientist, but if I remember right, radioactivity is the release of radiation from the nucleus of unstable atoms. They escape,' said Watkins, sitting down again. 'Maybe five hundred clicks a second, something like that.'

After a moment Itch said, 'Does Dr Flowerdew enjoy teaching, sir?'

'Why do you ask?'

'Well, he seems to hate every minute he's with us, that's all.'

Mr Watkins shifted in his seat. 'Oh well, we all have our moments, Itch, you know. You lot can be quite a challenge and, well . . .' He was considering his next comment when Flowerdew came in for the third time, now clutching a packet of batteries.

'How much darker has this rock gone, Lofte? Much darker? Slightly darker? Be more specific.' He glanced up at Itch as he unwrapped the new batteries.

Itch frowned as he thought. 'Well, when I got it, most of it looked like a dark Crunchie — you know, the honeycomb bit,' he said. 'If that helps.'

Flowerdew's look suggested it hadn't, but the batteries were in now and he tried the 'on' button again.

Whatever the three of them had expected, the torrent of clicks that emerged from the speaker on the side of the Geiger counter clearly took them all by surprise. Flowerdew swore. Watkins said, 'Good

Lord in heaven.' Itch's mouth was open but nothing came out. The needle on the front of the counter had jumped from 0 to 10,000 clicks per second. Its colour code went from green to blue to red. The needle was well into the red, pushing as far as it could go behind its plastic screen. They stood and stared and listened. Flowerdew moved the detector over the rock, and the constant rattle continued unabated. He switched it off and passed the machine to Watkins, who repeated the procedure, with the same results.

In the silence that followed, Itch was aware of both Watkins and Flowerdew switching their attention from the rock to him.

'I guess that's a radioactive rock, then,' he said.

'That'll be why it's hot,' said Flowerdew quietly. 'I don't recall you telling us precisely where you got this, Lofte.'

Itch, feeling increasingly as though he had done something wrong, said, 'I collect the table of elements, sir, and sometimes I buy stuff from a dealer I met in St Austell—'

'I had no idea you were a collector, Lofte,' interrupted Flowerdew.

That's because you never take any notice of me or my class, thought Itch, but said nothing.

'Do go on.'

'Well, that's it, really. He said he got it from a mate in Dorset or Devon or somewhere. Cost me ten pounds. Well, it will . . . I am guessing that it's not uranium. Maybe I should keep hold of my money.'

Mr Watkins started pacing again. 'Well, that's just it, Itch. It's not like any uranium I've seen dug up here. Or anywhere else, come to that. I think my friends at the mining-school team in West Ridge would like to see this.'

These words seemed to spark Dr Flowerdew into action. 'No. No. Not at all. We need to isolate the rock in a lead case or box as soon as possible. I have one at home. This is too dangerous to leave around school.'

'Well, you have a point,' said Watkins, 'especially after the greenhouse business. You'd better take it now, Nathaniel.'

And without waiting for a word from Itch, Flowerdew swept up the piece of rock and, holding it at arm's length, left the lab.

Mr Watkins, still staring at the door, said, 'How long have you had it, Itch? We should probably get you checked out.'

'Only since Saturday, sir, like I said. I haven't held it much either – it's been in my shed mainly.'

'Good. I'll seek advice from Dr Flowerdew as soon as he returns. I fear, however, that it might be some time before you see that stone of yours again.'

★   ★   ★

That afternoon Itch sat with Jack at the back of Mr Littlewood's history lesson. She was now fully up to date with what had happened with Watkins and Flowerdew at lunch time.

'But he can't just take it like that without asking you!' She started raking her hands through her hair – something she always did when she was annoyed.

'Well, he *can* and he has. Once the Geiger counter had done its stuff they were hardly going to let me walk around school with a radioactive rock measuring more than ten thousand clicks a second, were they?'

'I have no idea what that means, but it does sound dodgy. Does Cake ever sell you elements that are, you know, harmless? Things that you could bring to school and no one get hurt? Nice drop of oxygen maybe? Or gold would be good.'

A voice from the front broke into their discussion. 'I'm sure that's the finer points of German foreign policy you're discussing at the back.' Mr Littlewood was still writing on the whiteboard as he spoke. 'Sounds like Jack and Itch to me. Remind me, Jack, who the German Foreign Minister was.'

In front of them, many of their classmates turned round. Ian Steele was mouthing something at Jack, but it was impossible to make it out. However, unlike her cousin, Jack was on top of most of her subjects. 'Was it Von Ribbentrop, sir?'

'Nice one, Jack,' said Mr Littlewood, 'but I prefer

to hear only one voice in lessons. And that's mine.'

It was the class opinion that Mr Littlewood wasn't a bad teacher, but it was his first year and he was pretending to be tough to show who was boss. He would probably mellow a bit next term, they thought; most new teachers did. He looked barely older than some of the sixth formers, and provided an interesting contrast to Dr Flowerdew, who had arrived at the same time. They had been introduced at the same assembly. Unlike Flowerdew, Jim Littlewood had tended to the sickest members of Miss Glenacre's biology class as they lay outside the greenhouse, and had impressed many of the girls in Year Nine. Natalie Hussain, Debbie Price and Sam Jennings were singing his praises and seemed much keener on what Herr Von Ribbentrop had been up to than they had been before the incident. There was even a Facebook group dedicated to him, though no one knew if Mr Littlewood was aware of that yet.

At the back of the class, Jack and Itch resumed their note-taking. Itch's head was still full of the clicking Geiger counter and his hot rock. After being told that he wouldn't be seeing it for some time Itch had run to the window at the end of the corridor. He had watched in astonishment as Dr Flowerdew marched to his car, arm extended, clasping the rock with a handkerchief. Dropping it into his boot, he had then driven off at top speed.

Itch became aware that everyone else was writing. 'What's this we're doing?'

'Relations with Austria,' said Jack. 'Keep up.'

Itch then resumed what had become a familiar routine of taking notes from Jack, peering over her shoulder and trying to catch up with Mr Littlewood. The bell went with Itch still three paragraphs behind.

'A page please on relations with Austria by Thursday. That's a whole page and in normal-size writing, Colston, please.' Matt Colston feigned indignation but laughed with everyone else.

On their way out of history and downstairs to chemistry, Itch said to Jack, 'Fancy coming round for tea tomorrow? We could discuss, you know, German relations with Austria . . .'

'Wow, that sounds exciting. Got netball tomorrow. Wednesday OK?'

'Yeah, OK. I'll be a bit stuck otherwise. Thanks.'

They arrived at the lab and took their place on the end of the second bench next to James Potts and Craig Murray, the boy now famous for vomiting all over Flowerdew. Potts had been forced to find a new partner after he and Bruno Paul had been caught turning on the gas taps at the end of a lesson.

After five minutes there was no sign of Dr Flowerdew and the general buzz of conversation was rising. After ten minutes most students were wandering around the lab and sitting on the benches. Just as Tom Westgate was about to set off and report the lack of a teacher, Flowerdew appeared in the doorway, clearly trying to control his breathing. Still panting, he came into the lab, provoking a scurry of bodies returning to their proper places.

'I think you'll find it's *How Gases Behave*, page twenty-two. None of you are quite so advanced that you can afford to waste time so spectacularly like this.'

Ian Steele, behind Jack and Itch, could just be heard saying, 'And good afternoon to you, sir.' Those who heard smiled.

'Itchingham Lofte – here, please.'

Everyone turned round. Itch didn't need to look at the faces of Bruno and James to know that they were grinning. He walked up to the front and stood at Dr Flowerdew's desk.

To the class, the head of science said, 'As you have barely started, please don't think of stopping. *How Gases Behave*, page twenty-two. With three examples and diagrams.' He waited till all heads were down, then leaned very close to Itch's left ear, his voice barely louder than a whisper. 'I'll need it for a few days for tests. It's safe, but only where it is now.'

'When will I get it back?'

'Depends on the result of the tests.'

'What are you testing *for*?'

'What do you think, Lofte? Never seen so much radioactivity from a rock.'

'Mr Watkins thought *I* should be tested. For radiation.'

'You'll be fine,' said Flowerdew, already reaching for his textbook. 'That is all. Sit down, boy.'

Itch did as he was told. The rest of the lesson went by in a blur. His copy of *How Gases Behave* was opened at the right page but he couldn't concentrate on it. All he could see was the Geiger-counter needle pushing off the scale; all he could hear was the wall of noise from the thousands of clicks it emitted.

Just how much radiation had he been exposed to? Chloe had walked to school with him – had she been infected? He tried to remember how far radiation travelled and couldn't recall the details. Had he followed up the arsenic poisoning of his class by contaminating the *whole school* this time?

7

The coastal road heading north from the academy reaches open country within four minutes. It is a gentle climb till you reach the top of the cliffs, then it descends steeply to the next inlet along the coast, named St Anthony's Cove. It then widens into a dual carriageway, taking drivers on a direct route out of Cornwall.

There are only three houses around the cove; two stand together on the left as you drive through, and the other – a renovated fisherman's cottage – sits well back from the road on the right. It has a narrow driveway, a small, neat but nondescript lawn at the front and a steeply climbing half-acre of field at the back. A few apple trees form the boundary at the edge of the property before it becomes farmland. Although it is barely visible from the road, there is a new, substantial and glaringly modern extension behind the house.

This was where Dr Nathaniel Flowerdew had lived since losing his job at Greencorps – a major international oil company and sponsor of the Cornwall Academy. Although it was barely a ten-minute drive from here to the academy, the cottage was remote enough to avoid tourists, and certainly anyone from school. The other two houses in the cove were both second homes and usually empty. Even when the families were there, they showed no interest in their nearest neighbour – and that suited him just fine.

Flowerdew had built the extension almost immediately after moving into the property. He had filled it not with furniture, but with scientific equipment. It actually wasn't really an extension at all, it was a laboratory. With the exception of one corner, which housed a rowing machine and a treadmill, it was full of centrifuges, gas jars, blowpipes, models of molecular structures, computers and assorted machines packed closely together. Many displayed digital screens that blinked with the latest lines of data they had produced.

It was a beautiful evening, with one of the finest sunsets of the year taking place out at sea. A few cars had even pulled over to watch the last rays disappearing spectacularly into the Atlantic. However, this had gone unnoticed by Nathaniel Flowerdew. He was hunched over a beige glass machine, using two steel levers to manoeuvre

Itchingham Lofte's small rock into a metal chamber. He straightened up slowly, his hands on the small of his back, and gave a low whistle. Every other movement he made was as rapid and fluid as his protective clothing would allow. As soon as he had arrived home after school he had found his helmet, lead-lined apron and shiny-grey radiation gloves. At no time did he turn his back on the rock. This was the fourth experiment he had conducted that evening, and he had become more and more animated. After each test was completed, he moved over to a computer and fired off an email.

The same email to the same recipients.

Four times.

Flowerdew noticed a tremble in his hands, which he tried to still. Despite his exhaustion, his speed around the lab was increasing. He had started talking to himself too: 'You have got to be joking . . .' he said. 'What the . . .?' and, most recently, 'You . . . have . . . got . . . to . . . be . . . kidding.'

The lead case into which the rock had been placed during his brief trip home earlier in the afternoon sat on top of one of the workbenches, its lid open. He banged it shut as he passed and headed out of the door into the field. He removed his gloves and mask, and took a handset from his pocket. Hesitating only briefly, he dialled a number from memory. There was an international-length pause before he heard the ringing tone.

It rang just the once before a woman's voice answered. 'Hello, who is this?'

'It's Nathaniel Flowerdew in England.' He stopped, suddenly uncertain what to say next. 'It is imperative I speak to Mr Revere or Mr Van Den Hauwe. I wouldn't ring if it wasn't important. I have tried to email but have had no response. Please tell them it really is urgent.'

'One minute.'

At least she didn't hang up, thought Flowerdew, sitting down on a garden chair and looking up at the stars as they started to appear. A minute passed, and with no 'holding' music playing he had started to wonder whether he had lost the connection. Then the phone was picked up again and his heart lurched. But it was still the same woman.

'We have read your emails. Send another with all your results. Goodnight.' And she hung up before Flowerdew had managed to say anything more.

He jumped up, went in and grabbed a laptop from the lab, then ran outside again. (No mask, but he had spent only a very short time inside.) He sat again on one of the garden chairs, perched the laptop on his knees and turned it on. He waited impatiently for it to allow him access to his emails, his hands poised above the keys. As the page loaded, he fired off another, more detailed explanation of what he thought he had in his lab. He copied in all the results of his tests so far and attached a number of photos. The whole process took him ten minutes. He pressed 'send'.

He sat looking at his laptop, not sure what to do next. It was now completely dark, but the bright lights of the lab spread out into the field. He put down the laptop and reached into his trouser pocket for a coin. Absent-mindedly he worked it from his little finger to his ring and middle finger, twisting it up, over and under like a weaver at a loom. It reached his index finger and thumb, and then he reversed the process and the coin worked its way back again. With the exception of his fingers, he was quite still.

Ten minutes later the phone rang, sounding very loud in the garden, and Flowerdew jumped up, pocketing the coin.

'It's Christophe here, Nathaniel. How are you?' It sounded as if the French co-chair of Greencorps was just calling for a late-night chat, but Flowerdew knew that nothing was further from the truth.

'Good, thank you, Christophe. Well as can be expected here, anyway.' He stopped himself from grumbling about the academy; this was not the time and would not have been welcome either. 'Everything in the email is true. The rock in my lab is extraordinary. I have only basic equipment, of course, but it's pointing at 126. I know that's ridiculous, but I've checked and re-checked my results. And it's coming back 126.'

The Frenchman cleared his throat. 'Let us be clear what you are claiming.' His tone was half interested, half amused. 'When you say 126, you mean element number 126. The 126th element.'

'Yes, Christophe,' said Flowerdew breathlessly. 'I know—'

'When only 118 exist. Everything we know or can possibly think of is made from just the 118. I realize this is basic science, but maybe we all need a refresher course?' Revere chuckled. 'You seem to have forgotten much in Britain.'

There was a click, and Flowerdew assumed he was now on speakerphone. Some distant French and Dutch was being spoken.

Flowerdew decided to take the initiative. 'I know you are laughing, and I don't blame you. I would in your position too. But before you hang up, just look at the preliminary results I have sent you. Go get your experts, see what they say. I wouldn't have troubled you if I wasn't totally convinced that you *must* check this out.'

He heard another voice: 'Nathaniel, it's Jan. You know as well as I do that it can't be a new element. No one has discovered a naturally occurring element since 1937. That part of the table is complete. It's perfect. The new ones only exist in laboratory conditions, for fractions of a second, and I believe you need a particle accelerator. Are you seriously expecting us to believe that a new one has turned up in some kid's rock collection? And now it's just sitting there in your house? Unless you're rewriting the laws of science, you've lost your mind.' The Dutchman was always the more aggressive of the two, but even so, Flowerdew didn't like what he was hearing.

'I know how this sounds. But I'm not drunk and I haven't lost my mind. I'm telling you – I have a rock here which is behaving in a way I have never seen before. All the readings coming from it suggest it will fit into the Table of Elements at 126.'

'What about 119 to 125? Where are they?' asked Revere.

'Good question. No idea,' said Flowerdew. 'Think of it this way: if I'm right, I have in this lab here the most precious rock *ever*. *Of all time*. Worth more than any diamond. If there are others like it – and of course there will be – they'll pump out so much energy, Cornwall could declare itself independent by Christmas. New power stations from Bude to St Ives. Do you want to take the risk that I'm wrong?'

Christophe Revere spoke first. 'OK, we're interested. If you are wasting our time on this, you do know we will cut you off completely, don't you? We took a risk recommending you to the academy in the first place. We might be its chief sponsor but we had to push hard. Some of our other schools just refused. By rights, you should be in that prison with your colleague, Shivvi. If you become an embarrassment again . . .'

'I was aware of the risks of contacting you, yes.'

'Have you completed all your tests?'

'No, there are two more to do – but I would be surprised if they threw up any contradictory data.'

'Finish the tests. Send us all the results. Everything.' Revere paused. 'However, we really need to know more about where the boy got it from. It obviously won't be the only one. You say in your email he got it from a dealer.'

'I'll question him further tomorrow, but there are limits to what you can do if you are just a teacher.'

'We can make help available if necessary. Talk to the boy tomorrow and call back at this time.'

Jan Van Den Hauwe came on the line again. 'You have made us look stupid before. God help you if you do it again.'

8

At five a.m. the next morning, a good hour earlier than usual, Nathaniel Flowerdew was on his rowing machine. He could have started at four or even three a.m. as he had barely slept. The skies were lightening and the doors and windows of the lab were open as the air was already warm. While he rowed his usual ten kilometres, he gazed out over the field that rose up to the farmer's land beyond the trees. In the ten months he had lived there, he had only climbed it once, on his first day. A dozen sheep grazed on the grass that led up to the top of the hill, where the sun would soon emerge. Not that he would be there to see it.

He finished the 10k in fifty minutes, his manic energy from last night returning with every pull and glide. As he pounded his way through a further five kilometres he worked out what to say to the boy. He found himself smiling. This would be a good day.

He was the first teacher to arrive at school — something that had never happened before. He went straight to the chemistry lab, and realized from his timetable that he was supposed to be invigilating at an A-level paper in the old school hall at nine a.m. He left a note for John Watkins in the staff room saying that he wanted to see Itchingham Lofte at midday — could he come to the hall at the conclusion of that morning's exams?

Flowerdew spent the next three hours pacing up and down the hall in between the rows of students. They were his students — he had been teaching them for many months — but he barely noticed them now. He was imagining his return to Greencorps. The forgiven prodigal son returning. And with the geological discovery of the century. This was his way out of the wretched school; this was his moment, and no one was going to take it away from him. He had wondered if he would ever get the chance to resume his career — his real career, not this apology of a job — and it had arrived gift-wrapped.

He knew the science was bewildering. He knew there would be sceptics. But when they saw the evidence . . .

At registration Mr Watkins called Itch to the front. 'I have a note from our head of science. Here . . .' He passed it over and Itch read it.

'It'll obviously be about the rock,' said Itch. 'What do think he'll want, sir?'

'He's probably arranged to get your health checked out, I imagine.'

'No,' said Itch. 'He said I'd be fine.'

'Really? Just like that?' Watkins thought for a moment. 'Well, I haven't seen him today, but my next guess would be he'll tell you what you should do with the rock. If it's as radioactive as the Geiger counter suggested, then you'll need to find a home for it while it's being analysed. West Ridge would be my first call.'

'I'd like your opinion too, sir, really – if you wouldn't mind. You're the geologist, not him.' Itch hadn't intended it to sound quite so blunt and he blushed a little.

Watkins straightened. 'Hmm. That's what I've been thinking, to be honest with you. Dr Flowerdew said he had a lead container, so it made sense for him to take it as a precaution. Now that it is safely in its new home, there is no reason I can think of why the stone cannot be returned, or placed somewhere we can all study it. Come and find me when you've seen him.'

'Time is up, pens down, stop writing.'

The usual sighs and murmurs that greet the end of an exam broke out in the old hall. Flowerdew and Mr Hopkins, the physics teacher, collected the papers and the students left in threes and fours, comparing notes. Through the glass doors Flowerdew noticed Itch waiting outside and waved him in. All the students had now gone, and Mr Hopkins had handed a pile of papers to Flowerdew.

'Thanks, er, Chris. I'll take it from here.'

Flowerdew waited till the physics teacher had left the hall and then smiled at Itch. This had the opposite effect to what he had intended – he had never smiled at the boy before. It was a smile without warmth, and Itch was on his guard immediately.

'Well, I took your stone home and put it straight into a lead-lined box. Lead, as you probably know, is so dense it is very effective in stopping most kinds of radiation. It's safe. Remind me where you got it again?'

'As I said yesterday, sir – there's this dealer I see every now and again – he sells the stuff. He had it. I bought it from him for ten pounds.'

This made Flowerdew laugh. 'Ten pounds. My, my. What is his name?'

'He's called Cake, sir.'

'Cake? What kind of a name is that? Where does he live, this "Cake"?'

'I honestly have no idea.'

'Will you see him again soon? You see, if he has other rocks like this, he could be in danger. Scrub that – he *is* in danger. You saw how radioactive that one stone is.'

'But I'm not in danger?'

Flowerdew looked up. 'No. He'll have been exposed for longer. Relax, Lofte.'

While Itch was not about to 'relax', he realized his teacher had a good point about Cake's safety – even if he had no intention of telling him about the meeting with the dealer the next day.

'I'll try and find him, sir. But he seems to be always on the move. I'll look out for him.'

'I'd love to meet him if you think that might be possible?' That smile again.

'I'll tell him, sir. What happens to my stone now? Mr Watkins was talking about the West Ridge School of Mining. He said they could study it there.'

Flowerdew's smile tightened. 'I'm not sure that's the wisest step going forward. Their reputation was made in the eighties, and their analytical papers are not what they were. You need the sharpest minds on this, not some hillbilly local outfit. With respect to Mr Watkins.'

'Well, I'd like Mr Watkins to take care of it, sir, if that's OK. Now that it's safe in your box.'

Flowerdew stared at Itch. 'Right. Well, I'm afraid that won't be possible.' He straightened the exam papers in front of him.

'Why not, sir? He's the geologist!'

'I am aware of that, Lofte. But I have taken the precaution of sending it away for analysis. To labs in Switzerland, where I used to work. You'll get proper results there.'

Itch felt the colour rise in his cheeks and his throat tighten. 'You've done *what*? You've sent it to *Switzerland*? But it's mine, sir. It's *my rock*. You had no right!'

'I was considering the safety of the school and its pupils, Lofte, that is all. These labs in Geneva will provide an unbeatable service and world-class analysis. You really will be impressed. I'm sure that after the greenhouse affair Dr Dart will agree: the safety of the pupils should always be paramount. You see that, don't you, Lofte? You see that, I'm sure.'

Itch couldn't wait to get out of the hall. It had never occurred to him that Flowerdew would have got rid of it already. He knew he was a bad teacher and that staff and pupils all disliked him. He knew too that he was mean and vindictive – in an experi-ment about body mass he had reduced one of the larger girls to tears. But he had never thought him a thief.

He pushed through the doors and stopped, lean-ing his head against the wall and breathing deeply. 'He's a thief. He's actually a *thief*!' He headed out-side, muttering, 'The scumbag's a thief!' over and over again. He went round the hall and came to a large rectangle of concrete – the only remaining sign of the greenhouse. Around the edges lay a few leaves – all that was left of the plants – and tracks left by the bulldozers that had taken the building apart. A few students had come to look, among them Lucy Cavendish, the Year Ten girl who had brought Itch and Jack water when everyone was being sick. She smiled at him.

'Shame,' she said. 'What a waste.'

And all my work, Itch thought grimly. 'Yeah, you're right,' he said as he walked round it, leaving her staring after him. He had to tell Watkins what had just happened with Flowerdew.

On his way to the staff room, he went to his classroom and found Jack sitting on her desk, chatting with Sam Jennings and her friend Jay Boot. Itch thought that Jay seemed to spend all her time either eating crisps or picking her nose. Today she was managing both, one hand for each.

Classy, he thought.

Jack glanced up, caught the look on Itch's face and excused herself. She slid off the desk and came over. 'What's up, Itch?'

He beckoned her out of the classroom and they walked along the corridor towards the staff room.

'Flowerdew says he's sent the uranium or whatever it is to Switzerland. He took it home to make it safe, but then decided it should be examined by these labs he knows. I'm going to tell Watkins what's happened.'

Jack looked as though she was missing

something. 'Is that so bad? I mean, I know he's a jerk and everything, but if the labs are as good as he says they are, then maybe—'

Itch was astonished. 'The point is, it wasn't his rock to get rid of. He should've put it in his lead box and then told me. And Watkins is still the geologist and not Flowerdew, in case you'd forgotten.'

They had reached the staff room and Itch knocked loudly, saving Jack from having to reply.

Hilary Briggs, one of the ICT teachers, put her head round the door.

'I need to see Mr Watkins, please – it's urgent,' he told her. She disappeared again, and Itch continued where he had left off. 'Why would he send it away so quickly? What's the big hurry?' He turned to Jack, but she shrugged.

'No idea, but whatever he's done, it will be for the good of himself, I'm sure.'

The staff-room door opened again and Mr Watkins emerged. 'Thought it would be you. What happened with Dr Flowerdew?' He brought his tea with him as they walked down the corridor towards the entrance, past the head's office. Itch recounted his morning's conversation and Watkins listened with raised eyebrows. They pushed through the main door and stood in the sunshine. When Itch had finished, they stood in silence for a moment. Watkins turned to them both, having apparently come to a decision. 'Leave it with me,' he said, and set off back to the staff room.

The heads of geography and science met after school. Watkins had gone looking for Flowerdew earlier but couldn't find him. At the final bell he had cleared away slowly and, as the last students made their way out of school, headed for Flowerdew's lab. He only just caught him.

'Need a quick word if you don't mind, Nathaniel.'

'In a tearing hurry, actually. Can it wait?' Flowerdew had his briefcase in his hand and his jacket over his shoulder.

'Not really, no. Itchingham Lofte tells me the rock is on its way to Switzerland. An outcome he is very unhappy about – as am I. As his form tutor and his geography teacher, I'm the one he brought it to. You had an appropriate box for its safekeeping, but your jurisdiction finished there. You should have at least discussed this with me.'

Flowerdew put down his briefcase and removed his jacket, placing it on the desk. For a moment Watkins thought he was about to be hit. Flowerdew was tempted. He stared at Watkins.

'That's really what this is about, isn't it?' said Flowerdew. '*Your* territory, *your* empire. It's not about the boy or his rock at all. I've done what's best for the school, Watkins – you know that. Do you think the head needs another "school in peril" story out there? No, of course not. The further that piece of radioactivity is from the CA, the happier she'll be. Get over it, Watkins.'

Mr Watkins's eyes had been getting wider and his mouth more tightly closed as Flowerdew spoke. As usual, he had a biro in his hand, and now he pointed it at Flowerdew's chest. 'You're new here. We all know that. And that's OK because we all start somewhere. It's just a shame – for you and for us – that you had to start as head of science. Your inexperience has been obvious from the outset, and never more so than over this business. The plain fact is, this is theft. The stone is Itchingham's. If Lofte's family wanted to press charges, they might be successful. And Dr Dart certainly doesn't need that, either.'

Both men stood facing each other. A few students and members of staff wandered past, looking in at the windows.

'Well, it's all out now then, isn't it?' said Flowerdew. 'You've never liked me – you've always made that very clear – but I thought I could trust your professional judgement. I see now that I was wrong.' He started to put on his jacket. 'I am a very well-respected chemist, you know. I have dealt with minerals all my life; I have spoken around the world on the subject, and if I say this stone needs to go to the labs in Switzerland, it *does*. OK?'

Watkins took a deep breath. 'Wrong tense, Nathaniel, wrong tense. You *were* a respected chemist. Before you got sacked. That is what happened, isn't it? You don't leave a high-flying international job for the CA voluntarily. It's quite obvious you don't like being here – staff know it, pupils know it. Our assumption in the staff room is that you had something to do with that terrible oil spill. Would that be right? The one off Nigeria that led to the deaths of seventeen oil workers?' Mr Watkins's voice had been rising steadily, and Flowerdew's face drained of colour as he went on, 'Did you think we didn't know? Did you think we didn't connect the name of our sponsor and the name of your old company? You really do think we're stupid.'

'YES!' exploded Flowerdew. 'I DO! This crummy little school is going nowhere! Most of the teaching is second-rate and sometimes third-rate. You wouldn't believe the level of incompetence I see around me every day. And what passes for informed comment in the staff room is frankly laughable. If you expect me to accept—'

The door to the lab opened and Dr Felicity Dart appeared. She came in and shut the door behind her.

Watkins spoke first. 'Ah, Dr Dart. Do come in. Dr Flowerdew here was just giving me his opinion of the CA. Do go on, Nathaniel – you'd got to the bit

about third-rate teaching and general incompetence, I think.'

Flowerdew had regained some of the colour in his
cheeks but that was because he was clearly furious.

Before he could say anything, Dart held up her
hand. 'No. No. Not here. I will not have two of
my most senior staff rowing in a classroom. In my
office, now.' She turned and walked out, leaving
Watkins and Flowerdew to follow like two naughty
schoolboys.

'I was acting in the interests of the school, Dr
Dart. The radioactivity coming off that rock was
scary.'

The head had shown them to her small sofa, so
they were sitting uncomfortably close to each other.
Flowerdew, now more in control of himself, was
leaning forward to argue his case, forcing Watkins
to sit back. 'It needed to be off school premises as
soon as possible.'

Dart nodded. 'That is very true, and we are very
grateful you had a lead box to hand. Not many
schools would have been so lucky. But I would have
preferred it if you had taken Mr Watkins and
Itchingham into your confidence. It might be that
these Swiss labs are better equipped than West
Ridge, but there's no getting round the fact that it
wasn't your rock to send in the first place.' Watkins
looked impassive while Flowerdew's temper was

rising again. 'How long will they need to conduct the tests?' asked the head.

'I don't know; it depends what they find.'

'You need to get it back, Nathaniel, as soon as they have completed the tests. And to keep any complaints at bay – I *know* you were taking something dangerous off the school premises, but sending it abroad was uncalled for since it wasn't your property – you need to apologize to Itchingham Lofte.'

There was silence in the head's office. Then Flowerdew said, 'Very well,' and walked out.

Later that evening, as instructed, Flowerdew picked up the phone and dialled. It rang just the once, and Christophe Revere answered.

'The tests are complete,' Flowerdew told him. 'The results are the same. I've sent you the data.'

'And the boy? Did you question him?'

'Yes. He got it from this mineral dealer called Cake. He says he doesn't know where he lives but I'm on it, Christophe – I've asked to meet him.'

'We'll pick up the stone tomorrow. We'll send a courier. It'll be our usual firm.'

Flowerdew smiled. 'I remember. It'll be ready. Goodnight, Christophe.'

9

Last period Wednesday for Itch and Jack was English, with a teacher everyone called the Brigadier. His real name was Gordon Carter but no one used it. His nickname came from his large moustache and the fact that he seemed to want to march everywhere; no one knew whether he had actually been in the army or not. Today they were reading *Lord of the Flies*, and Itch hated every minute of it. This was partly because he struggled with essays – he always seemed to run out of things to say after the first paragraph – but mostly because it was about bullies. He couldn't help putting his own class on William Golding's island. Imagining 9W without a teacher or parents after a plane crash, he knew very well who would be first to be targeted by the class thugs.

The Brigadier was wrapping things up: 'Every-one to have finished this book by next week, please. You'll find it difficult to write the next essay if you haven't actually read the book. And I can spot a Wiki-cheat too. That is all. You may go.'

'But, sir, the bell hasn't gone,' said Sam Jennings.

'You may stay if you wish, but I have finished teaching and you have finished learning.' He picked up his case and strode out of the room. The class gathered their scattered books and bags and shuffled into the corridor a good three minutes ahead of the rest of the school. The bell rang as they were going down the stairs.

Itch and Jack waited outside Chloe's classroom. She came out with two of her friends, but seeing her brother and cousin waiting for her she said good-bye, and the three of them headed out of the reception hall and towards the school gates.

'You coming back for tea, Jack?' asked Chloe.

'Itch asked me. Tea is part of it; history home-work is the rest, I think.'

'I got a bit muddled, that's all,' said Itch. 'Anyway, Jack hasn't been round for a while.'

He spotted the usual problem of Bruno Paul, Darcy Campbell and James Potts hanging around by the gates, but they appeared to be studying a new piercing in Darcy's nose.

'It can only be an improvement,' said Jack.

'Let's hope it hurt,' added Chloe, and the three of them turned out of the gates without being noticed.

They headed through town and out towards the golf course.

'I just want to go via the beach huts, if that's OK,' Itch said. 'I need to pay Cake for the rock I don't have any more. Did you know Flowerdew apologized this morning? Well, sort of. He called me in and said that he realized it would have been better if we had discussed the advantages of sending the rock to Switzerland. Before he actually did it. He clearly hated saying it. Dart must have told him to — he wouldn't have volunteered.'

'Doesn't change anything though, does it?' said Jack. 'Still means you don't have it and he does. Or his people do.'

They had reached the section of the path that ran along the cliff edge, from where they could see the steps and the beach huts.

Itch squinted in the sunshine. 'I can't see him. Maybe he's asleep in one of the deckchairs.' They walked off the cliffs and down the paved steps to the huts. A few were occupied with some early holiday-makers brewing tea and reading books, but there was no sign of Cake. Five deckchairs were occupied, none of them by his mineral seller.

Disappointed, the three of them rounded the corner to take the road home — and practically fell over him.

Cake was sprawled against the wall of the public toilets. He was bleeding from the mouth and it looked as though he had a few teeth missing. His skin was white and blotchy and he had lost some of his hair. He hadn't changed his clothes since Itch had seen him last and his T-shirt was stiff with dried blood.

Jack and Chloe gasped. 'Cake!' shouted Itch, and dropped on one knee beside him.

'What happened? Who did this to you?' asked Jack.

'I should call an ambulance . . . Lean forward.' Itch put his sweatshirt behind Cake's head.

Cake opened his eyes and croaked, 'Itchingham Lofte.' He managed a smile and the bleeding started again. 'No one did this – don't call an ambulance.' He spoke in a half croak, half whisper. 'I have some information for you, but don't come too close. I'll try to speak up a bit.' He cleared his throat.

'Rest up. We'll get you a drink.' Chloe had a bottle of water in her school bag and she passed it to Itch, wide-eyed.

'Here, drink this.' Itch was going to tip the bottle up into Cake's mouth but he stopped him.

'Just put it where I can reach it.' He took the bottle himself and sipped the water. 'Now, I got stuff to tell you . . .'

'OK, OK,' said Itch. 'But first, that uranium – or whatever it is you gave me – is in Switzerland.'

Cake winced as he propped himself up. 'You what?'

'Dr Flowerdew, my chemistry teacher, ran a Geiger counter over it and it went crazy. He took it and sent it to some labs he knows from his old job. Says they're much better than anything here. It's caused quite a fuss, actually, but it's gone, that's the bottom line.'

Cake listened in silence and in pain. He swallowed more water and licked his lips. 'That's a disaster. A real gold-plated disaster. My God, what do we do?' He closed his eyes and drew his legs up, then put his arms round them and rocked back and forth.

Itch, Jack and Chloe looked at each other.

'Well, I'm mad about it, Cake, but why is it such a disaster? Presumably we'll get the test results through and then the rock will come back . . . ?'

Cake shook his head. 'No. No, no, no. It's never coming back. And Flowerdew . . . of all people to get their hands on it. How can we have let this happen?'

Now Jack spoke. 'I'm sorry, I'm not following this. What's happened?'

Cake opened his eyes and turned to look at her. 'Who's this, Itchingham?'

'My cousin, Jack. You met her at that Surfers Against Sewage thing at St Austell, remember? When I bought the arsenic. You can trust her.'

'We'll get you sorted, Cake,' she said.

'I remember now – a real-life Cousin Jack. You look like . . . You remind me . . .' Cake closed his eyes again and was silent for a moment, lost in some memory. At last he came to. 'OK. Well, this is where we are. These rocks are different. I'm not sure how, and I certainly don't know why, but that Geiger-counter reading you saw explains why I'm like this.'

'Whoa, whoa! Wait a minute,' Itch exclaimed in horror. 'You've got radiation poisoning? This is because of the rock? And you said *rocks*. You have more of these?'

Cake started to look agitated. 'This is all so wrong, so wrong. You kids mustn't tell anyone at all about this. *Anyone*. No mates, no parents, no teachers, no police, no government. *No one*. When word gets out about these rocks – yes, I have a few more – everything is going to change. Everyone will want them, you see. If these are as radioactive as I think they are, everyone will want to get their hands on them: energy companies, politicians, and probably some seriously bad guys.' He finished the water and dropped the bottle. 'And, yes, it's radiation poisoning. That's why you mustn't come any closer. My hunch is that my sweat and blood are worth avoiding.' The cousins glanced at each other and instinctively edged back a centimetre or two. 'And your man Flowerdew – I've heard of him before. I think he used to work for Greencorps. They're a big multinational energy company – and, well, let's just say they cannot be trusted; they absolutely cannot be trusted.' Cake grimaced at his own under-statement. 'Of all people to get their hands on that rock . . .'

'Wait,' said Jack. 'So if these rocks are so power-ful, why haven't you just got rid of them or handed them in or something?'

'Handed these in to who? *No one* can be trusted with them, guys. I'm trying to keep them safe and not go near them now, but I might be too late. It took me a while to find a safe container for them but they're OK for the moment.'

'How do you know about Flowerdew?'

'Oh, news went round pretty quickly – we all heard about him when he came here. I know some of the guys at the mining school, remember?' Cake started coughing and winced. 'And your radioactive rock is in a lab in Switzerland . . .' He paused. 'You're sure of that?'

Itch shrugged. 'That's what he said.'

'Well, he's moved very fast, then.'

Cake was speaking more slowly now, and Chloe said, 'I think we need to get you some help. Why can't we call an ambulance?'

'I'd never get out of hospital, little sister. I'd never get out. And they'll want my rocks too. I'd love something to eat, though, and some more water – I'll be OK if I can get home.'

Itch took some money out of his pocket. 'I was going to pay you for the uranium – or whatever it is. It's all the money I have on me. I could get you some sandwiches from the beach shop – they won't be up to much, though . . .'

'They'll be fine. Yes. Do it. Water and chocolate too.'

Itch ran off past the toilet block and the bus shelter towards the beach shop.

Chloe looked as if she had just thought of something. 'Back in a second,' she said to Jack, and darted off.

Cake lay still, with Jack crouched down a couple of metres away. 'How many rocks are there?' she asked.

'Seven more. Just seven. That I know of. But that's the thing, Cousin Jack, that's the thing. There won't only be seven or eight. There can't be. There must be tons of the stuff somewhere. But presumably a long way underground – otherwise that radiation would have done its damage by now.' Cake looked down at his bloody shirt. 'And people would notice that.' He closed his eyes again and was silent.

Itch and Chloe arrived at the same time from different directions, Itch with the food and Chloe, more slowly, with a plastic box and a bucket of water. 'Got this from the beach hut. Clean you up a bit.' She produced a small first-aid kit, found some cotton wool and pulled off a swab-sized chunk. Dipping it in the water, she held it up to Cake.

He shook his head. 'You're not touching me. Just leave it all there and I'll sort myself out.'

Chloe opened the kit and laid out a large piece of gauze, antiseptic cream, bandages and scissors. She cut the bandage into four lengths and rolled them up again.

'Is that a Guides thing?' asked Cake.

'It's a Scouts thing, actually,' said Chloe.

'Oh. Yeah, of course. Well, I'd rather do this when you've gone,' he said. 'Yeah?'

'Are you infectious, then?' said Jack. When Cake nodded, she said, 'Please let us call for an ambulance. You really—'

Cake started to get agitated again. 'No, no, no. I told you. We've done all that. You've done great, really. Soon as you've gone I'll sort myself out . . .' He paused. 'Listen — thanks, guys. Really. I'm feeling better. There'll be a bus soon and then I can go home.' And through a mouthful of bread, ham and cheese, he said to Itch, 'And you're right, these sandwiches aren't up to much.'

By the time the three of them reached the house it was nearly six and they were starving. They found a note from Jude Lofte saying she would be back around nine and to have the lasagne that was in the fridge. Chloe heated it up in the microwave.

They had left Cake in better shape than they had found him, but Chloe still felt they should tell

145

someone about his condition. 'It seems wrong to leave him like that.'

'Agreed,' said Jack, 'but you heard what he said. He doesn't want a doctor or an ambulance.'

'Where will he go?' asked Chloe.

'Don't know – but we did what we could,' said Itch, his mouth full of meat and pasta. 'I always get the impression that there's a group of mineral collectors who live near a big spoil heap. Or in it, maybe. Launceston way – St Haven, I think. And he knows all those guys out at the mining school. I bet they'd know what to do. Much better than us.'

Chloe looked reassured at this mention of grown-ups, and they all cleared their plates.

'German foreign policy time?' asked Jack.

'Guess so,' said Itch, and they started to remove school books from their bags, putting them on the kitchen table. Chloe went to watch TV.

'I've been thinking about Flowerdew, Jack. Cake knew about him. He said, *We all heard about him when he came here*. It sounds as if he was famous or something . . .' Itch fired up the laptop and waited for it to finish its opening routine. 'And that he and Greencorps were the very worst people who could get hold of the rock.'

'Yes, he seemed depressed about that,' said Jack. 'And Greencorps is one of the CA's big sponsors – their name is all over Dr Dart's notice board. I bet that's how Flowerdew got his job.'

146

'Unless Dart fancied him,' said Itch. Chloe laughed loudest at that.

He did a search for 'Greencorps' and 'Dr Nathaniel Flowerdew'. 'Wow. Have a look at this.' He scrolled through a number of old articles about Flowerdew's work at Greencorps and some academic papers he had written. '"The Principles of Stratigraphic Base Levels",' he read. '"The Oil/Water Interface". Bet those were bestsellers.'

'We should print off "Sedimentary Deposits: A Dynamic Correlation" and hand it in for our next homework,' said Jack. 'See what happens!'

There was nothing from recent years apart from links to stories about the Greencorps oil spill off Nigeria. Flowerdew's name did not appear in any of these articles, though a woman called Shivvi Tan Fook had gone to prison for manslaughter. Fifteen years. She was twenty-five and 'a senior oil analyst' with Greencorps, according to the report – though, in the photo supplied, she looked much younger.

'And soon after that we had a new head of science. Nice one, CA.' Jack was reading over Itch's shoulder. 'He lives down on the cove, doesn't he?'

'Yes, it's the house just behind the shiny BMW. It kind of stands out. Why do you mention it?'

Jack was thinking. 'When's your mother back?'

'The note says nine, but that's probably Mum being optimistic. I would imagine it'll be nearer nine-thirty or ten.'

'We've got almost three hours, then.' Jack was smiling. 'Why don't we go spy on him? We could take the bikes. We'd easily be back in time.'

'*Spy* on him?' said Itch. 'Are you mad? Peer at him through the curtains? We might see him in his pants. Or worse.'

'No – think about it. We knew nothing about him really, apart from the fact that he's a lousy teacher and everyone hates him. Now we know who he worked for and the kind of things they do. And he's taken your rock, studied it and sent it to Switzerland. All from the cove. We don't have to go near it – you could take your dad's binoculars. We need to know more about him, Itch.'

Itch hesitated. 'What about homework?'

'We'll be back before your mum. Shouldn't take long anyway – I can tell you all you need to know about Von Ribbentrop in twenty minutes.'

'What about Chloe?'

'Don't think so. She's great, but she's not the speediest on her bike. She can go to a friend's house, can't she? We'll need to hurry.'

'That might be tougher than you think – the bikes aren't up to much. Pretty ancient really. You can have mine; I'll use Gabriel's old one. Let me go talk to Chloe.'

It had taken longer than expected to set off, as the bikes' tyres all needed pumping up, and Chloe needed to spend some time telling them how stupid they were. But eventually they set off up the hill, pedalling hard. Itch felt a thrill of danger, but was also excited to be doing something himself rather than waiting for something to happen to him.

It wasn't such a steep climb up the cliffs, but both Itch and Jack were breathless long before they reached the top. They pulled over at a lay-by that had been built as a picnic spot. From here you could look south over the town and the beaches, west over the sea, and north down the hill to the cove, from where the road snaked its way up over the cliffs. It was still sunny and warm, and they would have light for at least the next hour.

'How are your brakes?' asked Itch.

'Just what I was thinking. Let's take this slowly.'

They squeaked and squealed their way down the long hill into the cove, their brakes full on but not making much impact on their speed. Itch was glad they weren't depending on a quiet approach just yet. They released their brakes at the bottom and pedalled slowly past the first two cottages, stopping when Flowerdew's cottage came into view. His steel-grey BMW was in the drive. He was in!

The butterflies really kicked in now.

'Sure about this?' asked Itch, knowing *he* wasn't.

'No, but let's do it anyway.' Jack pulled up her hood and Itch did the same.

'Where to now?'

'Follow me.' Jack headed along a path that led off to the right, about a hundred metres from Flowerdew's drive. They cycled part of the way, then dismounted and laid the bikes down behind a couple of old oaks.

'From here we can walk up the hill, and then if we keep low we can get to those trees.' Jack pointed at the small orchard at the top of Flowerdew's field. 'A perfect spying point, don't you think?'

They grinned at each other. This felt good.

They crouched low and started up the hill, keeping parallel with the edge of the field. Before they needed to cut left, Itch got out his dad's binoculars and peered down at the cottage. 'Can't see much from here. The spying trees it is.'

Crouching even lower among the stinging nettles and dandelions, they crept towards the apple trees that formed a barrier at the top of the field. Jack reached them first and Itch a few seconds later. They stood with their backs against the first two trees, panting and looking up at the sky. The clouds were a brilliant white, lit by the sun as it seemed to settle high above the horizon. The cousins' shadows merged into those of the trees as they lengthened up the hill.

They turned round and peered out from behind the tree trunks. They could see right down the slope and straight into the extension. The lights were on, and all the lab equipment was clearly visible. The door out onto the field was open but there was no sign of their chemistry teacher. They took it in turns to look through the binoculars. Itch's goes lasted longer than Jack's as he noted all the equipment, trying to identify each piece and what it did, giving the occasional low whistle or whispered 'Wow!' He lingered over the shelves of books and glass-fronted cupboards storing row upon row of what he assumed were various chemicals – though from the top of the field it was impossible to be certain.

Jack, by contrast, spotted three coffee mugs on the worktop in the middle of the room, and two bottles of water by the gym equipment. Clipboards and paper covered almost every surface. Outside, by a garden chair, lay a file of papers kept in place by another mug. The breeze lifted a sheet or two, but the mug was doing its job.

It was during Jack's third go with the binoculars that the door from the house into the lab opened and Flowerdew walked in.

'Itch! He's there! Look!' She handed the glasses to Itch, who grabbed them and focused again on the lab, his heart beating fast.

He gasped. 'And you'll never guess what he's got with him!' Itch's voice was still a whisper, but was forceful enough to make Jack grab the binoculars back. It was a few seconds before she identified what had got him so excited. On the floor beside the work surface stood a solid grey box with an adjustable handle. It looked like a piece of carry-on luggage, but with steel corners.

'Is that what I think it is?' asked Itch as he looked over her shoulder. Even without the binoculars he could see his chemistry teacher moving around the lab.

'What do you think it is?' Jack was alternating between following Flowerdew and studying the box.

'A lead-lined box. The kind you'd use if you wanted to store a radioactive rock. That sort of thing.'

Jack kept the binoculars a moment longer and then passed them to her cousin again. 'You look.'

Itch focused again. 'He's just picked it up. Looks heavy,' he said. A sharp intake of breath. 'And that's the radioactive symbol on it! Jack, that's our box!' Itch handed the binoculars back to her; she could clearly make out the bright yellow triangle on the side.

Itch sat back against his tree. 'It has to be heavy with all that lead in it. But what if he hasn't handed it over and my rock is still in there?'

'Why would he lie about that?' asked Jack, still not taking her eyes off the lab.

'Why is he such a git?' said Itch. 'I don't know. What's he doing now?'

'He's walking around talking on the phone. Looks like he's wearing washing-up gloves for some reason. He's getting a big protective thing from

152

behind the door to the house. Itch, it looks like a mask of some kind – it has a clear see-through panel! He's wandering about, talking and waving the mask-thing around. Now he's hung up and he's . . . I think you should watch this bit.'

Itch grabbed the binoculars in time to see Flowerdew approach the box, putting on the mask as he did so. His head, neck and shoulders were covered by the white, fitted fabric. Itch watched as he put the box on the work surface, undid four clips on the lid and lifted it off. He glanced in, then closed it all up again.

Itch had said nothing and Jack was getting impatient. 'Well? What's happening?'

He turned and looked straight at his cousin. Their trees' shadows were longer now, stretching almost to the top of the hill. Sunset was only half an hour away at most.

'He checked the box, Jack. He lifted the lid and looked inside. You don't do that if it's empty. My stone is *still here*. He lied to me, Jack! He's a thief *and* he's a liar.'

'And a git,' said Jack.

'And a git!' said Itch.

10

Although neither Itch nor Jack had mentioned stealing the stone back, each knew what the other was thinking. In the silence that followed Itch's last words, they sat with their backs against their respective trees. The light had taken on that orangy hue that often occurred before sunset, and the grass around them was damp with dew.

'What do you think?' said Itch.

'Same as you,' said Jack.

'That we would be stupid to try and take it back but we're going to anyway?'

'Pretty much, yes.'

There was a silence, then Itch said, 'I'm glad Chloe's not here.'

It seemed to Jack like an odd thing to say, but she said: 'Me too,' and knelt up again. She picked up the binoculars and trained them on the lab. 'Flowerdew's gone back into the house, though the box is still there. The outside door is still open, but if he closes it, that's it. If we're going to snatch it, we shouldn't wait too long.'

'Agreed. How shall we do it? Do we need a plan?'

'How about grabbing it and running as fast as possible?'

Itch smiled. 'I was hoping for something a bit cleverer than that. But essentially that's it.'

They were about to leave the cover of the trees when Flowerdew re-entered the lab to pick up the phone. He walked back into the house with it, again leaving the door open.

'Hell. Do we still go?' said Jack.

Itch nodded and set off diagonally down the hill at a crouching run, Jack a few metres behind. They couldn't run straight to the door as the lights from the lab lit up the first thirty metres of the field. If Flowerdew looked up from wherever he was in the house, he would see them clearly.

It took about twenty seconds for them to reach a pool of shadow formed between the cottage's back wall and the side of the lab. It was only a short run but felt to both Itch and Jack like the longest they had ever attempted. They huddled down and caught their breath. Itch started to get up, but Jack grabbed his arm and pulled him down again.

'What are we taking?'

'What do you mean?'

'The box or just the stone? The rock is yours but the box is his.'

Itch frowned. 'Hadn't thought of that. But we need the box for protection – remember the Geiger counter?'

'But,' said Jack, 'he'll notice within seconds if the box has gone. We'll never get away. If he doesn't know the rock is missing, we might have a chance.'

Itch nodded. She was right.

'Here, take this . . .' Jack handed him her satchel-style shoulder bag. He hooked the strap over his head and arranged it so that the bag rested against his back. He peered round the wall into the glass-fronted lab. Up close it was even more impressive. He was momentarily distracted from his task by the array of neatly labelled substances in the glass cabinets. It would take him a long, long time to acquire such a collection – his own seemed embarrassing in comparison.

Flowerdew's voice drifted through the door, and now Itch focused on the box sitting on the central work surface. From the door to the box was about ten metres. He would have to take a zigzag course because of all the equipment that blocked his path. Would they have time to open the box and remove the rock?

The lab door was half open. As Itch edged his way towards it, he heard Jack following right behind him. He could feel cold air from the lab on his face — the air conditioning felt fierce for an early summer evening. His heart was thumping in his chest and his hands were clammy with sweat.

Jack whispered, 'Come on!' just as they both heard a powerful motorbike approaching along the cove road and then slowing down. It idled for a moment before starting off again, the crunching gravel indicating its approach up Flowerdew's drive. Jack grabbed Itch's sleeve. 'Sounds like a courier! I bet he's come for the rock! Go!'

Itch and Jack reached the doorway of the lab just as Flowerdew, in the next room, looked up, hearing the approaching motorbike. On a still evening he had heard the roar from the bike half a mile away. It sounded familiar to him. He had once owned a Ducati Monster and thought he could recognize the sound now, even from this distance. He smiled: the couriers used by Greencorps always had the most powerful bikes on the market. He had forgotten how good the sound was. It was a sound that said: *You're back in the game.*

Through the window of his front room he watched as the driver checked the house from the road and made the left turn into his drive. It was indeed a Ducati Monster, all black and chrome, and even at five mph it made a beautiful, rumbling, controlled noise that seemed to fill the cove. He went to the front door and opened it just as Itch reached the lead-lined box sitting on the workbench.

As the sound of the superbike filled the house, Itch started on the first of the clips. He was relieved to find there was no lock, but the clips were tight-fitting and he had only seconds to get them open. Jack had positioned herself behind the now partly closed door into the house and peered through the crack. She waved a hand in a circular motion, indicating that Itch should hurry up. Itch didn't even see it. He had two clips undone and had started to prise open the third.

'He's outside looking at the bike,' said Jack in a shouted whisper, hopping from foot to foot, 'but he'll be back any second! Faster, Itch, you have to go faster!'

The last clip was open now and Itch looked around. Seeing a towel hanging over the rowing machine, he ran over and grabbed it. Back at the bench, he opened the lid. Inside was a small poly-styrene packing box. He shook it and felt the stone rattling around inside. He remembered what Flowerdew had been wearing when he was check-ing the rock and looked around again. He felt exposed, scared and thrilled, all at the same time. Spotting the shiny grey gloves, he grabbed the nearest one and slipped it on. It looked like a wash-ing-up glove, but it was very heavy – Itch guessed that it was lead-lined. He opened the polystyrene box with his bare hand and reached in with the glove. He'd forgotten how heavy the stone was – it rolled to the edge of his gloved palm. Recovering quickly, he closed his fist on it. The polystyrene went back into the lead box, then he wrapped the rock in the towel and shoved them both into Jack's bag.

'Nice bike,' said Flowerdew to the courier, who had removed his helmet and was shaking his long blond hair out of his eyes.

'Thanks, Dr Flowerdew. I'm Dougie. You have a package for me, I think.'

'Indeed. I'll get it. I used to have a Ducati Monster – beautiful machines, aren't they?'

Dougie smiled. 'I could bore you senseless, Dr Flowerdew, on the eleven hundred here – but this package of yours has to be on a plane at midnight. A swift turnaround needed. You'll need one of these . . .' He held out a plastic-coated steel chain with a small lock at one end.

'Of course. One minute,' said Flowerdew; he took the chain, turned and went back into the house.

'Too late! Hide!' Jack saw Flowerdew approaching, grabbed Itch, who was still shutting the clips, and pulled him onto the floor. They shrank back against the bench drawers, the bag between them. Reflected in the window, they saw Flowerdew stride into the lab and lift the box by its handle. He stopped abruptly when he noticed that one clip was open.

The cousins held their breath. There just hadn't been time to shut them all. Flowerdew shook his head, closed the last clip and wrapped the black chain around the box. It went round twice, and he clicked the two ends of the lock together, then left the lab. If the Ducati hadn't been making its beautiful noise, he would have heard two fourteen-year-olds release long-held breaths.

'Here you are. Guard it well. It's very precious,' he told the courier.

'I will, Dr Flowerdew.' The man snapped a plastic seal around the lock, lowered his cargo into the specially fitted box on the side of the Ducati and locked it. He put on his black helmet and opened the visor. 'Goodnight, sir.' He waved a salute and spun the bike round, spraying gravel in a neat arc.

Flowerdew watched as the bike roared down his drive and turned right onto the road. Its acceleration really was something to behold, and he stayed watching and then just listening as the bike disappeared northwards.

Itch and Jack had already reached their bikes when the sound of the Ducati disappeared from the cove. The sun was setting and they knew they needed to be back at Itch's house soon. They wheeled their bikes to the road and, without looking back, pedalled quickly up the hill, Itch with the radiation glove still on his right hand. Neither had spoken since fleeing the conservatory. This was partly because they had been running and were now cycling, but also because they were both struck with the enormity of what they had done.

They had stolen the rock back.

They had actually broken into a teacher's house and taken it. And with every passing minute, Itch was also increasingly aware that he had a dangerously radioactive stone in Jack's bag. The towel was no protection at all. Before he reached the top of the hill, he had come to the conclusion that he couldn't take it home. It was dangerous, and he didn't want it in the house.

He pulled over to the side of the road and hitched his bike onto the grass verge. He took Jack's bag off and placed it on the ground a couple of metres away.

'What's up, Itch?' asked Jack.

'We haven't thought this through. We can't take it home – bringing it into the house would be madness. We need to hide it, don't we?'

'We don't know what to do with it because, well, we had no idea we were actually going to steal it back in the first place. You're right about hiding it, though. Where do you reckon?'

Itch considered. 'There's this lay-by . . . the beach

hut . . . the golf course – anywhere really . . .' Every conceivable hiding place between here and home flashed through his mind. *I've got to get this right*, he thought. *This matters.*

'We need to decide quickly,' said Jack. 'It feels very exposed here.' She pointed at Itch's hand. 'Can we use that glove?'

'Of course! It's not much, but it's better than a towel. Don't know how much lead you can get in a glove – let's hope it's enough,' said Itch. He peeled off the glove and went over to the bag. Reaching in, he grabbed the rock, still wrapped in the towel, and lifted it out. Jack held the opening of the glove wide as Itch let it drop inside. She felt it fall as far as the fingers, folded the glove over and handed it back. Itch wrapped it in the towel again and put it back in the bag. 'Let's put it in the shed tonight and move it when we think of somewhere better.'

Jack picked up the bag and put it over her shoulder as they walked back to the bikes. Itch suddenly found his eyes prickling. After their argument last week he had wondered if they'd still be friends. Well, here was the answer: Jack knew the rock was radioactive, she knew it must be dangerous, but she carried it all the same.

'I'll take it, Jack. Give—'

'Shut up, Itch. Let's just get to your shed before we start to glow!'

11

The lead-lined, radiation-proof and empty box was in the Ducati top-box for just over two hours before the courier arrived at a private airfield. A Cessna twin-engined plane was waiting at the far corner of a triangle of runways, its lights glowing and flashing in the gloom; the bike headed straight for it.

The man leaped off the Ducati, unlocked the container and lifted out his cargo with both hands. He marched briskly over to a young Asian woman in a dark blue skirt and white shirt who had appeared at the door of the plane. She took it with only a brief nod to acknowledge the driver, and disappeared inside, strapping it into a seat next to her and calling to the pilot. Within a few minutes the Cessna was climbing into the night sky.

The pilot flew south-east, setting a course for Zurich. Below, the lights of Cornwall soon disappeared and the darkness of the Channel filled the plane. Roshanna Wing, the woman who'd taken delivery of the box, knew only that she had to hand it over to either Mr Revere or Mr Van Den Hauwe. No one else. She had been working for the Greencorps executives for two years, and these errands had become an increasingly common part of her job. They trusted her: she was efficient, and had a reputation for ruthlessness – an attribute that quickly led to promotion at Greencorps.

She dozed for most of the flight, so missed the lights of the French ports, the French interior and the mountaintops of the Alps as they crossed the border into Switzerland. The change in engine tone alerted her to their imminent landing, and she adjusted her seat and rearranged her hair. Instinctively she held out a hand to hold the box in position as they touched down.

A couple of hours later she was being driven through a small, deserted town. The car came to a halt at what appeared to be the old town hall, and she opened the door and climbed the steps to a large dark oak door, which opened as she approached.

Inside, the impression was of luxury – the carpet, furniture and paintings were top of the range – but the air had a chemical, metallic tang, and the light was harsh. She walked briskly past the abandoned offices and work stations. Every computer, every lamp, every machine was on. She walked straight into her office, throwing her jacket on the desk and, with the lead box in her left hand, knocked on a glass door with her light.

She could see the blurred outlines of the two men sitting at a long table. They appeared to be ending a video conference call, and Roshanna waited for them to call her in. She knew to knock only the once.

After less than a minute Christophe Revere opened the door and Jan Van Den Hauwe greeted her. Together they headed for a small laboratory, where she handed the Frenchman the lead box. He placed it on the table, and Van Den Hauwe took a key out of his pocket, snapped the plastic seal and unlocked the chain.

Two technicians in protective suits came in and carried the box through to a brightly lit, glass-walled booth. On getting a nod from the Dutchman, they undid the clips together, opened the lid together, and looked inside together. Then one of them pulled out the polystyrene case.

Taking the two halves apart, he found . . . nothing. He dropped both halves onto the table and tipped the box up. A few polystyrene chips fell out. The other technician rearranged some of them but, finding nothing, looked at the Greencorps bosses and shook his head. Removing his helmet, he brought the box out so that Revere could inspect it for himself.

After a brief glance the Frenchman picked up the box and hurled it through the glass door Roshanna had just closed behind her. She recognized some of the Dutch and French swearwords. Before all the glass had crashed and splintered onto the floor of the office, Revere was on the phone to England.

12

Chloe was finishing her breakfast when Itch came down the stairs. He hadn't slept well, his mind full of the events of last night. They could both hear their mother in the shower. For the moment it was safe to talk; Itch and Jack had briefed Chloe as soon as they got back.

'You can't leave it in the shed, Itch. Last night I Googled "radioactivity". It's scary stuff – you really need to take a look. The whole garden might be poisoned by now.'

Itch sat down at the table. 'I know that. Like I said, we never intended to take it back. We just saw our chance – that's all. And it *is* in a lead glove – that should protect us for a bit.' He got up to make some toast. 'You measure radioactive decay in Curies or Becquerels, I think. It sent the Geiger counter crazy, but how far the radiation spreads I'm not sure. I don't have the kit for that. But you're right about not leaving it in the shed. I'll move it before school.'

'Is there a safe way to carry it?' asked Chloe.

'Sure. All you need is a lead-lined box like the one we left behind.'

'So . . .' Chloe faltered. 'Moving it is pretty dangerous too, then?'

'Yes, I reckon so.'

She stood watching her brother make his toast. 'You need to tell Mr Watkins. He could get a box, couldn't he?'

'Yeah, I've been wondering about that. He could get one and then take it to his friends at the mining school. It's just that Cake said to keep quiet and tell no one.'

'Yeah, well, maybe Cake's wrong on this. Let's not fill the garden with Be— whatever you said . . .'

'Becquerels.'

'Right. Them. They sound nasty.'

The noise of the shower stopped, and Itch spoke more quietly. 'I'll get it on our way out. You haven't got an empty tin I could use, have you?'

'Got an old Hannah Montana pencil-tin, if you can face it.'

Itch grimaced. 'She's almost as toxic as the rock. She might even cancel out all the dangerous Becquerels.'

'Ha ha.'

'But that'll do, thanks.'

'Where are you going to put it?'

'Beach hut, I think. It'll just be for a few hours if Watkins can help us.'

'Is that any safer than the shed?'

'No one lives close to the huts, so yes, probably.'

'I'll go and get Hannah Montana.' Chloe went up to her room and Itch finished his breakfast.

Jude Lofte came into the kitchen wearing jeans and an old T-shirt, a towel round her hair. 'Morning, Itch. How's things?'

Itch wondered for a moment exactly how 'things' were. He *could* say: *Well, I broke into my chemistry teacher's house last night and stole my radioactive rock back. And it's currently wrapped in a glove and a towel – also both stolen – in our shed.* But he just said, 'Fine,' then added, 'No work today?'

'Got a paper to prepare – twenty thousand words – so I might as well work from home today. I can actually cook for you and Chloe tonight. How about that for a novelty?' She filled the kettle and found a tea bag. 'Any requests? I'm going to walk into town in a bit.'

This had Itch stumped for a moment. What *did* his mother cook best? 'One of your pies would be nice – you haven't made those for a while.'

'No, you're right. Not for years, I reckon. Dad always liked them, didn't he? OK, I'll see what the butcher's got.' She looked at the clock. 'You and Chloe should get off.'

While Chloe waited outside the front door, Itch headed for the shed with his sister's pencil-tin. He realized he was holding his breath and squinting, as though that might reduce his exposure to the radiation, which he pictured pouring all over the garden. He retrieved the towel and glove-wrapped rock from the empty paint pot he had put them in last night. Using a trowel, he tried to drop the whole lot into the pencil-tin, but the towel was far too bulky. Carefully, as if it might explode, he unwrapped the glove with the edge of the trowel, scooped it up and dropped it into the tin. He had no idea if that made it safer, but it seemed logical. He put on the lid and stowed it in his rucksack. He left the shed door open in case that helped get rid of the radiation — like it was some kind of bad smell.

He made Chloe walk twenty paces ahead of him, which she thought looked ridiculous – though she didn't complain. She stood guard while Itch opened the beach hut and hid the tin in a small saucepan they used for heating soup. He locked up and they walked past the other huts and onto the cliffs.

Chloe glanced at her brother. He looked pale and tired. His hair was a mess and his school shirt looked as though it was yesterday's. 'You OK?' she asked.

'Yeah, not bad, considering . . .' After a few paces he completed his own sentence: 'Considering I spent half the night wondering what Flowerdew might do next. I have him periods three and four.'

They were looping around the golf course now, quickening their pace – the beach-hut detour had cost them a few minutes.

'There is no way that he can connect you to the stone disappearing, though, is there?' said Chloe.

'Not unless he has CCTV in his house,' said Itch, 'and we didn't see any cameras.'

'I wonder if you're radioactive.'

'Thanks, Chloe. Let's hope not.'

Itch was sure Mr Watkins was the man to speak to. In fact, he was the *only* man to speak to. He knew his stones and he knew Flowerdew. In his many waking hours that night, Itch had decided that despite Cake's warning to tell no one, he had to get help, and his form teacher was the only candidate. He and Chloe arrived just as the 8.45 registration bell was ringing and they ran to their respective classrooms. Maybe he could get a word with Watkins before first period? He pushed open the classroom door but found Mr Littlewood taking the register.

Itch shuffled round to his desk and said quietly to Jack, 'I put it in the beach hut. Where's Watkins?'

'Invigilating an exam. Free at lunch time, I guess. You going to tell him?'

Itch nodded. He handed Jack her history books.

'Thanks, I didn't copy too much – honestly!'

Jack smiled. 'Let's hope not. Shall I test you on German foreign policy just to see how much went in?'

Itch laughed. 'Yes, that would go well!'

Suddenly James Potts shoved his head over Jack's shoulder. 'Some book-swapping going on in weird cousin-land, is there? I wonder if Mr Littlewood would like to know about that?'

'Go away, creep,' said Jack. 'Let me think now. Your last essay was a C-minus, wasn't it? Maybe *you* should try borrowing someone's work – if you can find anyone stupid enough to lend you anything.'

She got a sharp elbow in the ribs for that, but at least Potts went back to his bench and didn't say anything to Littlewood.

During break that morning, word spread of an interesting first two periods in Flowerdew's chemistry lab. The Year Eights were reporting that he hadn't turned up and that a whole period had passed before anyone came to sit with them. In the end Miss Glenacre had arrived to help out, and then Dr Dart. Apparently, they didn't know where he was, either. As Itch and Jack had chemistry next, they decided to turn up early to see what happened. Heading for the lab, they realized that the rest of the class had had the same idea. For the first time anyone could remember, every pupil was at their bench before the bell went.

As they waited for Flowerdew, Sam Jennings volunteered to be a lookout and stood by the door, poking her head out every ten seconds. After five minutes she flew back in, calling, 'Brigadier!' and had just reached her seat when their English teacher marched in. He put a pile of marking on the desk and was greeted by a forest of raised hands and a chorus of: 'Sir, where's Dr Flowerdew? Is he ill? What's happened to him, sir?'

Gordon Carter raised both hands for silence. 'The answer to all your questions is: "I have no idea." Sorry, but there it is. Now, I have a pile of marking to do, and intend to get on with it. I'm sure you have a chemistry textbook or something you can look at.' General groans greeted that. 'Or I could always set you a lovely essay . . . We could recap some of our *Merchant of Venice* if you prefer?'

Everyone opened their chemistry books at once, and the Brigadier smiled appreciatively.

Itch leaned towards Jack. 'This doesn't feel good, does it?'

Jack shook her head without looking up.

As period three ended and period four began, the Brigadier was replaced by Craig Harris, one of the games teachers. He was in his usual Scotland rugby top and tracksuit bottoms, and put a cup of coffee and two apples on the desk in front of him.

'I'm giving up my break for you guys,' he announced. 'And I know even less about chemistry than Mr Carter, so whatever it was you were doing for him, please feel free to continue doing it for me.'

Itch had started writing a bit more on his German foreign-policy homework; what he had done after their raid of the previous night was pretty sparse. They had history that afternoon, so this was a heaven-sent opportunity to add a paragraph or two. But he worked slowly, as he always did in history, and still had a few paragraphs to write when the bell went for the end of the period. Everyone got up to leave, but Itch told Jack he was just finishing off and would catch up with her at lunch.

Soon he was the only one left in the lab. Head down and writing as fast as he could, he was just finishing his last paragraph when he heard the lab door shut. He didn't look up immediately.

Then a voice said, 'Ah, Lofte. Just who I was hoping to see.' And Itch felt the blood drain from his face.

He looked up and saw Nathaniel Flowerdew standing at the front of the lab as if he was about to give a lesson. At first glance the teacher appeared the same as ever, with his expensive clothes and jewellery all in place. But his clothes looked crumpled and his hair shot out at all angles, as though he had, until recently, been wearing a hat. His face was flushed, his lips tightly together, almost invisible. He stared at Itch.

'Hello, sir.' Itch's voice sounded tight. He swallowed. 'You missed your lesson. Are you OK?'

'Come here.'

'Pardon?'

'You heard. Come here.'

Itch got up slowly and walked to the front of the lab.

'Where is it?'

'Where's what, sir?'

Flowerdew put his face right in front of Itch's. 'Let's get to the point. You came to my house last night and stole the rock. I want it back.' Then, very quietly, 'And I want it *now*.'

Itch swallowed again and then cleared his throat. 'You sent it to Switzerland, sir. You told—'

Before he had finished his sentence Itch felt a large hand around his throat. Flowerdew gave a roar of rage, and Itch was propelled, neck first, back towards the door. Flowerdew pinned him in the corner, out of sight of any passing students or teachers. Itch's eyes were watering as he stared wide-eyed at his teacher.

'Crying now, Lofte? Did you think I wouldn't know it was you?'

The hand round his neck tightened and started to lift him off the ground. He tried to cough, but the grip was too tight and bright lights started to appear in his eyes. Suddenly two Year Tens came into the lab and Flowerdew dropped him.

'GET OUT!' he shouted at them, and they jumped, then ran off.

Itch had crumpled and was now sitting slumped in the corner, shaking. Flowerdew knelt down beside him. From his pocket he pulled out a towel. Itch realized that it was the one from Flowerdew's house that he had wrapped the rock in. He had left it in the shed when he transferred the rock that morning.

Flowerdew saw Itch's expression change. 'Yes, I found this *in your shed*. Looks like mine, doesn't it? So I'll ask you again.' He reached out and grabbed Itch – by the shirt this time. He looked desperate – almost mad. 'Where is the rock, Lofte?' He lifted him up till Itch's head was higher than his own. 'I need it.' He banged Itch's head against the wall. 'I need it *now*!' He banged his head again. Itch cried out this time, and Flowerdew's other hand swiftly covered his victim's mouth. 'No, you're not calling out. The only thing you'll say is WHERE YOU PUT THE DAMNED STONE!'

Now the door burst open a second time, and Dr Dart, John Watkins and Chris Hopkins, the physics teacher, all ran in. Dr Dart screamed, 'Dr Flowerdew!' and Watkins grabbed Itch while Dart and Hopkins pulled Flowerdew's hands away from him. More students arrived – two Year Seven girls who started screaming. Then Jim Littlewood and Craig Harris came tearing in. Seeing Dr Dart and Chris Hopkins struggling with a manic Flowerdew, they jumped on the head of science and pinned him against his own desk.

Dr Dart ordered the students to leave immediately. 'And go to the staff room to get help!'

They left quickly, but another crowd was already gathering outside the lab, staring through the glass. Some started cheering as they watched Mr Watkins, standing in front of Itch, arms outstretched to form a barrier between Itch and Flowerdew. As soon as he thought the head of science was subdued he turned to find his pupil sprawled on the floor. He knelt down and tried to help him up, but misjudged his action so that Itch cried out as his head banged against the wall again.

'Careful with the boy, John!' called Dr Dart.

There were gasps from the watching students; every inch of window space was now taken by wide-eyed CA students, many of them with their phones pressed to the glass. A dozen blinking red lights shone into the classroom.

Meanwhile Watkins had removed his jacket and rolled it up to cushion Itch's head. Itch cried out in pain, and his teacher realized that there was a huge bruise swelling and distorting the back of his head.

'When you're finished, Jim, come and check here

please,' he said to their first-aider. But at the moment all the teachers were busy restraining Flowerdew. Hopkins and Harris held his legs while Littlewood pinioned his arms. But they were losing the struggle: Flowerdew was slowly but surely wresting his arms and legs free, yelling and hurling abuse at Itch as he threw his head from side to side.

A chorus of 'Fight! Fight!' had started in the corridor. Someone shouted, 'Detention for Flowerdew!' as the head of science turned to the head.

'He stole my rock! He broke into my house! It's gone and it's *his* fault! Search him – it's here, I know he's got it!'

Dr Dart, red-faced with fury, shouted back, 'I'll do no such thing! Consider yourself suspended immediately! You'll stay here till the police come!'

'In which case,' yelled Flowerdew, '*I'll* do it!' And he wrenched his arms free, turned and punched Mr Littlewood on the side of the head. The history teacher fell back, and now Mr Hopkins let go, leaving only the games teacher still with his arms around Flowerdew's legs. But Mr Harris shoved hard, just as he taught his rugby teams to, and Flowerdew toppled over. As he fell, he grabbed a glass flask from his desk and smashed it on Mr Harris's head, the shards flying everywhere. To screams and gasps from the watching pupils, blood started to pour through the games master's hair. He let go of Flowerdew.

Now free of restraints, the chemistry teacher stood and turned to Itch, who was still propped up against the wall, his head cushioned on Mr Watkins's jacket. Some of the pupils stepped back from the windows. A Year Ten girl shouted, 'Leave him alone, bully!'

'Get out of the way, Watkins, or make him turn out his pockets.' Flowerdew moved towards them, the neck of the broken flask still in his hand.

John Watkins was trembling slightly, but he didn't flinch and his voice was steady. 'We knew you were a terrible teacher, Nathaniel, but we never knew you were mad. You do realize you'll go to prison for this, don't you? Whatever career you're hoping for has gone.'

There was applause from the corridor – while Flowerdew advanced on Watkins, more like a street fighter than a chemistry teacher.

'Leave them alone, for pity's sake!' cried Dr Dart.

Flowerdew ignored her. 'Empty your pockets, Lofte.'

Watched by everyone, Itch took out the contents of his two trouser and three jacket pockets. Harris and Hopkins had no idea what was happening or what they were looking for, but stared at the items anyway – a few coins, three biros and some tissues.

No rock.

The large crowd of pupils watching from the corridor turned as they heard running footsteps. Six members of staff ran into the lab, led by Gordon Carter, the Brigadier. They all stood staring at the extraordinary scene in front of them, but before anyone could react, Flowerdew put his head down and charged. He crashed into maths teacher Sunil Mansoor, and Hilary Briggs from ICT, and pushed his way out of the door. The students scattered as he ran down the corridor.

Mr Harris, his head bleeding, made to follow him, but Dr Dart said, 'No, Craig, let him go. Just call the police. He's dangerous. Let him leave the school premises — they can arrest him later. And I suppose we'll need an ambulance as well. Oh my word . . .' And she slumped down in Flowerdew's chair.

13

Jim Littlewood and Craig Harris took Itch to the first-aid room. It was a basic affair with a low bed, sink and toilet. Two chairs stood by the door and there was a locked medicine cabinet above a small table. Littlewood showed Itch to the bed, but he opted for one of the chairs instead; Mr Harris took the other one.

Itch caught sight of his profile in the medicine-cabinet mirror. The bruise on the back of his head was enormous; it looked as though he had a small balloon inflated under his hair. It was pretty shocking, even to Itch; he dreaded to think what his mother would say. The school secretary was trying to get hold of her now.

'I really think you should lie down, Itch,' said Mr Littlewood. 'Bangs on the head should always be taken seriously, and yours looks mighty indeed. Do you have a headache at all?'

'Actually, yes, I do, sir. And maybe you're right about the bed.' Itch was suddenly feeling faint and dizzy, and Littlewood helped him over.

'The ambulance will be here soon, but let's hope your mother arrives first.'

'I'm not sure that I need an ambulance, sir,' said Itch.

'Well, one's coming anyway, and they can check Mr Harris out too while they're here.'

The games teacher's hair was thick with matted blood. He sat with an ice pack in one hand and a towel in the other, which he dabbed very gently on the back of his head.

The door opened, and a grim-faced Dr Dart came in, followed by Mr Watkins. 'How's he doing, Jim?' she asked. 'And how's that head, Craig?' She sat on the chair between Itch and Harris.

Jim Littlewood spoke first. 'OK, I think, but I'll be happier once the ambulance has been, just to get a proper analysis, to be honest. I'll go and look out for it.' He left the crowded first-aid room and Dr Dart turned to Craig Harris.

He looked at the bloody towel in his hand. 'Oh, it'll be fine, Dr Dart, really it will. The bleeding has stopped, though they'll need to make sure there's no glass in the wound.'

'Indeed,' said Dart. There was silence in the little room for a few moments.

'Can anyone tell me what all that was about?'

asked Harris. 'What was Flowerdew looking for? How come he was so mad? He'd totally lost it.'

Dr Dart and John Watkins looked at each other, and then at Itch, who had his eyes shut. The head nodded at Watkins, who explained what they knew.

'The bottom line, however,' Dart said, 'is that my head of science has just attacked one of my pupils and several members of my staff. A sackable offence. A criminal offence. The police can make the next move. Apparently he drove off at high speed. I'm sure he won't get far.'

There was a tentative knock at the door: a small group of students stood outside.

'We were wondering how Itch is . . .' It was Lucy Cavendish and a group of Year Tens, who nodded, peering in.

'Shaken and bruised, Lucy — the ambulance is on its way,' said Mr Watkins. 'Thanks for your concern.' He smiled reassuringly and eased the door shut.

Itch was wondering what he should do with the rock. He had an all-too-powerful image of it sitting in his beach hut, slowly filling it and the surrounding seafront with radiation. He had expected to be handing the stone over to Mr Watkins, but after Flowerdew's attack, he wasn't sure if that was wise. As far as Itch was concerned, he had merely recovered his own property — but would the police see it like that?

Itch considered himself an honest person. His mum and dad had always insisted on him and Chloe telling the truth. Occasionally he had felt the need to be less than direct, even slightly underhand when getting hold of some of the elements for his collection. He had claimed he was eighteen a couple of times, like when getting hold of some xenon. His mother had written the cheque and he had not told her of the age restriction.

Until the incidents of recent days, however, he had always assumed he was the sort who would own up to parents, teachers or the police if he had done something wrong. But he hadn't owned up to the arsenic affair, and Chloe and Jack had been unimpressed. Now he'd got his stone back. He was convinced he hadn't done anything *really* illegal, but everything seemed less clear.

'Itchingham's mother is here. And the ambulance is just behind.' Jim Littlewood had seen Jude Lofte hurrying up the school drive a few moments ago, and before she reached the academy entrance, the ambulance had turned into the drive, its lights flashing. He had run to the first-aid room to pass on the news, surprised to see Mrs Lofte coming up the drive. As far as he knew, they hadn't been able to find her. They had left messages to call the office at her home and on her mobile but none had been returned.

'Thank you, Jim,' said Dr Dart. 'Stay here with Mr Harris and Itchingham, will you? Mr Watkins, will you come with me, please?'

Down the corridor they could see a clearly agitated Jude Lofte pacing up and down outside Dart's office. The school secretary, Sarah Hopkins, was trying to calm her and get her to wait in the office. It was Jude who saw the approaching head teacher and head of geography.

'Dr Dart! Thank heavens! I've come straight here without ringing, I'm afraid – I—'

'Mrs Lofte, do come into my office. I'm so glad you're here. I'm glad you got our messages after all . . . I wasn't sure whether we had got hold of you or not.'

Jude looked confused. 'I'm sorry, I don't understand. What messages? And why are you glad I'm here?'

The two women stood staring at each other for a moment, then Dr Dart ushered Jude and Watkins into her office and closed her door. Everyone remained standing.

'We were ringing to ask you to come to the school because I'm afraid there has been a nasty incident involving Itchingham. He is OK, we think, but we have called the ambulance as a precaution. And the police are coming too.'

Jude Lofte turned white and reached for Dart's desk to steady herself. John Watkins grabbed her arm and helped her to a chair. She sat down quickly. 'An incident? Please tell me it didn't involve an explosion. Where is he? I need to see him!'

'You will, Mrs Lofte. Let me just explain what happened.' Dr Dart was, thought Mr Watkins, impressively calm. 'Itch is in the first-aid room and Mr Littlewood is with him. I regret to tell you that Dr Flowerdew attacked your son in his lab. He also injured two members of my staff. Itchingham received a number of bangs to the head. Mr Flowerdew ran off, and the police are looking for him. It would be best if the ambulance crew could see Itch as soon as possible—'

'Bangs to the head from what?'

'We think it was the wall, Mrs Lofte. His head was . . . banged against the wall.'

Jude gasped and tears flooded into her eyes. 'I have to see him,' she cried. Outside the office they could all hear footsteps running along the corridor – the ambulance crew.

'Just one thing, Mrs Lofte,' said Dart. 'If you didn't get our messages, why are you here?'

Jude's eyes welled with tears again. 'Because our house has been burgled, Dr Dart! Ransacked! I came back from town to find every room gone through – all our possessions scattered everywhere. I told the police I'd be here.'

Jude Lofte, Mr Watkins and the head stood

rooted to the spot, all looking at each other, unable to process all the information they had just received. Then, hearing a cry of pain from Itch, Jude ran from the office.

14

The whole Lofte family hadn't all been round one table since Christmas. In spite of the desperate circumstances that had brought them all together, Saturday morning breakfast was clearly being enjoyed. Nicholas had arrived on Friday evening, having received Jude's emergency email and catching the first available plane. The process of getting hold of Nicholas had become more complicated in the last couple of years; oil-rig health and safety, he had explained, had banned mobile phones.

Itch and Chloe's elder brother Gabriel had caught a bus down from Coventry and got home near midnight. It was now just after 8 a.m. and, early risers that they were, the Loftes were all sitting in their usual places around the kitchen table. Itch sat opposite Gabriel – it looked as though his elder brother had another piercing in his left ear. That would make a total of four in that ear and three in the other. He was Lofte-tall, of course, but appeared to have stopped growing just shy of his father's six foot four. His hair was darker and less wavy than Itch's but was considerably longer.

Coffee, juice, toast and cereal were passed around, and for the moment the conversation was light-hearted. There was news to catch up on from Gabriel's university and Nicholas's oil rig before they discussed the break-in.

'You guys know all this, I realize,' said Gabriel, 'but I'm playing catch-up here. Mum told me some stuff when she rang – but this . . .' He gestured to some of the contents of the kitchen which still lay in the corners of the room where they had been thrown. 'This is something else. This is shocking. I never realized it was so bad.'

'You should have seen it when we got back here on Thursday,' Itch said. 'Everything had been thrown around – cushions, books, CDs, DVDs, cutlery, food, plates, bedding, all on the floor. Mum's office was trashed too – the drawers emptied.'

'And my shoes were thrown everywhere,' said Chloe. 'My clothes too. Why would they do that?'

Her dad reached out and held her hand.

'It was quite late when we got back from the hospital,' said Jude, 'but the police were still here. They said it was a crime scene and that we shouldn't be moving anything till they had finished. We just sat here eating pizza. We were surrounded by pans, and packets of food were scattered all over the place, but we were only allowed to sit and eat. When they left we were too tired to clear up, so we just moved what we needed to get to our beds and started first thing yesterday.'

'What did the hospital say, Itch?' asked Gabriel, pointing at his brother's head with a piece of toast.

'I had X-rays and all that, which took for ever, but they didn't find anything.'

'What – they didn't find anything in your head at all?' asked Gabriel. 'That explains a lot.'

Itch flicked a crust at him and everyone laughed.

'They argued with Mum about letting me come home, but when she explained about the break-in, eventually they agreed. She was getting quite worked up, weren't you, Mum?'

'I think I might have been quite forceful, yes,' said Jude, recalling the events of Thursday night. 'But I did promise to get in touch if he went on having headaches or felt sick.'

There was a loud and jaunty knock on the front door.

'That can only be your brother,' Jude said to her husband. 'He and Zoe were here yesterday helping clear up. They said they'd pop back.'

Nicholas went to open the door and returned in conversation with his brother Jon, followed by Jack, and then Zoe Lofte carrying some fresh bread and a large bag of croissants. Jon was four years younger than his brother but looked older; his black hair was greying at the temples. He was, if anything, slightly taller than Nicholas, but stooped slightly, as though embarrassed by his height. He wore jeans and, as he always did, a T-shirt with SHOW OF HANDS, his favourite band, on the front. He smiled when he saw the family.

'Now that's a sight for sore eyes! You're all here and there's coffee too.' His voice was lighter than his brother's and the accent stronger. He greeted them all one by one. 'Good to see you, Gabriel – glad you could get down. Terrible thing here, terrible thing. How are you this morning, Itch? Your neck still looks bad.' There were deep red bruises where Flowerdew's fingers had squeezed it.

'Yes, it feels rough. It's the back of my head that hurts the most, though.' Itch turned his head, and Jack and her mother winced and gasped at the same time. The back of Itch's head was swollen and still bloodied, despite the treatment and dressing he had received at the hospital. A recently applied antiseptic cream was smeared over most of the swelling but blood was still seeping through where the skin had split.

Jack hugged Gabriel and sat down next to Chloe. Zoe put the croissants on the table and took a seat next to Itch. She was slim and serious-looking, with high cheekbones, and was dressed in three-quarter-length khaki trousers and a white shirt. Her shoulder-length dark brown hair was wet and left a damp patch on Itch's T-shirt where it brushed against him.

'Sorry, Itch – early morning swim. Let me look at you.' Zoe smiled as she peered over the top of her oval-shaped, steel-rimmed glasses. She shook her head slightly and patted Itch on the shoulder. 'That teacher needs locking up,' she said. Through full mouths and with nodding heads, it was clear everyone agreed with that.

'Tell me about him,' said Nicholas.

'Of course – you've never met him, have you?' said Jude. 'You haven't made a parents' evening for years . . .' After a brief pause she continued, 'Never heard a good word about him from either parents or children. I saw him before half term, and I swear if it hadn't been for Itch's name, he wouldn't have had a clue who he was.'

'Correct,' said Jon. 'He had no idea who Jack was when we met him. Just told us what they were studying and waved us away.'

'He's a jerk,' Jack confirmed. 'Everyone has always hated him. It's clear he can't stand being a teacher.'

'We can't stand him being a teacher, either,' said Itch.

Nicholas poured some more coffee. 'Actually, I *have* met him,' he said.

'What?' said Itch. 'You've met Flowerdew?'

'I only realized this morning. You described him

yesterday while we were clearing the place up a bit and I thought the name rang a bell, but it only clicked this morning. Years ago, when I was on my first rig, there was this curly-haired young idiot who was clearly being given special treatment by the company. They obviously thought very highly of him, as he was being given a crash course in everything. He only stayed a week or so but managed to annoy pretty much everyone in that time.'

'Yeah, that's him,' said Itch.

'Did you ever speak?' asked Jack.

'As I recall we did have words, yes. But this is many years ago and I assumed when the helicopter came to whisk him to his next place of education that it was the last we'd hear of him.'

'Shame you didn't push him in the sea,' said Chloe.

'If I had my time again . . .' said her father.

'How on earth did he get a job at the academy?' wondered Jon. 'And as head of science too?'

'It's Greencorps, Jon,' said Nicholas. 'They own the rigs, they own the tankers, they own the refineries, they own the petrol stations. Now they sponsor the academy. They run the whole show.'

'How can you stay working for them, Dad, if they're so horrible?' Chloé asked.

Her dad sighed. 'Basically, there's no one else. Unless you fancy moving to Russia or Greenland. That's where they're recruiting now.'

'Maybe not,' said Gabriel. 'Though Christmas in Greenland might be fun.' He smeared some marmalade on his toast. 'Do they think Flowerdew broke in here too? Surely that's crazy!'

Itch felt the back of his head again. 'But that's the point – he *is* crazy – and vicious too.'

'So, just to be clear,' said Jon. 'The police are working on the theory that Flowerdew broke in here, and then attacked Itch? Really? A teacher?'

'That's what they think, Jon, yes,' said Nicholas.

'And all over a rock,' said Gabriel. 'One of your collection, Mum said. Stolen from him by someone after he took it off you. What is it – gold or something? He must want it very much.'

'Well, apparently, yes.' Itch filled his brother in on the history of the radioactive rock – without the bits about breaking into his teacher's house or about the beach hut. 'The shed was trashed too, and the bulk of my collection was chucked around the garden. I've found most of it, apart from my titanium and aluminium, but they must be out there somewhere.' He pointed at his brother's new earring. 'Looks like you've got yourself some new titanium anyway, Gabriel – maybe I could just have that? I'm sure Dad would rather it was in my kit box than in your ear.'

Another family laugh. Normally his brother's piercings caused arguments, but not today. Itch could get used to this.

The day became a procession of visitors. The police came to question Itch about the assault and update them on the search for Flowerdew. Dr Dart came with the Chairman of Governors – no doubt because they were worried about legal action. Neighbours and friends called to see if they could help and asked after Itch. Reporters hung around too; local TV and radio were running reports of the assault – the *Western Daily Press* headline was: TOP TEACHER GOES NUTS. HORROR IN CLASSROOM AS SCIENCE BOFFIN ATTACKS PUPIL. Pupils' videos of the fight in the classroom had been uploaded to various websites, and stills had been used to illustrate the newspaper article. The front page showed a blurry close-up of a deranged-looking Flowerdew holding the broken flask.

Jon and Zoe bought fish and chips for everyone's lunch, and while the adults discussed the break-in yet again, Jack and Itch went up to his room, where Chloe joined them, also seeking an escape from grown-up chat.

'I like having your parents here,' she said, turning to Jack. 'They only come round when Dad's home.'

'I'm not sure our mums get on that well, really,' said Jack. 'They never call each other or anything.'

'When Dad said we were moving here, Mum never seemed that pleased, did she?' Itch said to

Chloe. 'It was always Dad's idea — he just seemed determined to get us out of London.'

'I don't remember any of that, really,' said Chloe, 'but I do remember Mum was a lot happier once she got her job in town. Maybe things will change now.'

'Maybe,' said Jack. The doorbell went again as yet more visitors arrived. 'I heard the police saying they thought there must have been more than one thief — or whatever it is we are calling them.'

'Which means Flowerdew had help,' said Itch. 'But who would help that toe-rag? It makes me so mad to think of someone going through all our stuff.'

Jack nodded. 'The whole thing sucks big time. This rock of yours, Itch, must have magic powers or something. What's so special about it that Flowerdew, plus his mad friends, would break into your house?'

'I'm not sure,' said Itch. 'But Cake was right, wasn't he? This is one popular piece of rock. So let's assume that he and Flowerdew are right and that it is something special — something to do with that Geiger-counter reading and the amount of radioactivity it's giving off. And also that Flowerdew and his mates are definitely the last people on earth who should get their hands on it.' He looked at Jack. 'We need to get it out of the beach hut. Flowerdew obviously doesn't know we have one, or that would be trashed too and he would have found it. I've cycled past a couple of times and it's fine, but he'll find out sooner or later.'

'Can't you just throw it into the sea or something?' asked Chloe. 'Surely it's caused enough trouble.'

Itch looked downcast. 'I know. I've been thinking about that. Throwing it into the sea isn't an option because, if it is radioactive, presumably it could pollute the marine life. But you're right about it causing trouble. If only Flowerdew hadn't attacked me I could have got it to Mr Watkins by now. But after what happened at school I can't just hand it over now and say, *Oh yeah, sorry, I had it all the time. Flowerdew was right. Sorry you got glassed in the head, Mr Harris.*'

He stood up and looked out of his bedroom window. It was a cool day with low cloud and light drizzle. He gazed at what was left of the shed: the door kicked in, and most of its contents scattered around the garden. He had retrieved his element collection over a few hours of searching through the flowers and bushes, and a lot of the smaller items were now temporarily re-housed in his rucksack; most of the larger ones would have to stay outside. He hadn't yet mentioned to his mother that he'd brought much of his collection back inside, but supposed he should do so soon. The rucksack sat by the side of his bed. He put his hand on it.

'You know,' he said, 'what with the trouble this rock has caused and the gas in the greenhouse, this little collection has caused a lot of grief.' He sat on his bed and looked at Chloe and Jack. 'Mass sickness, students and a teacher in hospital, a teacher with glass in his head – that's quite a price to pay for a hobby, don't you think?'

Chloe and Jack looked at each other.

'And now the break-in!' he continued. 'The whole house turned upside down and everyone's things thrown everywhere! That's my fault too!'

'But it's not like you did it on purpose or anything,' said Chloe. 'You didn't know what would happen with the arsenic, and the rock is all Flowerdew's fault.'

Jack found it hard to disagree with Itch's logic, even if Chloe was right about Itch not having meant for these things to happen. 'What do you want to do, Itch?' she asked him. 'The rock still needs to be moved – that's the most important thing.'

Itch looked up at her. 'You're right. And you know what I should do? Give it back to Cake. In fact, give it *all* back to Cake.' He stood and picked up the rucksack. 'I'm not sure I want to carry on collecting elements if this is what happens.'

Chloe looked stunned. 'But you've been collecting them for years, Itch. You love this stuff – you can't just give it all away!'

'And,' said Jack, 'there's no one else I know

with a collection like it. It's what you *do*, Itch.'

'Maybe,' said Itch, and sat down on the bed again. 'But let's get the rock and take it to Cake anyway. He can have it. I don't want it any more. He'll know what to do with it.'

Jack was looking at Itch's new Table of Elements poster. He had replaced the one that had been blown off the wall by the phosphorus explosion, and had again marked off the elements he owned.

'Where's uranium, then?'

'Number ninety-two,' said Itch without looking up. 'Bottom line, fourth from the left.'

Jack traced her finger along the final row, stopping at a picture of a piece of silvery-white metal. 'That doesn't look like our rock.' She studied it carefully. 'Not even close.' She scanned the assorted photos and pictures that accompanied each of the 118 elements. 'It looks more like lead . . . or iron.'

Itch stood up and joined Jack. 'It's not like a bird-spotting guide, Jack – but I agree, it doesn't look like uranium. All the radioactive elements are the high numbers. From eighty-four onwards. That' – he pointed to a photo of another silvery-grey metal – 'is polonium. It's what killed some ex-KGB agent in London.'

'I assume uranium isn't quite as nasty,' said Chloe.

'No. That's why the rock must be something else.'

'Where did you say Cake lived?' asked Jack.

'I think it's out by the St Haven spoil heap,' said Itch.

'That's a number twenty-two bus from the golf course,' said Jack, 'and a short walk once you get to St Haven. If you think you're up to it, Itch.'

'I'm fine now,' he told her.

'Is it safe to just carry the stone there?' asked Chloe. 'If it's as radioactive as you were saying, can't we put it in a box or something?'

Jack and Itch thought about that one. They had both felt extremely uncomfortable cycling home with it and didn't relish the prospect of taking it on a bus one bit.

'It's in the lead glove, but I wonder if we could make our own lead box too?' said Itch. He went downstairs, and Jack and Chloe watched from the window as he disappeared into what was left of the shed. He emerged waving a length of pipe in one hand and a mallet in the other.

'It's a piece of an old water pipe,' he said when he came back into the room. 'Used to be on the roof here. They made them from lead until they realized it was making everyone ill.'

Jack laughed. 'No, you really wouldn't want to go around poisoning people, would you?'

Itch smiled weakly. 'All right, point taken.'

The piece of pipe was a dirty grey colour and covered with dust and cobwebs. About thirty centimetres long and six or seven centimetres across, it was just wide enough for the rock to fit snugly inside. Itch wiped it on his T-shirt and blew down one end, sending a cloud of dust and grit over his bed.

'Mum will love that!' said Chloe.

'I'll blame Flowerdew.' Itch put the pipe on the floor. Gently at first, until he had worked out how much force to use, he started to hit one end with the mallet. As the lead started to dent and fold, he turned it slowly. In two minutes he had closed off one end completely.

'Will it keep the radiation in?' asked Jack.

This was what Itch had been asking himself as he bashed the pipe: the truth was, he had no idea. He shrugged. 'Yes. A bit. Don't know.'

'Very scientific answer, Itch,' said Chloe, and they all smiled.

'Right,' said Jack. 'Let's get that magic rock and catch the next bus to St Haven.'

15

They sat at the back of the bus. The rock, in its makeshift lead container, was now in a canvas bag and sat on a seat of its own in front of them. There were only four other passengers on the 22 bus heading south towards St Haven and then ultimately Launceston. An elderly couple sat silently at the front, and two middle-aged women were reading books a few rows further back. Nevertheless, all three cousins were silent for most of the journey.

They had recovered the rock easily enough, having checked that they weren't being followed. Chloe and Jack had stood guard while Itch opened up the beach hut and placed the glove and stone in the tube. He had sealed it with a few more well-aimed blows of the mallet and placed it in a canvas bag that Chloe had found. Carrying his rucksack – which still contained the more fragile elements in his collection – on his back, and the radioactive bag in his hand, Itch felt extremely vulnerable. He couldn't wait to pass the rock back to Cake.

The road to the spoil heap took them past the mine in Provincetown, and both Itch and Jack stared at it as they drove by. It looked busy enough for a windy day – plenty of visitors were strolling around the old mine workings. Jack noticed that some white trucks like those they'd seen when they were working there had pulled out in front of the bus.

'Those trucks again, Itch. We're in a convoy with them now,' she said. 'Never realized a mine needed so much maintenance.'

They continued in procession until they reached a T-junction, where two trucks went one way and two the other. The bus turned left, and as it slowed for the next stop, the pair of trucks they had been following disappeared from view.

'Nearly there, Chloe,' said Jack as the bus started up again. 'Next stop.'

Itch was grateful for his cousin's local knowledge, which was still so much better than his. He and Chloe were catching up, but there was still no one like Jack for bus route and timetable information. She had never quite stopped being their 'guide' to their new Cornish home. Itch had considered trying to dissuade Chloe from joining them, but she had insisted. Glancing across at her by the window, he was wondering if he had made the right decision.

She seemed older than her eleven years, but she looked tense and pale. He certainly wasn't going to let her carry the rock. With any luck they would find Cake, give him the rock and catch the 6.05 bus home. Itch had told his dad they would be back for dinner.

The bus slowed again as they arrived in St Haven, and then stopped. They were the only passengers to get off, and they looked around, wondering where the spoil heap was. St Haven was a tiny, if unremarkable, village with a church and a shop which they could see a few hundred metres ahead. There were a few modern houses on either side of the road, with the older cottages clustered nearer the church. They hadn't noticed any sign of a spoil heap on the way into the village, so they set off towards the shop to ask directions.

It was about to shut for the day: inside, a tall, middle-aged woman wearing a red and white apron paused with her keys in the door. 'Sorry – we're just closing,' she told them. She looked less than pleased to have this last-minute custom.

'We're looking for the spoil heaps,' said Jack. 'Are they near here?'

'No idea. What's a spoil heap?' She was speaking through the half-closed door, clearly thinking that if she opened it any further she might have to serve them.

'It's the stuff the mines throw out,' said Itch.

'They take the copper, tin or whatever and sell that, but the raw materials—'

'Itch,' Jack interrupted, 'she doesn't want a geography lesson.'

'Oh, sorry,' he said. 'Er, it's the piles of earth and—'

The woman raised her hand to stop him. 'The old mine works are in a field about half a mile that way.' She pointed south out of the village in the direction they had come from. 'Not a lot happens there. Just piles of waste. What d'you want to go there for? They're not safe, you know.'

But Chloe was pulling her brother away. 'Come on, Itch, let's go. Don't start explaining everything.'

They thanked the woman, whom they could hear shutting the bolts on her shop door as they turned and headed off down the road.

Itch was leading the way, still holding the stone-in-the-tube-in-the-bag, and Jack, bringing up the rear, now carried her cousin's rucksack over one shoulder. As the road curved round to the left, they walked single-file, with Chloe in the middle. The road straightened out and, as the land rose steeply, the old mine workings came into view. A couple of crumbling and grassed-over towers poked up above the top of the hill.

'That'll be it!' said Itch.

They found a path and set off up the hill. It took them ten minutes to reach the top. The view from there took in the decrepit old mine workings and, beyond them, the sparsely grassed slopes of the spoil heaps. The mine at St Haven had been very profitable in the nineteenth century, but nothing had been dug from the ground here for more than a hundred years. The cousins took in the ruins of many mine shafts and engine houses. In most cases just one wall or a corner survived, with brick somehow still perched precariously on brick. The grassed-over chimneys they had seen from the road looked stronger and taller, rising twelve metres from the sandy ground. And there were more of them. They counted eight scattered irregularly over the workings, which covered several acres of scrappy, stony fields.

They walked slowly down the hill towards the old mine. A low single-wire fence had been run around its circumference. At irregular intervals there were signs attached:

DANGER!
UNSAFE MINE WORKINGS
KEEP OUT!

'Anyone want to go back?' asked Itch. Jack and Chloe shook their heads. 'We'll tread carefully – come on.' And they ducked under the wire.

'Cake lives here?' asked Jack, looking from ruin to crumbled ruin. 'No wonder he doesn't look so great.'

They continued into what, a hundred and fifty years ago, would have been the heart of a bustling, noisy, smelly heavy industrial works employing hundreds of men, women and children. The shafts had been sunk wherever copper had been found, and were now tightly fenced off. Concrete pillars and chicken wire were hung with a warning triangle that had a picture of a man falling head-first down a hole.

'Doesn't Mr Watkins have a story about dogs falling down these old shafts?' said Itch. 'Pets disappearing – that kind of thing.'

'Yes, he does. Of course he does,' said Jack. 'A goat too, apparently.'

'That's nasty,' said Chloe, and they kept well clear of the nearest shaft.

In between the old, crumbling buildings, large spoil heaps of waste material had been thrown up. These were now grassy, sandy piles of stone and rubble as high as the chimneys themselves. On the spoil heap closest to them they could see the rotting wood of a trestle from an old tramway sticking out of the soil.

'I feel like we're the first ones to find this,' said Itch. 'It's as though the mine stopped working, everyone left, and no one has touched it since.'

'Like a ghost town,' added Chloe.

They walked around the spoil heaps rather than over them, as they looked unstable. Last year's earthquake had sent mini-avalanches down the sides of many of them, big rocky, sandy chunks of soil lying where they fell. The three of them rounded what looked to be the largest heap and stopped. There were more ruined outbuildings, a stone bridge which arched over a long-disappeared stream – and the unlikely sight of a caravan, settled under the part-ruin of an engine pump house. How it had got there they could not imagine, but if Cake still lived at the St Haven spoil heap, this must be the place.

They set off again at a faster pace now, Itch calling out, 'Hey, Cake! You at home? It's Itch!' They picked their way through the piles of old stone and slate, and he tried again. 'Cake! It's Itch – I've got something for you!'

As they got closer, they could see that the caravan was filthy, the windows covered with bird droppings and grime which had run off the roof. Brown curtains were pulled and hung on drooping string. Small rocks and pieces of slate littered the roof. The cousins slowed their pace again.

'Who could live in that?' asked Chloe.

There had been no answering call to Itch's shouts, and they approached the caravan in silence. They walked round what would once have been the tow bar and Jack gasped, putting both hands to her mouth. The caravan door was open, and the steps and surrounding ground were covered in blood and vomit; a huge swarm of flies and mosquitoes buzzed around. The smell was terrible, and Itch, Jack and Chloe stood staring at the open door.

It was Jack who moved first, edging slowly towards the gloom of the caravan interior. Chloe warned her to be careful as she stood by the door and peered inside. It took a few seconds for her eyes to adjust to the gloom, and only a few more for her to see everything she needed to. She made out a bed, a stove, a sink and a table by the window at the end. All were filthy, and there were more signs that the caravan's inhabitant had been very ill. The table was covered in stones, rocks and packages wrapped in silver foil. A few sealable plastic bags lay on the sofa, some containing small amounts of what looked like soil. Flies were everywhere.

'It's Cake's place, I'm sure of it,' said Jack, retreating quickly. 'It's full of all that stuff he sells to you, Itch. But he's not here.' As she headed back towards the others she noticed they were both staring beyond her. Following their gaze, she turned round and saw what it was that had taken their attention.

About two hundred metres away, at the foot of another spoil heap, they could see somebody lying on the ground.

'No, he's over there,' said Itch, and they all started to run.

Two hundred metres is not far, but they were

running without wanting to get there. They set off at a sprint, but as the horror of what they were running towards became clear, they slowed with every step.

Cake was lying face down in the rubble. He was stretched out, with his head tucked at an unnatural angle under his right arm – it was almost a sleeping position but for the way his head had twisted. His clothes were soiled; blood seemed to cover most of him. Here too a cloud of flies swarmed.

They had run silently but now Jack cried out, 'Cake! Cake! Oh, no! Cake, you poor . . .' She tailed off and looked away.

None of them had seen a dead person before, but they had no doubt that they were looking at one. They had reached the foot of the heap – Cake was ten metres away. They went no nearer – there was no point.

Chloe was sick where she stood, then sat down and started sobbing – deep rasping sobs, and Itch ran to her. He found that he was shaking, but he knelt down and hugged his sister. He found an old tissue and gave it to her.

'Itch, it's terrible! The poor guy! What has happened, Itch? We need to call for an ambulance . . . What do we do? He is dead, isn't he?' She blew her nose.

Jack sat down beside her, head between her knees. 'We should call for help, Itch,' she said.

Itch stood up and looked at Cake's body. Judging from the footprints and marks on the spoil heap, Cake had been at the top and had fallen; his neck was clearly broken. Jack and Chloe had barely known him, but they were the ones crying. Itch simply felt stunned.

He was about to take off his jacket to lay over Cake's head when he noticed a bright blue bundle, half buried in the rubble further up the slope.

Itch made his way past Cake's body and clambered onto the heap. The sandy surface gave way under his feet and he needed to put his hands out to support himself as he climbed. The blue fabric was wrapped around something that looked like a bag of potatoes, tightly bound with black cable. It had clearly been buried and then partially uncovered.

'Guys . . .' called Itch. He went closer and realized that the blue of the fabric wrapping was familiar.

Jack and Chloe were climbing up the slope behind him.

'What is it?' asked his sister.

'Another mystery,' Itch replied.

'Oh, great . . .' said Jack, bending down to examine the bundle. 'Is that paper underneath?'

The other two came closer and realized that Jack was right – there was a piece of paper jutting out from underneath the package. She tried to pull it free, but it was tightly bound by one twist of the black cable and started to tear. She carefully worked it free – a sheet from an A4 notebook, folded into four – then flattened it out and started to read the dense scrawled handwriting.

'It's for you,' she said, handing it to Itch. 'And there's a lot of it.'

Itch took the piece of paper and read fast. When he had finished he sat down. 'You're never going to believe this,' he said, and passed the note back to Jack, who read out loud:

'*Master Lofte, I hope it is you that finds this, but I'm sorry too for putting you in danger. Don't unwrap the parcel. It contains seven more pieces of uranium – if that's what it really is – like the one you already have. They are wrapped in a lead apron I stole from the hospital – but too late for me. The rocks are killing me, but I didn't realize it would be so bad – or so quick – till it was too late. Me of all people. I don't know how much protection the apron gives but it's a start. I don't know what this U is mixed with, but I've never seen anything like it. I've tried to find my mate who got the rocks for me but he's disappeared. I wish—*'

Jack broke off; the handwriting was almost illegible.

'*I wish I had never seen them and never got you one too. You need to get rid of them. I'm sorry, Itch, I really*'

*am. These rocks are dangerous. Don't trust anyone. Try
not to be scared. I'm sorry. God help me.'*

Jack folded the note and handed it back to Itch.
'So now what do we do now?'

16

'Let us assume he isn't an idiot,' said the Dutchman, Jan Van Den Hauwe. 'He wasn't an idiot when he was here – he can't have become an idiot just because he's in England.'

'Why can't he?' said Christophe Revere. 'He's desperate. Desperate to get back here. Desperate people do idiotic things. When I rang him to tell him his precious lead box was empty he erupted with fury before begging like a dog. He's out of control.'

On the screen that dominated one end of the boardroom were the figures that Flowerdew had emailed them after concluding his tests on the rock. They were being analysed once more by the chief metallurgist, Dr Joe Parris. He was tall, stooped and thin – his suit flapped as he walked. His thick white hair could have given him a genial grandfatherly look were it not for the austere wire-framed glasses halfway down his nose. He was well past retire-ment age but retained for his skills as the best analyst money could buy. And bought he most certainly was.

Van Den Hauwe continued, 'Either he has made all this up' – he waved at the figures on the screen – 'in which case he's insane; or we have here the evidence of the most remarkable substance we have ever analysed. Dr Parris?'

The metallurgist was pointing at the screen, following one particular line of data with his index finger, then rifling through the reams of paper in front of him.

'Essentially, yes.' His accent was pure Harvard, his manner brusque. 'If this data is not faked – and I would need to be persuaded of that – this subs-tance is revolutionary. It is brand new, gentlemen. Brand shiny and new. There are 118 elements, as you know. Well, this appears to be the 126th, exactly as your man in England claims.'

'He's not our man,' said Van Den Hauwe.

Parris continued, 'Even though it has never been seen before, we know precisely the readings we would be getting from such an element. The figures are on the screen. I can get technical if you wish, and tell you about the magic number of protons and neutrons it has – its doubly magic nucleus – but you may not thank me for it . . .' He waited for a reaction but both men indicated that he should carry on. 'I must say it's most likely a fake—'

'Never mind that, Joe,' said Revere. 'Assume the figures you have are correct.'

'In that case, based on this data, you have the scientific discovery of the century. Any century. And its power will be something to behold.'

There was silence in the room. Coffee and pastries had been brought in an hour ago, but nothing had been touched. Each man was alternately pacing and gazing at the information from Flowerdew's lab.

Van Den Hauwe spoke next. 'Would you guess, please, at its nuclear abilities?'

Parris took off his glasses. 'Unprecedented. Immeasurable. Extraordinary.'

The Dutchman considered this. 'Our business is oil, always has been. We've spent many years trashing nuclear power and highlighting its dangers. But if we get this rock, and the seam it comes from, we will be going nuclear, will we not?'

Parris rubbed his eyes. 'Two things: first, there is no seam; this will have come many, many hundreds of thousands of years ago, from an exploding star, a supernova. There may be other rocks, however; my guess is that would be likely. And secondly, yes, whether you like it or not, element 126 will be a strong neutron emitter – very useful as a start-up source for a nuclear reactor. The security implications are profound, of course.'

Revere looked up from his graphs and equations. Joe Parris walked the length of the table towards the co-chairs of Greencorps. He sat down next to Revere and leaned forward. He paused, collecting his thoughts, then spoke more quietly, as though he thought someone else might be listening.

'Even with a small number of these rocks there is enough power for any country, any organization, any terrorist group to go nuclear. Hell, *we* could go nuclear. Greencorps could become a nuclear player. This is a game changer, gentlemen.' He leaned back in his chair, looking from Revere to Van Den Hauwe.

'And would kill oil the world over.' Revere stared at the figures on the screen as though he might have missed something. 'Oil stocks would crash through the floor. As soon as word gets out of a new super-nuclear energy – nuclear two point zero, if you like – our whole industry could collapse. Who wants to dig a smelly, dirty well if a small piece of rock can do the job? We have to control this.'

'One more thing, if I may . . . ?' said Parris.

Revere nodded. 'Go ahead, Joe.'

'It's not just nuclear start-up. Pocket nukes – very small nuclear weapons – would become a reality. They are things of urban legend at the moment. But with this? If you could get a critical mass together, they would appear very quickly. These rocks are a nuclear start-up kit in a bag.'

'You say there may be more, Joe, but we only know of this one,' said Van Den Hauwe, pointing at the data.

'It seems unlikely to me that there would be only one,' said Parris. 'This started its journey with the enormous explosion you get at the death of a star – a supernova followed by a massive neutron explosion. It's hard to believe that it arrived on its own. Somewhere there will be others. When word gets out about what we are looking at here, there'll be a frantic search for more.'

'In which case,' said the Dutchman, 'we could be on the verge of a new Gold Rush.'

'With terrifying consequences if the wrong people get there first,' said Revere.

Van Den Hauwe smiled. 'You forget. We are the wrong people, Christophe.'

As soon as Dr Parris had gathered up his papers and left there was an urgent knock at the door. The Greencorps bosses looked up and saw the silhouette of Roshanna Wing waiting.

'Yes, Roshanna!' called Revere.

She came in carrying her laptop open on her palm. 'You need to see this,' she said, and swivelled it round on the table in front of them. It showed a page from the *Western Daily News*. Roshanna stood back as they both read the account of Flowerdew's assault on Itchingham Lofte and members of staff at the academy. They studied the photo of their former employee with the broken bottle in his hand.

Revere zoomed in on his face: strained, manic and wild-eyed. 'Well. There we are. He's lost it, Jan. There must be no link to us. Where is he now, Roshanna?'

'He's disappeared, sir,' she said. 'Apparently he took off after this attack and hasn't been seen since. I've called his house and mobile, but there's no reply from either.'

Christophe Revere spoke to Roshanna but was looking at his partner. 'We don't want anything more to do with Flowerdew, but we do want his rock. Go to Cornwall, Roshanna. Take help. Get the rock and make it safe for us.'

Van Den Hauwe nodded. 'Are you OK with that, Roshanna?'

'Of course,' she agreed. 'I'll take Berghahn and Collins – we'll leave in the morning.'

'No, I rather think you need to leave straight away – we've wasted enough time on this already.' The Frenchman dismissed her, and after she had left said to his partner, 'And when we have it? What then?'

'We make sure the *really* wrong people get a sniff, that's what. These are high stakes, Christophe, the highest there are. We play this right, we allow a rock

or two to find their way to a terrorist cell somewhere, and the nuclear boys will be sunk without
trace. For good. But if we play this wrong . . .' He
didn't need to finish the sentence. The two
Greencorps bosses looked at each other.

The Frenchman said, 'I still think it might be
nothing. But if it *is* something, it needs to be *our*
something.'

17

The cousins stood in the sandy waste and soil halfway up the spoil heap, with the body of Cake in front of them, and the radioactive rocks that had apparently killed him still half buried off to their left. Itch had finally placed his jacket over Cake's head and shoulders. His arm was round Chloe, who was crying again.

'We need to call for help, Itch,' she said, her voice raised. 'Who do you call when someone is already dead? Is it the undertakers?'

Jack shook her head. 'No, it must be 999. They can sort it out. Let's just tell them what's happened, Itch! Then it's over to them.' She took out her phone. 'No signal, of course,' she cried out in frustration.

Itch checked his phone, said, 'Same here,' and stood up. 'But before we call, what are we going to do with these rocks? We now have *eight*. I suppose we should take them.'

'Hang on, Itch,' said Jack. 'Why can't we just leave them all here? Come on, that's got to be the right thing! This is about as remote as we're going to get and there's no one about. We can explain everything when we ring 999.'

'But, Jack, you read Cake's note! *Don't trust anyone*, he said. *The rocks are dangerous*. If we leave them here, we don't know who'll find them. Flowerdew is still out there somewhere, remember!' Itch was frustrated at having to explain this. 'We *have* to make sure he doesn't get them!'

'Itch, no.' Jack was pleading now. 'I was scared of one, never mind *eight*. You saw what they did to Cake! Please – let's leave them here. We'll walk back into the village and call from there.'

But Itch had made up his mind. 'No – we just can't leave these rocks. Not after they've already cost Cake his life. He was my *friend*, Jack! I can't let him down now. I need to know what they are and why they are so important. *Then* maybe we can hand them over. Get them to Watkins, perhaps.'

'Only *maybe*?' said Jack. 'Only *perhaps*? Come on, Itch, let's—'

Itch interrupted her. 'Jack, listen! Cake specifically asked me to get rid of them, which I will, once I know how!'

'Promise?' said Jack wearily, suddenly in a hurry to finish this argument and get out of there.

'Promise.'

That seemed to be the end of it for now. Itch ran over to the blue parcel, and without any further comment from anyone he pulled it free from the ground. It was hot and heavy. It felt like there was something cooking inside. Cake had cut the apron to make the smallest package he could, but it was lead-lined, with the cable wrapped round most of it. However much protection the apron was giving them it was clear that the rocks were secure, and Itch had no intention of checking the contents. He pushed the bundle into the canvas bag.

At the foot of the spoil heap, they all hovered near Cake's body as if to say goodbye and pay their last respects. Jack and Chloe stood as Itch crouched down by Cake's covered head. He was trying to think of something wise to say when a loud, angry voice bellowed across the mine:

'WHAT THE HELL DO YOU THINK YOU'RE DOING?'

Itch, Chloe and Jack jumped up and swivelled round. Across the mine workings, by the largest spoil heap, stood two men and a woman. The man doing the shouting was short, barrel-chested; behind him stood a taller, older man in a cloth cap, and the woman – the one from the village shop. She was pointing at them.

The Lofte cousins, already upset and wired by the death of their friend, were now flooded with fear, guilt and panic.

This is bad, thought Itch, glancing from the adults to Cake's body to their bags. *And they'll think we did it.* 'Go!' he shouted, and he grabbed the bag and the rucksack and ran up the spoil heap.

'Where?' Jack followed Itch up the slope, taking the rucksack from him and pulling Chloe along behind her.

'Just follow!' yelled Itch as they scrambled over the top. The ridge crumbled under their feet and they half slid, half stumbled down the other side. There were two more spoil heaps off to the right, one to the left, and some more crumbling mine buildings and towers stretching off towards woodland about five hundred metres away. Itch focused on a network of engine houses and chimneys halfway between them and the woods. 'There!' he said, and took off across the open ground, avoiding the sand around the spoil heaps where their footprints would be all too visible.

They could hear the three adults shouting on the other side of the heap. From where they had been when they started yelling, they had a lot of ground to make up — at least a thousand metres, Itch thought. They then had to climb or go round the spoil heap. Itch wanted to make it to the buildings before they crested or rounded the heap. That meant going at a flat-out sprint.

Itch ran with the heavy canvas bag in his right hand, with no time to swap it to his left. Jack had

Itch's rucksack over her shoulders and Chloe running alongside. Jack could run faster than Chloe, but instinctively she settled at a slower pace, not wanting to let her young cousin fall behind. The ground was uneven, peppered with loose rocks and slate. They were terrified of slipping as they covered the ground between the last spoil heap and the mine buildings. All three of them stumbled many times, Jack twisting her ankle in one particularly deep hole, but they managed to stay on their feet.

About one hundred metres out Itch chanced a glance back over his shoulder. Jack and Chloe were at least a hundred and fifty metres behind him and it looked as though Chloe had a stitch as she was clasping a hand to her side. Her eyes were as screwed up as her running would allow – she was grimacing with pain. Itch reached the first wall, dropping the bag down on the other side of it. He then sprinted back to the others, grabbing his sister's hand. The three of them hurtled towards the cover of the wall. The shouts from the adults behind them were getting louder – their pursuers would come into sight at any second. Just a few more metres . . .

They threw themselves over the wall, Itch banging his head on the lead pipe in the bag, and the girls landing on top of each other. They lay motionless, gasping for breath, and as flat up against the wall as they thought was safe. It had crumbled to just over a metre high and looked as though it could collapse at any moment. They lay in the rubble, panting. Knowing that they had to do so as silently as possible made their recovery long and painful. Itch felt the back of his head: it throbbed and he was sure it was bleeding again.

The voices were coming ever closer, and Itch knew that they couldn't stay there for long. He pointed towards the nearest building – a tall, thin, three-walled ruin which had originally housed a shaft pumping engine. There was an empty door-way facing them, but they would have to cross open ground to reach it.

They could now identify two voices – a man's and a woman's. Peering through a crack in the wall, Jack saw that the older man was missing; presumably he had stayed with Cake's body. The short man and the woman from the shop had split up: the woman was walking up another heap and the man was heading towards their hiding place.

'He's coming this way!' hissed Jack.

Lying behind the wall, they could hear the man and the woman calling to each other. He was encouraging her but she sounded scared.

The man had stopped about five hundred metres away, and had turned back to face his companion on the spoil heap. While he was shouting to her, Itch nodded at Chloe and she crawled out from behind the wall and set off towards the engine house.

'Faster!' whispered Itch. The man might turn round again at any moment – but Chloe had disappeared through the doorway.

Itch realized that the man was reassuring the woman:

'You're doing fine, Mary – but careful near the top!' She called something back, and he was silent for a while. Then they heard him call, 'Hold on!' and he ran off. Itch and Jack took their chance: they both crawled as fast as the rubble, the rucksack and the bag would allow, across the gap into the engine house.

Chloe was wide-eyed with fear. She was sitting curled up tightly with her arms around her knees, looking smaller than Itch could remember. She looked eight or nine years old again. He and Jack dived into the corner next to her and Jack hugged her terrified cousin.

The three sides of the building gave them cover from the pair on the spoil heap, but between them and the woods that marked the edge of the old mine lay another two hundred metres of open ground, with only the last chimney for cover. It looked a very long way away.

Behind them, they heard a distant call. Jack edged her way towards a crack in the brickwork. Peering through, she saw the head and shoulders of the older man at the top of the spoil heap where they had found Cake. He was waving his phone around.

'It's the old guy. I think he's got a signal for his mobile! He's calling the others.'

She couldn't see the short man and the shop woman, but Itch could if he scrambled over to look through a crack in the other wall. Being careful not to dislodge any of the larger bricks or pieces of broken slate that now formed most of the floor of this building, he crabbed his way over to the crack that was nearest to him.

'They're climbing down,' he reported. 'Now they're looking over here!' Itch ducked just in case, even though he was sure they couldn't see him. After a few seconds of quiet he peered out again. 'They're running back to the old guy. I guess he's called the police, and wants them there. Hang on . . . he's stopped.'

The short man had stopped at the foot of the spoil heap and turned round, cupping his hands to his mouth. 'WE HAVE CALLED THE POLICE AND THEY ARE ON THEIR WAY. YOU WON'T GET FAR. THAT MAN IS DEAD! I'LL REMEMBER YOUR FACES!' The woman was calling him, and he turned and ran round the spoil heap.

'Itch! They think we killed Cake!' said Jack. Chloe started to cry again and Itch crept over to crouch next to her.

'Listen, Chloe. *They* might think we killed Cake, but no one else will. The uranium, or whatever this is, killed Cake. Radiation poisoning is easy to diagnose. He didn't protect himself until it was too late – everyone will realize that.'

She nodded, reassured. 'I know that. But they sound pretty mad.'

It was silent in the old mine and Itch looked out towards the woods. 'We need to make it to the trees and then get back to the road.'

'Where are we going?' asked Jack.

'Away from here,' said Itch. 'We'll make for that chimney first. Even if they see us, we'll be too far away. They're old.' He smiled at Chloe and got a weak smile back. He picked up the canvas bag and Jack hoisted the rucksack.

They were about to set off when Chloe cried, 'Itch – your jacket! You left it!'

Itch stiffened and sucked air through his teeth. He knew he had left his jacket; that had seemed the decent thing to do – they couldn't have left Cake uncovered. That wasn't what worried him.

'Please tell me your name isn't in it,' said Jack.

Itch said nothing. His mother had written his name on the back of the collar as he had lost his previous one on a school non-uniform day.

'Oh, help,' said Jack. 'We'd better get going.'

Itch checked that it was clear, and nodded. All three of them dashed out together towards the chimney. Like the others it was more or less intact and covered in ivy, but was slightly shorter than the rest. It was fatter too and so was wide enough for all three of them to hide behind. They reached it in twenty seconds and stood behind each other, with Jack looking ahead to the woods, now just about a hundred metres away. There was no sign of the adults; all was quiet.

'Let's just go for it,' said Itch, and they headed for the trees.

Gradually the loose stones and slate gave way to earth and grass. They crashed into the trees and bushes and threw themselves down, expecting to hear shouts, but none came. They lay still for what seemed like an age, then Itch turned to the others and smiled. 'Made it!'

They crawled through to where the trees were dense enough to hide them. When they couldn't see the mine workings any more Itch called a halt.

They sat with their backs against the tree trunks, facing a small clearing. A few early evening rays of sun made it through the leaves so they cast long shadows in front of them. They could hear faint traffic noise from the road they had left barely an hour before. They were all breathing heavily and drenched in sweat.

Itch knew his head was bleeding again and there was a steady throb from the back of his skull. He closed his eyes. He desperately needed to think. Where now, then? Instead of getting rid of his radioactive rock, he had ended up with *eight*. They were sealed, in a way, but he had no idea how effectively. It was more than possible that all three of them were subject to dangerous levels of radio-activity right now. Chucking the pieces of rock away or handing them in was very tempting – but couldn't he do better than that? He had read, collected, researched and obsessed about the elements for years – he should know what to do. Jack and Chloe were sitting with their eyes closed as they got their breath back, waiting for him to tell them what to do.

Itch stared at the canvas bag. The first rock had already sent Flowerdew crazy, but then he was clearly convinced that this substance was extra-ordinary – extraordinary enough to finish his career at the CA. Itch tried to remember all the other elements that had been found in uranium ore. He thought he remembered copper – but that wouldn't have produced such a hysterical reaction from Flowerdew. He guessed it must be gold, silver or platinum – something of extreme value. They wouldn't explain the high radiation count, but it just had to be something that could change the fortunes of the discoverer for ever.

Itch was sure Cake had realized that something weird was going on. He carefully took out the torn piece of paper that Jack had retrieved from the bundle and re-read it: *I've never seen anything like it . . . You need to get rid of them . . . these rocks are dangerous . . . don't trust anyone . . .* He folded it away again. How could you get rid of dangerous rocks, especially if you couldn't trust anyone?

His head was really throbbing now – he needed more painkillers. He checked his phone – there was a weak signal, but who should he call? His mum, dad and brother were all at home, but what would they say? *Ring the police, hand in the rocks and come home,* probably. He knew that was the sensible thing to do; Jack and certainly Chloe would be happier with that. But again he thought: *I can do better than that. I'm an element hunter, I have extraordinary elements. Deal with it.*

He would text his mum to explain that he and Chloe had been delayed, and Jack could text her dad. The parents wouldn't like it, but it would buy them some time before they started worrying.

As if reading his mind, Chloe asked, 'Shouldn't we be getting back? Or calling home?'

Jack looked at her phone. 'I said I'd be home for dinner. We do need to tell someone what's happened – that we didn't kill Cake.'

Itch nodded. Very soon the paramedics and police would be arriving and things would get tricky. 'Agreed. Let's ring when we're on the bus. I want to get away from here first.'

18

It took them twenty minutes to make their way through the woods to the road. When they were near the bus stop, Itch and Chloe hung back in the trees while Jack, a few metres further on, stood near enough to the road to look out for a bus. They were nervous and impatient to get away, but the Saturday evening bus service meant that it was another half-hour before one came along. Jack hailed it, and the others all ran towards the bus stop, arriving just in time for the driver to see them and stop. The bus was nearly full, but they found three seats together at the back, stowing the rucksack and canvas bag underneath.

The journey back took longer as the bus made more stops, but they still didn't have much time to decide on their next move. As if to underline the urgency of the situation, a police car rushed past them, lights flashing, presumably on its way to the spoil heap. They decided to call 999 using Itch's phone — the police would read his name on the jacket soon enough.

Itch did the talking — he was allowed to speak without interruption. Everyone knew all calls were recorded.

'Hello. We have just left the mine at St Haven. We found the body of a man called Cake. He was our friend. We think he was killed by radiation. He had some rocks, you see . . . Anyway, we were chased by some people who think we did it but we didn't.' He hesitated briefly, wondering if there was anything else he should add. 'We'll call again,' he said and hung up.

No one on the bus seemed to be paying them any attention. The combination of headphones, magazines and mobile phones meant that the passengers were immersed in their own world, which suited the cousins just fine. Even so, Itch spoke quietly, and Chloe and Jack leaned in to catch his words.

'I've tried to hand my rock over twice — the first time at school, but Flowerdew stopped it, and the second time today. Now we've ended up with seven more instead. We probably only have one more go at this before they are taken from us by people who *really* shouldn't have them. My original plan was to give them to Mr Watkins, and I think that's still the best idea. He'll know what to do.'

'If we can find him, yes. But it's Saturday evening, Itch. Where's he going to be?' Jack whispered. 'Do you know where he lives?'

Itch shook his head. 'No, that's just it. But there's that show at school tonight – the Year Tens, I think. They were selling tickets – remember, Jack? Mr Watkins goes to everything. He's bound to be there. We need to get him out of the hall and explain what's happened.'

Jack and Chloe both nodded. 'OK, let's do that,' said Chloe. 'But what if he's not there . . . ? What then?'

'No idea,' said Itch. 'How about giving the rocks to Paul, Potts and Campbell just to see what happens?' They all grinned, their mood lighter. It felt good to have a plan.

Chloe suddenly leaned back in her seat with her eyes closed, her hands resting on her stomach.

'You OK?' asked Jack. 'You're not looking so hot.'

'Not fantastic, no. A bit sick. It'll pass.' If Chloe had seen the look that passed between Jack and Itch, she would have been worried. They had both been waiting for signs of sickness. Cake's caravan had shown them what happens when you have radiation poisoning. They each held one of Chloe's hands, sent another text home, then sat in silence.

The Cornwall Academy came into view. All its lights were on, which confirmed that there was indeed something going on there tonight. As the bus slowed, five people stood up and gathered their things together. Itch, Jack and Chloe alighted just behind them and followed them into the school.

'Let's just go straight in,' said Itch. 'I bet Mr Watkins will be near the front.'

Jack put her hand on his arm. 'Do we all need to go in? Seems unnecessary, doesn't it?'

At the entrance to the hall, the last parents were buying their programmes and being shown to their seats by unusually smart-looking Year Tens.

'OK, I'll go, you wait here. Er . . .' He paused, looking at the canvas bag.

'It's OK, leave it here,' said Jack.

Itch put it down and ran inside. There was an expectant buzz of conversation as parents and friends waited for what the poster said was *An Unmissable Evening of Jazz and Blues*. The hall held around four hundred, and most of the seats were taken. Some in the audience read the programme, others were talking to their neighbours or twisting round to speak to friends behind. Out of sight, backstage, the sound of the school band warming up could be heard.

Standing by the door, Itch scanned the hall. In the front row he saw Dr Dart and her guests. Just behind was the teachers' row – he could see heads belonging to Mrs Jennings, Mr Hopkins and the Brigadier, but no Watkins.

'Hi, Itch – didn't expect to see you here. Want to

buy a programme?' It was the smiley Year Ten girl, Lucy Cavendish.

'Oh, hi,' said Itch. 'Sorry, no. Have you seen Mr Watkins?'

'He's just arriving. There.' She pointed to the second entrance at the front of the hall. 'How's things? Are you staying?'

'Er, sorry, no.' Itch sprinted round to intercept his teacher before he could take his seat, and grabbed him by the arm. 'Sir! You have to come with me! It's important. It's urgent!'

John Watkins looked at Itch, his face showing first surprise and pleasure, then irritation. 'Oh, come come, Itchingham – what on earth can be more important than an evening of light jazz with the Cornwall Academy's award-winning jazz band led by the very able Julia Nettles of Ten S?' He started to make for his seat, but found his way blocked by Itch, who had stepped into his path.

'Seriously, sir, please come outside.' Itch sounded desperate. 'We are in a lot of danger. And trouble.'

At this Mr Watkins stopped. 'Trouble? Danger? What's happened, Itchingham?'

Itch had his full attention now. 'Follow me, sir.'

Mr Watkins apologized to his fellow staff members and followed Itch out of the hall. Outside they found an anxious Chloe and Jack, who had moved round the corner of the hall to look out across the playing fields towards the sea. The sun was still high but the shadows were beginning to lengthen. John Watkins stood looking at them.

'Well? Speak, someone!' He looked from Jack to Chloe to Itch, then noticed the bulging canvas bag. 'What's in there? Itch, explain please.'

Itch didn't know where to start. 'Well, sir. It's like this. You know . . . You remember the rock that produced that reading on the Geiger counter?'

'Of course I do,' said Watkins. 'It started all this nonsense. Massive reading. Huge radioactive activity. In Switzerland . . . or not, apparently. What of it?'

Itch pointed to the bag. 'Well, it's in there, sir, along with seven others.'

Watkins's mouth dropped open. 'Excuse me, what did you say? *Seven others?* Please tell me they aren't radioactive too!'

Itch nodded. 'I think so, sir. They killed my friend, Cake, who had them in his caravan. He left us a note. But some people saw us and think we killed him, but we didn't – it was the radiation. We have to get these rocks put away somewhere safe, sir.'

Mr Watkins was a good teacher. His pupils liked him and his colleagues loved him. They had come to admire his eccentric clothing style, enjoyed his generosity in the canteen, and he was respected for his deep knowledge of geography. His world revolved around his pupils and his subject. But in all his teaching career, nothing had left him so completely bewildered. His mouth was open again.

'Sir?' prompted Itch.

The head of geography closed his mouth. Then he said, 'We'll sort out your story in a minute. What are the rocks in?'

Itch described the lead tube he had put together and the lead apron Cake had wrapped his rocks in.

'Well, it's a start,' said Watkins, 'but goodness knows how much radiation is leaking. We have to get them to the mining school. It's not far, and they will have the kit we need for this. Itch, come with me — you two stay here with your parents.' He started off in the direction of the car park, but Itch protested.

'Sorry, sir, but our parents aren't here. And we are all together, really.'

Watkins hurried on. 'Right! Everyone in the car! That's fine, we'll sort this out on the way.'

They ran in single file to the car park, with Jack and Chloe arriving last. 'Pile in,' said Watkins when he'd unlocked his Volvo. 'All rocks in the boot!' The canvas bag went in with the spare tyre and tool kit, and the rucksack was passed over to Itch again. He sat in the front with it at his feet, his sister and cousin in the back.

Watkins accelerated out of the car park, turning south. 'Safety first: we need to get the rocks locked up, then call the emergency services.' He threw his phone at Itch. 'Call Jacob Alexander and hold the phone to my ear.'

Itch found the listed phone numbers and pressed ALEXANDER, DR JACOB. It started to ring and Itch held the phone to his teacher's left ear.

'Jacob, it's John Watkins . . . Where are you . . . ?' He listened as he sped along the country roads. 'Well, I'm sorry, but you'll have to make your apologies and leave. Meet me at your office as soon as you can . . . Yes, it *is* an emergency. I have hugely radioactive rocks that need a safe house . . . Now. Can you do that? They might be responsible for one death already . . . Yes, really . . . Thanks, see you in a bit.' Itch removed the phone and cut the connection.

'Right now, you three. Ring your parents and explain what's happening and where we are going, please. They aren't going to believe it, but you need to tell them anyway. Say I'll call them from the mining school. Now, please.'

Itch and Jack took out their phones and were greeted by a string of beeps and squawks indicating a large number of texts and voice messages.

'Parents who need talking to by the sound of it,' said Watkins.

'Can we stop?' came a faint voice from the back.

In his mirror Watkins looked at Chloe who, even in the dark of the car, looked white as a sheet. 'Not really, Chloe, it's just— OK, maybe we should.'

The Volvo screeched to a stop and Chloe leaped out. She had been sick on the grass verge, wiped her mouth, blown her nose and turned round to get back in before Itch could even find a tissue for her. She fastened her seatbelt and Watkins drove off again.

'I'm stupid, of course,' said Watkins, sounding annoyed with himself. 'You must all be suffering from the radiation. I should have left you at the academy. Anyone else nauseous?'

'I'm all right,' said Itch.

'I'm fine so far,' said Jack.

They drove on at speed. With barely any traffic on the road, the teacher was taking the corners extraordinarily fast.

'Don't normally drive this fast,' he told them, 'but maybe it's just as dangerous to linger. No one seems to have rung their parents yet, so I will. Your phones, please – Itch, you know what to do.'

Jack passed her phone to Itch, who dialled her home number, waited for it to ring and held the phone to Watkins's ear. He waited. 'Answerphone,' he said, then, 'It's Mr Watkins from the Academy. Your daughter, Itch and Chloe are safe and with me at the West Ridge School of Mining. Please call when you get this.' He left his own number and hung up.

Itch passed him his own ringing phone, and heard his mother answer.

'Mrs Lofte, good evening, it's John Watkins from

the Academy. Your son and daughter are here with me, along with their cousin. You will need to pick them up from the West Ridge School of Mining this evening. Itchingham is fine, though Chloe has been a little unwell. Please be reassured that I will call you when we get there.'

Itch could hear his mother asking question after question – to no avail.

'I agree this is unusual, Mrs Lofte,' Watkins said. 'I only met the children at school tonight; they needed help and I am doing what I can. I will call you to say when you can pick them up.'

Itch removed the phone from Watkins's ear and ended the call.

'Your mother's not happy,' his teacher said, 'and I don't blame her.'

He still had time to dictate a text to Dr Dart explaining where he was going and why.

'She's going to go mental,' said Itch, typing the words into the phone.

'That is a distinct possibility,' said Watkins. 'Now, explain how we got here. We have about seven minutes till we are at West Ridge – tell me everything.'

So Itch, and occasionally Jack, related the whole story, from the first rock purchase to the raid on Flowerdew's house (this produced a whistle of astonishment from Watkins), and then to the discovery of Cake's body.

There was silence in the car when the story was

finished. Itch wasn't sure what his teacher's reaction would be. Eventually he said, 'I understand why you didn't call the police immediately, but call them again you must. They will want to question you. If this Cake chap died from radiation as you say, it will be obvious that you are innocent. We will ring as soon as we, and the rocks, are safely in the West Ridge labs. I imagine the ambulance boys will want to check you out.'

The car slowed down as they approached the outskirts of the old mining town of West Ridge. They had only passed a few of the outlying buildings when they saw a sign to the School of Mining. They turned left into a car park which led to a series of low-level, one-storey buildings.

The mining school was housed in an old further-education college built in the 1960s, and although from the road it appeared small, it was a warren of interconnecting rooms, lecture halls and labs. The car park was empty, bar the one vehicle parked by the front door. The college was in darkness apart from the reception area, where some neon lights illuminated the double doors and an enquiries desk. Watkins parked next to what they guessed was Jacob Alexander's car.

'Everyone out, and let's get this sorted.' Itch went to open the boot but Mr Watkins raised his hands. 'No, no, Itch – that's enough for you. Inside, and let's find Jacob.'

Itch hesitated. He hadn't gone through all this just to leave the rocks unguarded in a car park on a Saturday night, even if West Ridge was a quiet town. 'I'll watch the car — you find your friend,' he said.

19

Jacob Alexander's office was immediately behind the welcome desk and they could all see that the light was on and the door open. Alerted by the sounds of their arrival, he came out to meet his late-night visitors. He was a man of around sixty, broad and thick-set, with his remaining dark grey hair shaved close to his scalp. He was dressed in a suit with his recently removed tie draped around his neck. He smiled when he saw Watkins.

'John! Good to see you – even if you have taken me away from a dinner with my wife's book club.'

Mr Watkins hurried over and shook his friend's hand. 'Apologies and all that, but we need to get some very interesting rocks out of the boot of my car. Can you robe up for us?'

Dr Alexander looked over at the three cousins, who were watching the car.

'Who's this?' he asked.

'I'll explain later, but essentially the rocks belong to Itchingham Lofte there – the tall lad. And that's his sister Chloe and cousin Jack.'

'Ah, the Lofte clan. Of course,' said Alexander.

'Oh, you know them?' asked Watkins.

'Well, not exactly.'

'Anyway, please hurry, Jacob,' said Watkins. 'We've got eight rocks, and when I took a Geiger reading on just one of them, it gave me a reading of ten thousand clicks per second.'

The director stared at him. 'Heavens! Are you sure? From just the one rock? I'll get dressed.' And he disappeared back into his office.

When he reappeared, he was covered from head to toe in a white fabric suit, and carried a protective helmet under his arm – he looked as if he was expecting a chemical attack. He came over to the cousins.

'I feel a bit daft getting all this on, but if what John here says is right about the radiation count from your rocks, it seems a wise precaution.'

Itch, Jack and Chloe looked at their own flimsy clothing and wondered how much radiation they had absorbed. Chloe hadn't been sick again, but she still looked extremely pale.

Disappearing into another room, Alexander emerged with a large, heavy, white container like an oversized toolbox. 'This is what we use for our radioactive rocks – not that we've ever had eight here before – but it should do the trick. It's got a lead shield within thick high-density polythene. What are your rocks in?'

Itch, sounding almost apologetic, told him, 'Well, we had to make it up as we went along. One's in a lead tube, and the other seven are wrapped in a lead apron from a hospital.' He thought he'd leave out the word 'stolen' for now.

Dr Alexander nodded, put on his helmet and went outside. Watkins popped the boot with his key fob and watched as his friend placed the box on the ground, took off the lid, then lifted the boot and peered inside. With gloved hands, he picked up the canvas bag and placed it carefully in the lead box. He replaced the cover, tested its weight and shut the boot. Leaning heavily to the right, he carried it through the reception area. He paused to turn on a new set of lights, then called through the helmet, 'You can follow me,' and disappeared down a corridor.

They followed him down a number of corridors with darkened classrooms on one side and notice boards on the other. Itch checked out the posters and hand-written A4 sheets advertising ENGINEERING SOC, METALLURGY 2ND YEAR RESULTS and LITHIUM MINE TRIP TO BOLIVIA! SIGN UP!

They came to a T-junction, with labs running across the corridor. They turned left towards Labs 3, 4 and 5, and followed the lights as Alexander switched them on, going through two labs before arriving at their destination.

Alexander called out, 'Wait here!' loudly through his protective helmet. They all stood in the doorway and watched as the director stopped by a shed-sized container. It was made of white painted metal, its walls corrugated, with a door taking up one half of its front. He put the box on a workbench and pushed down on the compression door lock: the door swung open a few centimetres and he pulled it the rest of the way. He picked up the lead box and placed it inside on the middle of three shelves. From where the cousins and Watkins stood, it appeared that there were only two other boxes inside, one on each shelf. Alexander swung the door shut, and then lifted the handle. The heavy locking mechanism echoed through the lab. He turned round and removed his helmet before coming over to them.

'They are safe and we are safe, depending on how much radiation you have already been exposed to.' He beckoned them through to the adjacent lab. 'Sit down and tell me everything you know about these rocks that have so spooked my friend here.' He smiled at Watkins – who smiled back somewhat nervously.

'First I'm calling an ambulance,' the teacher said. Alexander nodded and they sat in silence as Watkins gave details of what had happened and where they were.

The director jumped up. 'I'll have a word.' He took the phone and, explaining who he was, walked out of the lab, pulling the door shut behind him.

'That doesn't feel good,' said Jack.

'They're on their way,' said Watkins.

'How long?' said Chloe.

'Didn't say, I'm afraid.'

After a few seconds Alexander strode back in and returned Watkins's phone.

'They understand the situation, I think. So . . .' He spread his arms. 'Begin.' And between the four of them, Itch, Jack, Chloe and John Watkins, sitting on stools, told him what they knew and told him fast. In under two minutes, they had finished their story.

'Right. Extraordinary. But you don't need me to tell you that.' Jacob Alexander had been pacing around the lab, but now he stopped in front of the cousins. 'My hunch is that you *will* get sick, I'm afraid. If the seven new rocks are as powerful as the first one and decaying in the same way, the lead apron wouldn't have been effective enough to protect you all. Chloe's sickness *is* probably caused by radiation.'

Jack put her arm round her cousin as she started to cry.

Alexander continued: 'We aren't equipped with any decontamination gear, I'm afraid. I can get some sent, but it will take a few hours. This is way outside what we would normally be dealing with here. Obviously.'

Itch said quietly, 'I'm so sorry, Chloe.' He looked at his sister, who was normally so strong and spirited, but now, in the harsh fluorescent glare of the laboratory, looked really scared.

Alexander smiled kindly, his tanned face creasing around his eyes. 'The hospital will sort you out, I'm sure, Chloe. You two will need to be checked as well, and I guess the police will be here shortly, once they've put everything together. And your eyebrows, Itch . . . Have they just fallen out? Because if so . . .'

'No, no, that was something else,' said Itch. 'It was an accident with some phosphorus a week or so ago.' He looked at his sister, but she wasn't listening.

'Oh. OK . . . Now, while we're waiting for the medics, let's see what you have brought us. I'd include you if I could, but we don't have the suits, I'm afraid. You can watch through the glass though, if you like . . .' And the director disappeared back into the lab where he had stored the rocks moments before.

They sat silently, their four stools close together, and watched him. Jack still had her arm round Chloe, who was leaning on her shoulder, eyes tightly closed. Itch sat with his head down, shoulders slumped, suddenly totally exhausted. If he stopped now to think about how much trouble he was in, he'd be paralysed. Soon he would have to deal with his family, and the ambulance and police when they arrived. He would look after his sister too, but she had her cousin at the moment, and right now he wanted to focus on the rocks. Once he knew what they were and what was going to happen to them, he would feel as though he'd done his duty to Cake. The note had said not to trust anyone, but that was never going to be practical. At some stage he had to hand them over to be tested, and if Mr Watkins thought that West Ridge and Dr Alexander were the best option, then that was OK with him.

Jack interrupted his thoughts. 'I'm just taking Chloe to the toilet, Itch. She's not feeling well again.' And she escorted her cousin out of the lab.

Itch found himself thinking about his grandfather's *Golden Book of Chemistry Experiments* and its advice to go and 'find out about things'. He wondered what its author would have made of this situation, with eight radioactive rocks being tested in one room and an eleven-year-old girl sick with radiation poisoning in another. It was the 'finding out' bit that was still driving Itch – he *had* to know what he had stumbled upon.

While lost in this vein of thought, he began to be aware of that feeling of combined dizziness and nausea he had felt in the greenhouse. It brought his thought processes to a crashing halt. *This is it*, he realized. *I know what's coming*. On the one hand he was surprised he'd been OK till now, but this was really the worst time to get sick. The rocks were finally being analysed; now was the moment he had to be well and thinking straight. Small beads of sweat appeared on his forehead, and he could feel his stomach tightening – there was no doubt what was happening.

He turned to his teacher. 'Sir,' he said, 'I think I'm going to be sick.'

Watkins looked grim. 'I'll check on the girls and then come and check on you. I'm sorry, Itch. Not much I can do to help. But the ambulance is coming, the paramedics will be here soon – you'll be in good hands.'

Itch nodded and dashed out, trying to remember where he had seen the signs for the toilets. If he hadn't been bent double with cramps and had instead been peering through the glass door into Dr Alexander's lab, he would have observed the director engaged in the most amazing analysis of his life.

It wasn't a tricky operation – just the transfer of eight stones into an X-ray fluorescence spectrometer, a two-metre-high green metal cabinet-style machine with a large console at the front. The effect was of an oversized and rather dull arcade game – operated by a man from outer space. Alexander had put his helmet back on and had taken the rocks out of first the canvas bag and then their protective covers. Once unwrapped, Itch's original one slid from the lead tube and the other seven were cut out of the lead apron. Their sizes varied from that of a large pebble to a medium potato, but all eight were jagged and charcoal black. They were staggeringly heavy for their size – much heavier than lead. Alexander's pulse kicked up a notch.

On closer inspection, he noticed small pewter-coloured flecks in most of them – they sparkled as they reflected some of the neon lights. He pulled out his phone and took photographs of each of them. Before placing the rocks in the spectrometer, he pointed his Geiger counter at them – and a volley of clicks rattled through the speaker so fast that it was just a solid wall of sound. In astonishment he looked at the meter – it was off the scale. John Watkins had told him this would happen, but it was astonishing to see. Adrenalin shot through his body – what *were* these rocks?

With a renewed sense of urgency, he set about transferring them one by one into the spectrometer. He needed it to get to work, bombarding the rocks with its X-rays. They would then react by emitting X-rays of their own, and from that the machine could determine their make-up. Before he keyed in the final instruction, Alexander turned to look at the glass door between the labs.

Itch's face was pressed against the window. His face was white and shiny with sweat, some of his hair plastered to his forehead, the rest sticking up at crazy angles. He had never felt as bad as this sickness had made him, but had been desperate to return to Alexander. He had been sick the once, then forced his trembling legs back to the labs – he was *not* going to miss this.

Alexander gave him a gloved thumbs-up – at which Itch raised his thumb to the glass in reply – then turned back to the spectrometer's keyboard and pressed 'Enter'.

There were no flashes, no bangs – just an instant row of black numbers and letters scrolling across a white screen. Itch watched as Alexander read, then re-read the figures. The director stood stock still for a moment, and then ran to grab some documents. Frantically he turned the pages of the largest file until he found what he was looking for. He held the chart he had found to the screen, his head moving up and down as he checked the results.

At first Itch thought a wasp must have found its way inside Alexander's protective outfit: he had started pogoing and leaping around the lab, his arms whirling like windmills. He ran around the spectrometer four times. Through the glass and the thickness of Alexander's helmet, Itch could definitely hear yelling.

He inched open the door. 'Dr Alexander? You OK?'

The director saw Itch, hastily put the rocks away and bounded over. Picking up some of the papers, he pushed Itch back through the door to the next lab, following closely behind. He removed his helmet, his face running with sweat, his eyes wide and staring. He was smiling broadly.

'Astonishing, truly astonishing! If I hadn't witnessed it with my own eyes I wouldn't have believed it. Astonishing! Never seen the like . . . It's what we've been hoping for!' He was talking at, rather than to, Itch as he started to pace again.

'Excuse me, Dr Alexander. What is it? What are they? What have you been looking for?'

The director stopped his pacing and turned to face Itchingham Lofte. 'It's *not* uranium. It's . . . It's . . . not anything we've seen before. It's new . . . It's . . . a . . . new . . . element! Well, an old element maybe . . . never seen on Earth since the Big Bang. It's what we've been looking for. But then—'

Frustrated, Itch interrupted. 'Sorry, but what? Dr Alexander! Can you start again?'

'OK.' He took several deep breaths. 'Unless my machine is on the blink, those rocks are made of a substance we've never seen before. The Table of Elements would put it at 126.'

'No, that's impossible,' said Itch. 'It stops at 118 – everyone knows that – and those at the end only exist in labs. They disappear in seconds. Your machine needs a kicking.'

'Trust me, I've kicked it!' said Alexander. 'Look, come through, *you* can kick it.' They walked back together into the next lab. 'You clearly know your stuff, Itch – I'm impressed. Your dad did well! Oh, congratulations, by the way, on getting the rocks here. You took what precautions you could, but this is absolutely where they should be.'

'You know my dad?' asked Itch – but they had stopped by the spectrometer and Alexander was pointing at the computer screen.

'Look, the results are clear.' He indicated the rows of figures. 'Each element produces its own characteristic X-rays, and these are absolutely unique to what we think 126 will be.'

Itch gazed at the numbers, dumbfounded. 'It's still not possible.'

Alexander laughed loudly. 'I know! Isn't it great!'

'OK,' said Itch. 'Assuming this' – he waved at the screen – 'is correct, what does it mean? What sort of things will these rocks be able to do?'

Alexander rubbed the stubble on his head vigorously. 'What a fantastically exciting question! Who knows! Let me give you an informed guess, based on what some elements at the top end of the table can do. Help with some forms of cancer. Detect oil down a well or gold down a mine – it's all down to the neutrons they give off. But I think that, when this gets out, most attention will be on their ability to start a nuclear reactor.'

Hearing footsteps, they turned and saw Mr Watkins helping Jack and Chloe back into the lab.

He was alarmed to see Itch in the same room as Alexander and the rocks.

'Itch! What are you doing? Jacob, are the rocks safe now?' he called.

The director thought for a moment and walked back through the door towards his friend.

'Are they safe? Well, I think so as I've put them back in their case. And the case is back in the can. And I've sealed the can. So, normally, yes – but I think we might have just said goodbye to normal . . .'

20

West Ridge is a small town set high on hills fifteen miles from the sea. Its college sits on the only through road. The lofty position and the single carriageway mean that it is vulnerable in winter, on the rare occasion of heavy snowfall, to being cut off. Seventeen years ago, following a freak storm, the town had been cut off for twelve hours. This Saturday evening in June, two road traffic accidents achieved the same result.

The first took place at a nasty bend in the road five miles to the south of West Ridge, a notorious accident black spot. A white Transit van skidded while cornering, lost control and overturned, spilling its load of drums of cooking oil. These split on contact with the road, leaving a slick which had spread across both lanes by the time the first car arrived on the scene.

Five minutes later, three miles north of West

Ridge, a broken-down old tractor was rammed by a blue minibus. The tractor's right rear wheel had collapsed, leaving it leaning on the crumpled coach. Fuel leaking from both vehicles had burst into flames, sending an explosion of light and smoke high into the evening sky. In the still, summer air, the sound carried to every house in West Ridge. In both accidents, everyone walked away from the scene unhurt – there were no casualties.

When the ambulances came from the north to get to the sick children at the mining school they found the road blocked by an impassable furnace; when the police arrived from the south, the road was blocked by twenty tonnes of Transit-van wreckage, six hundred litres of cooking oil and four cars which had skidded into each other.

The last two vehicles to reach West Ridge before the accidents were both black Audi A8s. In the one approaching from the south was a German – Volker Berghahn; the one from the north was driven by an American, Bud Collins, who turned to the smartly dressed woman in the passenger seat next to him.

'*Boom*. And boom again. Our turn, I think, Roshanna.'

21

In Laboratory 4 of the West Ridge School of Mining, its director was enjoying a moment of discovery he had thought he would never experience. He had served his time as a government climate scientist, as a metallurgist, and as a lecturer at Harvard. Although he was widely respected by his peers, he had always hoped to return to climate research. For him this was the most thrilling and important area of all science – indeed all education. But the big research jobs had come and gone, each with other people's names attached to them. Never his. Eventually he had taken the hint and moved back to his beloved Cornwall – to his last job before retirement. He had been promised the time and space to follow his own research, and so it had turned out.

And yet here he was with what he could only conclude was a revolutionary moment. Unless his spectrometer had gone as mad as Itch's chemistry teacher, the rocks sitting next door could change the world. Two questions ran round his head:

Are there any others?

Why have they appeared now?

Alexander found his head was spinning with it all. He was only brought back to earth by the sound of one of the children being ill. It was Chloe again. Jack was stroking her hair, Itch holding her hand while Mr Watkins started clearing up.

When he had finished, the teacher approached his friend and said quietly, 'Would I be right in saying that, whatever else it might do, your element 126 can make children very sick?'

Jacob Alexander nodded and turned away from where the cousins were sitting. 'I'm afraid so, yes. I'm just glad the ambulance is on its way because it is, frankly, impossible to know what we are dealing with here. These are extraordinarily powerful rocks – I've never seen their like before. So quite how much protection the children got from their makeshift containers is anyone's guess.'

Chloe had now fallen asleep, exhausted, and Jack was making her a pillow from her jacket.

Itch, though, was up and thinking again. 'Dr Alexander, you were talking just now about how these rocks could start a nuclear reactor . . .'

Watkins looked up. 'They can do what?'

'They are strong neutron emitters,' said Alexander, 'and small amounts can start up a nuclear reactor. We have more – so much more than that.'

Watkins said, 'So how many reactors could be started with that little lot next door?'

And Jacob Alexander was off again, pacing the well-worn channel between the workbenches. 'Impossible to say. Potentially, though? I'd hazard a guess at twenty or more.'

The enormity of what they were hearing was now sinking in.

'And weapons?' asked Watkins. 'Could they be used in nuclear weapons?'

'Yes, of course. For a nuclear weapon you need a critical mass of material, and that's what this is. It's deadly.'

Watkins now looked as pale as the cousins. 'You realize, Jacob, what we have here, then? Never mind every energy company and every government in the world wanting these rocks – every terrorist group will be after them! *Nuclear power in a box!* That's what we have! And available from Lab Four of your college!' He rubbed his eyes. 'Where are the police and the ambulance? I suddenly feel we are very exposed, very exposed indeed.'

Alexander looked at his watch. 'They said they'd be here soon, but it doesn't feel like it, does it?' He turned back to the children. Chloe was still asleep, her breathing shallow. Jack had fallen asleep too, her head on Itch's rucksack.

'*Trust no one* is what Cake wrote,' said Itch, 'and he was right. Who would you trust to do the right thing with that lot?'

The director sat down on a stool at the end of the bench. 'Well, in the right hands, you know, it could save the planet. When I was in the States, I worked with a man called Lovelock – James Lovelock. He developed an idea called the Gaia Theory – heard of it?'

Watkins nodded, but Itch shook his head.

'Doesn't matter. It boils down to this. Our Earth – Gaia – is the only *living* planet in the solar system and it behaves like a *living* thing. It looks after itself. Well, we need energy, and we need it quickly. Our natural resources are running out and our world is getting hot. And just look what we have here – a power source that can change the world, just when we need it.'

Itch looked at John Watkins to check if he was hearing straight but his teacher wasn't looking.

Alexander continued, 'I know I'm getting carried away here, but this is an evening for wild thinking, isn't it? We were all ridiculed for these ideas when they first started doing the rounds, but this is an extraordinary event, so I'm offering an extraordinary theory.' He was warming to his theme and couldn't keep still, so was up and touring the lab again. 'The Earth is hot, and getting hotter. In fact, it's moving to a new hot stage that we haven't seen for millions of years. I've always believed that, just as the Earth would look after itself, humans would have to look after themselves. But what if the Earth was, somehow, saying, *Here's your last chance. Here's the most extraordinary energy source you've ever had — green, clean nuclear power for all — surely even you guys can't mess this up!*'

It was Watkins's turn to speak, and Itch was waiting to hear what he made of what his old friend had said.

'I'm wondering if that's the old hippie we're hearing here, Jacob . . . You always were one for the sandals and brown rice. Surely you're not suggesting—'

But Alexander interrupted him.

'Oh, John! That's the old way of thinking! I've had all that hippie stuff thrown at me every time I went for the jobs that mattered. Well, who's looking stupid now? Next door lie eight rocks that could bring about a new industrial revolution on their own. This country could have all the energy it would ever need! And it's next door! In . . . in . . . that cupboard! Forget the oilfields. If we can share this knowledge and power, we might find a way through the new hot age that's coming.' His voice was starting to crack and Watkins offered him a bottle of water from his jacket pocket.

Watkins shrugged. 'Now maybe isn't the time for detailed argument, Jacob – I'm sure there'll be a proper discussion in due course. I really think we should call 999 again; the girls really don't look good.' They all turned to look at Chloe and Jack, both asleep, both deathly white. 'Why don't we start to move out to the reception area? It'll take us a while to get there. We might as well be ready when the ambulance arrives.'

Itch knelt down to wake his sister and cousin. He shook them gently by the shoulder. 'Guys. The ambulance will be here soon – let's get ready.'

Jack opened her eyes. 'Wasn't asleep. Just tired. That's some crazy stuff I was listening to.'

Itch smiled. 'Glad you were listening – I wasn't looking forward to explaining it to you.'

Jack sat up but Chloe hadn't moved, so Itch shook her more vigorously. She opened her eyes. 'Wassappening,' she said, slurring her words as she tried to sit up.

'We need to get you to the ambulance,' said her brother. 'It's on its way. Here, lean on me.' He hauled her up, with John Watkins helping from the other side. Jack didn't need any help; she passed the rucksack to Itch, and the party slowly set off for the front of the school. Alexander led the way, occasionally pausing to hold the doors open for Chloe, Itch and Watkins, as they retraced their steps.

'Dr Alexander,' said Itch, 'are you saying that the

Earth – or Gaia, as you called it – has really created a new energy source?'

He smiled at Itch. 'Sound unlikely to you?'

'Well, you could say that, yes.' Itch wanted to say it was the craziest thing he'd ever heard, but thought better of it.

'I know it won't be a popular idea, Itch, but it really makes sense to me. It's last orders for us; we have to get this right or we'll be toast – literally.'

They reached the reception area and peered out into the dark car park, which was still ambulance-free. Chloe sat down in an armchair and Alexander went into his office to call the emergency services again.

'Any reason I shouldn't ring my folks again, Mr Watkins?' asked Itch.

'No, good idea – tell them the ambulance is on the way, won't you? Maybe they should meet us at the hospital.'

Itch turned on his phone; it rang immediately, displaying an unknown number. 'Hello?' he said.

A man's voice asked, 'Is that Itchingham Lofte?'

'Yes, it is. Who is this?'

'My name is Detective Chief Superintendent Peter Ducker from Cornwall CID. There have been two accidents that have blocked access to West Ridge. This means we haven't been able to get to you, I'm afraid. We're now dispatching motorbikes, which should be there in fifteen minutes. Who is with you?'

Itch said, 'My sister, my cousin, Mr Watkins from school, and the director here, Dr Alexander.'

'Put Dr Alexander on, please.'

Itch went into the office, where the director had just finished his own call. 'It's the police,' he said, and handed him the phone.

'Jacob Alexander here. I've just heard about the accidents. We have three children with radiation poisoning and some highly radioactive material secure in my lab. The children need medical attention, and I need some security for the rocks. This is an issue of international importance, Detective, er . . .' Suddenly he realized he hadn't let the policeman speak yet.

'Detective Chief Superintendent Ducker, Dr Alexander, and if what you're telling me is true, those accidents are one heck of a coincidence. Make yourselves secure and we'll be with you as quickly as we can.'

There was the sound of activity in the entrance hall, and John Watkins called out, 'Er, Jacob, we have company. Someone's here, anyway. Doesn't look like police – did you order some cabs?'

The two Audis had arrived in the car park one after the other, the first from the left, the second from the right. They both stopped facing the entrance, headlights still on full beam, engines running. It was impossible to see into them, and all those in the building shielded their eyes from the dazzling blue-white xenon lights.

'Who are they, Jacob?' asked Watkins.

'No idea,' he replied. 'But not the police − the roads are blocked, apparently, and the police and ambulance can't reach us.'

'Well, they don't look local,' said Watkins, 'and they're not minicabs. Where does that leave us?'

Jacob Alexander turned to Itch. 'How many people could know about the rocks and that they are here?'

Itch considered. 'Well, no one knows that there are eight rocks except us. People at school know about the original rock − and Flowerdew, who took it in the first place. And who knows who he told . . .'

Alexander went over to the reception desk and hit a green disc by the phone bank. The double doors and revolving doors shuddered slightly as the locking mechanism clicked into place. 'Let's assume they aren't friendly until we know otherwise,' he said.

The passenger door of one of the Audis opened and Roshanna Wing stepped out. Whoever Alexander, Watkins and the Loftes were expecting, it wasn't someone like this. Tall and stylish, wearing an immaculate dark blue jacket, pencil skirt and high heels, she walked towards the entrance, smiling broadly and waving at Jack and Itch. Jack started to wave back, then stopped. The Greencorps woman walked up to the glass that separated her from the group inside and turned to the drivers, indicating that they should cut the engines. They did so immediately, and the headlights dimmed; the two men were now just visible.

'Dr Alexander? I'm Mary Bale, *International Herald Tribune*. Could we speak?' she called through the glass, holding up a press card.

'Yes, I'm Alexander – how can I help?' called the director.

'Well,' she said, 'we've been tipped off about a rather interesting rock that has been uncovered. Do you know anything about it?'

Jack turned to Itch. 'A journalist! How does she know about it?' she whispered.

'No idea,' said Itch, shrugging. The woman noticed the exchange and smiled again at the children.

Alexander called through the glass, 'It's not a good time. We're waiting for an ambulance – we have some sick kids here.'

Roshanna Wing looked concerned. 'I'm sorry to hear that. I won't keep you long. You are the Dr Alexander who was at Harvard till 2007, aren't you? I read your paper on tin mining – truly fascinating. I wonder if I could get a quick quote from you – be as non-committal as you like. I'll just get my pad.' And she turned and walked back to the car.

'I'll just say something boring and they'll go away. John, can you open the doors? The button's by the desk there.'

Watkins was not so sure. 'Since when did reporters drive Audis, Jacob?'

'Americans do things differently, John – you saw her card. The best way to kill the story is to be bland. I'm quite good at that. They'll lose interest, you'll see.'

Watkins pressed the button, the doors shuddered again, and Alexander went outside. Without thinking, Watkins locked the doors again immediately.

Roshanna Wing was bending down beside the Audi, apparently rummaging in her bag, as Jacob Alexander approached.

'Can we make this quick? I need to get back inside as soon as possible,' he said.

Wing stood up with her pad and pencil. 'Is it radiation sickness, Dr Alexander?'

'I . . . we . . . er, it's too early to tell . . .'

'So you *do* have it!' Wing exclaimed. 'We would love to get a quick photo of you next to it! This will go round the world – it will be *your* discovery, Dr Alexander! Think of that! Paul here is my photographer.' She motioned to the driver, and Bud Collins got out, doing up his jacket button as he came round to shake Alexander's hand.

'No, no, no,' said Alexander. 'This really isn't the time for photos. There are still many tests to do.

You wanted a quote – well, I'll give you one: No comment. There really is nothing to say. These sort of experiments happen all the time . . .'

Wing put her hand on his arm; she was still smiling but her voice had hardened. 'Sorry, Dr Alexander, but we know you have something special and we really do need a photo. We've come a long way for this and we have no intention of going home without one. It won't take long.'

Jacob Alexander bridled – a reaction John Watkins recognized through the glass. 'This might not be going well,' he said quietly.

The director of the West Ridge School of Mining drew himself up to his full height of six foot one and looked Roshanna Wing straight in the eye. 'Going home without a picture is exactly what you are going to do. You asked for a quote – well, you have one. If that doesn't suit you and . . . Paul here, well, I'm afraid that's just too bad. Goodbye, Miss Bale.'

He turned to go back in. Those waiting inside saw Roshanna Wing sigh and nod to her colleague. Bud Collins reached out with one hand and grabbed Alexander by the shoulder, spinning him round. With both hands the American hoisted Alexander onto the car's bonnet, where he lay sprawled, stunned.

Wing walked round to the front of the car and leaned in close. 'Just one photo. Let us in. Last chance.'

Inside the school, Jack grabbed hold of Itch as Watkins exclaimed, 'Oh my heavens! Oh my heavens! Oh my heavens!'

Realizing that they were all under serious threat now, Itch turned to look at Chloe, who was fast asleep again in the armchair. He ran over and tried to wake her, first by shaking, then by shouting. She stirred and opened her eyes. Itch told her as calmly as he could, 'Chloe, we are going to have to find the ambulances ourselves. Can you walk?'

Before she could respond, Jack cried out. Itch turned to see that Alexander had managed to direct a kick at the driver's groin; the man was now writhing on the ground, but had pulled Alexander down with him. The driver of the other Audi had come running over and was kicking the director in the stomach. From his waistband he had drawn a gun.

'Back to the lab!' shouted Watkins, and ran to help Itch carry Chloe along the corridor.

Jack, shouldering the rucksack, said, 'Itch, I'll help Chloe. You need to get those rocks, and you need to do it *now*!'

They swapped places and Itch sprinted off. He turned sharp left and then accelerated into the labs. He ran straight into Lab 5, where Alexander had tested the rocks on the spectrometer. He sprinted over to the large white metal container and, pressing down on the compression lock, swung the door open. On the middle shelf sat the white toolbox-style container that Alexander had put the rocks in. Picking it up, he felt them moving, rattling around inside, and he held it with both arms outstretched in front of him. He saw the canvas bag lying next to them, and put the box in that, then went through to Lab 4. A panting Watkins was settling Chloe down, while Jack held up her hand for quiet. From the entrance they could hear bangs and then the sound of shattering glass.

Watkins looked up. 'You both go. I'll stay with Chloe – we'll only slow you down. I promise I'll get her to the hospital and explain everything to your parents. There's a fire exit in the corner of Lab One.' Then, pointing at the bag Itch was holding, 'Hide them, get rid of them. Whatever you can do, Itch. God bless you both. *Go!*'

Itch and Jack stood and stared at each other for the briefest of moments, but long enough to catch the sound of running footsteps in the corridor and more yelling from the lobby. The running man – and it *was* a man as those were no high-heeled shoes pounding towards them – sounded too close for them to make it through to the other labs.

The merest hint of a smile was briefly noticeable on Itch's face. 'Jack, turn round and hold still!' Jack did so and Itch dived for the rucksack. Lifting the top flap, he found a small metal tin near the top. Then, turning to Watkins: 'Sir! Your cigarette lighter, please – now!'

Without comment but looking puzzled, the teacher felt in his jacket pocket, then reached in and threw him an orange plastic lighter.

Catching it, Itch put it in Jack's hand. 'You stand this side of the door, Jack.' He pushed her into position. 'Light it!'

The footsteps had reached the end of the corridor and were, presumably, about to make the left turn towards Labs 3, 4 and 5. Jack stood there wide-eyed, with the cigarette lighter flame held in front of her. Itch then climbed up onto some filing cabinets so that he was above and behind his cousin. Watkins and Chloe were staring at them both in alarm, but Itch shook his head and they got the message, resuming their patient and carer positions.

The footsteps stopped, paused briefly, then ran towards the lights of Labs 3 and 4. From there, whoever it was would be able to see Chloe and Watkins. The steps slowed and Itch tensed. Sensing the moment, Jack's hand began to shake, but the lighter remained alight in front of her.

'Lift your arm, Jack!' Itch said in a loud whisper. 'High as you can.' She held the lighter like an Olympic torch and stood stock still. 'When I say "*now*", shut your eyes tightly!' he told her, and she nodded. The footsteps were no more than a jog now, but were barely metres away from the door into Lab 4.

If anyone other than Chloe had been looking, they would have seen John Watkins with his eyes screwed up tight, his whole body rigid, as though he were about to receive a very painful injection. Her head still facing the teacher, Chloe's eyes were twisted round to follow what was happening at the entrance to the lab. She fixed on her brother, who was standing crouched and poised above Jack, holding the tin in his hands. He opened it and poured the contents into his palm. Her cousin stood rigidly, her arm aloft, the flame burning steadily. Then, through the doorway, the large frame of Volker Berghahn came into view, his gun held out in front of him. The German saw the teacher and the girl, and relaxed just a second too soon.

With Berghahn only a step away, Itch called, 'Now!', threw the powder at the flame and shut his eyes. Jack's arm wobbled and she too shut her eyes. The Greencorps man, still moving, did not close his, and was greeted by a blinding cascade of burning phosphorus. Brilliant white light filled the lab. Chloe looked away, but still had bright white shapes dancing in front of her eyes. Watkins opened his and turned to see what had happened.

The German had pulled up quickly enough to stop himself being engulfed by the fiery waterfall but had dropped the gun and fallen to his knees. Shouting in pain, he held his hands tightly pressed over his eyes.

Itch and Jack hadn't moved but were trying to blink the flash from their eyes. Watkins nodded vigorously at them and looked down the corridor in the direction of Lab 1. He mouthed, '*Go now!*'

With a quick glance at Chloe, Itch jumped down, picked up the canvas bag and the rucksack, took Jack's hand, and ran.

22

They found the fire exit without turning on any lights. Despite the white flashes in front of their eyes they could see the soft glow from the electric signs. They pushed down the metal bar on the door and burst through into the darkness outside. Clanging bells started ringing – they had clearly triggered an alarm of some kind – but they had to wait a moment for their eyes to adjust to the dark. Gradually they made out some sheds and out-houses, and a few trees silhouetted against the night sky. The only light was what spilled out from Labs 4 and 5.

The first of around a dozen sheds was directly in front of them – about twenty metres away – and they ran for it, ignoring the door that faced them and running round to the far side, where they stood with their backs to the wall.

'I bet he lost both eyebrows!' said Jack, taking the

rucksack from Itch, who laughed, far too loudly.

'Yes, but he'll be fine. In an hour or so. Cake would have liked that, I think.'

There was a brief silence, then Jack asked, 'Was that the replacement phosphorus he got you?'

Itch nodded. 'Told me to keep it for my birthday.'

'Nice one, Cake,' she said. Then she added, 'You OK?' Itch was alternately blowing on his hand and then putting it under his arm. 'You didn't overdo the phosphorus *again*, did you?'

'Well, I might have. I wasn't sure how much to use, so I used it all, just to be on the safe side.'

'Like last time!' said Jack, laughing now. 'And I'm sure "*I used it all, just to be on the safe side*" is not the greatest piece of scientific advice out there!'

'No, I guess you're right,' said Itch, who could now make out a large black patch on his hand, which was starting to throb. 'The other thugs will be close behind, so let's keep going . . .' He nodded in the direction of a large grey tank. 'That'll be the oil tank, I guess. There must be a service road near there for the tanker. Let's try that. You all right?' Jack was swaying slightly.

'Sure,' she said. 'Let's go.'

They jogged left towards the tank, Itch in the lead. The rocks rattled noisily around in their box; the canvas bag was very heavy now – he held it with both arms, cradling it close to his chest. His arms ached with the weight of it, made worse by the angle his arms had to adopt to run without dropping it. Jack followed close behind, the rucksack bouncing on her back.

The oil tank which served the college was huge, at least ten metres tall and twenty wide, and as they got closer, they saw that there was indeed a small rough track that snaked away through the trees to it. Itch turned the corner first and ran straight into the side of a large black car. Jack, at his shoulder, collided with him, and Itch banged his head on glass. From the other side of the car a man appeared, walking round the bonnet. The darkness was almost total, the tank blocking out any light from the labs, but Itch knew who it was from the first step. His insides looped the loop as Jack gasped and he heard that familiar elegant sneer.

'Of course, it's the freaky cousins. Who else?' Nathaniel Flowerdew moved round to stand facing Itch and Jack. He was wearing a black cloth cap over his white curls, a black linen suit and a very broad grin. 'Itchingham. Jack. What's that you have there? Pizzas? Mine's an American Hot. I do hope you're not going to disappoint me. Shall I check the bag?' He held out his hands; Itch didn't move. The sound of the emergency exit in Lab 1 crashing open again made Flowerdew jump, and he grabbed hold of Jack. 'Get in the car.'

He opened the rear door and pushed Jack in. Fleetingly, Itch thought of running, but with the

Audi team closing and Flowerdew holding Jack, he decided to join her in the car.

To his surprise, Flowerdew got in the back next to him and shouted, 'Drive!'

What had confused him was that the car, a Range Rover Sport, was a left-hand drive. A squat man with a ponytail fired the engine, flicked on the headlights and accelerated away from the tank.

The track was bumpy and full of potholes, but the Range Rover made short work of them, and within seconds they were through the trees and turning right. Jack had the rucksack, Itch had the rocks and Flowerdew was staring at the canvas bag. He had heard the dull cracks that came from inside Itch's box as he got in the car and had just realized what it meant.

'How many?' he said quietly, almost reverently.

Itch couldn't see any reason to lie. 'Eight,' he said.

Flowerdew laughed – quietly at first, but then louder and louder, until the driver turned round to check he was all right. 'Eight! You hear that, Kinch! We have eight of the blighters – and to think I was all excited about just one.' Flowerdew tore off his cap, folded it away in his pocket and fidgeted with excitement.

The driver, Kinch, turned again and nodded, smiling at him. It was a smile without knowledge, however; he clearly understood nothing of the significance of what they had just taken, but if his new boss was happy, then so was he.

As they sped round the back of the mining school, blue and white flashing lights lit the darkness. The Range Rover reached a junction of the service road. Turning right, they were able to watch the three police motorcycles and one paramedic roar into the car park.

'That should keep them all busy for a while,' said Flowerdew. 'But just in case, get on the floor.' He pushed Itch off the seat and Jack followed him down onto the mat. They sat there, surrounded by food wrappers and plastic bottles. 'Slowly past the cops, please, Kinch. And the medic.'

Kinch eased the Range Rover out onto the main road, and the two men turned to watch the police by the lobby of the mining school, standing amidst the shattered plates of glass. Both Jack and Itch thought of jumping out or trying to attract attention, but the automatic door locks had already clicked and the car's glass was all tinted. Itch was relieved to see the medic – Chloe could now finally get the treatment she desperately needed. Leaving her might have been the right thing to do, but he knew he wouldn't have done it if Mr Watkins hadn't been there; his teacher would make sure she was OK. Itch also wondered if the police would see off the woman and her two 'drivers', but was far from sure. Anyway, he and Jack had troubles of their own now.

Once clear of the mining school, they tried to sit up again, but Flowerdew shook his head. 'Stay down there, you two,' he commanded. 'Help yourself to some crusts. We waited a long time for you – we got through a lot of supplies, as you can see. I'm sure you'll find something tasty down there. Oh – and I'll have your phones, if you would be so kind.'

The cousins handed them over, and Flowerdew switched both off; then, opening the window next to him, he threw them out as far as he could. Out of sight and earshot of them all, both phones disintegrated on impact with the kerbside granite rocks.

'I was sure you'd end up at West Ridge eventually,' he told them. 'You love Watkins, and Watkins loves West Ridge. Where else would you run? You didn't disappoint, Lofte – though you took your time, I must say. Kinch here was beginning to wonder whether you'd turn up at all.' The driver shrugged, and Flowerdew went on: 'We were waiting at the back. As soon as those Audis swept into the car park I guessed they'd flush you out.'

The car accelerated away from West Ridge but slowed when it reached the smouldering tractor and minibus. The wreckage was still widely scattered across the road but a fire engine had put out the worst of the flames. Small isolated brush fires had sparked on both sides of the road but weren't preventing an ambulance from making its way slowly around the crash site. The Range Rover waited for it to negotiate the twisted, smouldering rubber and smoking metal. It was followed by two police cars, which flashed their thanks to the waiting driver. Kinch laughed but Flowerdew was not happy.

'They'll remember us now. You're an idiot, Kinch.'

Itch, losing feeling in his right leg, thought, *That's how Flowerdew talks to everybody. It isn't just us.* He glanced at Jack but she had her eyes shut.

'You should know we've all been sick,' he said. 'And I think Jack is about to be again. Could we sit up on the seats now?'

Flowerdew laughed. 'Play with things that are out of your league, Lofte, and you pay the price. In your case, radiation sickness is a very, very high price. How many times?'

'A few times.'

'Hair loss? Reddening skin?'

Itch wasn't sure, so said nothing.

'Your eyebrows have gone already – I can see that from here. It's just a matter of time, I'm afraid.'

Itch couldn't be bothered to correct him, and anyway, he now knew all too well what the next signs of sickness were. 'Where would you like us to be sick?' he replied, getting cross now, even though he knew that was probably unwise. 'On your leather seats or on your carpet?'

'How about on each other?' said Flowerdew,

provoking a sneering laugh from Kinch. 'OK, *she* can sit up, but you stay down.'

Itch gave Jack a shove, and she hauled herself up and swapped places with the rucksack, stowing it on the floor beside Itch.

They sped north, and soon picked up the major roads to head out of Cornwall. But as soon as they had put some distance between them and West Ridge, Flowerdew insisted that Kinch use the satnav to find a route with minor roads. He was still fuming at his driver.

'When they realize the rocks are gone, they'll be looking for a Range Rover seen leaving the scene, driven by a grinning simpleton with a ponytail.'

Itch was about to ask where they were going, but twisting round, he saw that the satnav showed an address in West London and a journey time of four hours, forty-five minutes. If they stayed on the B-roads, that would rise to at least six hours. He resumed the posture that was familiar from the times he'd tried to stay up late watching TV: if you don't move or say anything, everyone will forget you're there. It hadn't worked then and it didn't work now.

'You have no idea how many people will want what we have here,' said Flowerdew. 'The contents of that box are worth more than the crown jewels – more than all the Trident submarines this country owns – more than the total earning power of Canada.' He looked at Jack and Itch. 'I've done my homework, as you can see.' When this got no response, he kicked Itch in the ribs. Hard. 'Pay attention, Lofte! You always were one for drifting off.'

'Only in *your* classes. *Sir.*' This cost Itch another kick in the ribs, and he yelped in pain.

'Can I tell you how great that feels, Lofte? After all the pain you've caused me, to see you hurt is really rather therapeutic. I liked it last time, but then that fool Watkins interrupted.' He lashed out again. 'That's for Watkins.'

This time the kick landed lower than the first two, at the base of Itch's ribcage, and the sharpness of the pain flooded his eyes with tears. His determination not to cry out again made him screw his eyes up tight but the tears rolled down his face.

'A pathetic display, Lofte. You really shouldn't have stolen my rock, you know. Or broken into my house. I'm sure you'd like to say sorry, wouldn't you?' In the time-honoured way of teachers, he added, 'I'm waiting . . . I'd like to hear you *say sorry.*'

Itch was about to swear at him when he felt Jack's hand reach for his and, finding it, squeeze gently.

'Sorry,' he said instead.

'Sorry, *sir.*'

'Sorry, sir.'

'There. So much better. Now we are all friends again.' Flowerdew chuckled to himself as Kinch watched in his mirror.

Jack gradually fell asleep and Itch, with his rucksack to lean on, drifted off too. Itch's was a fitful doze from which he emerged sweating, nauseous and with his burned hand still throbbing hard. Lying there in the dark, he could see Jack asleep but with her head now on the seat where Flowerdew had been. He had obviously climbed over and was now in the front passenger seat, with the rocks at his feet. He had his laptop open and he was speaking quietly into his phone. Outside it was pitch black. Wherever they were had no street lighting and there appeared to be no traffic, either.

It was a while before Itch really tuned in to what Flowerdew was saying. Once he had shifted around to ease the circulation in his legs, he found a discarded water bottle under the seat which still had a few mouthfuls in the bottom. He quietly unscrewed the cap and sipped. The temptation to swig noisily was great but he didn't want to alert Flowerdew and Kinch to the fact that he was awake.

'No, Kazeem, listen. Trust me on this. I—' Flowerdew stopped, clearly interrupted by his caller. After a few moments he spoke again. 'I'll send you the data I have. Call me back when you get it.' He hung up, sent three documents via email and called another number. His greeting was in a language that Itch didn't recognize; it sounded African. '*Kedu!* It's Flowerdew. We need to meet up, Benedict. I have a present you should see. Can I send you details? Where to?' He quickly typed an email address. 'It's on its way.' The same three documents were attached and sent. Flowerdew closed his laptop and rubbed his eyes. 'Where are we, Kinch?'

The driver glanced at his satnav. 'Three miles from Bath. Do you want to stop?'

'No, but perhaps we should disappear for a while. Word is out about our cargo, but we don't have to be in London till tomorrow night. My old Nigerian friends won't be in place until then. We need to keep a low profile. The lower the better. Ideas?'

'There was a village called Abbotts a couple of miles back; we drove through it about ten minutes ago. It's full of second homes, all deserted and not alarmed. We could choose from about eight or nine, I reckon.'

Flowerdew smiled. 'It sounds perfect. Do it.' Then, as much to himself as to Kinch, 'These beauties change everything. Wars have been fought over less. And even if the authorities get hold of them in the end, nothing can be kept secret for ever. Even with the best intentions, it's the destructive power and terror these rocks have that'll win the day. That's what makes them so valuable.'

Itch thought it the most chilling thing he had ever heard.

Kinch said nothing but had already turned round. Within five minutes they were entering Abbotts again. There were a few streetlights, and they saw immaculate stone cottages lining the main street all the way to a church. Kinch pointed to the six or seven with bins outside their gates.

'They're the ones. Tell-tale sign – bins are empty, but there's no one at home to wheel them back in. Which do you fancy? You can take your pick.'

Kinch pulled the Range Rover to the side of the road and Flowerdew wound down the window. He looked up and down the row of well-kept Bath stone cottages, the honey-coloured brick lit only by the occasional security light. All windows were either shuttered or had curtains drawn. He shrugged. 'They're all the same. Let's take the end one.'

'The parking is round the back,' Kinch told him.

Flowerdew stared at him. 'You've done this before, haven't you?'

Kinch smiled. 'It's what you pay me for, isn't it?' He switched off the headlights and drove round to the side of the cottages, pulling up in a little service road that ran between the back doors of the cottages and their gardens.

'I'll be two minutes,' said Kinch, and slipped out of the car. Watching in the mirror, Flowerdew saw him lean against the back door and insert a number of thin steel objects into the lock. The door opened and Kinch disappeared inside.

In less than two minutes he had returned. Opening Flowerdew's door, he said, 'It's perfect.' Nodding at Jack, sprawled on the back seat, and Itch, apparently asleep on his rucksack, he asked, 'What do we do with them now? You've got what you wanted. They're just . . . in the way, really.'

'I know. But they know everything. Let's discuss this inside.'

Flowerdew picked up his briefcase and the bag containing the lead-lined box, and headed for the end cottage. He left Kinch to rouse Jack and Itch, haul them out of the car and into the house.

Kinch shut the door behind them, re-locking it. He'd put the lights on their lowest setting. They were standing in a small kitchen with an Aga cooker, a pretty farmhouse-style table and chairs, and marble work surfaces. In the corner of the room the door to a large pantry stood open. Assorted supplies were clearly visible inside and Kinch looked hungrily at them.

'Help yourself. I'm going to find somewhere to work,' said Flowerdew. 'Bring me a coffee – black, two sugars.' He turned and was about to walk out of the kitchen into the darkened house when he added, 'And don't let *them* out of your sight. Devious, lying, thieving children need all your attention, Kinch. Clear?'

Kinch nodded, and Flowerdew left with the bag and his briefcase.

Itch sat down at the kitchen table but then realized that Jack was swaying where she stood. He went over and steadied her.

'Need a bathroom,' she said.

'Both follow me,' Kinch ordered, and led the way up twisting pine stairs to a small landing. In front of them was a bathroom. Itch helped Jack in, found the light cord, kicked the door shut and got her to the toilet just in time. Kinch stood guard outside.

They stayed in the bathroom for half an hour, partly because Jack was really very ill but also because they hadn't been able to speak together for a while. After the sickness had passed, they both sat with their backs against the bath.

'Does this carry on or get worse?' whispered Jack.

'Well, I don't think we get better without help,' said Itch, 'and before you say it, we are sticking together. We left Chloe because she had Watkins. All right?'

'OK,' said Jack. 'I wasn't asleep in the car, you know – I heard Kinch say we were *in the way*.' She dabbed her face with a flannel.

'I suppose it's true. We *are* in the way now. Massively in the way.'

'And you heard Flowerdew. He said, *But they know everything*. Which we do.'

Itch stood up and opened the bathroom cabinet. Finding a tube of antiseptic cream, he smeared some on his burned hand. 'Apart from who he's trying to contact,' he said. 'It sounds like Greencorps have cut him loose, so he's calling all his old dodgy mates in the oil business who might be interested in the rocks.'

'Do you think we should assume that whoever comes for the rocks will be bad?' asked Jack.

'I think that's a pretty safe bet, yes. The chances of him giving them to any good causes is slim.'

Jack started laughing, and for a moment Itch thought she'd gone crazy. 'What's so funny?' he said.

'Just the picture of Flowerdew offering eight dangerously radioactive rocks to Oxfam to see if they would be of any use.'

Itch laughed too. 'And Oxfam becomes a nuclear power!'

'And bombs Christian Aid!' said Jack, and they dissolved into giggles.

This led inevitably to Kinch coming in and taking them downstairs again. It was clear that he had been busy working his way through the pantry. The table was littered with empty crisp packets, biscuit and chocolate wrappers and beer bottles. Kinch's T-shirt had crisp crumbs all over it from where he had wiped his hands.

Quietly – presumably so Flowerdew couldn't hear – he said, 'If you're hungry, there's plenty of stuff.' He went into the larder again, returning with a large packet of crisps. He chucked it at Itch, who caught it and opened it in one movement. Jack wasn't that hungry, but she nibbled a few and Itch devoured the rest.

'Any chance of sleeping in a bed?' he asked.

Kinch shook his head. 'Dr Flowerdew said you sleep in the dining room and I guard the door. The windows are locked shut there.'

Itch shouldered the rucksack and they headed for the dining room. In the gloom they could just make out a large table and some wooden chairs. At the far end there was one armchair with some cushions, and Jack slumped in it, curling up almost immediately.

Itch put down his rucksack and Kinch, watching him, said, 'Why do you carry that stuff around with you?'

'What stuff?'

'That stuff in your rucksack. He said to check it for weapons — scissors, knives, that kind of thing. But it's full of junk.'

'Is that what you told him?'

'I told him there were no weapons — just rubbish and weird boy stuff. He wasn't interested.'

'Well, I collect things, that's all. Metals, batteries — that kind of thing.' Itch was trying to make it sound boring and he clearly succeeded.

Kinch shrugged his sloping shoulders and left, muttering, 'Sounds fascinating.' He closed and locked the door.

Jack looked as though she really was asleep this time. Itch took a cushion she hadn't fallen on and made himself a makeshift bed from that, his rucksack and a tablecloth. He expected to fall asleep immediately but found himself still wide awake. He could hear Flowerdew talking somewhere nearby and it focused his mind. He and Jack were in a dangerous situation; and once these people Flowerdew was talking to realized what was on offer, it could only get worse. Whoever ended up with the rocks would not want two witnesses to everything. Itch wondered who these Nigerian friends of Flowerdew's were, and who they would tell. Before very long, Itch imagined that every mad group of terrorists and bombers would be heading their way. Suddenly, on top of all that, he was aware of the nausea returning.

He decided not to alert Jack or Kinch, but just sat in the corner of the dark dining room, the tablecloth gathered and ready in his lap, waiting for it to start. When it came, it shook him so violently it left him trembling, exhausted and wet with sweat. When the tablecloth had done its work, he lay down where he was and, silently, started to cry.

He was woken by Jack talking to him. He clearly hadn't been asleep long as it was still dark. It was a few moments before he remembered everything that had happened – though the vile taste in his mouth was all the reminder he needed. He was grateful for the cover of darkness to wipe his mouth and eyes with his shirt.

'You've been sick again, Itch – you should have told me! Why didn't you go to the bathroom? I'd have come with you,' Jack said.

'Yeah, well . . .' He couldn't really be bothered to explain his reasoning. 'It seemed too much trouble at the time. Sorry about the smell.' He stood up and went over to the shuttered windows. There was now a sliver of light from a gap above the shutter.

'If I slept through you being ill, I must have been really far gone,' said Jack. 'Did I miss anything else?'

'Just Kinch saying he'd been through my rucksack.' Itch's voice was thick and rasping.

'Really? What did he make of your collection? I hope you took him through it and told him all about atomic weights and electronegativities and so on. We've had to suffer – I don't see why a thug like Kinch shouldn't.' They both smiled and Jack added, 'Though I have to say the phosphorus did prove rather useful back at the mining school.'

Itch suddenly stood bolt upright, staring straight ahead.

'What is it, Itch?'

'You, Jacqueline Lofte, are a genius.'

23

Dr Nathaniel Flowerdew, in the lounge of the end cottage, had three customers interested in his business. One stood out from the others. He had sent each of them the documented results of his tests on the rock, but only one, a Nigerian businessman and politician called Agu Osiegbe, had delivered the million-dollar down-payment. Flowerdew knew that with more time he could demand any price he wished, and from any number of clients, but he didn't have that time, and only Osiegbe had delivered up front. He smiled to himself as he recalled how calls from Greencorps had been flooding in as the news spread, and he had simply ignored them – they had had their chance. Now they could just stand by and watch him succeed where they had failed.

'A pleasure doing business with you again, Nathaniel,' said the Nigerian down the phone now.

'I thought our trading days were over after the, ah, unfortunate oil spill.'

Flowerdew chuckled. 'Me too, me too, but then I never thought I'd be able to offer you anything like this. You've seen the stats I sent you from the tests. Nigeria can be a nuclear power – and under your leadership, Agu. As I recall, that was always your intention, was it not? You didn't spend all that time with the President's crooks and gangsters without craving power yourself.'

There was a second's delay on the line from Lagos. 'Who does not want such things?' said Agu Osiegbe. Then, 'And this is nothing to do with Greencorps, Nathaniel? I'm told they cut you loose. Just like they did your old friend, Shivvi. She's still in prison, of course. How *did* you get her to take the rap? She was just the diver, after all.'

Flowerdew spoke slowly. 'The issue here is *okwute*' – he used a Nigerian word for rocks – 'that is all – nothing else. And no, it's nothing to do with Greencorps. Except, of course, they want them too, and have armed thugs looking for them. But they had their chance and they blew it. Soon the rocks will be yours, and you will be the talk of the world.'

'Very well,' said the Nigerian. 'You have the down-payment. If the product is everything you say it is, we agree to a billion dollars and a thirty-per-cent stake in future earnings. And a bullet in the head if you're lying.' Osiegbe found this funny, but Flowerdew was silent. 'We are working on the transfer plan. I'm making arrangements for the pick-up. Do you still have that flat by the Thames? The "secret investment" you invited me to all those years ago?'

'Yes, of course. A good investment, and still secret.'

'Good. We'll speak later today. So long.'

Flowerdew stood up and walked around the room. He was both irritated and elated by the call, but if his old Nigerian colleague was true to his word, in a few hours all the loose ends would be tied up. He weaved a coin between his fingers as he paced. He noticed the coffee Kinch had brought in earlier, now stone cold, but he didn't want to talk to his driver, and he certainly didn't want to talk to the kids. As Kinch had pointed out, they had become a problem – one with only one solution. As he considered what the next few hours would bring, it occurred to Flowerdew that all he had to do was 'oil the wheels' of a reaction that was already underway. Extensive exposure to radiation led to death sooner or later, and with the eight rocks in his possession he could make sure that it was sooner. He smiled.

Feverishly, with his painful, burned hand, Itch was emptying his rucksack. It seemed an eternity ago that he had filled it with his collection for safe-keeping, but now his elements could stop being a hobby and start doing some work. The phosphorus had bought them time in the mining school, allowing them to escape. Maybe what Kinch had called his 'weird boy stuff' could help them again.

'Here's to being weird!' he said out loud.

Plastic bag followed plastic bag, as one by one Itch's elements were assembled on the dining-room carpet. Jack watched as her cousin turned each over in his hand, muttering a stream of numbers and words to himself.

'You all right?' she asked.

'What? Oh, sorry, yes. Old habits . . .'

'Found anything useful? What's that you've got?'

'Sadly, a useless piece of titanium that used to reside in Gabriel's ear.' He picked up some other bags. 'Manganese – no; copper coins – no; chromium forks . . . maybe. At least they're pointy.'

Jack looked unimpressed. 'Come on, Itch – we need some magic from somewhere! Anything! We haven't got long, it's getting light. Look.' The first real sunshine of the morning was brightening their room but bringing with it a growing sense of fear about the day ahead. 'From the top, Itch, just start— Oh, help.' Jack stopped and looked at her hand, which had been in her hair. Clumps of it had just come away and she held it out to Itch. Tears pooled in her eyes, then streamed down both cheeks. 'Last chance, Itch. Find something,' she said quietly. 'I'll take the fork, but it's hardly a plan of action, is it?'

Itch looked at his cousin. Her face was deathly white and sweating, and her hair was matted; two small bald patches had appeared above her left ear. He nodded and opened his mouth to say something supportive, but nothing came. So he just smiled and went back to his elements.

The last item out of his bag had produced from Itch what his dad would call an 'oil-rig word'. In his hand was a brass-coloured capsule with a pointy end. Bullet-shaped but about four times as big.

'What is it, Itch?'

'It's xenon. Number fifty-four. Atomic weight 131.293. Density five point nine. Melting point minus 111.8 degrees Centigrade, boiling point minus 108 degrees Centigrade . . .' He paused and looked up. 'You've normally stopped me before I get this far.'

'Yeah, well, this time I'm quite interested in what you've got say,' she told him. 'What can it do?'

'Well, if I remember correctly, Jack, it's an anaesthetic.'

She looked at him with her tired brown eyes. 'Now *that* sounds like a plan of action,' she said.

Christophe Revere and Jan Van Den Hauwe had told Roshanna Wing that the word was out about the new element 126; and that it was, as they had suspected, *rocks* they were now looking for, not just one rock. They knew it was many, but not how many, and they also knew that the rocks were now in the hands of their old colleague, Flowerdew, who was no longer answering their calls. The questioning of Alexander, Watkins and Chloe Lofte was being held in secret; the reports were highly confidential but, as ever, the information was available for the right price.

Greencorps could pay that price and so, it seemed, could many others. The Frenchman and the Dutchman warned Wing that news of the rocks had spread globally. Soon that corner of south-west England would be home to any number of crazies who fancied nuclear energy in a bag.

They had explained all this after Wing had told them what had happened at the mining school and how Itch and Jack had got away. After much cursing she had been put on hold. She paced the motorway service-station car park where they had holed up. She knew that losing the rocks, the Loftes and Flowerdew was bad, and it was only the bleep every five seconds that told her she was still connected. Two minutes passed before contact was resumed.

'You've a head start on the crazies,' said Revere. 'It's not much, but it's something. We want those rocks, Roshanna – you know that. That's priority one. But if you can't get them, it may suit us if the mad guys win the race. What mustn't happen – what absolutely *mustn't* happen – is for the authorities, the police, the government, the scientists, the establishment to get their huge grabbing hands on them. Then we really will be sunk. Am I clear?'

'Yes, Mr Revere, absolutely.' Roshanna knew she hadn't entirely kept the surprise out of her voice and was annoyed with herself.

Van Den Hauwe clearly thought more explanation was needed and came on the line. 'You know how it is, Roshanna. Ideally we'd place a rock or two with a group we can trust. They'll go and commit some outrage somewhere and no one will trust 126 again. Our company, our industry needs this, Roshanna. Oil is what matters to Greencorps, and oil is what will always matter if we get this right.'

'Yes, Mr Van Den Hauwe, I do understand. Obviously we still don't know where they are at the moment. We could trawl the minor roads if you wish, though I feel certain Flowerdew will head for London. Do we have help there?'

'Absolutely. We agree with your analysis. Flowerdew can't stay holed up down there – he needs to get to where the players are. Preparations are in hand. Go to the London office and we'll talk then.' They hung up.

One Audi now sped to London; the other was left in the service station. Berghahn still couldn't drive – his eyes needed more time to recover from the phosphorus flash – and Wing planned to spend the journey phoning, emailing and messaging all her London contacts, building up a picture of who the players were in this increasingly dangerous game. Where would Flowerdew go? Who would he sell to? And what would he do with the children?

The sign said: LONDON 120 MILES.

The stench in the cottage's dining room was overpowering, the heat of the new day working its way into the contents of the tablecloth and filling the room. However, the only occupants were oblivious to it, talking and planning. Itch and Jack sat with their backs to the armchair, passing the xenon canister between them. They handled it gently, as though it was a bomb, despite the fact that it had been thrown around in the rucksack for hours and survived without a scratch. It was ten centimetres long and about the thickness of a large candle. It was a dull brass colour with small, smudged lettering around the bottom. They had both tried to read it but it appeared to be in a foreign language – Russian was Jack's guess. It had the feel of an aerosol can but without any operating instructions.

'Where did you get it?' asked Jack.

'A medical suppliers in Antwerp – they were getting rid of stuff, I think. Closing down.'

'And they sell this stuff to kids?'

'Not knowingly, no. I said I was a medical researcher working on a PhD in bio-sciences. I ordered a bunch of stuff, but this was the best thing they sent.'

'How does it work?'

'I'm not quite sure how anaesthetics work. More to the point, I don't know how to make this particular anaesthetic work. There's no button to press, no ring-pull and no screw top. It's obviously supposed to be used in a machine connected to breathing apparatus and so on. Stuff we don't have.'

'Doesn't look very big, either, does it? Will there be enough gas in there to take out two men? And how can we make sure it doesn't take *us* out at the same time?' Jack sounded scared again.

'You're right, it doesn't look like much. We'll need a small space. The smaller the better. And, to be honest, I've no idea what we're going to do with it, but it's all we have, Jack. It's better than just having a fork, anyway.'

Hearing footsteps in the hall outside, they scrambled to their feet and hastily repacked the rucksack, leaving the xenon canister near the top. They sat down again, expecting Kinch or Flowerdew to appear, but the footsteps carried on into another room and then stopped. Itch and Jack heard a knock and then a distant, 'Yes.' So it was Kinch going to see Flowerdew. The day was beginning.

Kinch had expected to find Flowerdew asleep in an armchair or on the sofa and was surprised to find him sitting at a small desk, typing furiously with the index finger of each hand. He was scowling, his face pale and drawn, his eyes puffy. He didn't look up, speak, or acknowledge Kinch's presence in any way. Kinch shuffled his feet but there was still no reaction, so he started to look around: wall-to-ceiling bookshelves; a small, old-fashioned television; and a flowery three-piece suite. The canvas bag containing the rocks sat on an armchair.

Nathaniel Flowerdew suddenly glanced up from his laptop, looking surprised to see Kinch.

'I was, er, just wondering what the plan was today. And would you like some tea or breakfast or something?'

'Yes, tea would be good.' Flowerdew held out his mug, which was still full from Kinch's last visit.

'Are we staying here or moving on?'

'We are waiting.'

'Right.'

Kinch returned with a mug of tea and hovered, wondering where to put it. Flowerdew took it from him with one hand, continuing to type with the other.

'What shall I do with the kids?' asked Kinch. 'They could do with some food, I guess.'

'Fine, fine,' said Flowerdew.

'Will they be coming with us when we do leave?'

'If they're still conscious.'

Kinch turned and left the room, shutting the door behind him. He went over to the dining room and turned the key. As he opened the door, the smell made him recoil. Covering his mouth, he peered in. He saw Jack and Itch sitting together, the rucksack between them and the sodden tablecloth stuffed into a wastepaper basket.

'Stone me,' said Kinch. 'Why didn't you call me? You could have done that in the bog, not here. Bring it out.'

He held the door open, and Itch and Jack slowly got to their feet. Itch took the rucksack and Jack the wastepaper basket and they filed out into the kitchen, where Kinch then shoved the soiled table-cloth into the bin. He offered them both tea, which neither of them usually drank but they took anyway. Kinch's breakfast appeared to be a tube of BBQ Pringles, which he did not share, though he tossed a packet of cheese biscuits at them. They were stale, but they both ate a few.

Flowerdew called out from the lounge and, checking again that all doors, windows and shutters were locked, Kinch left the kitchen.

'Is this room small enough?' whispered Jack. 'It's pretty airless. If we could get them both in here . . .'

'And then stab the canister with a fork? I don't know, Jack – it still looks too big a space for one can of xenon to be effective. And there are draughts from doors and windows. I think xenon is much denser than air, so it'll stay low. The kitchen won't work.'

'How about the car, then?' suggested Jack, and she could tell from the look on Itch's face that she might be on to something.

'Yes, of course, the car! It's big, but it's the smallest space we all sit in, assuming we're not staying here. And the air con will circulate the gas around it . . . Brilliant work, Jack!'

Easily observed against her pallid skin, Jack flushed slightly. 'So now all we have to do is open the can and get out of the car without inhaling any ourselves,' she said.

'Yes, that's pretty much it,' said Itch.

'We move now,' said Flowerdew, gathering his papers together. 'And assuming the radiation hasn't finished off those meddling Loftes, we'll have to take them too. But I want them tied up and gagged; they're bound to try something stupid. OK?'

Kinch nodded. 'Sure. Where are we going?'

'The deal's come good, Kinch, the deal's come good! It wasn't supposed to happen till tonight, but everyone suddenly seems in a frightful rush. We meet Comrade Osiegbe at an address in Paddington at one p.m. He and his people have a lab there to confirm my tests. And you know the sweetest thing, Kinch? You know the sweetest thing?

They give us the money, and we give them the rocks *and* the kids. They've agreed to take them as part of the deal. Makes it all so much . . . neater, don't you think?'

'What will they do with them?'

'Well now, let's just say you'd be surprised how much you can sell a child for these days. And leave it at that.'

24

Flowerdew had insisted that Kinch dump the Range Rover and find another car. They needed to use the motorways, but everyone would be looking out for the Range Rover, so a suitable alternative needed to be pressed into action. Kinch trawled round the village and finally chose a silver graphite Lexus RX 450H, which had proved the easiest to spring. It also had the advantage of a silent hybrid engine, meaning it was able to leave the quietest road in the quietest village, disturbing no one at all.

Flowerdew sat in the front with the bag and his briefcase at his feet. Jack and Itch sat in the back, hands tied in front of them with black masking tape. Kinch had advised against gags, given that they'd been sick, and Flowerdew had reluctantly agreed. The rucksack, with its canister of xenon anaesthetic just under the top flap, lay at Itch's feet.

It was a hot day and the air conditioning was already working hard. As they pulled onto the M5, Itch was counting the number of air vents and noting where they were pointing. He could see six at the front, and he and Jack had two pointing straight at them. The satnav was estimating three hours, and 175 miles to Paddington, which suddenly didn't seem like very long or very far. Even if Itch could work out how to empty the xenon into the car, they couldn't do it when they were driving along at ninety-eight mph.

The M5 became the M4, and the miles to their Paddington rendezvous counted down. Flowerdew seemed in an exultant mood, conducting furiously to the classical music on the radio. Under cover of the extraordinary volume of sound put out by the car's sound system, Jack and Itch were able to conduct brief, unnoticed conversations.

'We've only got about ninety minutes left, Itch! Come on — last chance!'

'I know! Still thinking.'

Thirty minutes later: 'Him being in such a good mood means trouble, doesn't it?'

'Reckon so.' And then, forty miles out from the capital, 'How are you feeling?'

'Terrible. Rubbish. Like I'm going to be . . . sick . . . again.' They looked at each other and, very slowly, smiled. A proper ear-to-ear smile. They had both thought of the same thing at the same time, and turned away, looking out of the window in case Kinch or Flowerdew glanced in the mirror.

As the end of the motorway approached, the traffic slowed and Flowerdew's mood changed. He became tense, and switched off the radio. The final few miles of motorway passed in silence. As they joined the steamy queues of West London, the satnav said four miles to destination. The tailbacks around the Hammersmith roundabout moved inch by inch towards one set of traffic lights and then another. As the Lexus slowed again, Jack started groaning.

'Shut up,' said Flowerdew. 'We're nearly there. Don't start now.'

Itch leaned forward, teeth gritted. 'It's called radiation poisoning,' he snapped. 'It's not something you can stop and start. You get dizzy, nauseous, then you're sick. Next is hair loss, fever and maybe blood in your vomit. You're the brilliant scientist. What would you suggest? I don't know, but from where I'm sitting, if she's sick like yesterday, it's going all over your head, Flowerdew. Whoever you're meeting to flog my rocks to, I'm sure they'll love you with puke in your hair.'

Flowerdew spun round and glared at them. Anger flashed in his eyes, but he knew Itch was right.

'Damn! All right. Pull in, Kinch – there's a place just there . . . Let's get this over and done with.'

They pulled off the road, leaving the slow-moving traffic to wend its way towards Shepherds Bush. They were in a small cul-de-sac with parking for a dozen cars, and Kinch pulled into the first space he came to. Flowerdew produced a pocket knife and, reaching behind, roughly cut the tape that bound Itch and Jack's hands. He nicked the skin on Itch's left wrist with the point of the blade. 'Oops,' he sneered.

Itch ignored the cut, undid his seatbelt and leaned over to undo Jack's.

'Make it quick. We have an appointment in Paddington. All of us. So stay where we can see you,' said Flowerdew, reaching for his phone. Itch opened his door and jumped out. He dropped his rucksack on the road and felt for the xenon canister. For a moment he thought he'd lost it, but his hand closed around the warm metal casing under the flap of the rucksack. He quickly went round to help Jack out of the other side of the car. As she sat on the pavement, her head between her knees, Itch went back to open the door on the other side of the car and looked at the hinge. It was surprisingly small: a flat black metal connector which ran from the door to the body of the Lexus. The canister would sit happily on top. He glanced up. Kinch was watching Jack, Jack was retching, and Flowerdew was on the phone. Now was the moment.

He balanced the canister on the hinge and, with his heart thundering and his head pounding, he slammed the Lexus door shut with every ounce of strength he had. There was a sharp metallic screech, and then a crunch as the heavy-duty door made contact with the xenon. It bounced open again. The canister was bent, twisted and dented – but not punctured. The xenon was still inside.

Flowerdew and Kinch spun round. 'What the—?'

'Sorry!' called Itch. 'Got the seatbelt stuck in the door!' He held up the metal buckle and put on a 'silly me' face. They appeared to accept this and turned back. Itch adjusted the canister slightly so that the weakest-looking part of the casing would take the full force of the steel door. He slammed it again. He felt the door close a little further, but it still didn't shut. As he opened it once more, the canister fell onto the car floor and rolled slowly under Kinch's seat. Itch watched it as the mangled metal rotated twice and then stopped. At its base, where the unreadable words were, was a small but clearly defined gash. Shutting the door quickly – it clicked this time – Itch ran round the front of the car and knelt in front of Jack.

'I think I did it! I slammed the door on it and I think it's been punctured, but I can't be sure . . . And I used all of it, in case you were wondering.'

Jack snorted and coughed. 'Was there gas coming

out when you shut the door?' she asked from between her knees.

'It's colourless and odourless, Jack. I was hoping for a hiss or something, but I couldn't hear anything. We'll find out sooner or later.'

'How long does it take to work?'

'Don't know, but keep this up anyway. If it's going to work it'll be in the next few minutes.'

'How many is a few?'

Itch put his hand on Jack's shoulder and looked up at Flowerdew, who was still jabbering into his phone. Catching Itch's eye, he was waving them back into the car when Jack really was sick. Flowerdew watched and then resumed his conversation. Itch offered her the bottle of water he'd been given at breakfast, and some tissues, then moved round to sit next to her on the kerb. She took both and leaned against him, her eyes closed. Itch looked at Kinch and Flowerdew and sat up, nudging Jack. He was laughing.

'It's worked! Jack, look, they're out of it! Ha!'

He helped Jack to her feet, and they both stood staring at the occupants of the car. The driver and passenger looked as if they had just parked up for a nap. Kinch's head was wedged up against the driver's side window, his mouth wide open. Flowerdew had slumped back, his head lolling uncomfortably towards Kinch. The xenon had emptied itself into the car and, distributed by the powerful air-con system, had been inhaled by Kinch and Flowerdew in sufficient quantities to render them unconscious in two minutes. The cousins stood transfixed by what they had done.

For a few seconds they took it in turns to stand in front of the car and call Flowerdew every bad word they had ever heard, but feeling they might be attracting attention, Jack pulled at Itch's shirt.

'Come on – get the rocks. We don't know how long they'll stay like that and we have to open the door to get the box. Let's go.'

Itch held her back. 'No, wait a bit. Let the xenon do its work. They'll be going deeper, I think. In a few minutes we could operate on them and they wouldn't wake up.'

'Now that is tempting,' said Jack as they stood shakily and counted out about two minutes.

'OK, let's get the rocks,' said Itch, not able to wait any longer. 'This needs to be quick. Hold your breath.' He opened the front passenger door and pulled out the lead-lined toolbox, still in the canvas bag, out from under Flowerdew's feet. Next to it, he spotted the briefcase and took that too. Then he leaned across and removed the key from the ignition, shut the door, and then locked the car. Itch threw the key into a nearby bush.

'Sweet,' said Jack. 'Now can we go? Give me the rucksack.'

Itch chucked it to her and she shouldered it.

He picked up the canvas bag and its familiar weight cut into his hands. 'Can you take this too?' he asked, handing Flowerdew's briefcase over.

'That's stealing, Itchingham Lofte.'

'We'll give it back,' he said, grinning. 'Let's go.'

As quickly as they could, they left the car with its sleeping occupants behind and headed in the direction of the last tube station they had passed.

Hammersmith underground was five minutes away; they ran there in two. Flying past the shoppers and tourists, they enjoyed the anonymity – no one looked twice at two teenagers with a rucksack and a couple of bags, even if they were in a hurry.

To reach the tube platforms, the cousins ran into a large shopping centre. It offered many fast food restaurants and Jack slowed and then stopped, pulling on Itch's arm.

'Itch,' she panted. 'Toilet. Now.'

He didn't argue and they went inside the brightly lit burger bar. The neon lights made them both feel even more exhausted and pale, but they tucked themselves into a booth, with a table between them. As soon as their bags were safely stowed Jack excused herself and headed for the toilet.

Itch opened Flowerdew's briefcase and then shut it immediately. Making sure that no one was watching, he took another look. A laptop, its light still on, Flowerdew's black cap, some papers and a lot of money. He removed the cap, putting it on straight away, and the laptop, which he laid on the table. The shopping centre offered free Wi-Fi, and Itch spent a few minutes Googling for train times, making some scribbled notes on a paper napkin. He stopped as Jack appeared, shoving the napkin in his pocket. She walked slowly and unsteadily to the table. He didn't need to ask and she didn't need to say.

Itch took a ten-pound note out of the briefcase and went to get some water and two large portions of chips. He didn't think they'd feel like eating, but in minutes every chip had disappeared.

As Jack drank her water, some of the colour came back to her cheeks, but she had started to shake again. 'I need to stop, Itch. I'm where Chloe was last night – I need to stop . . .'

Itch didn't respond, and she added, 'I'm tired.'

Itch didn't need to be a doctor to tell that Jack's self-diagnosis was correct. She had had enough and she needed help.

'OK, Jack,' he said, 'we'll get you help, but I need your help one last time. I have a train to catch and I might not make it without you. Last time. Promise.'

Jack's eyes were filling with tears. 'Of course – I'll try. I'm just sorry to let you down.' She reached for a napkin and dabbed at her cheeks. 'Remind me why this isn't the end, though? Haven't we done what we needed to?'

Itch dug into his pocket and pulled out Cake's note. He read out loud: '*You need to get rid of them. These are dangerous. Don't trust anyone.*' He handed it to Jack, as if for verification, but she pushed it away.

'And what if he's wrong? What if you actually *can* trust someone? And what if it's the police you can trust? We could call them now and they would come and get us. Then we'd be safe – and so would the rocks.'

'I wish that was true, Jack, I really do. But look what's happened. Cake is dead. We're sick, Chloe's sick. Flowerdew and Kinch were happy to see us poisoned and probably dead. Those people back at the mining school – whoever they were – had guns. That's five people in twenty-four hours who would kill for these.' Itch tapped the canvas bag. 'What's more, they are still out there. And others too who haven't found us yet. These rocks are a curse, Jack. Look here.' He looked at Cake's note again. '*I wish I had never seen them. You need to get rid of them.* That's what he wrote.'

'But Dr Alexander told us how brilliant they were and how much good they could do. In the right hands,' Jack pointed out.

'Does it feel like that to you? He also said the Earth had provided us with a gift! Ha! Some gift.'

Itch slurped on the remains of his water. 'Flowerdew said wars have been fought over less, that even with the best intentions it'll always be the destructive power of these rocks that wins the day.'

'He said that?'

'In the car, on the phone. Scary stuff. What's that old sixties song your dad sings? *Return to Sender*? Well, I reckon that's about right.'

'What do you mean?'

'Not sure yet. But I made the wrong call over the arsenic, Jack. I put everyone in our class in danger. I'm not going to make the wrong choice this time.'

'You can't compare—' started Jack.

'I can. I was protecting myself, that's all. I keep wondering what would have happened if they had got worse. I could have done something – just rung the hospital, even – but I didn't.' Itch looked at his cousin. 'I'm going to put that right. Return to sender.'

'But all that stuff about an exciting new energy source . . .' Jack was struggling to keep much force in her argument.

'Jack, we can't look after what we've got, never mind bringing this stuff along. It's too much, it's too powerful. Do you remember when we found Cake by the beach huts?'

Jack nodded. 'That seems such a long time ago.'

'Yeah, well, he said something about how

everything would change – everyone would want this stuff and we shouldn't tell anyone. Not friends, not parents, not governments. I think he was right. It's too late to keep it a secret, but it's not too late to stop everything changing.'

As Itch was speaking, Jack glanced through the burger bar's large front window. Four policemen had just run into the shopping centre. 'It's make-your-mind-up time,' she said.

'Already made it,' said Itch.

A passing policeman on his way to Hammersmith police station noticed two sleeping men in a Lexus that had been reported stolen. Back-up arrived quickly; they had, after all, only two hundred metres to travel. Knocking on the driver's window produced no reaction, and when the passenger proved impossible to rouse too, a passing ambulance was flagged down. One officer broke the driver's window, reached inside and opened the door. Both occupants stirred as they were handcuffed, the driver then becoming abusive and head-butting an officer. CS gas was sprayed in his face. A quick examination of the car revealed the battered and pierced canister under the driver's seat, and the senior policeman reached for his radio. When an old lady came out of a nearby flat and mentioned seeing two young men with bags and a rucksack running towards the station, the officer spoke quickly to his controller and they all headed for the underground.

Two miles away, near Paddington, the figures of Christophe Revere and Jan Van Den Hauwe appeared on the conference screen at Greencorps' London office. Standing in a rough semicircle, watching, were Roshanna Wing, Bud Collins and Volker Berghahn, now with his sunglasses off, revealing livid red blisters around his eyes. His short brown hair was singed even shorter, with little lighter burned hairs littering his shoulders like dandruff. The three of them stood together at one end of the room, and they had been joined by a small number of suited security officers, whose job it was to protect the interests of Greencorps in the UK. They looked like security men the world over: alert, poised, suspicious. Each of them – Wing counted eight – had cropped hair and an earpiece. They looked suspiciously at the new arrivals, but Van Den Hauwe made the pecking order very clear:

'This is Roshanna Wing; she reports directly to Mr Revere and me. She takes instructions from us and gives them to you. I'm sure you all understand that. She will tell you more about what – and who – we are trying to locate. Some context from me, and then I'll leave it to Roshanna. Time is not on our side.' The Dutchman paused, looking uncertain for a moment, then continued. 'It is possible the whole of our industry is threatened by these rocks. Therefore Greencorps is threatened – your jobs are threatened. A former colleague has already been taken into custody, we understand. We won't be seeing him for a while. Find the rocks, gentlemen. Failing that, make sure the agents of the British government don't get hold of them.' He smiled. 'It's as easy as that. Best of luck.' The screen went blank.

Roshanna Wing turned to address the men, who were now looking at her. 'In the last few minutes we've picked up reports indicating that former Greencorps chemist Dr Nathaniel Flowerdew has been picked up by the police in Hammersmith. It sounds as if he was drugged with an anaesthetic and the two kids ran off with the rocks towards Hammersmith tube station. Let us assume they are heading for one of the mainline stations or possibly Heathrow. We need at least one agent in every station. We are looking for a needle in a haystack, but two tall teenagers carrying a rucksack and a large canvas bag between them is at least something to go on. It is likely that there will be others looking for them. We think Flowerdew was in London to trade – almost certainly with one of the Nigerian outfits you have faced before. They will want these rocks very, very badly, and will stop at nothing to get them. However, as you heard from

Mr Van Den Hauwe, even this is preferable to the British police or MI6 getting them. Use force only as a last resort – usual Greencorps protocol applies. Bud Collins here will tell you where you are going. Reports to me, please. Now, go.'

25

Itch and Jack watched as the four policemen ran into the shopping centre, causing heads to turn everywhere. The sight of Met officers racing towards a tube station entrance caused instant alarm, and when six more arrived a few moments later, many shoppers decided to leave.

'Come on,' said Itch, and they joined the exodus. Itch headed straight for the taxi rank. 'I was going to use the tube but that's not going to work now,' he said.

'Where are we going?'

'To spend some of Flowerdew's money on a taxi.'

There was a small line of black cabs and no queue. The first one was driven by a woman, who smiled as she saw the two teenagers struggling with their bags and jumped out to help.

'All right, loves? Where to with this lot, then?' She was a large woman in her mid-fifties, dressed in a tracksuit with FULHAM FC on the front.

'It's OK,' said Itch, but she insisted.

'I'll just put these here, shall I?' She indicated the front of the car next to her, but Itch shook his head.

'No!' It came out louder than he had intended. 'No – in with us, please.'

'OK, suit yourself.' And she hoisted the canvas bag into the back of the cab. Jack and Itch climbed in with the rucksack and briefcase.

'Victoria Station, please,' said Itch.

'Right you are, loves. I must say—'

But Itch cut her off by switching off the intercom and pulling the glass divide across. She looked at them both in the mirror, shrugged and pulled out into the London traffic.

Itch sat on the folding seat behind the driver, facing Jack. He leaned towards his cousin and spoke very quietly.

'This is your last stop, Jack. You need a doctor and I need to disappear. With them.' He pointed to the canvas bag. 'And even if you were OK, I'd have to do this last bit alone.'

Jack looked puzzled.

Itch continued, trying to sound more certain than he was feeling. 'Listen, I'm going to try and get rid of them. I think I know of somewhere that might . . . well, take them in. But since there are so many people who want to get hold of them – pretty nasty people too – then it's better if I'm the only

324

person who knows where they'll be.' He gulped. He'd thought his plan through, but saying it out loud made it sound much more scary. He hoped Jack hadn't noticed the new tension in his voice.

She coughed and wiped her forehead with her sleeve. 'I don't know what to say, Itch,' she murmured. 'I know I'm sick. I do need help, but you can't do that on your own! Maybe I can come some of the way—'

Itch cut in. 'No. Really, no. You can't, Jack. I started this whole thing and I have to finish it without anyone else.' Realizing he might be sounding ungrateful, hurtful even, he carried on swiftly, 'It's just that' – he closed his eyes to make sure he got this next bit right – 'it's just that they won't stop, Jack. These people with guns will still want the rocks and will still have guns when I'm done. If you don't know where I've gone, you'll be in less danger. I think. That's how it seems to me anyway.'

Guns, Itch thought with a shiver. How could his hobby have come to this? Men with guns were chasing them, and he had no doubt they would use them. Everything depended on him getting the next few hours right; he knew his plan was a logical one, but he doubted if he had the guts or the skill to make it work. Had he ever done anything brave in his entire life? He didn't think so.

After a pause, Jack nodded her understanding.

'OK. I won't argue any more. What happens when we get to Victoria?'

'I disappear. You can't see me buy a ticket or anything.'

'What do I do?'

Itch thought. 'You go to a newsagent's and wait twenty minutes – if you can – and then find a phone and call 999. Hopefully, if the timetable I've checked is correct, I'll be gone.'

They both looked out of the window as they passed Buckingham Palace. The royal flag was flying – the Queen was in. 'Maybe we should just leave them with her,' said Jack. 'She'll have some-where to put them.' They both laughed.

'I'm sorry, Jack, for all this. I never knew . . . If I'd known . . .'

Jack put her hand on his knee to silence him. 'Of course you didn't. Of course you didn't. I just hope we'll all be OK. Hope that Chloe's OK. You've decided what you have to do, and maybe you're right.' She wiped more tears away. 'You're the bravest person I know, Itch. I'm proud to be a Lofte.'

Itch put his hand briefly on hers and stared at the teeming London traffic, his own eyes swimming with tears.

The congestion around Victoria delayed them another fifteen minutes, and Itch started to wonder how much radiation was leaking out of the container. He hoped he wasn't infecting the cab driver, but he had done what he could, and now had no choice but to see this through.

Itch and Jack sat in silence. It was the silence of two friends who, though they had already been through a lot, were more scared of what the next few hours might bring than either of them wanted to admit. Itch was worried for his cousin and his sister, and whether he could dispose of the rocks on his own. Jack was worried that she was going to die.

They finally pulled in beside the station and, having paid the fare with a twenty-pound note – receiving another suspicious look from the cabbie in the process – Itch and Jack stood on the kerb looking at each other.

'Do we say goodbye now, then?' asked Jack.

'No, let's go inside,' said Itch. 'We need to rearrange the bags a bit.'

Jack hoisted the rucksack onto her shoulders one more time, while Itch picked up the canvas bag. He had to switch hands constantly as he now had blisters on most of his fingers from the bag's stretched fabric handles. Flowerdew's case was lightweight in comparison and swung from Itch's other hand.

They walked swiftly through the corridor of shops and coffee outlets to the high glassed ceiling of the main concourse. Tourists milled around looking lost, jostled by Londoners hurrying to their trains. The smell of pastries and coffee mixed with the unmissable scent of steamy, sweaty travellers. Itch and Jack stopped again, causing a stream of people to swerve around them, tutting and shaking their heads in annoyance. Oblivious to everything else, the two cousins stood there, awkwardly aware that the time for farewells was now.

'You said you wanted to rearrange the bags.'

'Oh yes,' said Itch, looking for the nearest toilets. 'Give me the rucksack, and I'll come and find you in W H Smith's. By the magazines.'

Jack slipped the rucksack off her shoulder and passed it to him. He headed for the toilets, balancing the three bags. Jack watched him all the way to the stairs with the MEN sign above them, then wandered over to the news-stand. It felt strange to have nothing to carry, her shoulders light and relaxed. Nevertheless she walked with her hands pushed deep into her pockets and her head down, convinced that everyone would be looking at the whiteness of her scalp where her hair had fallen out. In truth this had still only happened in the two small areas around her ears but it felt to her as though she were almost bald.

She walked past the jumbo-sized chocolate bars and sweet multi-packs and found the magazines just past the paperback books. She stood staring at her favourite reads: X-FACTOR FASHION TIPS!, FREE LIP GLOSS INSIDE!, SECRETS BOYS KEEP! ran the gaudy headlines – and realized she couldn't find an ounce of interest in any of them. She was weary beyond belief and had started to shake again, but she was determined to stay the course until Itch had made his escape.

She had decided to pick up a *Just 17*, merely to blend in with all the other customers, when she caught a familiar smell. It took her a few seconds to place it, but then, as it came to her, her insides lurched.

It was burned hair.

It was only faint, but the memory of the phosphorus explosion in the lab was fresh in her mind and her nostrils. Someone with burned hair was standing close by.

Frozen to the spot, she forced herself to turn round slowly. Immediately behind her was a long queue of customers that snaked towards the tills. This shielded her from the newspaper browsers: amongst them she spotted a tall, broad man wearing sunglasses, his head turning first one way, then the other. It was, she was sure, the man from the mining school who had kicked Jacob Alexander in the stomach. The man who had then walked into the burning phosphorus.

Jack drew a sharp breath and held it. The line of customers was getting shorter, and she had to leave before her cover was gone completely. As the man began another sweep, she walked as casually as she could along her side of the queue, past the tills and out onto the station concourse. As she left, she broke into a sprint. She hadn't meant to — it felt like a spontaneous, final, desperate race for survival. She ran straight through a snaking line of foreign students and hesitated only a fraction of a second before bursting into the men's toilets.

It was busy, but no one paid her any attention — her height and short hair meant that she passed a casual inspection — and she headed for the cubicles. This was no time for embarrassment, and she started knocking on the locked doors. There were four rows of six, and as she knocked and called, 'Itch! It's me!' she received a number of cross and angry replies. The end cubicle opened slightly and Itch's head, still wearing Flowerdew's cap, looked out.

'Jack! What's up?' he said, standing with the cubicle door partly open. She could see that he was in the middle of repacking the rucksack: many of his elements were spread out on the floor.

'One of the men from the mining school! The one with the burning hair! He's here!'

'Did he see you?' Itch looked alarmed.

'Don't think so, but he could come in here any minute!'

Heads were now starting to turn and Jack went into the cubicle next to Itch's, bolting it shut. She sat down on the toilet seat as she heard Itch re-bolt his door.

'I've got the rocks into the rucksack,' he said through the graffiti-covered partition. 'It's tight, but they're in. Had to put almost all of my collection into the canvas bag. Guess you'll have to take it, if that's OK. I'll keep Flowerdew's briefcase for now, but here's some of his cash in case you need it.' He slid some twenty-pound notes under the partition. 'And for many, many reasons,' he added, 'let's hope no one is watching this!'

The humour was lost on Jack. 'Can't think I'll need money, but OK.' She wasn't arguing with anything now – she just wanted it all to be over. She'd help Itch escape, then crawl into a corner and wait as long as she could before calling for help.

The canvas bag was pushed under the partition; it now contained an assortment of powders, pieces of rock and corked tubes where the radiation box had been. Jack wanted to say she'd look after his element collection but didn't think she was in a position to promise anything. She said nothing, picked up the bag and sat with it on her lap.

'You all right?' said Itch.

'Never better,' she said. 'What do we do now?'

'Er, we say goodbye, I suppose.'

Itch had the re-packed and straining rucksack on his back and the briefcase in his hand. He leaned against the partition, with Jack on the other side.

'I'll go and get a ticket – that means I'll be

turning right. You go left and hide out somewhere as long as you can. But call the ambulance as soon as you need to. I'll be fine.'

'OK.'

'You wear the cap.'

'OK.'

Flowerdew's cap came through from Itch's side and Jack put it on. There was a silence and they both realized there was nothing else to say.

'Let's go,' said Itch, and they both emerged slowly from their cubicles, peering round the doors, checking for the man with burned hair. The toilets were busy, but there was no sign of him. They headed for the exit, Itch in the lead. They both pulled up as it opened and three men came hurrying in, but the burned-hair man wasn't one of them. They looked at each other and Itch nodded slightly. Jack leaned forward and kissed him lightly on the cheek. Then she opened the door, turned left and disappeared.

Itch waited ten seconds and followed her out, turning right. The large ticket office was a hundred metres away, with the self-service machines just in front. He headed for the nearest shop and worked his way towards the machines by pretending to be a customer at each stall or sandwich bar on the way. From behind a counter selling Cornish pasties, he searched the faces of the hundreds of passengers walking in every direction. There were more police-

men than usual, he was sure, including four standing by the entrance to the tube. However, seeing no
sign of Jack or burned-hair man, Itch walked the
final twenty metres to the first ticket machine,
where he paid cash for a ticket to Brighton.

26

Itch stood behind a steel pillar near Platform 10, his eyes everywhere. He could hear police sirens, but nothing was happening near him. He had five minutes till his train left. It had pulled in a few moments ago, but he had not wanted to sit on it any longer than necessary. He was waiting for a group to board the train together so that he could mingle unnoticed. None had come. He thought he had checked every single passenger who had got on the train: burned-hair man wasn't among them.

'Can't be seen. Can't be noticed. Can't be seen. Can't be noticed,' he repeated to himself over and over. If his plan had any chance of succeeding, he had to ensure that no one saw him board this train – that no one even knew in which direction he was heading. Or at least that no one *remembered* him. He had to make the rocks disappear without anyone seeing him. He had never minded being tall – over the years it had put a few bullies off – but he was suddenly aware that he wasn't just a teenager with a rucksack, but a very *tall* teenager with a rucksack. Instinctively he hunched over a little and shrank back further behind the pillar.

As the time for the Brighton train's departure came closer, more passengers got on. A small party of middle-aged women had gathered at the turnstile, apparently waiting for another friend to join them before they boarded. Itch had started to walk towards them when he realized that the radiation sickness was back. He froze halfway between the pillar and the platform, knowing that, whatever happened, he mustn't be sick in full view of all these people. It would guarantee that his plan failed.

'*Can't be seen, can't be noticed.*'

He looked around, eyes wide, as he tried to control what was happening to his body. He knew he had only a few moments to make himself discreet but all the toilets were too far away now. The photo booth was no good – the curtain was too short; the flower stalls and coffee vendors wouldn't do – they were busy and full of customers. But he was out of time. Walking swiftly towards the other platforms, he noticed a stairwell behind a pasty stall. The narrow steps led to some bars and cafés, but the stairwell was quiet; most customers used the main, grander stairs. With no time left and all the bodily control he could muster, he ran into the small space and crouched down, pretending to tie his lace. With his rucksack still on his back and the case in his hand, he braced himself against the wall.

Afterwards, he was wet with perspiration, shaking and dizzy, but the sickness was not quite as bad as it had been at the empty cottage. He reversed out of the stairwell and straightened up, nearly fainting. Steadying himself against the wall until his head and vision had cleared, he then set off again, a little shakily, for Platform 10.

'*Can't be seen, can't be noticed.*'

In the end there were no last-minute passengers, so he boarded on his own and stood for a moment by the recently slammed doors. Would he be more or less conspicuous if he sat on his own? Should he sit in the busiest compartment or the quietest? Itch didn't know, couldn't work it out, so he sat in the first seats he came to. He was in the rear carriage, in a double seat with a table in front of him. Only three other passengers could be seen: two men and a younger woman. They paid Itch no notice, seemingly intent on consuming as many cans of beer as they could in the one hour that the journey made available to them.

Itch placed the briefcase on the table and the rucksack on the seat next to him. He hooked one arm through a strap as a precaution, but soon realized that, as he was at the end of the train, there would be no one walking past him at all.

If he was lucky, he might just be left on his own.

He unhooked his arm and opened Flowerdew's briefcase to remove the laptop. He hadn't had time to look at all the loose papers in there before, but it was soon clear it was a chemical analysis of the rocks. Itch found the last page. Flowerdew had come up with the same conclusion as Dr Alexander, though he expressed it differently. Itch read the last few sentences:

> *It is my opinion that element 126 places previously unheard-of power in the hands of those who control it. It is beyond price. Whoever has it will dominate the energy market for the foreseeable future.*

Although Itch had heard all this before, it still took his breath away to see it written down, spelled out in black and white. He looked at his old rucksack. It was blue and black nylon with white plastic edging, and stained by biro leaks in the front pocket. It had LOFTE written in black marker in his mother's handwriting on the flap. He couldn't remember how long he'd had it – it might even have belonged to his brother first – and all things considered, Itch thought, it was unlikely to be handed on to his sister. It seemed utterly preposterous that its contents would 'place unheard-of power' in the hands of whoever owned it. Before last week his rucksack had usually contained only school books, pens and cheese sandwiches.

Thinking of his sister and brother, and seeing his mother's handwriting made Itch feel suddenly, desperately, unbearably lonely. Sad too – but mainly he had an unshakeable sense that although he had to do this on his own, he would have given anything to have had company. He wondered what Chloe would have said; what Gabriel would have done. He thought of Jack and hoped she had found help by now. He imagined his father might have offered up a prayer for their safety, so Itch tried one himself.

He wondered if he could use Flowerdew's laptop to send an email. The signal was OK – the laptop screen indicated an erratic but regular connection – but were they traceable like a phone call? He wanted to email as much of the contents of Flowerdew's laptop to someone . . . Mr Watkins, maybe? He could then add a personal message to his family. He set about copying and pasting everything he could find from documents, emails and contacts. Not all of it was in English, but he was sure it would all be of interest to the police, the Cornwall Academy, and anyone else who needed to know about the past of Dr Nathaniel Flowerdew.

There were hundreds of photos. He skimmed images of luxurious rooms, London streets and views of the London Eye; buildings and landmarks presumably in Nigeria; oil installations and rigs from all angles; some photos of Flowerdew's house in Cornwall, and many of his lab.

He came across a file marked VT DEVIL LOL and clicked on it. It opened with twenty-five pages of reports and analysis of a disaster off the coast of Nigeria. It was a Greencorps document that detailed the extent of the pollution caused by a rig blow-out two years ago. Following the report were email exchanges, in which Flowerdew was clearly furious at being named in the report as the main culprit. The 'chief science executive' had concluded that it was Flowerdew's advice to push the oil well deeper that was the main factor in causing the catastrophe. Photos of oil-covered beaches, dead wildlife and grief-stricken families came next. A brief TV news clip showed harrowing scenes of dead and injured oil workers being brought ashore.

The Brighton express train rattled on through the stations of Surrey as Itch was lost in a world of sadness from Africa. The final exchanges referred to the 'fall guy who'll take the rap' – presumably, thought Itch, the woman called Shivvi he and Jack had looked up back at his house. Then there was Flowerdew's last comment, which he had added for his own amusement: *And so, the devil finally falls! Farewell!*

Itch closed the laptop and looked, unseeing, out of the window. They entered and then left a tunnel, but he barely noticed. He wanted to make sure that

Flowerdew went to prison for a long, long time. He wanted everyone to see the documents he had seen, but as he looked at the faltering 3G signal, he became increasingly worried that an email might be traced. If anyone worked out which train he had caught, his plan was in serious peril, and so was he. He wanted to send a note to his family saying he was OK – but not if it meant that those eight rocks of 126 ended up powering some madman's nuclear ambitions.

Reluctantly he closed the documents and contacts and deleted the email he had composed.

'*Can't be seen, can't be noticed*,' he muttered again.

He found a pen in the briefcase, and had started to draw a diagram he had found online, when one of the drinking party at the end of the carriage kicked at their table, causing many cans of drink to tip over. The beer poured onto the floor and over the trousers of a man called Kevin. Itch knew this from the laughter that came from the other two and their shouted comments of 'Kevin's wet himself!' and 'Look at baby Kevin, he needs his nappy changed!' Kevin, a tall red-haired guy in a checked shirt, punched his two friends in the face. The punches weren't hard but, in combination with the lager, proved very effective. The pair slumped to the floor, momentarily concussed. When they came to, both had bloody noses and started yelling. As Kevin shouted back and the girl kicked out a bulb, causing all the lights in the carriage to blow, Itch knew he had to act. If they, or one of the other passengers, pulled the emergency cord or attracted the guard, his plan was in trouble again.

'*Can't be seen, can't be noticed.*'

His instinct was to reach for his rucksack, but of course his collection was now with Jack in the canvas bag. Wherever she was. Wherever it was. If he tried to walk past them, through to the next carriage, he risked provoking Kevin and his drunken friends. He needed them out of here . . .

And then Itch gave a little smile.

His rucksack could help after all. He hadn't removed *quite* everything. He reached for the front pocket and undid the flap. Inside were three small tubes he had acquired at the same time as the xenon. When a store is closing down, they want to sell everything, quickly. Jeans, shoes, chemicals – same rules apply. They also make fewer checks on the buyers, so Itch's story about being a researcher was taken at face value. That is how Itchingham Lofte, aged fourteen, had come to own a selection of stink bombs. He now only had three left, one each of three different kinds.

These weren't the usual small phials of hydrogen sulphide that you find in joke shops. One was labelled WHO ME, another SBM, and the last, PARKIA SPECIOSA. All three caused a stench, but the first two were US government issue and particularly extreme.

'WHO ME' was the name given to a top-secret Second World War stench weapon. When used, it smelled of human waste but suffered from the weakness, so Itch had read, that the user of it ended up smelling as bad as the victim.

SBM stood for 'Standard Bathroom Malodour', and was a slightly more efficient version of WHO ME but smelled the same. Itch and his family had found this out the hard way.

The third tube — the one labelled PARKIA SPECIOSA — contained dried green pods. Their Latin name was rarely used; most people called them 'stinky beans'. Itch had been told that they were edible, but he wasn't interested in the culinary uses. When you stamped on the pods they released a powerful gassy smell. He had tried this back in Chloe's bedroom when he had first received the shipment. The stink was repulsive, and his sister had shouted at him for a long time. The train compartment was enclosed enough for them to work again, he concluded, and reached for the grey metal tube.

The drunken shouts were getting louder, and Kevin aimed another swipe at his friend, but only succeeding in smashing another light fitting. Itch had to move swiftly. He thought of the mainline map again: two tunnels had been marked, the first going under the M23 and the second labelled as the Balcombe tunnel. Hadn't they gone through one tunnel? Itch thought they had — in which case the second was due soon. He sat back and watched Kevin and friends push each other around. The girl had had enough and slumped onto her seat, but the men were still fighting when the carriage went black. With the lights out, they collapsed onto their seats. Itch grabbed the phial and poured all the beans into his hand. Feeling his way along the carriage, he counted eight seats and stopped. He bent down and placed the beans on the floor, then stamped hard. The dried pods crunched under his feet.

'*Parkia speciosa*,' he muttered, grinning, and felt his way back to his seat. The methane stink hit him before he got there, and he covered his nose and mouth with his hand. It was as if the carriage had been sprayed with rotting cabbage. Itch gagged, coughed and laughed all at the same time. As he sat down, the train left the tunnel and light flooded the carriage. Kevin and his friends had all started coughing and retching. Looking at each other in horror, they started blaming each other for causing the smell. Just when it looked as though they were about to start another fight, Kevin stormed out of the carriage, a handkerchief over his face, and the other two followed him.

When their arguing and fighting faded into the general, gentle clackety-rattle of the wheels on the track, Itch returned to planning what he needed to do on arrival in Brighton. As he sat alone in the carriage – and the smell of the stinky beans meant he was likely to remain that way – the enormity of what he was planning was beginning to dawn on him.

He was staking everything on a Watkins story. His geography teacher had told many tales about the schools he had taught in, but one in particular had stuck in Itch's mind. It was an astonishing account of bravery, determination and tragedy. He hoped it was true; he really *needed* it to be true. A teacher wouldn't exaggerate to make a good story, surely? If Watkins had made up any of his tale, then Itch would be wasting his time. He needed *every* fact to be *exactly* as Watkins had described it. He wished he could ring him up and ask him, but that was impossible. The plan would have to remain a secret; Itch was the only one who could ever know about it.

He consulted the online bus timetable. He was tempted to take a taxi – he still had plenty of Flowerdew's money to spend, after all – but the bus would, he thought, be more anonymous. They appeared to be regular and left from outside the station, so that clinched it. If the timetable was accurate, he could be at his final destination within the hour . . .

His nerves jangled as he wondered again if he was up to the task. His sickness would get worse all the time, so he had to move fast. It seemed to come on in waves, with the gaps between the nausea becoming shorter and the convulsions more violent. He closed his eyes and wondered how long he had before his strength left him completely.

The train was slowing down as it approached the outskirts of Brighton, and he closed the laptop and considered its weight. Did he need it any more? He knew what he had to do and where he had to do it – the task would require all his strength, and Flowerdew's briefcase would only be in the way. He would have loved to hand the computer, with all its incriminating evidence, to a prosecuting lawyer, but that wasn't about to happen. So if he didn't need it but had to make sure that it didn't fall into the wrong hands, he had only one option.

He removed the money from the briefcase and shoved it in his back pocket. He knew he was alone in the carriage, but with one final check anyway, he walked to the train window. He pulled it down as far as he could, and leaned out. They were still travelling at what Itch guessed was around forty mph, processing through the neat gardens and allotments that often backed onto rail tracks. He couldn't see anyone watching the train – and no one was leaning out of it, either. Picking up the laptop with both hands, he held it out of the window. He hesitated, knowing that throwing things out of trains was stupid, dangerous and, more to the point, likely to draw attention to yourself. But he needed the laptop destroyed, so he threw it out as far as he could, back along the tracks. It flipped, opened and spun in a low arc before hitting the concrete at the side of the cutting and bursting open. Itch just had time to see the battery fly out and the screen shatter before they turned a corner and it disappeared from view. The briefcase followed, landing amongst tall weeds, rubbish and shrubs at the side of the track.

He returned to his seat as the brakes squeaked and the train slowed and then stopped. This was it, then. He picked up his rucksack, feeling the rocks shift again, and hoisted it onto his back. He stood as straight as he could and waited by the door, feeling like a skydiver waiting for the green light before a jump into the unknown.

27

The 22 bus weaved its way around the roads of Brighton's town centre, and then headed east towards the open country of the South Downs. The afternoon sun felt hot through the filthy windows, and the air in the bus smelled of sweat and sun cream, sand on the floor showing where many of the previous passengers had spent the day.

Itch's insides were churning with a mixture of terror, nervous energy and radiation-induced nausea. He was sweating profusely, but so was everyone else on the bus. He had tucked himself away at the back and avoided eye contact.

Can't be seen, can't be noticed.

He watched the neat houses passing by, their gardens full of playing children and smoky barbecues. That last family meal together seemed a thousand miles away and a million years ago. Itch screwed his attention back to what he had to do. He had been looking on the left side of the road as that was where all the buildings had been, but now, up on the right – the coastal side – he spotted what he had been looking for. It was a large old Victorian school building, a converted workhouse, its heavy, austere, square exterior looking more ramshackle and dilapidated the closer you got.

Above the fence, a small sign read THE FITZHERBERT SCHOOL, with smaller writing underneath that Itch couldn't make out. Twenty or more years ago, a young geologist called Mr John Watkins had taught there. Itch picked up his rucksack and pressed the 'Stop' button.

He climbed down from the bus, crossed the road and stood looking at the Fitzherbert School. It was the sort of building that seemed designed to strike fear into the heart of any child who entered its doors. There was no decoration, no ornament – nothing to make any visitor or pupil smile. Even with happy modern teachers, whiteboards and computers, it would still feel like a prison.

Itch leaned on the fence and studied it. A drive led from the main road to the large double doors. It appeared to have three floors, with big bay windows on the ground and sash windows on the upper floors. A more recent but just as rundown series of buildings extended away from what Itch assumed was a side entrance. Shutters and curtains covered all but the top windows. There were no parked cars and no signs of life.

Itch looked around. The traffic continued to rush past – no one glanced at a boy with one foot on a school fence or noticed when he climbed up and over it.

He stayed close to the hedge which marked the school's boundary with the neighbouring scrubland – it seemed unwise to walk up the drive to the front door. As he walked around, he started to wonder if it actually still was a school. The paintwork on the windows had peeled and flaked away, exposing rotting wood and frames which looked as though they would cave in with the lightest gust of wind. Most of the bricks around the side and back were covered in a green fungus, and a darker mould spread from the ground up towards the windowsills. The back door was made of glass and rotten wood, but was held shut by a new brass padlock fixed across the frame. Next to it, a boxed window had one frame painted in whitewash and the other boarded up with wood. The school certainly seemed unloved and uncared for. Itch knew he needed to find the woodwork room – he just hoped there still was one.

He walked over to the box window, its ledge level with his chest. The thin piece of board had been nailed across it and he pushed hard with both hands. The frame and board gave way, falling in and thudding onto what sounded like bare floorboards. Itch peered inside.

It was a classroom – and clearly still in use. Posters of Roman soldiers and maps of ancient Rome filled one wall, while various punctuation guides decorated another. Six tables had been pushed together in the middle of the room, with the teacher's desk immediately in front of the window. Glancing over his shoulder and swallowing hard, Itch removed the rucksack and swung it through the gap and into the classroom. He lowered it onto what he assumed was the teacher's chair and then scrambled in after it.

Easing himself down, he glanced around. It looked like weekend classrooms always do – everything neatly put away, trays of pens and pencils laid out in readiness for Monday.

Itch had shouldered the rucksack and was making for the classroom door when, without warning, he vomited a stream of blood onto the floor. He fell to his knees, unable to stay upright, his whole body convulsed with the sickness. His head spinning with pain, his throat burning, he lay down on the floorboards and was sick again and again. Panic-stricken, his eyes wide in horror, he tried to get up, but his legs had stopped working. He edged his way over to one of the desks, lying up against it. He watched the bile and blood pool on the floor in front of him; then a great fog descended in front of his eyes.

★　★　★

It was the shaking that woke him up. His whole body was trembling. In the near-darkness of the room he couldn't see where he was lying, but he could feel wood, hard against his ear. He was lying on his rucksack, which had slipped from his shoulder, forcing his head, pulsing with pain, against the table leg. His mouth was lined with dried blood and sick, and he spat what he could onto the floor. Gradually he shuffled away from the table and stopped, his eyes slowly adjusting to the darkness of the classroom. He was lying on his back a metre or so from the door, twilight illuminating the area of the room nearest the pushed-in window. Itch wasn't sure how long he had been unconscious, but it must have been several hours. He reckoned he must have passed out and then slept. His clothes stuck to him and his hair plastered his face.

On the bus he'd wondered how long he had left. The obvious answer now was: *not long*. The gaps between his bouts of sickness were getting shorter – less than two hours between the Victoria Station one and here. How long before the next? Ninety minutes? An hour?

He had to get up, he had to press on, and he certainly didn't want to think about the impli-cations of vomiting blood. Rolling over, he forced himself onto all fours and then, using one of the desks, dragged himself to his feet. But his head immediately swam with giddiness, and he sat down on the desk. Slowly his head cleared, and, with no adverse reaction this time, he stood up and walked slowly towards the door. He tried the light switch but nothing happened. Moving out into a pitch-black corridor, he groped his way along a wall till he found another switch — still nothing.

'Great. Just great,' he said aloud, his voice harsh and rattly. The school had no power. He was going to have to perform his miracle blind.

Slowly he made out other doors — more class-rooms, each as dark as the next. Knowing it was pointless, he still tried each light switch, but without success. Returning to the corridor, he felt his way along the wall towards a looming dark shape which cast a long wide shadow back towards Itch. As he got closer he saw that it was a vast staircase, which disappeared into the gloom of the first floor, a threadbare carpet reaching as far as a small land-ing. Thin beams of light seeped through a small window above the front door as Itch followed the curve of the bottom stair.

Suddenly he jumped and called out in terror as a pale figure, arms outstretched, appeared beyond the staircase. It must have been at least two metres tall, and he suddenly realized that it was a statue. Feeling stupid, he edged closer. The Virgin Mary, he guessed, from the robes and the smile. Like the rest of the school, this Mary had seen better days. She had lost an ear, half of her nose and some fingers. The blue paint of her robes was chipped and flaking.

'You look how I feel,' he said to her.

Itch was in the entrance hall: from here, corridors led off east and west as well as north and south. He knew which room he needed, but there was no helpful sign pointing him in the right direction. He decided to head towards the rambling extension that snaked its way into the grounds.

He crossed the hall past the figure of Mary and into the dark corridor heading east. A handrail appeared, and gratefully he guided himself along. Eventually he came to where the main house finished and the extension began. Here the corridor zigzagged round to the left, and the rapidly disappearing light was countered by its larger windows. Itch saw a number of posters pinned to the wall – his heart started to pound again. He could just make out the words: RULES OF THE WOODWORK AND METALWORK ROOMS, the first one was headed. STRICTLY NO RUNNING! said another. SCIENCE LAB SAFETY FIRST, ran the headline on the last one. This was it, then.

'Done it!' said Itch. 'Now to find the well.'

The story of the Woodingdean Well was one of John Watkins's best. It was the kind of tale that pupils enjoyed because it always wasted half a lesson in the telling – maybe a whole lesson if questions were allowed. Itch had heard it within weeks of joining the Cornwall Academy, and then regularly since. He had recounted it to his father on one of his trips home and remembered the thrill of impressing him – not something that happened often.

According to the story, underneath the wood-work room was a well. The school had been built as a workhouse for the poor of the area: 'Like in *Oliver Twist*, where he asks for more,' Watkins had explained. To ensure a fresh water supply, a well had been dug, sometime in the late 1850s. Water was not found where the miners had expected, so they had just kept going. Teams of diggers had operated in shifts, twenty-four hours a day, every day, for four years before water was struck. The depth reached – Itch remembered Watkins holding up both hands for total silence and dramatic effect – was an astonishing 1,285 feet. This made it the deepest hand-dug well in the world, as deep as the Empire State Building was tall.

This fact always got the biggest gasp; even pupils who took no interest in anything sat up and took notice then. Itch remembered being amazed that it was possible to dig down so deep, and just for water! Not gold or silver, just water. He had drawn his own version of Watkins's whiteboard illustration on his book covers: a vertical drop for 400 feet, then a horizontal line of thirty feet at sea-level, and then another drop to 1,285 feet. His teachers had told him to stop drawing lightning bolts everywhere, but he had explained that they weren't lightning bolts – it was the Woodingdean Well.

In time Itch elaborated on his drawings. They now featured little earthworks and small figures working like ants down a pit. He had drawn the image so many times he could close his eyes and see it still. It was like a flash bulb that had burned its way onto his retina.

Four hundred feet; sea-level for thirty feet; a total of 1,285 feet. A lightning bolt into the earth.

Watkins also described the conditions the men had endured, and the many accidents. With a mixture of relish and horror, he related how the teams had dug by candlelight, often naked in the extreme heat and the confines of a four-foot circle. They bricked the well as they went, building a chimney into the earth from the top down. The earth was passed up in buckets by winchmen, who stood on small platforms cut into the side of the shaft. There were many tales of the well being haunted. Some said a nun's body was at the bottom; others said it was one of the winchmen who had fallen to his death.

Watkins would finish the story by recounting how, at a change of shift one Sunday evening in 1862, one of the miners had noticed the bottom of the well bulging upwards. It was only gradual but the Earth's crust had appeared to be buckling. The alarm sounded, and the four diggers began their mad scramble to the surface. As they raced upwards, they shouted to the winchmen they passed to leave their buckets and platforms and get out as quickly as possible. Soon the men were climbing ladders faster than they had ever climbed before, listening out for the roar of a surging wave of water breaking through the piston head at the foot of the well.

It took the men forty-five minutes to make their escape. When the crust did break, flooding the shaft, it took only two minutes for the water to reach the surface, just seconds after the last exhausted miner had climbed out at the top. The water brought with it a murderous tidal wave of machinery and tools left over from four years of digging, scattering the terrified men in all directions as buckets, ladders and bricks also cascaded out of the well.

'That part of the school,' said Watkins as he finished his story, 'was always pretty scary.'

There was an awed silence for a few seconds, before the hands went up and questions were called out:

'Did you see the ghost, sir?'

'Did you ever go down there, sir?'

'Did you ever throw anything down there, sir?'

Watkins always smiled at the last comment. 'Only pupils who really annoyed me,' he said.

A teacher's joke, funny only to teachers.

The question Itch now wished he had asked was: 'How much of all that was true, sir, and how much have you made up to impress us?'

However, it was too late for that now. He had gambled that John Watkins was telling the truth. He had remembered the story and 'the lightning bolt into the earth' he had drawn so many times as he and Jack were being driven to London by Flowerdew and Kinch. He had immediately known where he was taking the rocks. He knew where they had to go.

They had come from deep in the Earth, and that was where, rampant radiation poisoning permitting, they were returning.

28

The final section of corridor did indeed lead to the woodwork room, the metalwork room, and finally the science lab. Each room had two large windows onto the corridor so some murky light found its way into them. Leaving the rucksack by the notice board, Itch jogged over to the woodwork-room windows. Peering through, he could make out the workbenches with their lathes; short planks of wood leaned against the wall near the door. In the metalwork room he could see the racks of tools in glass cabinets. The science lab had its wooden work surfaces with gas taps for the Bunsen burners. Behind the teacher's desk, rows of chemicals in assorted jars were lined up neatly.

According to Watkins it was the woodwork room that contained the well, but there was absolutely no sign of it. Itch darted around the shadowy benches and machinery, peering under desks and moving chairs. Why would you hide it? More to the point, *how* could you hide it? The world's deepest hand-dug well must leave a mark, surely, even if it had been finished a century and a half ago. Itch didn't know if he was expecting to smell a huge unused well, presumably full of stagnant water, but he couldn't detect anything other than sawdust.

He tried the metalwork room, with its anvils and cold forge. The cabinets behind the desk housed some of the more dangerous-looking tools and drills with assorted bits, but there was no sign of any well. The science lab had all the familiar gassy smells of the one at the CA, but it was very small, and a quick inspection revealed nothing. Even though it was almost dark, Itch was sure he hadn't missed it.

He paced furiously back to the woodwork room. The dreadful thought that Watkins had made the whole thing up was beginning to grow in the back of his mind. Itch dismissed it as best he could and tried to remember what his geography teacher had actually said. He must have missed something. *You just cannot hide something this big*, he thought. Then, out loud: 'Come on, *where are you*?!'

He was sure Watkins had said something about 'the entrance of the woodwork room', and he got down on his hands and knees. A close-up inspection revealed scuffed floorboards, a stone threshold and nothing else. He stood up, feeling sure that, somehow, the answer was here but he had missed it.

He shook his head, as if to dislodge unhelpful ideas. He went over it again:

The entrance to the woodwork room.

He was there now. No well.

Sure?

Positive.

Had it always been the woodwork room?

No idea, but it wasn't in the other rooms, anyway.

Had the entrance always been in the same place?

An electric charge of excitement passed through Itch's tired body and he felt the adrenalin kick in.

Got it.

He ran back to the wall where the notice board was. Behind the wooden frame was the un-mistakable outline of a door. Or where a door had once been: the original door to the woodwork room.

He looked down. He was standing on a threadbare piece of carpet about four metres square pushed up against the wall. That's what had been nagging him – the change in the floor he was standing on. He'd been so excited to see the posters he hadn't properly registered what was beneath his feet.

He dragged the rucksack off the carpet, propping it against the wall. He pulled at the carpet, but it was heavy and it shifted only slightly. Kneeling down, he started to roll it up instead, hands shaking with excitement. As he reached the place where the old door had been, the flooring changed. Instead of the lino of the corridor he saw old floorboards. He continued rolling up the carpet until it was one long tube along the woodwork-room wall.

Itch stood up. He had revealed eighteen floor-boards, each about four metres long. They had been nailed down and glued together. He ran back into the woodwork room, grabbing an assortment of hammers and chisels, and set to work. Chipping at the glue and prising out the nails, Itch removed the boards one by one. The first four on each side revealed only concrete, but that changed when he reached the middle ten planks. As he lifted them up, he saw a huge, riveted, square metal plate with a recessed centrepiece.

'You beauty,' said Itch.

As John Watkins told it, there were occasional visits to the well, with pupils allowed to peer into the gloom, thrilled and fearful. Itch assumed this seal hadn't been in place then – it wasn't the kind of well-cap you could just whip off any time you wanted to tell your story. The steel plate was at least three metres across with a recessed circle in the middle – Itch guessed the central circle was about a metre in diameter, with a raised handle, and secured by eighteen large screws around its circumference. The plate itself was riveted into what he assumed was concrete.

He had a selection of screwdrivers ready: he took a large Phillips and walked out onto the steel plate. Kneeling down, he placed one hand in the centre of the circle, momentarily imagining the vast hole beneath him and shuddering. One by one, he started to work on the screws. They had been in position for years and most were, unsurprisingly, stuck fast. When one proved too much, Itch moved on and tried the next. Completing the circle, he had only removed four screws – each one about four centimetres long. Reaching for the largest hammer, he hit the circular panel next to the remaining screws. The metallic clanging echoed down the corridor and around the school, but Itch barely noticed. This was all taking too long. His own time-clock was ticking, and he had no idea how difficult this final task was going to be. Occasionally he coughed to clear his throat, and dark blood speckled the steel plate.

The sharp jolt of metal hammer on metal plate dislodged enough rust and grit to loosen the screws, and Itch worked away at them as fast as he could. As each one came free, he put it carefully in a pile near the wall. When they were all out, he knelt at the lip of the circle, reached for the handle and, taking a deep breath, pulled hard.

Nothing.

The cap didn't move.

He tried again. He knew he was much weaker

than usual, but the cap wasn't shifting at all.

He stood up and was halfway to the metalwork room in search of some extra leverage when he changed his mind.

'Idiot,' he said to himself, and ran back. Once more he knelt at the edge of the disc, leaned over, put both hands on the handle and *twisted*.

It moved.

'Got it!' he shouted. Millimetre by millimetre, working it first clockwise then anti-clockwise, he started to rotate the well-cap. It was becoming looser all the time, each movement making it screech as the thread of the cap released itself from the thread of the plate. Slowly the cap edged up – Itch worked his hands round and round, moving one over the other, twisting and pulling. It now sat a few centimetres above the plate, and Itch straightened his back. He wanted to be ready for the moment it came free – he didn't want to lose his balance now.

One more revolution.

Two more.

A third, and then suddenly there was more movement and the cap came free and shifted sideways. A horrible stench, filthy and dark, hit him like a punch in the face. He gagged and turned his head away, his eyes shut. Inch by inch he pulled the cap from the hole, the steel scraping noisily but eventually crunching down onto the metal plate.

Itch backed away from the hole. The smell of rotting vegetation rose like a gas and filled his nostrils, the hall, the corridor, and probably the whole school. Sitting back now, he could actually see the air above the hole shimmer and move. He half expected the ghost of the winchman or the nun to appear.

Slowly he edged towards the hole again, his heart pounding, his head thumping, and looked over the edge. He could see only darkness – what light there was in the corridor certainly didn't penetrate more than the first few centimetres of the well. He realized he was holding his breath, but the smell had now changed to something more like cooked cabbage and sewage. It was hideous, but he could tolerate it. The train carriage with its crushed stinky beans had been a good rehearsal.

Retrieving two of the screws, he dropped them down the well. One by one they disappeared. He waited for a splash but heard nothing. He needed something bigger, and found a one-kilogram brass weight in the metalwork room. Holding it dead centre of the hole, he let go. It disappeared into the blackness and Itch waited. How long to fall 400 feet? Only a few seconds. Silence.

Sitting back by the notice board, Itch wasn't sure what he had expected; that the water would be lapping at the top of the well? He hadn't actually thought beyond finding the well and then throwing the rucksack, rocks and all, down into the depths. He could still do that – but what if they got stuck halfway, what then? No, he knew he needed to put them out of reach for ever. If criminals, terrorists and governments were as desperate to get hold of them as Cake and Alexander had claimed, climbing a few metres down a hole wouldn't deter anyone.

Slowly the reality of what he faced began to dawn on him. Exhausted, bloodied and weak with radiation poisoning, he was going to have to climb down into the well. He didn't know how deep he would have to go in order to ensure that the rocks disappeared, but he was going to have to try. Wearily he dragged himself to his feet, and tried not to think about the last time anyone had gone down this well. Images of men scrambling for their lives came to his mind.

Back in the metalwork room, he searched for a light. Even the diggers of the nineteenth century had candlelight. The forge and the blowtorches would be gas-powered, and in the cupboards behind the teacher's desk he found what he needed: four canisters of camping gas, three red ones with '47kg' on the side, and one small, grey, tennis-ball-tube-sized one. An old cigarette lighter was lodged in the top of one of the red containers, and behind them lay a tangled pile of tubes and blowtorches.

It took him ten precious minutes to pull everything over to the hole and attach the canisters, tubing and blowtorches together. He put the small canister in a side pocket of the rucksack and arranged the big ones at regular intervals around the hole. Turning on the gas from the first one, he sparked the lighter. An orange and blue flame from the blowtorch filled the corridor with a flickering, dancing light. Pausing briefly, realizing he should have at least considered the possibility that there were flammable gases in the room, he lowered the flame into the hole.

The rubber tubing took the swaying flame a metre below the surface, and Itch lay flat, his hands on either side of the hole. He looked down again. The metre-diameter hole in the plate sat on a two-metre-diameter well, and as Itch lowered his head he could see the bricks that walled the shaft. Some were cracked and crumbling, and most were lined with moss, but it looked solid – and drier than he had expected. As he turned his head around the circumference of the well, he tried to guide the light of the flame to where he was looking. He strained his neck to look under where he was lying and he saw the one thing that he had hoped for and dreaded in equal measure.

There was a narrow metal ladder that started just below the lip of the well and disappeared into the depths. By the swaying gas light, Itch's eyes followed it down about five metres before it disappeared. It looked solid enough, but who was to say it wouldn't collapse with the first foot that touched a rung? Again he thought of just throwing the rucksack down the hole, closing the well-cap and getting to a hospital. But no matter how often he told himself that 400 feet would be plenty deep enough, a voice in his head came back with *1,285 feet*. That's why he was here. The deepest well: that was the point.

He had decided. *He was going down.*

'Last-minute shopping,' said Itch, and he switched off the gas. He then ran back to grab some of the short lengths of wood from the woodwork room. Thirty seconds later they were dropped down the well, disappearing noiselessly like the brass weight and the screws before them. Next he found a towel by the sinks in the science lab. As he stuffed it down his shirt, his attention was caught, as it so often had been, by the array of chemicals in jars and bottles in the glass-fronted cabinet behind the teacher's desk. On the top shelf stood a thick, clear-glass bottle. The label said *Na*, but Itch already knew what it was from the soft, silvery chunks that lay submerged in a clear oil. It was sodium – one of the most explosive metals, which was why it was kept under oil. If it was exposed to the air for more than a few seconds, it would start to react, fizzing and turning pink. In lessons, teachers always used a disappointingly small slice of sodium to illustrate their experiment, dropping the sliver into water with a 'pop' as the hydrogen gas caught fire.

'Guess I might need all of it,' said Itch, and he opened the cupboard. He picked up the jar, made sure the top was secure and hurried back to the well.

Itch didn't stop now. He knew if he did he might just have second thoughts and back out. He checked the positioning of the gas canisters and tubes, the blowtorches dangling over the edge. He then put the sodium jar in the rucksack front pocket, where the tubes of WHO ME and SBM were still wrapped in foil, and hoisted it all onto his back. Checking the lighter was in his trouser pocket, Itch walked to the edge of the well.

His head swam and he started to shake again. He could no longer tell where the terror ended and the radiation poisoning started. He walked round the well till he was opposite the ladder and sat down, swinging his legs over the edge. *Over the abyss*, he thought. He lit one of the blowtorches again, and lowered it down into the hole. He waited till it had stopped swaying and checked the other two large gas canisters. Their tubes hung down on the other side, and he turned on the taps, releasing their gas, unlit, into the well.

'Wish me luck!' he called to no one in particular, but maybe to the ghosts of the well or the statue of

Mary. Or maybe just because it felt good to shout. Lying face down with his feet over the well opening, he shuffled and wriggled his body closer to the drop. His legs slid into space and he started kicking and swinging until they found the ladder. He walked his feet down the rungs, testing their strength. Satisfied, he eased himself below the surface.

For a moment Itch froze, staring at the bricks and mould that surrounded him. The smell of gas reminded him to reach for the lighter and, stretching up but looking down, he lit one of the gas-emitting blowtorches. All the gas which had flowed into the well ignited in a ball of flame. Itch heard his hair sizzle but kept his eyes looking down. The brilliant flash lit the walls properly for the first time, and momentarily he saw the planks of wood he had thrown down, tiny, distant and splayed in a rose pattern hundreds of feet below. The familiar smell of his burned hair stayed with him for only a second.

The illumination of the fiery gas ball was brief, but the three burning torches provided Itch with a steady light to start his descent. He was at the top of a ladder that disappeared into the darkness below. He didn't know how far it would take him, but slowly, rung by rung, he climbed down into the unknown.

29

Four hundred feet; thirty feet; 885 feet. Down, across and down again: 1,285 feet. That's all he knew – that's how Watkins had taught it. He would keep going deeper till he found water, or couldn't go any further.

The burning blowtorches hung still now, and provided a steady, if limited light for Itch to descend by. He moved slowly to start with, his body taut, his grip frantically tight. His burned right hand was badly blistered, but the pain had eased. The expectation that every rung was about to give way made progress slow, but as they proved solid, he picked up his pace. He also noted that the bricks were still dry. He couldn't see, hear or smell water. Wherever the water level was, it hadn't been up here for a long time.

He developed a rhythm as he climbed down – left foot, right foot, left hand, right hand, test ladder.

Whoever had had the task of constructing and then fixing the ladder to the wall appeared to have done a good job, and he was grateful.

After he had been climbing down for a few minutes, he came to a recessed ledge cut into the side. Just a step in space away from the ladder, it was big enough for a boy and a rucksack to rest up if necessary. Itch wondered if this would be the place for the small gas canister to do its work. He had thought of using it at the bottom, but maybe it could be just as useful here. He looked up and then down again. No, he hadn't come far enough. He'd taken a few chances already; he'd risk another.

As he descended deeper, the rungs of the ladder became increasingly damp and the surrounding bricks were taking on a green hue. Pausing briefly, he ran his finger down the wall; it was wet with moisture and slimy with algae. Hands tight on the ladder, he looked around. The dark green moss was everywhere, the bricks now lost behind it. While it made for a more dangerous descent – his feet were slipping on the wet rungs now – at least he knew water was near.

He came to another ledge cut into the wall. These mini-platforms were presumably where the winchmen had operated from, pulling the endless buckets of soil up to the surface, then guiding them down again. Itch wondered if this was the ledge the winchman had fallen from. The hole below him was black and looked endless. The lights from the top were dwindling. He needed more.

Itch stepped out and off the ladder. The alcove was just deep enough for him to turn round with his rucksack on, and he stood only a few centimetres from the drop as he took out the small gas canister, tubing and blowtorch. He turned the nozzle and the gas hissed. The lighter did its work, and Itch positioned the canister so that the tube and torch hung free, its light spraying out and down. He put on his rucksack again and climbed back onto the ladder.

Each step needed extra care now, and his rate of descent had slowed. After fifteen minutes that felt like days, he spotted the top of one of the pieces of wood he had thrown down. Excited that he had reached the bottom, he picked up speed, his legs and arms working faster again. But he was now skipping the 'test ladder' part of his routine, and suddenly he felt the left side pull away from the wall slightly. Itch froze. He stared at the rivets that held the ladder in place; one of them sagged slightly in the mossy brick. Unsure how long it would hold, he hurried on.

In the near darkness, the ends of the planks loomed into view. Itch was trying to judge how far he still had to go when the rung he was standing on snapped.

His right foot had only just touched it when

it gave way, shattering clean down the middle.

The impact on the next rung as his foot jerked downwards caused that to snap too.

The third, fourth and fifth ones gave way, the cracking and splitting iron sounding like rapid-fire gunshots.

Itch had fallen nearly two metres in a second.

Terrified, he grabbed onto the side of the ladder to slow himself down, the rust and screws tearing into his fingers. In desperation he cried out, his voice echoing and rebounding up the well.

By leaning into the ladder and pressing with his arms into the metal, he slowed his fall but his feet were flailing, scrabbling, trying to find the rungs again. *I'm not going to make it!* he thought as an image of his body falling into the depths flashed through his mind. He continued to slide, his hands squeaking like brakes on the ladder before his feet finally found a rung that held, and he came to a halt.

The skin on his arms burned and bled but he didn't look at them. His hands were lacerated but his mind shut out the pain. He looked down. He was up to his thighs in water.

The planks of wood had embedded themselves at the bottom – in mud, presumably – and only the tops were above water level. This meant that the bottom was only a little way below them. Instinctively Itch looked up. He could see the small canister's orange flame burning steadily, but the ones at the top were tiny, like three stars in the sky. The gas would soon burn up, and Itch had little enough time anyway.

Four hundred feet down, Itch looked around and saw only shadows and faint shades of grey and brown. He climbed three steps so that he was out of the water – dark black and rippling out from where his legs had just been. He watched as the ripples passed around the submerged planks and disappeared. Visibility just over a metre, then.

Itch knew that there was a tunnel that led off from where he was standing, but the water was too deep to tell where it was. He saw again the lightning-bolt shape he had drawn; this horizontal tunnel would run for about thirty feet before the well dropped again into the bowels of the Earth. He guessed it wouldn't be on the ladder side, but that was the easiest to check. He removed the towel from inside his shirt, laying it over a rung. He noticed how bloody it was – his hands were ploughed with deep cuts with split skin on all his fingers and palms. He mopped up what he could.

Next he slipped off the rucksack and, holding it in one hand, removed his shirt with the other. He looped the sleeves through the rucksack's straps and then knotted them tightly onto the ladder. He took off his trainers and socks and chucked them at the far wall, where they bounced and fell into the water, the ripples folding back to the ladder.

Itch stepped back down the three rungs into the water and reached for the nearest plank. It was a roughly cut piece of pine and he tugged it free of whatever sludge it had stuck in. Holding the ladder with his left hand and the wood in his right, he stepped down another rung. Filling his lungs with air, he descended the next two. When he reached the third, he was completely submerged, and holding the end of the plank, he started poking and prodding. He quickly realized that — as he had suspected — there was nothing but brick on the ladder side of the well. The tunnel to the final drop led off from elsewhere.

He climbed out of the water again, and got his first hint that the sickness wasn't far away. His stomach tightening, he grabbed as many of the planks as he could reach and bundled them together, laying them flat on the water. He launched himself on top of his makeshift surfboard. With a plank in his hand, he started stabbing clockwise round the well, the wood darting backwards and forward under the water.

He had turned through ninety degrees and found only brick; another ninety degrees took him back to the ladder, and he started to get worried. If the well ended here, just four hundred feet below the ground, he had been wasting his time. Increasingly frantic, he paddled past the rungs and spun round to 270 degrees. His father had been right – paddling *was* a useful skill, after all.

Last chance. He closed his eyes. There was no mistaking what was coming. The sweats and shaking were beginning again as he pushed the wood under the water. He felt it glance off what could be a corner piece, and then it shot forward, disappearing out of his hand. Grabbing another plank, he tried again a little further round and, sure enough, the wood met with no resistance. This was the tunnel that led to the final drop, thirty feet away.

As Itch got onto the ladder and climbed back up a few rungs, his whole body shook. He hoped he still had the strength for what he had to do. He knew he couldn't swim underwater along thirty feet of tunnel, drop the rocks down the remaining 885 feet and make his way back to safety. He couldn't have done that if he'd been fit; with a heavy dose of radiation coursing through him, he knew it wasn't even worth trying.

If *he* couldn't push the rocks over the edge, though, he knew something that could. He reached for the front pocket of his rucksack and removed the silver foil from the tubes of WHO ME and SBM, the stink agents. Unfolded and stretched out, the foil was about the size of an A4 piece of paper. Finding the glass jar of sodium, he removed the stopper and threw it in the water. He laid the foil out on his left hand, and clumsily, his shaking hands slowing him down, poured the soft chunks of metal onto the foil, the oil leaking away over his fingers.

Even in the shadowy darkness four hundred feet down, Itch could see the reaction begin. The silvery sheen was turning pinkish-white as he folded the foil over to make a parcel. He sealed the edges by pinching them together, as if making a Cornish pasty. It already felt hot on his hand, his open wounds making him gasp. Crimping the seals as tightly as he could, he held the package in his teeth and released the rucksack from the shirt's knots, then tied the sodium parcel in its place. With enormous effort, he hoisted the rucksack onto his bare shoulders and stepped back into the water.

Using his last reserves of strength, he trod water in front of where he knew the tunnel mouth was. Holding onto the planks of wood to balance the pull of the rucksack, he dived. He only needed to go down a few centimetres to reach the tunnel, and he half swam, half pulled himself along the ceiling as far as could manage. He wanted to go as far in as possible. The closer he could get to the final drop, the better the chance of sending the rocks to the bottom. But in the underwater darkness, he lost all sense of how far he had gone. As his body weakened, the rucksack pulled him deeper, and he knew he had reached the end.

Four hundred feet below the earth, in a flooded

nineteenth-century well shaft, Itchingham Lofte let go of his rucksack.

Corkscrewing round, his chest bursting, he felt his way back to the tunnel entrance. As he broke the surface, he inhaled deeply, his breath rasping and ragged. He knew he had only seconds left to finish the job. Grabbing the sodium from his shirt sleeves and ignoring the heat searing into his damaged hand, he dived down for the tunnel a second time and took the parcel as far as he dared. Letting go, he spun round and swam back for the ladder.

How much time Itch had now depended on how tight he had made the seals in the foil. He started up the rungs, his bare feet pushing as fast as they could. He needed the water to be kept away from the sodium for as long as possible. He reached the rungless section where he had crashed through the rusted iron; but he didn't slow down. Pulling himself up with his hands, Itch was flying.

Maybe the body finds untapped reserves when it needs to; maybe the fear of dying makes it do extraordinary things. As he climbed, he muttered, '$2Na + 2H_2O = 2NaOH + H_2$; $2Na + 2H_2O = 2NaOH + H_2$.' Over and over, like an incantation, he repeated the formula of the reaction he was both escaping from and depending on. Sodium added to water leads to sodium hydroxide and hydrogen gas. Bang.

'$2Na + 2H_2O = 2NaOH + H_2$.' Louder now, as

if appealing to the chemistry gods that controlled all reactions, Itch screamed it at the top of his voice, yelling through the well, his voice bouncing, rebounding, magnified:

'$2Na + 2H_2O = 2NaOH + H_2$!'

Rung by rung, foot by foot, bloody hand by bloody hand, Itch climbed away from the water. He knew his sodium would blow eventually – the water would find its way through the silver foil and the reaction would be instantaneous. Molten sodium, caustic soda and flame would explode in all directions. He needed the eruption to be big enough to blow the rucksack along to the end of the tunnel, where gravity would take it to the very deepest point – 1,285 feet below the Earth's surface.

But he also wanted to live.

The ladder cut into his bare chest, his feet and his hands, but his eyes were focused on the small winchman's platform, which was now only a few steps away. Three rungs. He'd stop there.

Slowing, Itch was shaking with nausea and fear; the sweat was blinding him. He wiped it away with his bloodied hands.

He made the next rung. He was getting closer to the light from the small canister, but it was no brighter – its supply was running dangerously low.

Another rung.

The convulsion felt as though it started in his feet and worked its way up through his legs, his hips and his stomach. Refusing to stop climbing, Itch hauled himself up to the last rung and threw himself off the ladder and onto the ledge as the sickness took him again.

Flat on his back, he saw the little canister flame flicker, fade and go out. In the darkness, the five stars of the blowtorches at the top still flickered. That wasn't right, of course – there should only be three.

Itch had just started to count the flames again when there was a low rumble from deep in the well, followed by the roar of water being thrown out of the tunnel at huge pressure. The ledge shook and some of the bricks crumbled, the pieces scattering over him. Water rushed up the well, pushing mud, rocks and his planks of wood with it.

It was an underground tsunami. In the tight confines of the tunnel, the explosion threw the water out with extraordinary force. Itch had no time to brace himself as filthy, foul-smelling water crashed over him. He was lifted, spinning round and upwards, like a whirlpool in reverse. Burning, choking water stung his eyes and poured down his throat. Then, as quickly as it had risen, the water level crashed down again, tossing Itch back onto the ledge, where he lay like a broken doll.

With the sound of the sodium explosion still reverberating and the waves slapping the well's sides a hundred feet below, Itch, choking and gasping, felt his body shutting down. It hurt. It all hurt. He turned to face the wall. He was burning up and shivering at the same time. He wrapped his arms around himself and curled into a ball. He squeezed his eyes shut to keep out the light and heat which were coming from somewhere.

He saw his sister smiling at him and he smiled back.

'Sorry,' he said.

He saw Jack waving and tried to wave back.

'Sorry,' he said.

His parents called to him.

'Sorry,' he said. 'Sorry for everything.'

30

The car came for Nicholas and Jude Lofte, waiting outside the house while they packed. They didn't need much, but it had taken them a while to realize that. Carrying a small bag each, they approached the car, and the driver jumped out. He nodded at them and opened the rear door. They fussed with the seatbelts and armrests while the driver watched in his mirror.

'Shall we go, Mr and Mrs Lofte?'

'Yes, sorry. We're ready,' said Jude, and the car pulled away.

'Music?' asked the driver.

'No, thank you,' they said together.

He nodded. 'I'm Steve, by the way.'

'Oh. Nicholas, Jude,' said Nicholas, pointing unnecessarily at himself and his wife.

They set off into the night.

Itch's parents spent most of the journey in silence.

Jude sobbed quietly and Nicholas stared out of the window. Occasionally they held hands.

'They haven't really told us anything,' Jude said.

'I'm sure they will when we get there,' said Nicholas. 'They promised they would, remember?'

They both made calls to Chloe to check that she was OK – she was still in hospital but equipped with her phone. They promised to call when they had something to tell her.

'She sounded upset, Jude,' said Nicholas.

'Not surprising really, when you've been through what she has.' Although they'd both asked the same question many times, Jude said again, 'Do you think one of us should stay? It's not too late.'

'We've been through this. She said to go. We need to do this together.'

'OK,' said Jude, and she took a deep breath, letting it out very slowly.

Three hours later they came to the grey five-metre-high gates marked MINISTRY OF DEFENCE and STRICTLY NO ADMITTANCE. It was the early hours of the morning, but when they parked outside an imposing red-brick building, all the lights appeared to be on and staff were bustling everywhere. The driver jumped out and opened their door.

'Follow me,' he said. 'It's not far.'

The Loftes walked with their heads bowed, avoiding the gazes of the people they passed; the sympathetic glances made them feel awkward. Everyone seemed to know who they were and why they were there.

Steve's idea of 'not far' turned out to be a five-minute march through a bewildering series of neon-lit corridors. Finally they reached two large steel doors with a guard outside. The guard was armed.

'If you wait here,' said Steve, 'someone will be with you shortly.' He nodded at them both – almost a bow – and left. Jude and Nicholas sat on two plastic chairs and waited. Nicholas reached for his wife's hand.

'Our boy . . .' he said quietly, his eyes glistening.

The doors opened and they both jumped. A smiling, curly-haired woman came over to them.

'Hello, Mr and Mrs Lofte, I'm Patty Hammond. I hope your journey was comfortable. Please – this way.' She gestured back through the steel doors, and they all went in, the guard banging them shut behind them. She turned to face them. 'Are you ready to see your son?' she said. They both nodded and Patty Hammond pushed open the next door.

They were in a hospital ward. It was a long room and had been divided into two. Their half was equipped with sinks, a shower and blue robes hanging on pegs. Through tinted glass they could peer into the other half. There were four beds on either side, each with screens and partitions, but only one, at the far end, occupied. A robed and masked doctor sat beside a patient surrounded by tubes, drips and monitors, and with blankets pulled up to his chest. Nicholas and Jude cried out as they saw their son.

'You're about to have some visitors.' Dr Jim Fairnie spoke quietly, but it was enough to wake Itch.

'Just dozing,' he said groggily.

'Your folks are here.'

Itch smiled. 'It's been a while.' He tried to sit up, and Dr Fairnie helped him, rearranging his pillows. The doors from the other room opened and two tall, blue-robed figures came in. They stopped as if waiting for permission to approach. Itch waved at them.

Running now, Nicholas reached the bed first, his wife just behind, then pulled up, not sure what happened next.

'He isn't infectious,' said the doctor, a small man in his forties with a neat moustache, 'but *you* might be. No embracing, I'm afraid. For now. He has a long way to go – he only came round this morning. Please sit.' Dr Fairnie indicated two seats, one on each side of the bed.

'Oh, Itch,' said Jude. 'What have you done? We've been so worried. Look at you!' She was studying what was left of his hair. It had fallen out in clumps, leaving tufts on top of his head and at the back of his neck. Her hand covered her masked mouth; her eyes sparkled with tears.

'I know – not pretty,' said Itch, his voice hoarse. 'It was a shock to me too.' They sat in silence, not sure who should speak next. 'Hi,' he said.

'Hi,' his parents said together through their masks.

After a moment his dad blinked and swallowed hard. 'Look, son, we are just thrilled you're OK. I know there's lots to say, but now isn't the time. We thought we'd lost you . . . Love you, son.' An embrace should have followed, but they had to make do with tears. The doctor handed paper handkerchiefs round and took one himself.

'What about Chloe and Jack? I've asked, but no one will tell me. Are they OK? Please tell me they're OK.'

Jude looked at Nicholas. 'Yes, we think,' he said. 'Chloe is still in hospital – they want to keep her in for tests but don't think there's any lasting damage. Jack is in hospital in London – they're worried about her immune system. She's lost her hair too.' He smiled.

'My immune system is stuffed, apparently. Dr Fairnie will tell you.'

'Dr Fairnie will indeed tell you,' said the doctor, 'but not just now. We think Itch'll be fine, but it's been touch and go. You can have a few more minutes, and then General Keyes needs a word.'

'General Keyes? Who's he?' asked Nicholas.

'Top man on campus,' said Dr Fairnie. 'He'll

explain the, er, security situation.' The Loftes looked baffled. 'Two minutes, then.' And the doctor busied himself checking the monitors.

'I'm sorry for all of it. Everything,' said Itch quietly. 'I was only doing what I thought was right.'

His mother looked like she was about to say something but checked herself. 'There's plenty of time for all that,' she said, smiling thinly.

Itch closed his eyes; he was getting tired. His parents got up to go.

'Hey, Mum!' he croaked, feeling his face. 'At least I kept my eyebrows this time!'

Jude laughed and blew a kiss to her son, then Patty Hammond reappeared to take them both to meet the general.

Dr Fairnie sat down next to Itch. 'There's a lot to talk about. Up for it?' He smiled, his moustache twitching.

Itch nodded. 'Two questions from me first.'

'Shoot,' said Dr Fairnie.

'How did I get here and how long was I out for?'

'Well, I can tell you how long you've been unconscious, certainly. You've been gone a week, Itch. Seven days in all – the first three in Crawley Hospital in Sussex, then you were transferred here to the Mason Military Hospital. We're part—'

Itch interrupted. '*Crawley?* Where's that?' His astonishment was noted by Fairnie. 'How did I get there?'

'A real mystery, that one – we were hoping you would help us. Crawley is the nearest hospital to Gatwick Airport. You were left there, Itch, on a stretcher. The receptionists say they looked up, and there you were, laid out by the front door. You were unconscious and in a mess. A real mess. And someone had stuck a radioactive symbol on you. A correct diagnosis, as it turned out.'

Itch was mulling over the implications of what Dr Fairnie was telling him.

Someone had found him.

Despite everything, someone had found him. They had saved his life, certainly, but someone now knew where he had been and, almost certainly, what he had been doing. Everything now depended on who it was and what they intended to do next.

Who knew?

'We've pieced together a lot of the story. We know you acquired a piece of radioactive rock which was then taken by Dr Nathaniel Flowerdew. He analysed it, sending his findings to his old employers at Greencorps. We believe they sent agents to get their hands on it. That's who you met at the mining school. Jacob Alexander and John Watkins – they're fine, by the way – told us that you actually had eight rocks altogether. I've seen the analysis. Unbelievable. Extraordinary. No wonder everything started to get a little busy.'

'Hang on,' said Itch. 'Are you a real doctor? You sound more like the police or something.'

Dr Fairnie smiled again. 'Army medic originally. And Intelligence. You'll be seeing quite a lot of me. Sorry about that.' Itch motioned for him to carry on. 'Well, Flowerdew and his sidekick were taken to hospital under arrest after you'd effectively anaesthetized them. Neat trick, that, by the way. And then you and Jack disappeared. When we got hold of your cousin, she was near Marylebone Station in the middle of London—'

'Wow,' said Itch quietly.

'Why "wow"?' asked Fairnie.

'Nothing. Go on.'

'Well, Marylebone Station runs trains to Stratford-upon-Avon, Leamington, Wrexham — places like that. So we assumed you'd gone north-west. But you were totally off-radar until you appeared at Crawley Hospital. They worked on you; then, when you were stable, they transferred you here.'

'Why?'

Fairnie stood up and checked some of the monitors, adjusted a drip and sat down again.

'You're a wanted man, Itch. The *most* wanted. Seriously, you have no idea; while you have been out cold, the world has come knocking. You had in your possession the most powerful and valuable rocks ever. *Of all time.* And now you don't. That's where everyone gets interested.' He consulted some notes. 'But first things first. Did you succeed?'

'I'm sorry?'

'Did you succeed in disposing of the rocks?'

Itch nodded.

'You're sure? Because if you failed, we have a potential global catastrophe on our hands. Every government in the world – including Her Majesty's, by the way – wants to know more.'

'They've gone,' said Itch. 'Trust me.'

Fairnie waited for more, but none came. 'We have tested extensively, of course, for unusual and unexpected radiation levels which might suggest you failed, but have found none.'

'I didn't fail.'

'Good. However, every crime syndicate, every terrorist group you have ever heard of – and many you haven't – would like to know where you put them. What you've done with them.'

'Wow,' said Itch again.

'Precisely,' said the doctor. 'Many high-level people – good people – will try to persuade you to tell them. My hunch is they won't get very far.'

'I didn't . . . do what I did . . . just to tell everyone. If I'd thought they'd been safe, I could have rung the Prime Minister or someone. The whole point was to keep it secret.'

'Does Jack know?'

Itch shook his head.

'Who rescued you?' asked Fairnie.

'I have no idea. Really. And they might want to keep quiet about it, don't you think?'

'If they are wise, yes. And pray that no one works out who they are.' Fairnie gathered up his papers. 'You've had enough. I'll leave you for now. One of my colleagues will stay with you.'

'What did you mean when you said I'd be seeing quite a lot of you?' asked Itch.

'I've been put in charge of your security. When you are done here and you've had all the blood transfusions, I'm moving to Cornwall. We're going to be neighbours, Itch. When you decide you *do* want to tell someone where the rocks are – and I think you will – I'll be right next door.'

Itch stayed in the military hospital all summer. He had suffered all-over radiation poisoning and burns to his back. He needed a bone-marrow transplant and several blood transfusions as his immune system had been in meltdown, but he recovered more quickly than his doctors had expected.

'By rights, you should be dead,' said Fairnie on more than one occasion, 'but there must have been something unpredictable about the emissions of those rocks. Obviously we don't know for certain what the long-term effects of exposure to a new element will be. If only we could study them . . . Where did you say you left them?'

This always made Itch laugh; it had become their running joke. Many senior military men, energy experts and politicians had tried to persuade him to reveal the rocks' whereabouts. The government's chief scientific officer had lectured Itch on his duty. Bribes had been offered, or 'rewards for your gallant effort', as the Home Secretary had put it. Itch explained over and over that he wouldn't have risked his life to get rid of them, only to reveal where they were in exchange for a new family house. (He hadn't told his dad about that one.)

With Jim Fairnie it was different. He knew Itch would never tell where they were, so would just drop 'Where did you say you put them?' into their conversation two or three times a day. Itch had come to rely on him since being admitted to the military hospital. He had become adviser, teacher and physiotherapist as well as doctor and guard.

His mum came as regularly as she could; his dad was back on the rig. To his delight, Chloe was able to visit when she was out of hospital; his first visitor after his bone-marrow transplant.

'Mum, Dad and Gabriel offered to donate some, but they had found a donor already. Apparently it was the Prime Minister who hurried things through.'

'Another bribe,' he said.

'But you won't tell, will you, Itch?'

'Course not.'

Chloe looked pale, but her smile was the broadest he'd ever seen. She explained how the police and ambulance crews had taken Watkins, Alexander and her to hospital. Itch then told her as much as he thought was sensible about his story – it didn't take long.

When Dr Fairnie called that their time was up, Chloe gathered her things together to leave.

'Itch,' she said, looking straight at her brother, 'do you trust him?'

Itch thought about that; he was surprised it hadn't occurred to him before. He had come to rely on Dr Fairnie for information, advice and news, and he realized that he had accepted his advice and counsel the way he would if Mr Watkins had delivered it.

'Yes, I suppose I do,' he said. 'He's kind and knowledgeable. He tells the truth, I think. And he's in charge of my security, so let's hope he's good at his job too.'

Chloe smiled, nodded and kissed her brother on the top of his shaved head.

It was a little longer before Jack could visit. Her immune system had also been badly mangled by the radiation, but she had not needed a bone-marrow transplant. They spoke on the phone and messaged each other, but it was three months before she was allowed to make the journey. Steve was the driver in charge, as he had been for all the family visits.

When she walked into the ward – masks and robes no longer needed – they had looked at each other and burst out laughing. They had identical close-cropped haircuts. At first it had been essential to mask the uneven loss of hair, but now they had grown used to it and had decided to keep it just as it was. Jack had lost weight, but the sparkle was back in her eyes.

Conversation hadn't been easy. Itch had assumed they were being listened to – indeed assumed all their communications were monitored. Any proper chat was going to have to wait, but they made a start.

'So,' said Itch. 'Marylebone Station.' His voice was flat but he looked amazed. His hand gestures said: *How did you manage that?*

Jack worked out how to explain what had happened without giving anything away to eaves-droppers.

'I took a cab. Burned-hair guy had spotted me and was in the cab behind. He'd been following me since . . . for a while. The traffic was terrible and I was sure he was going to snatch me from the cab. When I saw a school party heading along Baker Street, I jumped out and joined them. Pushed my way into the middle of the students and stayed next to the teacher. Burned-hair man had got out too, but couldn't exactly take me from there, so he followed from a distance. I decided to tell the teacher that I was being threatened by the man in the leather jacket and could she call for help. She spotted a policeman near Marylebone Station. When she called to him, burned-hair man ran off. Apparently that was when I collapsed and the policeman called for an ambulance.'

'If he hadn't followed you, he'd have got me,' Itch said.

Jack nodded. 'Guess so.'

'Jack, I'm sorry for getting you so ill.'

'Shut up, Itch.'

'OK. They say they'll talk to us about any long-term side effects in time.'

'Yes, they said that to me too,' said Jack.

'I hope it was worth it. I think life will be quite different now.' Itch had explained what Fairnie had told him about the protection he was going to get. 'I decided on the way to—' He almost said Brighton but stopped himself at the last minute. They exchanged wide-eyed glances. 'I decided to try a bit harder with the whole friends thing. That might be tricky now, with all the security. Maybe you could help?'

'I'll try, sure. Anyway, at least Potts, Paul and Campbell might leave you alone now,' said Jack. 'Maybe they'll pick on someone their own brain-size.'

'Well, it's a start,' said Itch. He waved as he

caught sight of his Uncle Jon and Aunt Zoe. 'Time to go, Jack – your folks are here. I hope they're still speaking to me.'

When Fairnie stopped by next, Itch had a science question for him.

'All the elements at the top end of the table – the high numbers – have only existed in the laboratory for tiny amounts of time. Fractions of a second. There aren't any photos of elements 114, 115, 116, 117 and 118 because they haven't existed for long enough. So how come 126 just sat there in lumps for thousands of years? Doesn't make sense to me.'

The doctor rubbed his moustache thoughtfully. 'I'm not a chemist, but I have been briefed. Although you are right – all the high-end elements are fantastically unstable – it has been thought for a while that, higher up the table, there exists something called the "island of stability".'

Itch's eyes widened. 'You've made that up!'

'No, really,' said Fairnie. 'The island of stability. It's true. They think it's possible that a few elements on this "island" could become more stable and decay much more slowly – maybe over millions of years rather than fractions of seconds. I can only imagine, Itch, that your 126 comes from the island.'

'OK, if you say so,' said Itch, lying back. 'Whatever. It sounds like you've been reading too many dodgy science websites. Or just made it up.'

'I'll get the chief scientific officer to call by again to explain it all, if you like.'

'No, no, I give in,' said Itch. 'I believe you!'

There was one more visitor Itch was waiting for. John Watkins had come up as soon as school broke up for the summer. He looked older but just as boisterously enthusiastic about life. He was someone else Itch thought he needed to apologize to, but Watkins was having none of it.

'My dear boy. No, no, no. I know it was rough back at the mining school, but I'm so grateful that you showed me those rocks. Everyone – *everyone* – is talking about them. When colleagues find out *I've actually seen them*, they just flip. I've had calls from around the world and even done an interview with *National Geographic*.'

Itch smiled. Then, looking around as if to check for spies, Watkins coughed to clear his throat and spoke in a loud whisper. 'You know what happened to South-West Mines, don't you? Just been nationalized. The government have taken it over.'

'What? Why?' Itch was flabbergasted. As Watkins leaned closer, he could smell the tea and cigarettes.

'Well, I've had this from Jacob – who's back at the mining school, you know. Apparently Bob Evert had struck gold. Literally. He wasn't supposed to, but because small amounts had been found at the South Carreg mine nearby, he dug deeper than he was supposed to and found small amounts too. His mate the mayor made sure it kept ticking over as a tourist attraction, while keeping the gold quiet. They had big dreams, Itchingham, and they got greedy. They kept digging. They'd reached extraordinary depths. To hide all the earth and rocks they were bringing up – they obviously couldn't pile it up at South-West Mines – they hired trucks, vans and lorries to scatter it around the old spoil and slag heaps.'

Itch was now sitting bolt upright in bed, wide-eyed with surprise. 'The rocks came from South-West Mines! You are kidding! No!' He stared at nothing in particular and remembered Cake explaining how he had got the rocks from a mate who had been sifting and scouring on another spoil heap. A mate he hadn't been able to trace since.

'So that mine we went down must have been a front! That whole "working mine" and tourist-attraction stuff was a con!'

'Not to start with,' said Watkins. 'We think it was genuine until they found the small amounts of gold, and then they spent all their time in the other shaft. They dug for riches, Itch, and found the most valuable rocks in the world – but didn't realize. Now the mayor has resigned – "to spend more time with his golf clubs" or something – and Evert has retired early so everything will be hushed up. The government boys are in the mine already – no one can get near it. Local news says it's over "security con-cerns", but Jacob says they're digging for more 126. For the moment, at least, there are only the eight samples you had.'

'And good riddance,' said Itch.

'Yes, yes, as you say. Though Dr Alexander might say "produced when we need them the most",' said Watkins.

'Yes,' said Itch slowly. 'He would, wouldn't he?'

'Dr Alexander also says that his students always worked with South-West Mines until a few years ago, when relations suddenly soured and they felt unwelcome. Presumably that's when they found the gold.'

'That figures,' said Itch. 'And why they got rid of the old miners as guides.'

Watkins said brightly, 'And now I've had to sign the Official Secrets Act, so you and Jacob are the only people I can ever talk to about any of this! I shall, as you can imagine, find that quite a challenge.'

'Do you expect more of 126 to be found, sir?'

'Yes, but nothing about this is normal. All rules appear to be . . . *in the balance*, shall we say. This isn't normal − none of it is.'

'I've been hoping,' said Itch, 'that instead of the *first* of a new strain, it turns out they were like the *last* of an endangered species. That they had existed since for ever but had all gone back into the centre of the Earth and got melted down again.'

'Except that from what I'm hearing, the guess is that the rocks weren't as old as that. Certainly tens or hundreds of thousands of years old, but no more.'

'So how come they came out of a mine?'

Watkins smiled. 'Who knows, Itch, who knows? Earthquakes can move things around quite a lot, you know. Maybe they've been thrown away before.'

There was silence in the room.

'That would be quite a story, sir.'

'Indeed. And if you put that in an essay I'd have to put a red line under it. *Preposterous*. Anyway, Jacob says the HazChem boys have been everywhere. They've followed the trail your rocks left from South-West Mines to a spoil heap in Dorset, then back to us. Before they were put in Jacob's radiation box they left quite a trace, those rocks of yours.'

Itch shook his head. 'Not mine now. Nothing to do with me, sir, nothing to do with me.'

Watkins got up to go, but Itch had one more question. 'Did I do the right thing, sir?'

Watkins thought for a while and Itch jumped in again. 'I messed up with the arsenic in the green-house and let everyone down, so I—'

'Yes, yes, we know all about that — we pieced it together in the end.' Watkins waved a hand

400

dismissively. 'Itchingham, you did what you believed to be right. It was I who told you to get rid of them back at the mining school. I share in your decision – though have none of your bravery.' He smiled kindly. 'Yes, I think you did the right thing. Let's hope so. We shall have to wait and see.'

In the days leading up to Itch's release from the military hospital, there was a marked increase in activity and change in security. Itch asked Jim Fairnie what was happening.

'Two things. Firstly you're going home, and secondly . . .' He hesitated for just a second. 'Secondly, Flowerdew's escaped.'

Itch put down his magazine and stared, open-mouthed, at Fairnie. 'You are kidding me, right?'

'Sorry, Itch, I'm not. He was sprung while on his way to a new detention centre. An Audi pulled out in front of the prison van and a woman threatened to spray everyone with gunfire. They handed him over. Our security sources believe they had access to a private plane which was thought to be on course for Tashkent.'

'Remind me . . .?'

'Uzbekistan.'

'Oh. Well, good luck there. Expect a dive in chemistry results from Uzbek schools very soon.'

Jim Fairnie laughed, but not for long. 'He's another part of the problem now. We seriously

401

considered moving your whole family into hiding, but that was deemed inappropriate. You are about to become the most protected boy in the world. Your security detail won't be far off the US President's. We believe there will be active threats against you for the foreseeable future.'

'Maybe I'd better just stay here.'

Itch was joking, but Fairnie wasn't. 'We considered that too. The general vetoed it. Instead we have bought the house next door to yours and are in the process of moving our people in.'

'What happened to the Cole family? I liked them.'

'They quite liked our offer and have moved closer to the golf course. Apparently Mr Cole was very keen.'

'I bet he was. When do we go?'

'Day after tomorrow.'

'It'll be nice to get home,' said Itch. 'I was wondering, Jim, before we go, if you could help me with something.'

'Sure. You seem very calm about everything, Itch. I'm impressed.'

'I'm just happy to be alive. I've been through some bad stuff, met some bad people who hurt me and my family. I . . . had a rough journey, I suppose. And after all that, I'm not sure I'm too worried about anything. Not yet, anyway. I do wonder every day who found me and took me to the hospital. I've gone through everyone I know and like, and none of it works out. No one knew. Jack was in London, sick, being followed by burned-hair man. Watkins and Alexander were miles away and in hospital. My family knew nothing.'

'Which leaves the people you don't like.'

'Precisely,' said Itch. 'But Flowerdew and Kinch were gassed and then locked up. I'm sure the Greencorps team couldn't have found me. I was the last one on the train, Jim, and in the last carriage. I'd have seen any of them get on, I'm sure of it.'

There was a silence before Itch shrugged.

'Getting sloppy, Itch. You haven't told me about a train before,' said Fairnie, smiling.

Itch looked horror-struck, his mouth open.

'I wouldn't worry. It's hardly a revelation. We'd guessed that much, anyway. Now, where did you say you left them?'

Itch was too cross with himself to smile at the joke this time.

'Look,' said Fairnie. 'It could be that your rescuer might just stay hidden. Maybe we'll never know.'

'Maybe. Or maybe someone is waiting for the right moment to get in touch.'

'In which case we'll be there to help. OK?'

Itch nodded.

'Good man,' said Fairnie. 'Now, what is it you needed me to help you with?'

Itch, with a smile back on his face, handed him his magazine.

'Of course,' he said. 'The element hunter is back.'

'What else would I do, Jim? I've got to rebuild the collection. I thought while I was here . . . you might be able to get your hands on some thallium. It's just that it's quite difficult to—'

'Ah, there was one more thing,' Fairnie interrupted. 'Our chief scientist reports that if we do find the rocks and the fuss ever dies down, it is quite likely that element 126 will be given the name *lofteium*. Its symbol will be *Lt*.'

Itch's face flushed as his jaw dropped. No sound came out.

'Just thought I'd mention it.'

The most protected boy in the world had a slightly different trip to school. He still walked out of his house, down the hill and across the golf course into town. He still walked with his sister. It was just that he did so surrounded by four very tall men wearing earpieces and bulging jackets. A car tailed them, and a van with blacked-out windows was always in the school car park.

The most protected boy in the world had a slightly different time when he was *at* school. He still took chemistry, English and French. He still struggled with history. It was just that every lesson had a security man at the back of the room, and another by the door. All teachers reported less disruption and better grades.

And on his back the most protected boy in the world appeared to be sporting a brand-new rucksack.

With 118 pockets.

Sussex, England
June

The worn black carpet was back in position underneath the notice board. It had resumed its job of
hiding the bare floorboards from inquisitive
children. The eighteen planks had been glued
together again and laid carefully in the space cut
from the old lino. The steel cap that fitted into the
plate had been replaced and screwed down.

In the darkness of the well, the dry Sussex brick
descended into the chalk and soil. A white rim of
caustic soda had appeared three hundred feet down,
indicating a recent high-water mark. Just below, the
iron ladder was broken and five rungs were missing.

The water that filled the horizontal tunnel and
the final 885-foot drop was perfectly still, unmoved
by even the smallest eddy or current. It was a
mixture of rain water and lye solution – sodium
hydroxide, evidence of a recent sodium explosion.

This had blown much of the weed, mud and loose brick out of the tunnel, and it had settled in the nooks and crannies of the deep well, or bounced and continued its descent in slow circles.

At a depth of 900 feet, the bricks were still holding together.

At 1,100 feet the water had worked its way into the cement and started to pull away at the rock.

At 1,200 feet the walls were starting to collapse, the bricks crumbling and dissolving with age.

And at the bottom of the well a polythene and lead radiation box, closed and sealed, lay in a metre of mud. It was surrounded by rusted winch machinery, rotten wooden planks and pieces of melted rucksack.

Inside the box a small dark cluster of rocks lay together, 1,285 feet below the school notice board.

And waited.

Author's Note

I know that many people hate science. I hated science. It took me till my forties to realize I was wrong. While writing about Itch, Jack and Chloe, I was constantly aware of readers who just want to get on with the story and may just skip the elements stuff. Fair enough really. If, however, you could do with a bit more background to some of the ideas in Itch's world, here are a few top facts.

THE PERIODIC TABLE/TABLE OF ELEMENTS

The heart and soul of Itch's world and this book. The somewhat baffling lines of boxes, letters and numbers are indeed everything that there is in the known universe. And unknown universe, come to that. You can see from the chart that it is a bit like the castle that Jude observes, with hydrogen and helium being the turrets and the rare Earth elements as the moat at the bottom. If you can think of a better description, please let me know!

It was all put together in this form by a Russian chemist called Dmitri Mendeleyev in 1869. The elements are listed in order of increasing atomic number (the number of protons in the atomic nucleus – this gets tough quickly!). The 'period' bit refers to the horizontal rows where there are recurring or 'periodic' similarities between the elements. The vertical columns or groups are more important, and often the elements in these 'families' have very similar properties. When Alexander is checking his charts and figures, he would have found that element 126 fits under the Fe, Ru, Os, Hs column (iron, ruthenium, osmium, darmstadtium).

Of the 118 elements, 92 are found naturally on Earth; the rest have to be made in labs, with expensive things like particle accelerators. Chances are your school won't have one. And if it does, keep it a secret.

The island of stability

Yes, it really does exist! Or at least, I didn't make it up – it has been talked about for many years. All the elements at the top end of the table are fantastically unstable and some have only existed for seconds or fractions of seconds. There are scientists who think that there may be some, as yet undiscovered, elements that will be sufficiently stable and courteous enough to hang around for long enough to be quite useful; element 126 would be one of them.

COUSIN JACK

This is the name of a wonderful song by Show of Hands (Jon Lofte's favourite band – hence the T-shirt). It is also the name that was given to Cornish miners when they migrated around the world to countries like Canada and Australia, taking their skills with them. Some think that the term became widespread, as miners would often call each other 'Cousin', and Jack was the most popular Christian name in Cornwall.

MINING IN CORNWALL

A great Cornish tradition, especially copper and tin mining. It dates back to between 1000 and 2000 BCE, when metal traders called Britain 'Cassiterides', meaning 'the tin islands'. Cornwall and the west of Devon provided the bulk of the UK's tin, arsenic and copper. As Mr Watkins says, the geology of Cornwall is still something of a mystery! Who knows what is down there? The Romans came to Britain because they'd heard there was gold here. There is certainly some at the South Crofty Mine near Cambourne, and many like Bob Evert who fancy getting their hands on some.

GAIA THEORY

Anything with 'theory' attached is usually pretty boring – but hang on a minute. This is the idea of James Lovelock, 'one of the most original and influential living scientists', to quote the Astronomer Royal, Martin Rees. Lovelock suggests that the Earth should be thought of as one big living thing, not a billion different ones; that the Earth is alive and looks after itself and disapproves of much that humans do. I know it sounds crazy – and Itch and Jack think so too when Jacob Alexander explains some of his ideas. But James Lovelock is widely respected now and has changed the way many view the Earth.

Acknowledgements

There are many fine brains who helped me put *Itch* together. Grateful thanks to a gallery of talent. To Hilary for telling me to get on with it and pointing out that *Itch* was a pretty cool title. To Charlie Fletcher, who helped steer me in the right direction when I was lost in the belly of the beast. To Jo Wroe, who encouraged me to write it in the first place. To my friend and enthusiast Martin Wroe for telling me about Stephen King's *On Writing* – what a book! To Helen Kanmwaa and her punctuation skills. To Senior Vice-President of the Geographical Association Bob Digby for all Cornish and magma-based knowledge (no, Mr Watkins is not him!). To nuclear physicist Professor Paddy Regan at Surrey University, thanks for all the advice, and the use of the white coat and the X-ray fluorescence spectrometer. To UCL's chemist extraordinaire Professor Andrea Sella, who first told me about the 'island of stability'. To all the scientists I interviewed while at BBC Radio 5 Live, particularly the extraordinary James Lovelock, CH, CBE, FRS. I'm not sure Jacob Alexander is his best disciple! To Dr John Lee FRCA for his knowledge on anaesthesia To Ian Rankin who, in a wonderful Twitter exchange, found me Sam Copeland at RCW, who believed in *Itch* from the off. To all at Random House, especially Kelly Hurst, for whipping me and *Itch* into shape. To Theodore Gray's *The Elements*, an extraordinary book and source of the 'everything you can drop on your foot' quote which Itch mentions to his mother. To the original Itchingham Lofte and Nathaniel Flowerdew, I am in your debt. To the 'radioactive boy scout' Daniel Hahn, who showed what one boy was capable of. To Caroline Chignell and Emily Rees Jones at PBJ Management for reading and liking *Itch* in the beginning. And to Ben, Natasha (neat idea!) and Joe, who put up with a possessed wannabe author they weren't quite expecting.

Any mistakes are, of course, all my own work!

Coming in 2013:
The story continues in a new
exciting adventure:

Turn over for a taster . . .

deserting her. The two bunks above her were silent and the stack of three opposite were still too, save for an occasional grunt and mutter from deep in someone's dream. The three new arrivals slept on tattered mats on the floor, their arms and legs tangled with a number of plastic bowls. The mouldy remains of beans and cassava were scattered everywhere.

She was about to make for the door when she heard a key in the lock. She held her breath as it turned slowly and the ancient pin-tumbler mechanism strained and then clicked. It seemed deafening to Shivvi and she tensed, glancing around the cell, but no one stirred. She counted to twenty, then moved to the door, pushing against its steel panels. It opened slowly, and light from the prison landing fell on one of the new arrivals. A squinting face looked up at Shivvi who, turning round, drew her finger sharply across her neck. The girl understood the threat well enough and lowered her head to the mat. Shivvi slipped out of the cell.

She had memorized her route to the outside world so many times. She knew the corridors she had to slip down, the rooms she could hide in and the doors and gates that would be open. She had paid enough. The bribes were at last coming good and soon she would be free. Crouching low to avoid being seen from any of the cells, she ran towards the two metal doors at the end of the corridor; she could already see that they were slightly ajar. Her bare feet were noiseless as she sprinted and then slowed down, slipping through them both in a second.

Her wing was on the fourth floor of a block that ran parallel with the front gates of the prison. But as she flew down the flights of stairs – the steel doors stood open at each floor – she knew she was heading in the other direction. There were three staff entrances: one for the caterers and cleaners at the side of the prison, and two for the wardens and guards. She had paid for the nearest one to be unmanned and unlocked. She would be there in one minute; the deal was that it would be locked again in three.

The stairs came out at a courtyard which was at the centre of the prison. The air was warm and humid, but in comparison with the fetid stench of the prison, Shivvi thought it was the freshest thing she had ever smelled. She inhaled deeply. She had exercised here many times, but as she looked across to the far side where her open door would be found, she realized she had never seen it empty before. As she checked her route around the cobbled periphery, she briefly caught a familiar stale perfume and whirled round. The vast bulk of Zuma, one of the senior guards, was hurtling towards her. Shivvi jumped sideways – but not quickly enough to escape Zuma's grabbing hands, which closed around her ponytail. Attempting to throw her to the ground, the guard pulled down sharply, but Shivvi had been here before. In countless street fights and prison battles she had found herself attacked by bullies and thugs who assumed that because of her 1.6-metre, 45-kilo frame, she would be a pushover. They were wrong. As Zuma tugged her down, Shivvi smashed her palm into the guard's face, splintering her nose instantly. It was her speciality. Zuma let go and put her hands in front of her face, gasping as blood poured between her fingers. Shivvi ran behind her and kicked at her knees. Zuma's legs buckled and she fell to the ground, groaning.

'Lie down. Lie down, Zuma, or I'll smack your nose again,' she half whispered, half shouted in the guard's ear. Zuma did what she was told. 'You stay here for ten minutes. You don't make a sound.' Shivvi bent down and looked her in the eye. 'You made my life a misery for three years. I hope you go as mad in here as I have.' And using Zuma's head as a starting block, she sprinted for the gate.

The altercation in the courtyard had cost Shivvi some crucial minutes, and as she approached staff entrance A, skipping round open doors and ducking under lit windows, she recognized the silhouette of the guard who had been unlocking the doors for her. With keys in hand, she was about to close up.

'No!' called Shivvi, closing fast, and the guard, looking up, stood aside. They exchanged the briefest of glances, and the former Greencorps oil analyst, convicted polluter and killer squeezed her way out of the prison and onto the dark back streets of Lagos.

Hiding behind a garden wall, Shivvi Tan Fook retied the band in her black hair and produced a pair of sandals from under her shirt. She slipped them on and looked around, smiling. If anyone had been watching, they would have marvelled at the effect that one smile could have on a face. Despite her twenty-five years – the last three spent in one of the most notorious prisons in Africa – she could still look like a teenager.

'Now,' she said out loud. 'Dr. Nathaniel. Flowerdew.' She spat the words. 'I believe we have an appointment.' And she started to run through the still dark streets, away from the prison and towards the harbour.